The Perfect Princess

Tales of Dragon Magic
and Royal Romance

E.D. BAKER

Bloomsbury Publishing, London, New Delhi, New York and Sydney

This omnibus edition first published in Great Britain in January 2014
by Bloomsbury Publishing Plc
50 Bedford Square, London WC1B 3DP

Dragon Kiss first published in the USA
by Bloomsbury Children's Books in 2009
Text copyright © E.D. Baker 2009

A Prince among Frogs first published in the USA
by Bloomsbury Children's Books in 2010
Text copyright © E.D. Baker 2010

The moral right of the author has been asserted

Illustration of dragon and title page art by Carrie Gifford

A CIP catalogue record for this book is available from the British Library

ISBN 978 1 4088 4693 3

MIX
Paper from
responsible sources
FSC® C020471
www.fsc.org

Printed and bound in Great Britain by CPI Group (UK) Ltd, Croydon CR0 4YY

1 3 5 7 9 10 8 6 4 2

www.bloomsbury.com
www.edbakerbooks.com

This book is dedicated to Ellie, my first reader and a marvelous author in her own right; to Kim, my horse expert and the one who makes my Web site possible; to Victoria, from whom I've learned so much; and to my wonderful fans, who are so encouraging.

Contents

Dragon Kiss

One

"What do you mean, you're going after that girl?" demanded Audun's grandmother. She set the sack she'd been carrying beside the pile of the family's belongings waiting at the mouth of the cave and turned to look at the fifteen-year-old dragon. "You know she's really a human!"

Audun looked at her in surprise. After everything that Millie had done for them, he hadn't expected anyone to object to his plans.

"I thought all of you liked her," he said, glancing from his grandmother to the rest of his family.

"We do," said his mother while his father nodded. His grandfather just shrugged and looked apologetic.

"Liking her has nothing to do with this," his grandmother, Song of the Glacier, replied.

"You can't have forgotten that she saved our lives!" protested Audun.

"We know what she did," said his grandmother. "And we appreciate it, but that doesn't change the fact that she

1

isn't a dragon. Just because she has magic doesn't make her one of us."

Audun shook his head. "I don't understand why that's a problem. I mean, I've heard about dragons that can change into humans. What's wrong with a human who can turn into a dragon?"

"I'm not arguing with you about this, Audun," said the elderly dragoness, "and I'm not giving you my permission to run after that girl like some lovesick albatross. Now go help your grandfather gather the rest of the sacks. We'll be leaving in a few minutes."

"Then you'll be going without me," Audun declared. "I love Millie and I don't want to live my life without her!"

Audun's mother, Moon Dancer, gasped and gave her son a horrified look. In the dragon world the elderly were revered, especially the dragonesses; no one ever talked back to them.

"I can't believe you spoke to your grandmother that way!" exclaimed Audun's father, Speedwell. "Please accept his apology, Mother. He's young and foolish."

Dragons were honest at heart and found it nearly impossible to lie. Once in a while, however, Audun wished that he could lie, just a little. "I didn't mean to be disrespectful, Grandmother," said Audun, "but I can't apologize when I don't mean it." He stepped to the ledge that fronted the cave they called home and turned to look at her once more. "I just wanted to tell you where I was going

2

before I left. I thought you would understand, but I guess I was wrong. Safe travels." When Song didn't respond with a similar farewell, Audun spread his wings and leaped into the frigid mountain air.

He tried not to look back, but he couldn't help himself. Swooping one last time around the mountain-ringed valley, Audun glanced down at the ledge as he worked to gain altitude. Only his parents had remained outside to watch him go. Seeing the sad curve of their necks even from a distance made him wonder, for just a moment, if he was doing the right thing. But then he thought of Millie and how much she meant to him. She had left only the day before, yet it already seemed like an eternity. His parents would understand with time; it was Millie he had to go see now.

Since the hour he was hatched, the only time Audun had been separated from his family for longer than a few days was when they were trapped in the walls of a witch's ice castle. It was Millie who had set them free. Audun had been fascinated by the lovely green dragon from the moment he first saw her, and had fallen in love when he discovered how sweet and good and brave she was, despite the fact that she was really a human. Dragons often fell in love at first sight. His parents had done it and so had the parents of some of his friends. It was usually with someone the dragon king had chosen for them, but it was true love, regardless. However it happened, once dragons fell in love, it was for the rest of their lives.

Audun's grandmother often accused him of acting without thinking first. He admitted to himself that he might have been hasty in leaving his family the way he had, but he already knew that Millie was right for him. It was true that she was a human part of the time and a dragon only when her magic changed her, but she was the most beautiful human Audun had ever seen and she wasn't at all what he'd expected of a creature with only two feet. Brought up to believe that humans lied, cheated, stole, and thought only of themselves, he'd been delighted to meet Millie, who was as honest as a dragon and even more caring.

Audun was certain that all he had to do was encourage Millie and his grandmother to spend some time together and the two of them would get along. Two such wonderful females would have to like each other, wouldn't they?

ᡭ

Dragons have an unerring sense of direction, and more acute senses than humans, especially their vision and sense of smell, so it wasn't hard for Audun to locate Millie's trail. Every dragon's scent was unique, but Millie's was more unusual than most. Part smoky musk of a dragon and part flavorful undertones of a human, her scent varied according to whatever form she was in. Because she'd been a dragon when she flew south, Audun smelled more of her dragon than of her human scent.

4

Starting out the day before would have been better for tracking her scent on the air currents between the mountains, but he hadn't wanted to leave without spending some time with his family after their experience in the witch's castle. Audun's long neck wove from side to side as he followed Millie's scent between the mountains and over the pass leading to the foothills beyond. He circled above a large outcropping of rock where he thought he detected the smell she'd given off when she was a human, but the scent was old and the storm that had scoured the mountains the day after Millie arrived had nearly erased it. A short distance away he spotted a snow leopard, which ran in fear at Audun's approaching shadow.

Picking up her dragon odor again, he followed it above the foothills and across the lush forests and rolling grasslands that made up much of the Kingdom of Bull-rush. The countryside was lovely, although Audun preferred the glittering ice and pristine snow of the Icy North. The air was warmer here, too, and uncomfortable for a dragon from a land where the ice never thawed and the snow never melted. When Audun noticed a river flowing beneath him, he didn't think twice about landing at the water's edge.

Drawing his wings to his sides, he curved his neck to the river and hunched down to gulp gallon after gallon of cool, fresh water. He closed his eyes in pleasure, dunking his head until he was submerged all the way to his shoulders, and didn't open his eyes until a change in the current told him that something large was close by.

A pale face with wide-open, staring eyes engulfed in a cloud of some sort of green weed drifted toward him. Audun jerked his head back, certain it was a drowned human. Although he didn't want to touch it, he thought he should take it out of the water in case someone was looking for it. The current was carrying it past quickly, so he grimaced with distaste and reached out with one clawed foot, pulling it from the river to the soft mud of the shore.

Audun jumped back in surprise when the body jumped to its feet and shouted, "What do you think you're doing, you brute?"

"Sorry!" said Audun. "I thought you were dead."

"How dare you!" exclaimed the young woman, flicking the dripping strands of her long, green hair over her shoulder. "That has to be the rudest thing anyone has ever said to me!"

Audun didn't know what to do when the woman hurled a clump of mud at him before bursting into tears.

"I know I've been looking a little pasty lately and I have taken to floating aimlessly, but still . . ."

"I said I was sorry," said Audun. "I don't know very many humans. I've never seen one with green hair before and the way you were staring at me—"

The woman stopped crying to give him a nasty look.

"Haven't you insulted me enough already? I'm not a lowly, smelly human. I'm a water nymph and this is my river!"

"I didn't realize . . ."

"It's not your fault. I haven't been myself ever since that horrible troll ate two of my favorite fish. What is the world coming to? Trolls stomping across river bottoms, stirring up my nice silt and polluting my lovely, clean water with their awful stench as they devour my little darlings! Then humans clutter my riverbank with rafts . . ."

Audun didn't hear the rest of the nymph's complaints once she gestured to a raft lying on the shore only a dozen yards upriver. Raising his head to sniff, the dragon smiled as he recognized Millie's human scent. He was sure he would have noticed it sooner if he hadn't been so distracted. The nymph was still talking when he turned away and trotted to the raft. Although the logs were old and battered, the vine holding them together looked fresh.

Audun bent down to give the raft a thorough sniff, paying special attention to the side Millie had touched. He also found the scent of the boy, Francis, as well as that of the obnoxious troll. The nymph was right about the troll's stench.

"I've been talking to you!" shrilled the nymph, who had followed him to the raft.

"Right . . . ," Audun replied, still not paying attention to her. He was pleased to have found the raft. It was a connection to Millie, something she had touched and used.

"I've got to go," he said, as he spread his wings. Although he'd known he was on the right track, it was good to have the knowledge confirmed. She seemed that much closer now; his search might almost be over.

Audun took to the air and recaptured Millie's dragon scent. It took him across the river to a land of scrubby grass and rolling hills that grew taller with each passing mile until they became mountains. These were different from the mountains that he was used to; they weren't as high, and there was snow only on the tops of the very tallest, but even there the air flowing past them seemed warm and gentle.

He almost lost the scent at times, and had to cast back and forth for it, but when he reached one of the mountains farthest to the south it became so strong that it seemed to fill his nostrils. Following the curve of the mountainside, Audun began to see signs of humans: a rough path zigzagged down the side of the mountain, following its contours to a village on one side, and a castle perched on a pinnacle of rock on the other. Millie's scent was strongest near the castle, both as a human and as a dragon, so he descended, hoping to see her.

He was flying over one of the squat, sturdy towers when a shout went up and arrows began to whiz past him. Dodging the arrows was easy at first, but then the archers' assault intensified and he had to fly higher to get out of range.

"Millie!" he roared, turning this way and that as he struggled to avoid the flood of arrows. "Millie, are you there?"

A figure seated on a broom shot from the top of the tower, and Audun was certain that it was Millie. But then another figure joined it and the two of them steered their brooms toward Audun. They were talking to each other as they flew and he could hear what they were saying even before they reached him.

"Hey, Ratinki! Will you look at that!" said the younger of the two witches in a voice so loud that Audun thought they could probably hear her back in the castle. "I've never seen a white dragon before. Have you?"

The old witch shook her head and replied in a raspy voice, "Nope. He's a good looker, though. I wonder what he wants with our Millie."

"He was calling her name. He must want to talk to her," said the younger witch.

Ratinki looked exasperated. "You're such a ninny-head, Klorine! Of course he wants to talk to her. Maybe we can find out why." Using one hand to shade her eyes from the sun, the old witch shouted, "You there!" and flew higher until she was facing Audun. "What do you want with Millie? None of your dragon tricks now. We're powerful witches and can turn you into a flea in the blink of an eye."

"I just need to see her. Is she here?"

"Maybe she is and maybe she isn't. We're not telling you a thing until you tell us why you want her. Go on, you can tell us. We're friends of the family."

"I'm not telling you anything," said Audun. "It's personal."

Klorine eyed him as she flew up to join them. "She met you on her adventure, didn't she? We were dying of curiosity, but she wasn't here long enough to tell us anything. Her parents whisked her away right after she got back."

"You simpleton!" snapped Ratinki. "I was going to make him tell us all about it. Now we'll never know what happened!"

"Maybe Millie will tell us the next time we see her, although I don't expect that to be for a good long time. I've never seen Emma and Eadric so upset."

"If she were my daughter, I'd lock her in a tower and throw away the key," said Ratinki.

"If she were your daughter," said Klorine, "she would have locked herself in the tower and thrown away the key."

Audun couldn't wait any longer. "Where did they take her?"

"Home, I suppose," said Klorine.

The old witch snorted with disgust. "You're going to blab everything, aren't you? So much for keeping secrets from the enemy!"

"I'm not your enemy," said Audun. "I love Millie. I

would never hurt her. If you could just tell me where she lives . . ."

"Greater Greensward, of course."

"Klorine!" shouted Ratinki. "Don't tell him that! Who knows what he has in mind."

"Don't be silly, Ratinki. He said he loves her. I think true love is so romantic!"

"Between humans! But he's a dragon. For all we know he might want to eat Millie!"

Klorine pursed her mouth in disgust. "Now who's being a ninny-head? This is a nice young dragon, not some ravening beast. Don't pay her any mind," she said, turning back to Audun. "Just head south over the forest and the river. Millie's mother is the Green Witch and a Dragon Friend. Any dragon can tell you how to find the castle. There are lots of dragons in Greater Greensward. You'll feel right at home there."

"I doubt it, but thanks, anyway," said Audun.

Two

When it began to rain, Audun searched until he found a cave where he could spend the night. He finally found one that was big enough, but was disappointed to see that a family of wolves already occupied it. Fortunately, after he went in to look around, the wolves decided to go somewhere else to sleep, and he spent the night undisturbed. Even so, he had trouble falling asleep. All he could think about was Millie. He'd never met anyone like her before.

Every time he was ready to drift off, Audun saw Millie's face. He remembered how her eyes had lit up when she smiled at him, and how frightened she had looked when she'd found him frozen in the ice with his own noxious gas swirling around him. He remembered how she'd melted the ice with her dragon fire and had taken the flames into herself when his ice-dragon gas exploded. After she had saved his life, fire had nearly consumed her and she'd had to dive into a valley filled with snow to put it out. The snow had melted and she was sinking in the water when he dove in after her. Audun rubbed his forelimbs, remembering what it had been like to carry her. He wished he could touch her again, if only for a moment, and he went to sleep only after he'd promised himself that he'd be with her very soon.

The sky was clear the next morning except for a scattering of clouds in the distance. He had no trouble finding Millie's scent again, but he hadn't flown far before he lost it. This didn't worry him at first. Turning on a wing tip, he retraced his flight path, returning to the spot where he'd last smelled her. He continued on, more carefully this time, and lost the odor at exactly the same place. Audun tried again and again, each time becoming more agitated as well as more determined not to give up.

Eventually, he caught the faintest whiff of another familiar scent, one he had smelled for the first time in the castle near his home. It had been the Blue Witch's castle, and although his family had been trapped in the walls, it hadn't been the witch's doing; she had been a prisoner as well. He couldn't remember the old woman's name, but he did know that she and Millie had become friends of sorts. It was possible that she might even know Millie's whereabouts.

Following the new scent, Audun flew toward a part of the forest where the trees were older and taller. As he passed over a clearing, he glanced down and saw a nymph with long, green hair paddling in a small pond, while a unicorn drank from the shallower water. At Audun's approach, the nymph slipped into the depths of the pond. The unicorn snorted, shook its mane, and turned to run.

The dragon flew on and soon the old witch's scent drew Audun to a clearing where nodding bluebells surrounded a small, well-kept cottage with a newly thatched roof and a gently puffing chimney. Three white-haired women sat in the shade of the only tree in the clearing, sipping from cups shaped like half-opened tulips. Not wanting to startle them, Audun landed at the edge of the forest. He was about to call out a greeting when the woman in the muddy-colored gown glanced over her shoulder and said to her friends, "Don't look now, but there's a dragon sneaking up on us."

The woman in gray lowered her cup. "If you won't let us look, Mudine, you'll have to do the looking for us. Is it anyone we know?"

Mudine shook her head. "I've never seen a dragon like this before. He's white."

" 'Never trust a dragon you don't know,' my old mother used to say," said the woman in gray.

"Don't be ridiculous, Oculura," snapped the smallest woman. "I had the same mother as you and I never heard her say such a thing! She wouldn't have trusted any dragon, living or dead!"

"You're older than I am, Dyspepsia. You left home years before I did. I had to listen to a lot of mother's adages before she choked to death on that fried radish."

14

"Can you two stop arguing long enough for us to deal with this dragon?" asked Mudine.

"That's easy enough," said Oculura. "A wall of flame should chase him off. It worked on my last husband when he wouldn't stop coming around."

"That's even more ridiculous!" said Dyspepsia. "This is a dragon we're talking about. They love flames! Why don't we try something like this . . ."

Rising to her feet, the little old witch swept her arm in a grand gesture while muttering under her breath. With a rumble and a *whoosh!* a torrent of stones rose out of the ground and flung themselves at Audun's head.

Befuddled, Audun half-turned, lifted his tail, and swatted the stones aside. He hadn't done anything to provoke these humans, yet they were attacking him. All he wanted to do was talk to the Blue Witch about Millie. Maybe they didn't understand . . .

"Excuse me!" he called, taking two steps closer to the old women. "I just wanted to . . ."

"Well, that didn't do a bit of good," said Oculura. "The beast is still coming to get us. Maybe if I do this . . ." Speaking under her breath, the witch held her hands in front of her, then thrust them apart as if she were trying to move something heavy.

Audun yelped as the ground opened beneath his feet. He spread his wings and was about to fly away when Mudine said, "And I'll do this!" Smiling with glee, the old woman fluttered her fingers at his feet and said something Audun couldn't quite hear. Vines erupted from the hole in the ground and wrapped themselves around Audun. "Go ahead and use your fire on those, dragon!" she shouted. "Those asbesta vines will never burn!"

The white dragon roared in surprise, jerking at his trapped feet and flapping his wings. Suddenly the door to the cottage burst open and a fourth white-haired lady stepped out, blinking at the sunshine. "What's this racket about?" she demanded. "I thought you were going to let me take a nap."

Taking a deep breath, Audun exhaled onto the vines, which immediately turned a sickly shade of yellow and shriveled. Free again, he rose into the air and cupped his wings so he could stay in place. He would have flown away if he hadn't recognized the woman who had just stepped outside as the witch he had come to see. It was plain that she recognized him at the same time, because her eyes grew wide in surprise.

"What are you doing here?" she asked. "I never thought I'd see you again."

"I'm looking for Millie," said Audun. "Do you know where I might find her?"

"Why?" the witch asked, sounding suspicious.

"Because I love her," he replied. "I don't want to live without her."

The Blue Witch snorted and said, "You sound like you want to propose."

"I do," said Audun. "I want her as my mate. I want to spend the rest of my life with her."

Slapping her knee, the Blue Witch chortled. "Now if that doesn't beat all! That's got to be the funniest thing I've ever heard."

"I wasn't joking," Audun said, giving her the sternest look he could muster.

"Then you're in for a big disappointment," said the witch, sounding a lot less cheerful. "Her family would never let her marry a dragon! You'd have to be a human before you'd get even a glimmer of a chance."

The crest on the back of Audun's neck wilted. "So you're saying there's no hope for me?"

"I didn't say that," said the Blue Witch. "Dragons can do lots of things, some that come naturally, and some that have to be taught. Your elders figure they'll teach you what you need to know once you're old enough and smart enough to handle it. If you're serious about Millie, go talk to your king and his dragon council. They're the only ones who can help you."

"I'll do that if I have to, but I want to talk to Millie first. Do you know where she went? I was following her scent until I lost it over the forest."

"You won't be able to find her. Millie's mother used

17

magic to whisk her away to someplace where they could talk with no one interrupting them. Even I couldn't follow them if I wanted to. I doubt Millie would want to see you now, anyway. She's in a lot of trouble and having you there would just make it worse. Nope, your best bet is to see your dragon council. If you're lucky, the members might have a soft spot for true love—if you really love her, that is. You do, don't you? I'll be angry if I helped you like this and you weren't sincere."

The Blue Witch wouldn't let Audun go until she was convinced that he meant what he'd said. After that, she made her friends apologize to him for attacking him with their magic, and by then they were all declaring how hungry they were and made him stay to eat. While they shared a meal of leftover stew (giving Audun all the meat), the Blue Witch began to reminisce about life in the Icy North, making the white dragon tell her friends about it as well. It wasn't until late afternoon that she finally let him go with a sack of dried fish and the good wishes of four white-haired witches.

༄

Audun's wings were heavy as he flew away from the witches' cottage. He had been so looking forward to seeing Millie again that he hadn't allowed himself to consider the fact that she might not be findable. Dipping one wing, he started to turn in the direction of the Icy North, but changed his mind. Although he might not be able to see Millie, at least he could see the castle where she'd grown up. Even that much contact with something of hers might ease the ache in his chest.

The castle wasn't hard to find once he left the forest where the witches lived. Scanning the horizon, he soon saw green pennants snapping in the wind atop the tall, slender towers of a castle. With the sun at his back, he sped toward the castle and landed in the courtyard. A stable boy was nearly dragged off his feet when the horse he was walking saw Audun. Screaming, the horse fought to get away, but the boy held on and got the animal under control long enough to get it out of sight of the dragon.

Audun was wondering if he should leave when an older woman with gray-streaked auburn hair swooped out of the sky on a magic carpet and landed in the courtyard beside him. "May I help you?" she asked.

"I wanted to see Millie," said Audun. "I'm a friend of hers."

The woman's lips widened in a warm smile. "I'm her great-aunt Grassina. Wait just a minute and I'll see if she's here."

A flicker of hope lit up Audun's eyes. "Do you mean she's home?"

"A little bird told me that she got back a few hours ago," Grassina said over her shoulder as she headed for the door. "She might be resting, though. I'll just go up and—"

The door flew open and Millie came racing out, shrieking, "Audun!" Dashing across the cobblestones, she threw her arms around the dragon's neck and clung to him.

Audun smiled, curved his neck around her, and said, "I told you that you couldn't keep me away." Millie turned her head and he saw that her lovely green eyes were red from crying and her cheeks were streaked with tears.

Two other women appeared in the doorway, neither of whom was smiling. The older woman had golden hair like Millie's, but it was sprinkled with white. She was beautiful, despite the cross expression she was wearing. "It's that dragon, the one she was telling us about. He shouldn't be here, not after all the horrid things Millie said."

"I didn't say anything horrid, Grandmother," Millie cried, before turning back to Audun. "I just told them how much I care about you," she said, looking into his eyes.

"No human should love a dragon," said her grandmother. "It isn't right."

"That isn't fair, Mother," said the other woman. "Eadric loves me whether I'm a human or a dragon, just as I love him no matter what I am. I simply don't understand how Millie could feel so strongly about Audun after such a short time. Unless it's her dragon side . . . Flame Snorter swears she fell in love with Grumble Belly the first time she saw him."

This woman looked remarkably like Millie and it occurred to Audun that this had to be Millie's mother, who was not only a princess, but also a witch and a Dragon

Friend. Audun squinted his eyes and could see a rosy glow around her, the fabled sign of a true friend to dragons.

"I'm honored to meet you, Dragon Friend," he said, bowing his head. "I've come to court your daughter."

Millie's grandmother's hand flew to her forehead and she swayed as if she'd been struck. "This is worse than I thought," she said in a strained voice. "We can't let this happen. We'll be the laughingstock of all the kingdoms. Or worse yet, the object of their hatred. If we let dragons marry into the family all the neighboring kingdoms will consider us unsuitable to rule. We'll have armies marching on us from every direction."

Millie's mother sighed. "I wouldn't go that far, Mother. No one has complained about my dragon side. However, Millie, we can't let you marry a dragon just because you're attracted to him. I'm sure you think you love him," she said, holding up her hand when Millie started to speak, "but you hardly know him. You can't truly love someone you don't really know."

"That's not true, Mother. Audun and I have been through so much together! I know him enough to know that I do love him!"

At Millie's words, Audun felt a warmth growing inside him like he'd never experienced before. While he'd known that he loved Millie, he hadn't been sure that she felt the same way about him. Now that he was sure of her feelings, he knew that nothing in the world could keep them apart.

"I'm sure you think you love him, darling, but there's only one way to know for certain. Give it time and see if you both still feel the same way."

"Oh, we will," Millie said.

"Did I forget to mention that the test works better when you aren't together?" her mother asked. Dust began to swirl around Millie's legs, tugging at the hem of her gown.

"No, Mother, don't do this!" Millie exclaimed, looking at her mother in horror.

"It's for your own good," her mother's voice said over the rising wind. She was standing only a few yards away, yet she sounded as if she were a long way off. "You'll appreciate what I've done someday."

"Millie!" Audun shouted, as he felt her being pulled away. And then both she and her mother were gone, leaving Audun with Grassina and Millie's grandmother.

"Don't look at me that way," the older woman told Audun. "It's for the best. You never should have come here. Now go back to wherever it is you're from and leave my granddaughter alone." Turning abruptly, she strode back to the castle door. "I'll see you inside, Grassina," she added, then firmly closed the door behind her.

Audun felt as if a giant had swatted him out of the sky into the side of a mountain. He turned toward Millie's great-aunt, certain that she was waiting to tell him how his love for her niece was hopeless and that he should leave and never come back. She was wrestling with her magic carpet, however, and was more intent on shaking off the dust that had covered it when the wind had carried Millie away than she was in telling Audun anything.

"Let me help," said Audun.

Grassina stepped aside as the dragon picked up the edge of the carpet with his talons and flapped it until the dust puffed free and drifted across the courtyard. "Thanks," she said, nodding her approval. "You know, you don't have to listen to everything Millie's grandmother says. My sister, Chartreuse, is a very negative person and can never see the good in anything. My husband is a wonderful man. He was an otter for many years, although I fell in love with him when he was human," she said, half to herself. "Chartreuse still doesn't like him and is always making unnecessary comments about smelly otters and how she expects him to lick his fur. He hasn't done that in years—at least, not in public. All I wanted to say was that if you really love each other, you shouldn't let anything stand between you. If you want to be with Millie, I'm sure you'll find a way."

Three

It took Audun three days to reach the part of the Icy Sea where King's Isle was located. On the final day he'd flown above frigid, choppy waters where jagged glaciers provided the only places to land. A storm chased him for the last few hours, catching up with him shortly before he reached the island. Fighting against the buffeting wind and freezing rain, he saw little of his goal in the stormy darkness and would have flown past it if a flash of lightning hadn't reflected off the island's icy crags. He didn't notice the dragon sentries who flew out to meet him until their wings actually touched his. Flying wing tip to wing tip, they guided him to the only opening into the home of the ice-dragon king, leaving Audun at the highest spire.

With ice-coated wings and aching muscles, Audun was so tired that he staggered as his claws finally touched the ground. When the door opened and another dragon appeared to escort him to a place where he could rest, Audun could only nod his thanks and stumble after him to an empty chamber where a ledge along the wall served as a bed. Curling up on the ledge, he slept the rest of that day and well into the next, too tired to open his eyes when dragons came to check on him. He dreamed of Millie and of what their lives would be like once they were together. When he finally woke, it was to the sound of the door creaking open and talons clicking across the floor.

Raising his head, Audun blinked in surprise at the pair of young dragons who stood by the door, watching him. They were both females, one was probably nine or ten years old and the other's age was closer to his own.

"He's awake!" the younger dragoness whispered to the other.

The older dragoness had been staring at Audun in a way that made him want to squirm. "Welcome to King's Isle," she said, giving him a radiant smile.

Although Audun had never visited King's Isle before, he knew quite a bit about it. It was the stronghold of the king of the ice dragons from the day he was chosen to rule until the day he died. Dragons lived for a very long time, so the selection of a new king happened once every few hundred years. The current king had been selected nineteen years before, after the death of the previous ruler, who had been so old that his scales were dull and brittle and his teeth worn down to nubs. The stronghold was also the home of the king's councillors, as well as of the dragons and dragonesses who made up his court.

Because far fewer female dragons than males were born, females were treasured and treated with great care. At the age of eight, dragonesses were brought to the court of the dragon king to be raised until they were old enough to start a family with their own mates. It was the responsibility of the king to select their mates as well as to see to the education of the dragonesses. Both Audun's mother and his grandmother had spent their formative years living on the island. Audun was sorry he had ignored most of their stories. It would have helped if he'd learned what the dragons on the island did, especially those like the dragoness eyeing Audun.

"My name is Hildie," she announced, letting her eyelids droop in an odd sort of way. "I'm glad you're awake. Dragons our age rarely visit the island. Have you come to petition the king for a mate? Say you have. All the others who have come are so old. I'd hate to end up with one of them."

Audun shook his head, saying, "I'm here to ask the king and his councillors for their help. I'm not looking for a mate."

"That's too bad," she replied, turning so that her tail rubbed against his leg. Wetting her lips with her tongue, she looked him up and down, her gaze lingering on the muscles in his legs and the ridge along his back. "The king is very busy now," she said. "One of the old councillors died and King Stormclaw has been meeting with her replacement. You probably won't get an appointment for days."

"Is there anywhere that I can—," Audun began.

The door slammed open and a burly dragon, over twice Audun's height, ducked his head and squeezed through the doorway. There was a silvery tinge to his scales, and he had a ridge as sharp as dagger blades and the longest talons Audun had ever seen. Audun stepped back from the anger flashing in the huge dragon's eyes; Hildie just looked disgusted.

"What do you think you're doing here?" the dragon growled at her. "I leave my post for two minutes to help Iceworthy and you sneak past."

"We were waiting in line for our turn on the ice chute when we heard that *he* was here," the younger dragoness announced, pointing at Audun. "Hildie wanted to come see him up close before any of the other dragonesses could. She thinks if she meets him first, she'll have first claim on him. She shouldn't be here, though, should she, Frostybreath?"

Hildie turned on her companion and scowled. "Be quiet, Loolee. No one asked you."

Loolee smiled sweetly at Audun and skipped out the door. Frostybreath growled at Hildie until she started to leave as well. "You'll have to forgive Loolee," she said, pausing in front of Audun so she could tilt her head, making her neck look long and slender. "She's just a child and doesn't know what she's talking about."

"Hildie!" snapped Frostybreath.

The dragoness made an exasperated face and smiled at Audun one last time before she, too, left the room. Frostybreath squeezed through the doorway again, shaking his head and muttering to himself.

The door shut with a click. Audun sighed. He'd been about to ask if there was somewhere he could go to get something to drink, but he hadn't had the chance. Thinking that he would look for a drink himself, he opened the door and was halfway out when a deep growl made the ridge along his spine rise.

"Get back in there, squirt," said Frostybreath, baring his fangs.

"I was just—"

"I don't care what you were doing," said the dragon. "You're not going anywhere until I say you can."

Audun was puzzled. Although he hadn't known what to expect when he'd arrived at the island, it had never occurred to him that he'd be treated like a prisoner. "I really just want—"

"Yeah, yeah. That's what they all say. Then the next thing I know you'll be flying off with Hildie or another young dragoness and I'll have to go out in the wind and rain to haul you both back. I don't like the rain, boy, so don't even think about it. Now go in that room and don't come out until I say you can."

Frostybreath took a menacing step toward Audun and the young dragon backed into his room and shut the door.

He was studying one of the walls of ice, wondering what would happen if he licked it, when the door opened and an elderly, narrow-faced dragon official, wearing rings on every talon and a medallion in the shape of the king's head, stepped inside. The dragon carried a stylus in one set of talons and a stiffened parchment in the other. Peering down his long, thin nose at Audun, he said, "My name is Iceworthy. I understand that you want to ask the king and his councillors for help. What, precisely, is the nature of your request?"

"It's personal," said Audun.

"I see," murmured the dragon as he wrote. "P-e-r-s-o-n-a-l. And what exactly is this personal request?"

"I'd prefer to ask the king."

The dragon raised a brow ridge and twitched his tail. "You would, would you? Apparently you don't understand how things work here. King Stormclaw is a very important dragon and cannot talk to just anyone. My job is to make sure he isn't bothered by minor nuisances like you. Nothing gets to King Stormclaw without my approval. You either tell me now, or I'll have Frostybreath throw you off the island. Which shall it be, hmmm?"

It was obvious from his expression that the old dragon wasn't going to give in. The young dragon sighed. "I want to ask how to become a human. I was told that I should go to the king and his council for help."

"Human, eh? Well, I'm sure you have your reasons, although no one in his right mind . . . Ah, well, that's neither

29

here nor there. What is your name, young dragon? I'll have to write my report, then turn it in. You should hear back from the council in a few days. A week at most."

Audun sighed. "I'm Audun, son of Moon Dancer and Speedwell, grandson of Song of the Glacier and High Flier and—"

The dragon grunted and gave Audun a peculiar look. "Enough!" he said, lowering his stylus.

The old dragon's bones creaked as he turned around. Audun followed him to the door, saying, "Please, sir, before you go, if you could just tell me where—"

The door shut in Audun's face, leaving him even more puzzled than before.

Although the young dragon tried to distract himself in the empty room by counting the number of his reflections he could see on the ice walls and finding cracks in the ice that looked like animal faces, it wasn't long before all he could think about was how thirsty he was. Rather than lick the wall and risk getting his tongue frozen to it, Audun used his talons to gouge out a piece of ice. He was just about to place it in his mouth when the door opened and Frostybreath came in, carrying a platter of newly caught fish and a jug of fresh water.

Seeing the ice in Audun's talons, the guard shook his massive head, saying, "I wouldn't eat that if I were you. An old sorcerer used magic on it to keep it frozen for as long as there are dragon kings. Put it in a closed vessel and it will freeze any liquid around it. You wouldn't want to see what it would do to your blood if you ate it."

Audun dropped the chunk of ice. Frostybreath smiled and set the platter and jug on the floor. "Eat hearty, squirt. You're meeting with the king and his councillors in the morning. I'd get a good night's sleep, too, if I were you. You'll need your wits about you tomorrow."

After the guard had gone, Audun squatted on the floor beside the platter, drained the jug of water into his mouth, then picked up the chilled fish and dropped them onto his tongue, one at a time. He thought the whole thing was too confusing. First he was a prisoner, then he was about to be kicked off the island, now he was getting just what he wanted sooner than he'd thought possible. *If only I could get someone to tell me what's going on,* he thought, yawning until his jaw made a cracking sound. *If only I'd listened more when Mother and Grandmother told me about living on the island.* He picked up the empty jug and shook it. *If only I still had some water left!*

He was settling down on the ledge when he bumped the piece of ice he'd broken off the wall. It skittered a few inches, but Audun reached out and caught it before it could fall off the ledge. *Magical ice might come in handy,* he thought, and tucked it into the pouch that all ice dragons have under a flap of skin between the base of their wings and their back.

Although Audun didn't think he'd be able to sleep that night after having slept most of the day, he lay down to

31

rest and didn't wake up until Frostybreath brought him more fish in the morning. The dragon guard grunted a greeting, and handed Audun a platter and another jug, saying, "Hurry up and eat. I'm supposed to take you to the council chambers right away, but I don't want you fainting from hunger at the king's feet."

While Audun ate his breakfast, Frostybreath stood by, tapping his talons impatiently against the ice. Audun was licking the last fish scale from his lips when the dragon beckoned him to the door. "Come along. The sooner I have you delivered to the council, the sooner I can get back to my real job."

"I thought guarding newcomers like me *was* your real job," said Audun, as he trailed Frostybreath out the door.

The big dragon shook his massive head. "Not at all. I'm just filling in for a friend who had to get a broken fang fixed. My real job makes use of my talent. I can freeze things just by blowing on them. I'll show you. Spit."

"What?" said Audun. "Here, you mean . . . now?"

"Right here. Don't worry. No one will mind."

Audun shrugged. "If you say so." Gathering moisture in his mouth, he spit at the wall in front of him. Just as the fluid left Audun's mouth, Frostybreath exhaled. The air crackled and shimmered; a small chunk of ice hit the wall with a *thunk!* "Wow!" said Audun. "That's some talent."

Frostybreath looked pleased by the compliment, but he shrugged as he lumbered down the corridor. "That's nothing compared to what the king and his councillors can do. King Stormclaw can call up storms—"

"I've heard that," said Audun.

"Here we go. We'll take this ramp down to the lower levels. See how much brighter it is now? The storm must have stopped."

Audun had not seen any windows, but the ice was translucent and let in daylight when the sun was out. The walls that had seemed gray and dismal the day before now looked as bright as the ice on the mountains back home. The ramp was wide enough for two ordinary-sized dragons to walk side by side, but Frostybreath was far bigger than average. Audun had to follow him down the ramp, staying well back to avoid the other dragon's swinging tail.

"And one of his councillors, Frostweaver, can make intricate patterns out of frost," Frostybreath continued. "They say that the newest councillor . . . Hey, watch where you're going!" the big dragon shouted, as a pack of giggling young dragonesses raced past in the opposite direction.

Audun thought he saw Hildie and Loolee in the group, but they were gone before he got a good look. "Where are they headed?"

"To the top of the ice. They'll take turns riding down the chute that winds around the outside of the stronghold. You wouldn't have seen it, coming in when there was a storm the way you did, but it is pretty impressive if I do say so myself. Took me nearly a year of my days off to make it."

"You made it by yourself?" Audun asked.

"The little ones needed something to do when the weather is bad, seeing that it's bad most days. Ice floe tag isn't safe for the youngest during a storm. Sliding down the chute has become their favorite game. Ah, look, I was talking so much that I didn't realize we were almost there. You go right through that door and wait for the councillors to send for you. Shouldn't be long now."

"Thank you," Audun called, as the bigger dragon continued down the ramp.

"My pleasure!" Frostybreath rumbled over his shoulder.

Four

Following Frostybreath's directions, Audun closed the door behind him and took a seat on a ledge. He was curling up to rest his chin on his foot when a door opened and a dragoness who wasn't much older than he was peeked into the room. Gesturing for him to follow, she stepped aside as he slipped through the door.

"What do I do now?" Audun whispered. He had entered the largest chamber he had ever seen. A hundred dragons could have spread their wings and still had room to move around. At the far end of the room five great slabs of stone rose from the floor in a half circle with the open side facing Audun. The center slab was higher than Audun's head, with the rest only a foot or so shorter. Carvings of dragons in flight covered the slabs and each slab supported a life-sized statue of a dragon.

"Answer their questions," said the dragoness, and she disappeared into the room he'd just left, pulling the door shut behind her.

Audun looked around the room. It was more dimly lit than the antechamber had been, and encased in so much ice that the sunlight didn't penetrate as well as it had at the upper levels. He assumed that another door, near the slabs, was the entrance for the king and his councillors. Keeping his ears perked for the sound of approaching feet, he padded across the stone floor, trying to see what famous dragons the statues might depict. Audun was only a dozen yards away when the statue in the center moved.

"That's close enough, young dragon," boomed a voice that seemed to make the walls shake.

Suddenly the torches on the walls flamed brighter and Audun realized that the shapes on top of the slabs weren't carvings at all, but real dragons. And if they were real, then the one in the center must be King Stormclaw and the other four could only be his councillors.

Uncertain how to act before the king, Audun bowed so that his forelegs were bent and his chin almost touched the ground.

"You may rise," said the king.

Audun glanced up. He'd heard that the king was always chosen from among the older dragons, but he didn't think that King Stormclaw looked that old. His neck still supported his head proudly, his back was still straight, and his wings showed no tears or gaps; the only evidence of age was the dullness of his blue-white scales and the shortness of his fangs. He was an imposing dragon and must have been exceedingly handsome when he was young.

Audun dropped his gaze when he realized that the king was studying him just as carefully. Finally, Stormclaw spoke, although he wasn't talking to Audun. "So, Song, I finally get to meet your grandson. He looks a lot like you, although I can see High Flier in him as well."

Startled, Audun looked up and let his gaze follow that of the king. Two elderly dragonesses were seated to the right of King Stormclaw. One of them was a stranger to Audun. The other was his grandmother.

Audun was confused. When he'd last seen his grandmother, she'd been with the rest of his family on the way to their cave overlooking the sea. No one had mentioned that they were going to visit the king. He couldn't imagine what might have happened to bring them here. Before he could ask, however, King Stormclaw turned to him and said, "I've been asking your grandmother to join my council for years, but she's only just relented. You should be very proud of her. She's a remarkable dragoness. A talent like hers is rare."

Audun nodded, but the king wasn't finished yet.

"Young dragon, why have you come to see me? Are you here to make sure that I'm treating your grandmother well? As one of my councillors, she'll be among the most respected dragons in the kingdom."

It took Audun a moment to realize that the king

was waiting for him to say something. The problem was, Audun wasn't sure quite how to phrase his request. Although the other councillors were watching him with interest, his grandmother's gaze was as impassive as if *she* were the stranger. He had a feeling that he wasn't going to get any help from her.

Audun was still trying to think of what to say when the pale gray and white dragoness seated beside the king leaned toward Stormclaw and whispered something.

"Ah, yes," said the king, nodding. "I remember now. Iceworthy mentioned something about your wanting our help. Something about becoming a human, as I recall."

"That's right, Your Majesty," said Audun.

King Stormclaw frowned. "A peculiar request, and one I'm not often asked. Why do you want to be a human, boy? Isn't being a dragon good enough for you?"

"Being a dragon is the best thing in the world!" said Audun. "I don't want to give up being a dragon altogether. It's just that, well, there's this girl . . ."

"Ah, I see," said the king, the furrow in his brow relaxing. "You met a dragoness and you want to impress her. I can understand that, but there are far better ways to impress a girl than by turning into a human."

"That's just it," said Audun. "The girl is a human, or at least part of the time. She can also be a dragon and when she is, she's the most beautiful shade of green—"

The king snorted and twitched his tail. "There's no

such thing as a green dragon, and even if there were, no human could possibly turn into one without . . ."

Song of the Glacier leaned toward the dragoness beside her and whispered into her pointed ear. The two councillors carried on a short, whispered conversation before they both turned to the king.

"Do you have something to tell me, Song?" said King Stormclaw.

Song nodded. "I've seen the girl myself, Your Majesty. She can indeed turn into a green dragon. You were right in that no natural dragon is green, but she is a dragon through magic, which might explain her . . . unusual color."

The king's brow ridge rose in surprise. "A human who could do that must be able to harness some powerful magic! Why have I never heard of such a one before?"

"She isn't from the Icy North," said Audun. "I followed her trail south to a kingdom called Greater Greensward. She is a princess of royal blood as well as the daughter of a powerful witch who is a Dragon Friend." The hiss of indrawn dragon breath nearly drowned out Audun's next words. "Whether a human or a dragoness, she is a brave and true friend and . . . more than that, to me. I love her, Your Majesty, and I've learned that the only way I can ever be with her is if I can be a human just as she can be a dragon. I've been told that you might be able to help me. Can you, Your Majesty?"

King Stormclaw scowled even more fiercely than before, but it wasn't Audun who received the first taste of his anger. "Did you know of this, Song of the Glacier? Did you know that your grandson is enamored of the Green Witch's daughter? She is the only human living who dares to call herself Dragon Friend and if she is friend to the fire-breathers, she is no friend of ours. You have sorely neglected your grandson's education if he doesn't know of the enmity between us."

Song of the Glacier raised her head and looked directly at the king. "What happened between our kind and theirs took place long ago. Few living today feel as you do about the fire-breathers, Your Majesty. I did not teach my grandson such a lesson because it is not a bias that I would want a young dragon to learn."

The dragon king narrowed his eyes in anger and the other members of the council gasped as the crest on top of his skull rose. Only Song of the Glacier didn't seem intimidated by his aggressive stance. "You would not say such things if the fire-breathers had killed members of your own family," growled King Stormclaw.

"But they did!" exclaimed Audun's grandmother.

Glancing at the others in the chamber, the king shook his head. "We will talk of this another time." He took a deep breath and his crest relaxed, making him seem less formidable. Turning to Audun, King Stormclaw said, "You ask for something I will not give. You may spend one more night in the stronghold, and leave in the morning. Now go, before my temper rises again."

Audun felt as if someone had stuck an icicle into his innards and twisted it. He toyed with the idea of fleeing the island to go find Millie before King Stormclaw could stop him, but then he saw a peculiar look pass between the king and Song of the Glacier. Apparently something was going on here that he couldn't understand.

Worried and upset, Audun left the antechamber. He had no sooner stepped onto the ramp when a gaggle of young dragonesses rushing up the slanted floor surrounded him and carried him along with them.

"Wait!" he said, trying to work his way through the crowd. "I have to—"

Someone nudged him back into the middle of the group of dragonesses. "You have to go with us!" Hildie announced from beside him. "We want you to try the chute. You've never seen anything like it."

"But I'm really not in the mood for—"

"Then we'll put you in the mood," said Hildie.

Loolee danced around him, nimbly avoiding the other dragons' feet. "You have to come with us, Audun! Please?"

"All right. I'll do it for you, Loolee," Audun replied, smiling down at the little dragoness.

The dragonesses' enthusiasm was so contagious that by the time they reached the top of the ramp, Audun was nearly as excited as they were. They had passed countless corridors on the way up, but there was nothing at the highest point of the ramp except a level platform and a smooth tunnel angled steeply down.

"I'm going first this time!" Loolee shouted, as she ran to the edge of the platform. Amid a storm of protest from the other dragonesses, the little dragon girl carefully tucked her wings to her sides and hopped off the platform and into the tunnel. "Hoowee!" she shouted, as she disappeared from sight.

"Audun is next!" Hildie cried. She shoved him to the front of the still-forming line.

"What should I do?" he asked, teetering on the lip of the platform.

"Go!" shouted all the dragonesses. Half a dozen of them pushed him from behind.

Audun stumbled off the edge . . . and fell. "No!" he shouted. His heart seemed to climb into his throat, but the ice that formed the twisting, turning chute was so smooth that he couldn't have stopped, no matter what. Opening his wings was out of the question—there wasn't enough room. He raised his head once, bumping it sharply against the ceiling of the chute. After that he remained crouched as he hurtled down the incline on all fours, using his tail to keep his balance.

The chute wound steeply around the island, doubling back and looping through the center at least twice. There was no way out until the bottom, but soon the drop that had been terrifying became exhilarating and Audun didn't want it to end. Finally, the ice-filtered daylight gave way to the absolute darkness of stone, and his ride was over. Sliding out of the chute onto a smooth stone floor, Audun glanced up at the wavering torches and saw Loolee waiting for him in the long, narrow room.

"Did you like it?" the little dragoness asked, her eyes bright.

"That was great!" said Audun.

Loolee grabbed his arm and pulled. "Come on, then. We can do it again, but we have to get to the top before anyone else or they'll make us go to the end of the line."

Audun stood on wobbling legs and said, "Lead the way." Loolee grinned, and Audun grinned back. He looked around as he followed the little dragoness up the ramp and was surprised by how deep into the heart of the island the chute had carried them. "What's down here?" he asked, as they passed the first of the corridors.

"Not much," she replied. "King Stormclaw's lair is one level below this, but you can't get there from here. Even if you could, it's off-limits to just about everybody. They say he keeps his treasure in a pit below his lair and it's filled with precious gems. His councillors all have their rooms on this floor. They have meeting rooms and stuff on the floors above this. The audience chamber is on the floor above those. I don't like it down here. It's too dark even with the torches. I like the ice levels better. It's always brighter up there, except during the really bad storms."

"Are the councillors' chambers off-limits, too?" asked Audun.

Loolee shrugged. "I suppose not, but nobody ever wants to go there. Why do you want to know?"

"Because my grandmother is the king's newest councillor," Audun said. "I'd like to go see her if I can."

"You're related to a councillor! That's so chilled! I wish I was!"

Audun chuckled at the little dragoness's enthusiasm. "So," he said, "if I wanted to see my grandmother, which way should I go?"

"That's easy. Go back to that hallway," Loolee said, pointing to the corridor they had just passed, "and turn right. You'll know you're almost there when you run into the guards. But I've got to go if I want to be first again. See ya!"

While the little dragoness ran up the ramp, Audun followed her directions and went the other way. The corridor was wide, and it made abrupt changes in direction that soon had him completely disoriented. He slowed when he heard voices ahead, one of which was familiar.

"And then I told her, 'Of course my feet are cold. I'm an ice dragon, aren't I?'"

Audun recognized Frostybreath's voice and wondered if the rough laughter that followed his joke belonged to the guards Loolee had mentioned. Rounding the next corner, Audun found Frostybreath talking to two equally huge dragons wearing medallions bearing the insignia of the king's guards.

"Halt!" cried one of the guards, the smile on his face changing to a scowl as he arched his neck and spread his wings to make himself look even bigger and more intimidating. "What business have you here, young dragon?"

"I've come to see my grandmother," Audun replied. "I heard her rooms are on this level."

"That depends," said the other guard. "Who is your grandmother?"

"Her name is Song of the Glacier," said Audun, looking from one guard to the other.

"It's true," Frostybreath said, when the two guards looked skeptical. "Iceworthy told me so this morning."

"Then you're in luck, young dragon," said the first guard, as he lowered his wings. "Your grandmother returned to her rooms not ten minutes ago. Someone will have to escort you to her, however, and we're not allowed to leave our posts." The dragon gave Frostybreath a meaningful look.

The big dragon sighed. "I suppose I can take him. But you owe me for this, Tailshaker, just like you owe me for guarding him while you had your fang repaired."

"I'll pay you back next week." The guard laughed. "You can count on it."

❧

Audun was impressed by the size of his grandmother's rooms. There were three of them and each was bigger than the largest room in his family's cave. The first two rooms were furnished with dark woods and rich fabrics that rivaled the colors of his grandfather's jewels. The bathing pool in the third room was big enough to fit his entire family at once and still would have left room for guests. Even so, what he noticed most as his grandmother gave him a tour was the stiff way she held herself and the cool tone of her voice; it was clear that she wasn't pleased with him.

"Why did you come to see me, Audun?" she asked. "You can't think that I'm going to help you by influencing the king's decision."

"I must admit that I was hoping you would," said Audun, "but the real reason I came is to find out why you're here. At first I thought Grandfather might be with you, but I haven't smelled him or seen any of his things in your rooms."

There was sadness in Song of the Glacier's eyes. "No," she said, "he didn't come with me. The king asked me to come to the island and didn't include my mate in the invitation."

"How did you become one of the king's councillors?" Audun asked.

"King Stormclaw wasn't exaggerating when he said that he'd been asking me for years. I'd turned him down every time because I never felt that he really needed me until now. Even so, when I heard that one of his councillors was dying and that he'd need a replacement soon, I'd hoped to avoid coming here by taking our family and fleeing the Icy North, but after what happened in that witch's castle, I knew that I couldn't put you, your parents, or High Flier in danger just because I wanted us to be together. You left before I could explain what I had to do."

Audun nodded, but there was still something he didn't understand. "Did you know Stormclaw before you came here?"

His grandmother sighed. "I met him the first time I came to the island. His father was in charge of the guards and his mother had died in a storm just the year before. Stormclaw had nowhere else to go, so the old king let him live here. We became friends and later . . . more than friends."

"When did you meet Grandfather?"

"Old King Bent Tooth had chosen your grandfather, High Flier, for me. Dragonesses must marry whomever the king chooses, and my parents made it clear that I would be no exception. You must understand, I care for your grandfather, but back then I loved Stormclaw and I still do."

"So they made you leave Stormclaw and marry Grandfather."

His grandmother nodded. "We hadn't spoken in years because I thought it would be too painful. When he was chosen as the new king and first asked me to be one of his councillors, I didn't want to come because I wasn't sure what would happen if I saw him again. I've spent most of my life trying to be a good mate to your grandfather, while knowing that someone else was my true love. It's hard for someone your age to understand, but I hope you will, someday."

"I think I already do," said Audun. "It's why I need the king's help. It's why I need your help, too, Grandmother."

Song of the Glacier twitched her tail in agitation. She began to pace in front of him, her scales making a swooshing sound. "Ordinarily, I would do whatever I could to help you, but a human and the daughter of the Green Witch? Are you sure it's really love, Audun, and not infatuation? Any dragon would be attracted to someone who saved his life, but that doesn't mean you have to spend your entire life with her. Humans aren't like us. I've told you many times that they lie, cheat, steal, and think only of themselves. They can be cruel to members of their own species and twice as cruel to species they regard as animals, including us."

"But Millie isn't like that. She put her own life in danger to help us. And she's honest and caring ... I love her, Grandmother, and it isn't just because she saved our lives. She is the one I want to share my life with. I will never love another dragoness the way I love her."

"Perhaps not, Audun, but have you really thought this

48

through? I've seen what living among humans can do to dragons. If you get your wish and learn how to change your form into that of a human, you will always have to hide who you really are and what you can do. You'll live in constant fear of discovery."

"It wouldn't be like that for me," said Audun. "Millie is already a dragon part of the time and the people in her kingdom accept her the way she is. Her mother is a Dragon Friend, which means that members of our own kind accept and respect her."

"Fire-breathing dragons, perhaps, but you heard what King Stormclaw said. Our kind may not revile her as he does, but neither would they accept her. It's true that the feud between us is old and mostly forgotten, but the king could make trouble for you should you even desire to remain friends with the girl. If you pursue this relationship without his approval, King Stormclaw will banish you at the very least."

"What happened between the fire-breathers and us, Grandmother? No one ever told me."

"It happened hundreds of years before I was born, so I don't know precisely, but apparently, by chance, the ice dragons discovered a cave rich in gems. Considering the love of jewels that all dragons feel, this was a marvelous find. Although the cave was in a distant land, we mined it for years undisturbed, bringing the jewels here to the stronghold, and enriching our kingdom's treasury. When

49

the human king of the distant land discovered what we were doing, he threatened to bring the wrath of all humans down on us. Instead, we made a pact with him wherein we would continue to mine the gems, and he would receive a share.

"Once again, all was well, until the fire-breathing dragons learned of our pact with the human king. They tried to find the cave, forcing us to take ever greater measures to hide its location. One day they managed to waylay the dragons bringing the gems to the stronghold and stole a vast number of them. There was a great battle and many were injured on both sides. It happened so long ago that most families have recovered from their loss. But some, like the family of King Stormclaw, hold too tightly to their grudges."

"And that's why he hates Millie's mother?"

Audun's grandmother nodded. "He's a good dragon, but he can be rash at times as can most dragon kings. That is why they have councillors, like me. You do realize, Audun, that even if you lived in a kingdom where you wouldn't be persecuted for what you are, you would be throwing away a promising future among dragon kind. I'd always hoped that someday you might aspire to a high position, perhaps even the central platform in the audience chamber."

"I don't want to be king, Grandmother. I just want to choose my own mate. Is that really too much to ask?"

"You sound like I once did, more's the pity. No," she said, sighing again. "I don't think it's too much to ask. But what about your talent? I know you haven't learned what it is yet, and you may not for many years, but what if your talent is something you can use only in the Icy North or that you can't use around humans? If I didn't live among glaciers, I would never have known that I can hear them speak."

"That's true, Grandmother, but a lot of ice dragons have talents that have nothing to do with where they live. Grandfather can fly high wherever he is and Mother's graceful all the time. I bet Frostybreath could freeze things even if he was someplace hot. I just hope my talent is a good one, but whether it is or not, it will have nothing to do with Millie."

Song of the Glacier stopped pacing and turned to face him again. "If you truly love Millie, there is one other thing you need to consider. Dragons live for hundreds of years while humans have a much shorter life span. We never have more than one mate. Are you sure you want your mate to be someone who will not live as long as you will? If you marry her, you will do so knowing that you will outlive her and have to endure many years of grieving once she is gone."

"I understand that, Grandmother. It is a price I am willing to pay if it means I can have even a few years with Millie."

"Then I hope she loves you as much as you love her, my dear grandson."

"Will you talk to the king and the other councillors for me?" Audun asked.

Song of the Glacier sighed. "You're very persuasive, Audun. I'll do whatever I can to help you."

Five

Once more it was Frostybreath who came to tell Audun that the king had summoned him. "But I thought he didn't want to see me again," said Audun, rubbing sleep from his eyes.

"A king can change his mind, just like everyone else," the big dragon replied. "But be careful what you say. He seemed mighty worked up about something."

"I hope he *has* changed his mind," Audun said, suddenly feeling much more hopeful. "Why did you come for me? Still filling in for your friend?"

"I was on my way to the top," said Frostybreath. "So I told my friends that I'd save them the trouble. I'm adding a curlicue to the first part of the chute. I thought an extra flourish would be fun."

"I went down your chute with Loolee yesterday. I don't think I've ever had so much fun before. It's great that you can use your talent to make other dragons happy," said Audun.

Frostybreath grunted. "I do what I can. It seems to me that a talent isn't worth much if you can't use it to help others."

Audun waved good-bye to the dragon as they parted ways. He hadn't discovered his own talent yet, but then few dragons did until they reached their twentieth year. Although he wasn't worried, he hoped that his talent would be something worthwhile. His grandfather could fly higher than anyone else. His father could fly faster. His mother was as graceful as a drifting snowflake. But his grandmother's talent was so subtle that she didn't seem to do anything except sit with her eyes closed, so that she almost appeared to be asleep. When she finally opened her eyes, she would tell Audun and his parents what the glaciers were saying deep in their depths. Sometimes she said they talked about the changes in temperature or what was in the water around them. Sometimes it was about the creatures that lived in the sea nearby. When two or more glaciers bumped into one another, regardless of whether they thundered or whispered, they usually talked about one another.

As a little dragon there had been times when Audun thought that his grandmother didn't really have a talent and that she was making it up, but everyone else seemed to believe her and she always did know when a glacier was about to move or when there were new fish in the area. Sometimes dragons came to ask his grandmother for advice and she would go off by herself to listen to a glacier. Eventually, Audun came to understand that she really was special, but it had never occurred to him that the king might think so as well. The more he thought about it, however, the more sense it made that a talent like his grandmother's could be valuable to anyone who watched out for the welfare of dragons who lived on and around glaciers.

Audun had almost reached the audience room when he began to wonder what talents the other councillors might have. He'd been so concerned with getting the king to agree to help him that it hadn't occurred to him to ask his grandmother about the other dragonesses. Although most dragons knew about the king's history, little was generally known about the dragonesses who advised him. Audun hadn't paid much attention to them the last time he was in their presence, but he did seem to recall that they were older than Song of the Glacier, and at least one of them had looked at him with kind eyes. Perhaps she would help Song of the Glacier change the dragon king's mind.

Audun was about to enter the chamber when a dragon wearing the satchels of a messenger strapped to his back emerged, looking harried and tired. He nodded at Audun who waited until the exterior door had closed before opening the door to the audience chamber.

King Stormclaw wasn't seated on his stone pillar as he'd been during their last interview. Instead, he was pacing the length of the room, his tail twitching in agitation. The king stopped when he spotted Audun waiting nervously by the door. "Come in, young dragon. No need to stand there looking like I'm about to rip off your head. You'll be pleased to hear that I've reconsidered. At first I thought you were crazy for wanting to learn how to turn into a human so you could be with a human who can turn into a dragoness. I'd never heard such a thing! And knowing who the dragoness is, I must tell you that I was tempted to lock you away for your own good. However, out of regard for your grandmother, I have reconsidered your request and am willing to give you the opportunity to show me that you deserve to be taught how to turn into a human. You will have to complete five tasks to prove your worth." He gestured toward the dragoness seated farthest from Song of the Glacier. "Frostweaver will tell you what you must do."

Audun turned to the dragoness and bowed, so excited at the good news that he couldn't help but grin. The old dragoness was smiling at him when he looked up, and he could see that at least two of her fangs were missing. The flesh on her jaws was lined with wrinkles and her white scales were dull and yellowed with age. Her blue eyes bore a filmy cast but, even so, he saw excitement gleaming in their depths. Frostweaver looked so fragile that he couldn't help but wonder if she could still fly.

"Good day to you, Audun, grandson of my new friend, Song of the Glacier. It gives me great pleasure to tell you of your task and to set you on the road to achieving your goal." When the old dragoness waved a talon before her face, Audun thought she was about to fall over. It took a moment before he realized that she was using frost to draw a map in the air as if she were writing on ice. The frost shimmered and grew more solid, until he thought he could almost reach out and touch it.

"Far from here," said Frostweaver, "lies the kingdom of Aridia. In the southern half of the kingdom you will find the Arid Desert. Although many believe that the shifting sands harbor no life, we dragons know that is not true. You must fly to the Arid Desert and look for the rarest of all birds, which can be found only in the driest of lands." With a swipe of her talons, the map faded away, and the picture of a bird replaced it. The bird was ugly, with a bald head and small, piercing eyes. It looked scrawny at first, but as Audun watched, its body filled out until it looked like a different bird entirely. "You may find the desicca bird in either of its phases, but it is not the bird itself that you seek. Locate the bird and follow it to its nest, buried deep within the burning sands. Retrieve one of the eggs and bring it back here. If you are to succeed at your task, you must ensure that the egg remains intact and that the chick inside lives. Upon successful completion of this test, you shall receive your next task."

Audun nodded, relieved that the task was so simple. Find a bird and bring back its egg. Yes, he could do that.

He studied the picture as it faded, then bowed once more to the old dragoness, and turned to leave.

"Just a moment, young dragon," called Frostweaver. "You will need to take this with you." Audun glanced back to see the old dragoness weaving strands of frost in the air in front of her, creating a band of silver and white. The band grew, becoming a square as wide as her wings could reach. When she finished, she tapped the center of the square and it shrank until it was no bigger than the span of the outspread talons of one foot. Pinching the square between two talons, she handed it to Audun, saying, "This will keep the wearer whatever temperature he needs to be and will grow or shrink to the necessary size. Remember what I said about the egg. I'll be looking forward to your return. Dragonspeed!"

Audun took the square from Frostweaver and bowed once more. He was tucking it into his wing pouch as Song of the Glacier came forward. "I wish you well, Audun. Be careful in the desert and don't eat any spoiled meat. Safe travels!"

It was the farewell he had longed to hear when he left his family only days before.

❧

The young dragon was on his way up the ramp when Hildie ran after him, calling his name. "Is it true you're leaving?"

she asked, coming so close that the scales of their legs brushed together as she matched her pace to his.

Although Audun had had plenty of friends while growing up at the edge of the Icy Sea, they had all been boy dragons. All the dragonesses he'd ever known had been adults, so he wasn't sure how to react when Hildie persisted in touching him. It made Audun feel uncomfortable and he moved aside to give her more room. She followed him, staying just as close until he was bumping against the far wall.

"Where did you hear that I'm leaving?" he asked, picking up speed as he tried to put space between them. "I only just learned it myself. Does your talent allow you to see into the future?"

Although he was half-joking, Hildie seemed to take him seriously. "Actually, I don't have my talent yet. Frosty-breath told me that you were leaving. A dragon charged with cleaning your room for the next visitor told him so."

"Things move quickly around here," said Audun.

Hildie shrugged. "They usually do, although I wish they hadn't moved so quickly this time."

"Audun, do you really have to go?" cried a voice, as a small dragon launched herself onto his back.

"I do, short stuff," Audun said, laughing as he spread his wings. The little dragoness slid down just as she would the chute. "There's something important that I have to do."

"Will I ever see you again, Audun?" Loolee asked, but Audun could see that Hildie was waiting for his answer, too.

"I'll be back before you know it, little one. This shouldn't take long at all."

Six

Audun decided that Frostweaver must have done something special to the map; he could recall the way to the Arid Desert as if it were etched on the air in front of him even as he flew, and his memory wasn't usually so precise. The sun had been shining when he left the island, but the sky darkened only a few miles out and rain began to fall. Fighting his way through a vicious squall that lashed the southernmost shoreline of the Icy Sea, he followed the curve of the land until he reached the range of mountains that defined the western edge of the Kingdom of Bullrush. He skirted the mountains and went inland, turning west again before reaching the mountains of Upper Montevista. It took him two days to get that far. Another day of flying carried him across the desert of East Aridia where it was so hot that he began to sweat with his tongue and from the bottoms of his feet.

It was night when he passed over the castle in the center of a huge city. The castle was wide, with tall spires and pennants flying everywhere. Row upon row of soldiers were lined up around the inside perimeter of an enormous courtyard in the middle of the castle grounds. Bright torches edging the courtyard showed that a mosaic depicting an older man with flowing, white hair covered the very center. A man with a shining bald head stood at the edge of the mosaic beside a man who looked remarkably like the one pictured. When the bald-headed man raised his arms, the crowd grew quiet. He paused, as if for effect, then performed an intricate gesture with his hands. Audun realized that the man must be a wizard when the mosaic seemed to come to life, blinking and opening its mouth to speak. The man in the mosaic talked about the bravery of his army and congratulated the officers who had led the soldiers into battle. He spoke of the conquest of another kingdom and of how much the subjects in East Aridia would benefit. Audun thought that the man who looked like the mosaic might be doing the actual talking, but he couldn't tell for sure without going closer.

As Audun circled overhead, the face in the mosaic stopped talking and grew still and lifeless once again. The soldiers cheered, saluting the man with the flowing hair. They held their spears aloft and shook them; the glint of metal in the torchlight reminded Audun of the soldiers who had shot arrows at him in Upper Montevista, so he turned once more and headed back over the open desert.

On the fourth day he reached Aridia. A dry, hot wind

was blowing, slowly moving dunes of golden sand across the land below him. Growing up in the Icy North, he had seen countless snowdrifts, but none so wide that they stretched as far as he could see. The heat radiating off the dunes parched his throat and made him wish for the rain that he'd battled only days before.

Audun closed his inner lids to protect his eyes from the biting, wind-carried sand, but even though he flew high above the ground, he could hear the sand hissing against his scales and feel it scouring away the grime he'd acquired while traveling. By dusk he still had not found any birds, let alone the desicca bird he'd seen in Frostweaver's image.

Audun stayed aloft until long after the sun had set and the searing heat of the sand had cooled enough that he could land. Settling on the ground, he welcomed the night chill that enveloped the desert, and fell into a fitful sleep where images of Millie crying as her mother whisked her away made him growl and twitch his wings.

The heat returned with the morning and once again Audun took to the air. He hadn't gone far before he saw an enormous bird flying far off in the distance. Even in the Icy North, dragons had heard of rocs, but it was the first time Audun had ever seen one. He wondered what other kinds of creatures might live in the desert and was surprised when a short time later he glanced down and saw the ground moving. Drawing closer, he spotted a horde of insects with daggerlike stingers arched over their backs scuttling across the sand. As he passed over wind-eroded ruins, he saw an enormous snake with an arrow-shaped head investigating the remains of a collapsed wall.

A little farther on, he watched as a huge cat nearly the color of the sand slunk along the ground, stalking its prey. He would have thought nothing more of it if he hadn't seen what the cat was hunting. Three human children were shuffling across the sand, looking forlorn and bedraggled. The boys, who weren't very big, were half-carrying, half-dragging a girl even smaller than themselves. Audun might have continued on if the little girl hadn't glanced up just as he flew overhead. She looked terrified, but what made Audun want to stop and help them was the girl's blond hair and the shape of her face: the little girl looked much the way Millie must have when she was very young.

Audun was too far away to hear what the girl said when she pointed up at him, but he could see the frightened looks on the boys' faces. The older boy dropped the little girl's hand and reached into his waistband for a forked stick. Audun didn't know what he was going to do with it until the boy set a stone on a leather strap tied to the prongs of the stick. He was pulling back on the strap when the big cat wiggled its rump and charged. Not wanting to see what happened when the cat reached the children, Audun tucked his wings close to his body and aimed for the beast. The younger children began to scream just as Audun opened his mouth and roared. The boy let the leather sling go as the dragon flew over their heads and the stone bounced off Audun's neck. The young dragon barely felt it as he flew past them and landed in the big cat's path. With its fur bristling, the cat pulled up short. Faced with an angry dragon three times its size, the animal turned and ran.

To Audun's surprise, the boy turned to him and bowed, saying, "Thank you most kindly, gracious dragon. I apologize for thinking you meant us harm when you were really defending us from that horrid lion. I never thought I'd see a dragon here. My name is Galen and these two are my brother Samuel and my sister, Shanna."

All three children had straight hair bleached to a pale blond, but while Galen had blue eyes, the other children's were a warm brown. With their straight noses and squared chins, Audun would have known they were siblings even if Galen hadn't told him so.

"You are most welcome, young sir," said Audun. "I am Audun of the Icy North. If I may ask, how is it that you can talk to dragons?"

The little boy shrugged. "We had a tutor who had some magic. He taught us many things."

"Where is your tutor now? Why are you here without an adult to protect you?"

Shanna pulled a piece of cloth from her sleeve and clutched it to her chest. Audun noticed that it had a wooden head and was roughly shaped like a human. "We ran away," she said, and popped her thumb into her mouth.

"We had to," said Galen. "We lived in Desidaria, the city that surrounds the royal castle of King Cadmus, although the castle no longer belongs to him. He was killed in the war."

"There's been a war?" Audun remembered the throngs of armed people he'd seen in the courtyard in East Aridia.

Galen nodded. "It ended just a few days ago. King Beltran of East Aridia sent his soldiers to attack Desidaria. They defeated our soldiers and ransacked the city. A lot of people were killed, including our king. His brother, Dolon, swore fealty to King Beltran. Dolon sits on the throne of Aridia now."

Shanna pulled her thumb out of her mouth to tug at her brother's sleeve. "What about Owen? Can the dragon help us get Owen back?"

"We have to go," said Samuel. "Owen could be hurt."

"Who is Owen?" asked Audun.

Galen rubbed the side of his head and frowned. "He's our older brother. After King Beltran left, there were a lot of orphans and nobody knew what to do with them. Dolon said that they could all come live in the palace. He put us with them until Owen was able to sneak away from where he'd been in training and come for us."

"Owen rescued us!" said Shanna. "He was very brave!"

"Owen helped us get out of the city," said Samuel. "He was taking us to our aunt's home on the other side of the desert when the roc came."

"It came down, *whoosh*!" Shanna said, demonstrating with her hand. "And took Owen away."

"We were going after him when you found us," said Galen. "It's what he would have done if one of us had been carried off."

"Do you think he's all right?" Shanna asked, her brown eyes big and round.

"I'm sure he is," Galen said, but he didn't sound very convincing.

"We have a problem, though," said Samuel.

Audun raised a brow ridge. "Only one?"

"He means we're lost," said Shanna.

"Owen was the one who knew the way," explained Galen. "I thought I knew which way the roc took him, but I've been getting all turned around . . ."

Shanna rubbed her eyes with a grubby hand, wiping away a tear. "I want to go home, Galen!"

"I know, Shanna," said her older brother, as he put his arm around her. "That's what we all want. But we can't go back to Desidaria now."

"I can take you to your aunt's home," said the dragon, "as long as you can tell me where it is."

Samuel shook his head. "We have to get Owen first. We can't go anywhere without him!"

"Could you help us find him?" asked Galen. "We could find him faster if you were looking for him, too."

"You have wings!" Shanna said through her tears.

"We'd go with you," said Samuel. "If we were all looking—"

"I can't take you with me. You'd be in the way. And I can't leave you here. It isn't safe. I'll take you to your aunt and come back and look for Owen."

"No!" cried Samuel. "He's *our* brother. *We* have to go rescue him!"

"Take my help the way I offer it, or don't get it at all. It's up to you. I have my own task ahead of me, so if you don't want my help . . ."

"But we do!" Galen said. "You and I could take Shanna and Samuel to our aunt's home, then I could go with you."

"Galen!" shouted his brother and sister in unison.

"That wasn't what I offered," said Audun.

"Then we accept your offer as it was given," said Galen through stiff lips. Audun thought he looked as if he wanted to cry.

Audun crouched down and bent his neck so the children could climb on more easily. "We'd better hurry," he said. "I have a lot of flying to do."

⌒

With the map that Frostweaver had shown him set in his mind, Audun was able to use the children's scanty memories of the way to their aunt's home to head in the right direction. It took him longer to find the town than it had to cross the desert, but when he did he landed on the outskirts and refused to go into the town itself. Although the children assured him that their aunt would want to thank him, Audun couldn't help but remember the reception he'd gotten from other humans.

"Do you know the way to your aunt's home from here?" Audun asked as the children clambered down.

Galen nodded. "I came to visit her last year. I know right where she lives."

"You're going back for Owen, aren't you?" Samuel asked, his brow creased with worry.

"I'm going to start looking for him now," said Audun. Dipping his head to the children, he spread his wings, pausing only long enough to say, "I'll bring him back if it's at all possible."

"Are you sure I can't go with you?" asked Galen. "Two pairs of eyes can see more than one."

"That's true," said Audun. "But dragon eyes can see farther than human eyes. And trying to take something away from a roc won't be easy or safe. If you go with me, I'll have to worry about you as well as your brother. You don't want me to be distracted when I'm trying to rescue him, do you?"

The little boy looked at the ground and muttered, "I guess not."

"Besides, your brother and sister need you to take them to your aunt. Someone bigger and stronger than them has to show them the way. Samuel and Shanna are depending on you."

"That's true," Galen said, glancing at the smaller children. Shanna was rubbing her eyes again and it was obvious that she was having a hard time keeping them open. Aside from two bright red spots on his cheeks, Samuel looked pale and shaky.

"Take care of each other," Audun said, backing away so he could flap his wings without knocking the children over.

"Thank you!" Galen shouted as the dragon took off.

Audun didn't know much about rocs, other than that they were big. He'd heard that they might fight dragons if provoked, but no one he knew had ever fought one and he didn't want to be the first. If rocs were as territorial as a lot of other birds he knew, there probably wouldn't be too many in one area, which meant that the bird he had seen before might be the very one he had to find now. With the wind shifting the sand, it wasn't easy to find a certain spot in the desert, but Audun was sure he had come pretty close. He flew in the direction that he thought the roc had gone, looking for any sort of sign that a big bird had passed that way.

It was late in the day when he saw the first droppings. Something big had created the huge black and white speckled piles that littered the desert floor like half-melted globs of snow. The enormous feather resting on the sand beside them was as long as his wings were wide.

A penetrating scent grew stronger as he flew on. The ground below him began to change. Instead of sand, he saw rocky outcroppings with occasional withered plants growing in the cracks. The outcroppings became taller and more misshapen the farther he went, until a bizarre garden of weirdly shaped formations lay before him. Having been blasted by wind and sand for many years, the stones had taken on outlines unlike anything else in nature. Fantastic protuberances, curves, and spires stood sentinel, casting their shadows on the land as the sun prepared to set.

Still following the scent of the roc, Audun eventually came upon a tall spire with a nest made of entire trees stacked and woven together on top. Vines as big around as a human man's waist helped to hold it together. Audun was impressed by the enormous distances the roc must have flown to bring such big trees to build a nest. He was even more impressed as he drew closer and could see the nest's actual size. A dozen dragons could have slept in the nest without any one touching another.

At first the nest appeared to be empty, but then he saw movement: a down-covered baby roc three times the size of a baby dragon waddled from one side to the other. Audun had flown close enough to spot another fledgling when he heard a loud squawk and saw a shadow pass overhead. The mother roc was back, bringing food for her babies. With the enormous bird approaching, Audun didn't have much of a choice; he could hide or fly away and hope she hadn't seen how close he had been to her nest. Because he still didn't know if Owen was there, hiding seemed like the better choice.

Audun put on a burst of speed and flew under the nest to latch on to one of the tree trunks with his talons. Hanging upside down beneath the nest, he turned his head to the side as rotting bark became dislodged, pattering around him as it fell. There was another painfully loud squawk and the entire nest dipped down when the adult roc landed. The nest continued to shake while she walked across it, chirruping softly to her babies. Audun tried not to make a sound as he fought to hold on.

Something heavy hit the nest as the roc dropped whatever she had brought to her babies. There was more thrashing only feet above Audun's head, making more debris rain through the cracks. Peering through the gaps in the interwoven trees, the young dragon could just make out the patterns of a two-foot-thick snake that reared up when one of the babies pecked it.

With the snake hissing just above his head, Audun moved to the other side of the nest, looking for something to indicate that the boy, Owen, had been there. He was halfway to the outer edge when both babies attacked the snake at once and the mother joined in to help them, making the nest bounce and shake.

Stopping to peer up through the tree trunks every few feet, Audun eventually reached the far side of the nest and began to move along its rim. He was working his way around a thicker cluster of branches, trying to see through some still-attached foliage, when a face appeared and two vivid blue eyes blinked at him. The face was that of a human boy about the same age as Millie and her friends, and his hair was the same shade of yellow as that of the three children Audun had just met.

Audun hadn't expected to find the boy as easily as this. "Are you Owen?" he whispered.

The boy looked stunned. He drew back, but the branches wouldn't allow him to go far. "How do you know my name?" he asked.

"Your brothers and sister sent me to find you. I'm here to take you to them."

Hope lit the boy's eyes. In his excitement, his voice was louder than before. "You've seen them? Are they all right?"

"Shh!" said Audun. "Not so loud or the birds will come looking. Galen and the others are fine. They're just worried about you. Is there any way down from there?"

"You mean a hole through the bottom? I don't think so. I was looking for one, but this is all I've found. It's sort of a pocket between the trunks. The little ones can't reach me, but I won't stand a chance if a big one comes looking for me. There are two adults. The one that brought me has been gone for a while. I thought I could wait until night and climb down if I could find a gap big enough to let me through."

Audun turned his head and stretched his neck to see what was below him. The nest was on a pedestal of stone with sheer drops on every side. Unless the boy was a very good climber, he wouldn't have made it, especially in the dark.

"I wouldn't recommend it," Audun whispered to the boy. "I can't get to you from here, but if you climb onto the nest I can carry you away."

"Why should I trust you? How do I know you really helped my brothers and sister?"

"I didn't come to steal you from a roc's nest so I could eat you, if that's what you're thinking. Do you want my help or not?"

A tree trunk groaned as the adult roc settled her weight on it. The sun was going down. Although Audun was looking forward to the cool of the night, he wasn't so sure how well a human would fare. The other roc would probably be back soon, making it that much harder for Owen to sneak out of the nest.

"If I draw the adult roc away, do you think you could climb out and hang on to the bottom of the nest until I come back to get you? I'll be as fast as I can, but we should do this now."

"I think I can," said Owen. "I used a branch to keep them off me before. How will you draw the big one away?"

"That," said Audun, "will be the easy part."

Audun's talons wouldn't let go at first, after having gripped so tightly for so long. When he could finally move them, they were stiff, but he was able to work his way to a spot where there weren't any protruding branches to get in his way. Finding a clear space below him, Audun let go of the nest and fell, opening his wings with a snap. Gliding out from under the nest, he beat his wings when he was past the edge and rose up so that he could look inside. The two babies lay beside their mother, their bellies full and rounded. At the sound of Audun's wings, the adult bird opened her eyes and looked him full in the face. "Awk!" she cried, nearly deafening Audun.

Throwing his head back, Audun roared, the sound of his voice almost as loud. Then, before the roc could react, he flew straight at her head, slapping it with his tail as he flew up and over her.

The nest tipped abruptly as the adult roc launched herself into the air. She came after Audun as if her tail were on fire, her shrill screams echoing off the rock in front of him. Audun angled his wings and began to climb. The roc was right behind him, her heavy wings pounding the air with a *whump! whump!* Veering this way and that around the bizarrely shaped spires, Audun led the giant bird away from her nest. Miles of ground sped by below him, yet he could still hear the roc screaming.

He was at the very edge of the formations when he glanced back. The roc was finally out of sight, so Audun angled his head and body and took off back toward the nest, faster than most dragons and much faster than any bird as big as a roc could ever fly. Circling around, Audun sped back to the nest but was only part of the way there when he saw another roc far off in the distance, heading in the same direction. Audun didn't have much time. He focused on the nest ahead, and put all his strength into going even faster.

"Climb on!" Audun shouted, as he reached the boy. "Hurry, the other roc is coming!"

At the sight of a dragon, the baby birds squawked and fluttered to the other side while Owen scrambled onto Audun's back.

"Hold on tight!" ordered the dragon. He beat his wings and flew as fast as he could until they were well over the desert.

Audun had slowed to a more comfortable pace when Owen finally tried to talk to him. "Where are you taking me?" he asked.

"To the town where your aunt lives. It's where I dropped off your brothers and sister. They said it was where you were headed when the roc took you."

"I don't know how to thank you," said Owen. "I still can't believe a dragon is helping us. Why are you here, anyway? I've never seen a white dragon like you before."

"I'm from the Icy North. I've come looking for a desicca bird."

"A what? No, wait! I've heard of them, although I don't know very much. They're really rare, even more rare than rocs. The only place they've ever been seen is around oases. I guess that's where you should look. I wish I could tell you more."

"Actually, you've helped a lot. I'll head for an oasis as soon as I drop you off."

"It will be night by then. It gets awfully cold in the desert at night."

"I know," said Audun. "I'm looking forward to it."

Seven

When Audun woke the next morning the sun was already up and the sand was uncomfortably hot. As he flew over the desert, the light reflecting off the sand made his head hurt, but he'd already used up an entire day helping the children and didn't want to lose any more time.

Audun's head was pounding when he finally saw an oasis, small, yet with a glint of water, and an islet of stunted trees. He licked his dry, cracked lips, but despite the pain in his head and his ever-growing thirst, the young dragon was reluctant to land for fear that the oasis was either a mirage or a trap. The water looked so tempting, and the shade so inviting, however, that Audun circled the oasis, high enough that anything on the ground would have difficulty seeing him, but low enough that he could see if something moved.

When the oasis didn't disappear and he didn't spot anything dangerous, he flew down until he was close enough to see an ant waving its feelers from the tip of a nodding leaf. Audun settled to the ground and sniffed the water. It smelled as clean and pure as it looked, so he took a chance and sipped. The water was warm, but delicious. As it trickled down his throat, he gave up all caution and submerged his head, taking one enormous gulp after another. Fortunately for Audun, the pool of water was small and he had emptied it before he drank enough to make himself sick.

With water in his belly and the shade of the trees cooling his back, Audun would have been happy to stay and rest, but he knew that his blue and white scales would stand out against the gold and green of the oasis and were sure to frighten away the bird he had come to find. Spreading his wings again, Audun took off. Perhaps he'd find a desicca bird at the next oasis.

For the briefest moment Audun wondered if the desicca bird might not exist and if the king and his councillors were just trying to get rid of him. He might have given the thought serious consideration, if his grandmother hadn't promised to help him. Even if she wasn't happy with his choice, he knew that she would never betray him in such a way. And certainly Owen would have had no reason to lie. If the boy said the bird existed, Audun was sure that it did.

The sun was still high in the sky and Audun was beginning to feel thirsty again when he spotted something flying in the distance. Because it didn't move quite like a bird, Audun grew curious and swerved in its direction. As he drew closer he realized that it was a man riding on a magic carpet—the same bald-headed wizard he'd seen making the mosaic talk. Intent on following a pair of vultures, the wizard didn't seem to have seen Audun.

The young dragon watched as the man gestured at the sky. A small, dark cloud appeared overhead, scudding just above the vultures. Suddenly, a bolt of lightning shot from the cloud, forking to strike both vultures at once. Stunned, the birds tumbled to the ground. The wizard gestured again and sand rose into the air, shaping itself into a braided net which scooped up the birds and hauled them onto the magic carpet. Not caring to see what the wizard would do next, Audun turned and sped back the way he'd come.

The wind was beginning to pick up when Audun finally spotted an oasis even smaller than the first. As he spiraled down toward it, he saw a fat, yellow-brown bird with a bald head tottering awkwardly through the meager foliage surrounding the tiny pond. It looked just like the bird in the image that Frostweaver had shown him.

Not wanting to frighten the creature, Audun swerved away, but it was too late. His shadow had fallen on the desicca bird, which looked up in alarm. A moment later, the bird took off, flying away on broad, sturdy wings strong enough to support its chunky body. Audun followed the bird, hoping it would lead him to its nest, but instead it veered into the increasing wind. Soon the wind was so strong that Audun had to fight for every inch, yet the desicca bird was able to fly into it with no apparent difficulty.

When the stinging sand made his eyes tear despite their inner lids, Audun turned his head away and struggled to gain altitude, hoping to climb above the storm.

Afraid that the wind might tear his wings before he could escape, Audun strained to get above the blowing sand until he was so high that the air was thin and he had to fight to breathe. The golden cloud roiled and churned below him as he fought to stay above the storm. When the wind finally died away, Audun spread his wings to their fullest and let himself glide down to the hot sand.

Too tired to move, Audun lay on his side, dragging air into his aching lungs. He was still there when the sun went down, letting the night bring its welcome chill.

∽⌒

As the sun came up, Audun raised his head and groaned. Another day of searching. Another day of little to drink and nothing to eat. At least now he had seen one of the birds. He even had a good idea of where he should start looking.

The storm had changed the face of the desert, erasing dunes here, creating new ones there. Once again Audun took to the sky, looking for the oasis where he had seen the desicca bird. He found it more quickly this time, for now he knew where to look. The precious patch of greenery and water had been ravaged by the storm, but not destroyed. Audun was certain that this was where the bird would appear. All he had to do was wait.

A new dune had formed close to the oasis. Landing halfway up, Audun inched backward so he was partly buried in the concealing sand, yet could still see everything that happened near the water. As the morning wore on, the sand became hotter, until Audun felt as if he were roasting alive. To his surprise, however, the spot between his back and his wing wasn't hot. In fact, it was the only spot that was comfortable.

It occurred to Audun that it might be the effect of the never-melting ice that he had stuck in his pouch, so he took it out and held it against his forehead, easing the ball of pain that had been forming between his eyes. Even without the ice, however, the area between his back and wing felt fine, so he reached in the pouch once more and removed the rest of its contents, including the square of woven frost. Although he'd assumed that he was meant to use it to keep the egg warm, he wondered if it would also work to keep him cold.

After returning the ice to his pouch, Audun spread the square over his back. Within a minute or two he began to feel cool all over. Comfortable now, Audun shifted back and forth, letting the sand cover him until only his head was free. He waited through the heat of the day, dozing now and then, and was rewarded for his patience when something flew past his face. The desicca bird had returned.

Audun kept perfectly still as the bird landed at the edge of the pond. It looked fatter than he remembered it and was even more ungainly as it waddled into the water. Stretching its neck, the bird's throat convulsed and, to Audun's surprise, a fountain of water gushed out, mixing with the water that was already there. As more and more water emerged from the bird, its sides shrank until it was as thin as the first image that Frostweaver had shown him. When it was finished, the desicca bird waddled out of the pond, which was now considerably larger.

Audun's stomach churned as he thought about what he'd just seen. He had drunk water from a pond just like that only the day before. It had tasted fine then, but the thought that it might have come out of a bird's stomach was revolting. He was trying not to gag when he noticed that the bird had gone to the base of a dune on the far side of the oasis and had begun to preen its feathers, leaving them with a glistening sheen that seemed to glue them together. When it finally seemed satisfied, the bird turned to the dune and began to dig, scrabbling at the sand and shooting it out behind in a constant stream. It continued to dig until its body was buried in the sand, yet it didn't show any sign of stopping. When it had completely disappeared into the dune, Audun realized that the bird was creating a round tunnel as wide as it was tall.

Although the bird was out of sight, sand continued to shoot out of the tunnel. When it stopped, Audun expected the bird to emerge, but at least five minutes passed before he saw movement and then it wasn't the bird at all, but a mottled brown and gold egg, rolling out of the tunnel as its mother pushed it from behind. The bird emerged only long enough to place the egg beside the water before returning to the tunnel. Twice more it brought out an egg, and each time Audun thought about rushing down to grab one, but curiosity made him stay where he was, waiting to see what would happen next.

When the last egg had rolled to a stop beside the water, the desicca bird tapped it with her beak once, twice, three times. Suddenly the egg began to rock wildly back and forth. A crack appeared in its side and a sharp yellow beak appeared. As the first baby emerged from its shell, the mother tapped the second egg, eliciting the same response. The third egg was a disappointment, however, for despite the mother's tapping, the egg remained motionless and no baby bird appeared.

Audun was mentally kicking himself for not taking one of the viable eggs before they hatched when he noticed that the babies were following their mother into the pond. Scrawny and yellow, the freshly hatched chicks staggered into the water and plopped down. While their mother stood beside them, chirruping softly, the babies sat patiently, gazing at each other and the new world around them. Audun wondered what was going on. Then he realized that even though they weren't visibly doing anything, the chicks were growing plumper. It wasn't until he saw the waterline receding that he understood what was happening.

The chicks had hatched from the eggs of a bird that carried water in her body and could deposit it at will, and now they were absorbing the water she had brought.

That's one way to give your babies water in a desert, thought Audun. *And that's why they're seen only near oases. They don't come to the oases. They make them!*

The two chicks were as round as snowballs when Audun's gaze returned to the last egg. He was going to have to visit another oasis in the hope that a second desicca bird might come along. And if none came . . . The remaining egg rocked slightly and Audun gasped. The baby inside was alive after all!

Moving carefully, Audun crept out of the dune, hoping the mother desicca bird wouldn't notice the sand trickling down the slope, or the continued rocking of her egg. She was still absorbed in examining her hatchlings so Audun dashed down to the water's edge, pulled the square off his back, and threw it over the egg. Picking it up in his talons, Audun leaped into the air, climbing high with powerful beats of his wings. The desicca bird squawked, but Audun was already far away, with the egg clutched to his chest.

Twice in two days he had stolen something from a mother bird. The first time he had felt triumphant. This time he couldn't help but feel guilty.

Eight

Word of Audun's return must have reached the council members the moment he set foot on King's Isle because he was taken directly to the audience chamber where they were already waiting. He had yet to relax his grip on the egg he carried; it was almost with reluctance that he unwrapped it from its covering and held it up for the king and his councillors to see. The older dragons leaned forward to get a better look. After a moment, Stormclaw turned to Frostweaver and raised a brow ridge.

The old dragoness gestured to Audun. "Bring the egg to me, young dragon. My eyes aren't as good as they were when I was your age."

Audun stood on his hind legs to show the egg to Frostweaver, and sand trickled from the spaces between his scales, dusting the floor. Although the sandstorm had polished the outside of each scale, it had also left him with sand in every crack and crevice. He'd already decided that the desert was a nice place for an ice dragon to visit, but he, at least, would never want to live there.

The sand crunched under his feet as Audun held the egg higher, being careful not to lose his grip. The dragoness leaned so close that the tip of her nose almost touched the egg. Turning her head to the side, she placed her ear against the egg and listened. When she finally sat back and turned to the king, a smile split her wrinkled face.

"It's a desicca bird's egg all right, and I can hear the chick moving inside," she told the king, as Audun covered the egg to keep it warm. "We can't waste any time. He has to take the egg to her now."

Stormclaw nodded. "And he will, soon enough. But first I want to hear what happened. Did you have any difficulty finding the bird?" he asked Audun.

The young dragon shook his head. "Not once I knew where to look, but if the human boy, Owen, hadn't told me, I'd still be combing the desert right now."

"When did you see a human?" asked Song of the Glacier.

"I saved his brothers and sister from a lion that was about to eat them. They were the ones who told me that a roc had carried off Owen. It was after they escaped from Desidaria right after the war."

The king's brow ridges came together in a frown. He glanced at the dragoness seated between him and Song, but all she could do was shrug. "There's been a war in

Aridia?" he said, turning back to Audun. "Who were they fighting?"

"The East Aridian army invaded the city. A lot of people were killed, including the king."

Frostweaver gasped; Stormclaw and his advisers exchanged glances. "That explains why there was neither a delivery nor a message," said the king.

"What else can you tell us about this war?" Song of the Glacier asked her grandson.

Audun told them everything he could remember, and when he was done he told them in greater detail about the lion and the roc and finding the desicca bird. The king had come down from his pillar to pace while the young dragon talked about the orphans in the city, but he didn't interrupt until Audun was finished. "You've done well, young dragon. Better than we expected. The news you brought has given us much to think about."

"Stormclaw," prompted Song of the Glacier.

"Ah, yes. Your second task," the king continued. "Because you have been so resourceful, and have shown real concern for the chick within the egg, we believe you are the ideal dragon to take care of this for us. Wave Skimmer will tell you what to do."

The dragoness seated between Frostweaver and the king waved at Audun to get his attention. She was plumper than Frostweaver and not quite as old, although her scaled face bore more wrinkles and creases. "I'm over here, young dragon," she said. "King Stormclaw seems to forget that you don't know who we are. My name is Wave Skimmer and my talent lets me see things far away, provided they're under or on top of water. And if the weather is good. And if I'm feeling up to it. Sometimes my back aches so much that—"

"Wave Skimmer!" interrupted the king.

"Oh, right. You're in luck today. I think we'll be able to see just fine. We need you to take the egg to the sea witch Nastia Nautica, and exchange it for a musical instrument called the Sea Serpents' Flute that she keeps in that rotting hulk she calls home. Here, I'll show you."

Picking up a wide bowl resting beside her, she spread her wings and stepped off the slab, landing on the floor with a thump. The bowl was filled with water that sloshed over the rim when she set it down. "Now watch," Wave Skimmer said, sticking her talon in the water and stirring it. A picture formed in the swirling water. It was hard to make out at first, but as Audun watched the image became clearer. An old mermaid with pale, nearly transparent hair and dark green scales on her lower half was holding a long, thin tube with holes running down two sides.

Wave Skimmer flicked her talon at the mermaid. "That is Nastia Nautica, and that," she said, circling her talon tip around the tube, "is the instrument you have to bring back."

The mermaid in the image looked up when Wave

Skimmer said her name, almost as if she had heard her. She began to look around, peering under tables and into chests. When she didn't see whatever she was looking for, she flipped open the curved lid of a sea chest and tossed the instrument inside. Bubbles escaped from the chest as she shut the lid and turned to sit on it.

"What's she doing?" Audun asked.

"Don't ask me," said Wave Skimmer. "She's as crazy as a sea serpent stuck in a waterspout."

Nastia Nautica spun around, her dark, empty eyes looking frantically from one side of the room to the other.

"Do you think she can hear us?" Audun asked.

The mermaid darted to the empty panes of the large window at the back of the room. Sticking her head out, she peered around, seeming disappointed when she pulled her head back in, her mouth working in a scream that Audun was thankful he couldn't hear.

"Huh," said Wave Skimmer. "I hadn't thought of that. Sure looks that way, doesn't it?" The old dragoness took her talon out of the water and the image vanished. When she stuck the tip back in, Audun could see rolling waves as if he were looking down at the water from above. "That isn't right," muttered the old dragoness. "Maybe if we go this way . . ." When Wave Skimmer angled her talon to the side, the image shifted as well. Now it looked like the waves were coming head on, as if the dragons were bobbing on top of the water. Audun noted that they were near an island with oddly shaped trees and what looked like a magic carpet on the sand. An old man was dancing around the carpet, waving something green in the air while sunlight glinted off his bald head.

"It's that wizard again," muttered Audun. "I wonder what he's up to now."

"Slush!" exclaimed the dragoness, and jammed her talon in the water until it scraped the bottom of the bowl. This time the image raced down to the bottom of the ocean until all they could see was brown muck.

"I went too far," murmured Wave Skimmer, pulling her talon back just a bit. "There, that's better." The image of an old, round-bellied shipwreck appeared, the timbers broken and half-covered with seaweed. Brightly colored fish darted in and out of the openings while a long, thin creature like a flat snake undulated past. "It's not much to look at, but the old witch has lived there for years," said the dragoness.

Suddenly, Nastia Nautica shot out of one of the larger openings, frightening a school of small, bright yellow fish that darted out of her way. The sea witch looked wildly around, but didn't seem to see anything. Shaking her fist at the ocean outside her door, she retreated into her wreck.

"Where is this?" asked Audun.

"That's easy," said Wave Skimmer, taking her finger out of the water. "Go due south for three days. When you see a cone-shaped island puffing smoke, head west until you see three islands in a straight line. Look for the sea witch's wreck near the island shaped like a seagull's head."

"Why don't you show him a map like I did?" asked Frostweaver.

Wave Skimmer glared at the older dragoness. "You do things your way and I'll do them mine. Now, if you don't have any other questions . . . ," she said, turning to Audun. When he shook his head, she flew back to her perch atop the slab, her wings creaking with each beat.

"You forgot the amulet," King Stormclaw reminded her.

"Oh, right! Silly of me. He's going to need that." Peering down at Audun she told him, "Now, I'm sure that like most ice dragons, you can hold your breath underwater for a good long while. However, you won't be able to hold it while you talk to the sea witch, so you'll need this amulet I'm going to give you, if I can just find it." The old dragoness patted her slab. "Let me see . . . No, it's not . . . I know! I must have put it in my pouch." Her voice became muffled as she buried her face under her wing. "No, it's not . . . Ooh! What's this? Tsk, tsk. I'd better have a doctor look at that before it gets any bigger. Now let me . . . Here it is! I was sitting on it. This is your amulet."

Snagging the chain with his talon, Audun held up the embossed amulet so he could examine it. Waves surrounding a round bubble rolled across the amulet. For a moment, Audun thought the waves were moving.

"That amulet is yours now, so put it on and don't take

it off. It will let you breathe underwater for as long as you're wearing it. Take it off and you'll drown. If you're underwater, I mean. Any questions?"

"Just one," said Audun. "I'm supposed to take the egg to the sea witch and trade it for that flute. Does she know I'm coming?"

"Nope. She has no idea," said Wave Skimmer.

"Is there anything I should know about her?"

"You shouldn't trust her. Nastia Nautica's a slippery one. Any *other* questions?"

Audun shook his head and the old dragoness sat back with a soft grunt. "Well then, as I said before, you need to hurry. The chick won't stay alive in that egg forever. I don't know why the old sea witch wants it, but she won't trade for the egg unless the chick is still alive."

"I'll leave right away," said Audun, but King Storm-claw was talking to his councillors again. Audun heard a few words: ". . . send someone to find out . . . ," and ". . . no one who can . . . ," before his grandmother called him over. She gestured for him to follow her behind her slab so they could have a moment of privacy.

"I wanted to tell you that you did very well with your first task," Song told him. "Just be careful around the sea witch. Nastia Nautica has no scruples. She'll do anything to get what she wants."

☙

Audun had a lot on his mind as he climbed the ramp to the top floor and the exit of the island stronghold. He was grateful to his grandmother for taking his side and worried that the king might never see why he had to be with Millie. And what about Millie? Her mother had taken her away because of him. He didn't know anything about her mother, except that she was a princess, a witch, and a Dragon Friend. Was she good to Millie? Had she taken her away to punish her? What was she doing right now? Was he wasting his time hunting for an egg and negotiating with a sea witch when he should be rescuing his beloved?

Audun wasn't looking where he was going as he left the ramp and almost ran into two dragons that were blocking his way. One was Hildie, looking bored. The other was an older male dragon he had never met before. "Audun!" cried Hildie, her face lighting up. "I heard you were back. Are you staying long?"

"No, I'm on my way out now, actually," he said, trying to edge past.

Hildie frowned ever so slightly, then quickly sidled up to the older dragon and stood so that their sides were touching. "Wait, you have to meet my suitor, Ice Rider. He got his adult name last year, isn't that right, dear?" The adoring look she gave him was so unlike the bored expression she'd been wearing just a moment before that Audun was surprised. Apparently Ice Rider was as well, but he seemed to like it; he lifted his tail and wrapped it around hers in a possessive way.

"That's right, sweetness," he said, smiling at her.

Turning to Audun, Hildie said, "He's the champion ice floe rider. He can ride a floating piece of ice for miles."

"How nice," Audun told the dragon. "I'm sure that comes in handy at times." As he squeezed past them, trying to keep the egg he cradled against his chest from getting squashed, he noticed the look of disappointment in Hildie's eyes.

"Audun!" squealed Loolee, as she barreled off the ramp. "I heard you were back. Do you want to ride down the chute with me? I had so much fun last time."

"I'm sorry, Loolee, but I can't today. I have to go somewhere now. Maybe I'll be able to slide with you when I come back."

"All right," the little dragoness said, her crest drooping.

"And we'll talk, too, then, won't we, Audun?" called Hildie as he neared the door to the outside.

"Of course," he said, but instead of thinking about talking to Hildie, he was already wondering what he could possibly say to a sea witch.

Nine

A udun may not have had a map this time, but he did know how to follow directions. He flew due south for three days, stopping to catch fish and to drink from rivers, and later to catch even bigger fish from the ocean. He took time out to sleep twice, once amid the ruins of a castle, after getting permission from the banshee who lived there, and once on a tropical island whose only occupants were crabs and seabirds. Both nights he had difficulty falling asleep because he was thinking about Millie. Audun took good care of the egg, carrying it gently and making sure it was wrapped in the square so that the temperature was just right.

If it hadn't been for the smoke, he would have missed the cone-shaped island that Wave Skimmer had mentioned. He'd been looking for the smoke for the last half day, but he smelled it before he saw it. Turning west, he began to look for the three islands all in a row, but didn't spot them until late in the day.

Not wanting to face the sea witch in the dark, Audun spent the night on the island shaped roughly like a seagull's head, although he thought it looked more like a crow. He was worried about the baby bird because it had been in the egg for much longer than its nest mates, so every once in a while he pressed his ear against the egg and listened. If he waited long enough, he was rewarded with the smallest of sounds, and so knew that the baby was still alive.

He woke early the next morning when the sunlight turned rosy outside his eyelids. After breakfasting on a plump fish, he flew out over the water, the amulet's chain around his neck. Unlike the murky water in the Icy North, this water was clear and he could see far into its depths as he skimmed the tops of the waves.

Audun circled the island. When he reached the spot where he had started and still hadn't found anything, he widened the circle and searched again. He did this three or four times, until he finally saw the wreck just beyond an enormous bed of seaweed. The ship had sunk in one piece. It had been a large ship, and sturdily built, although time and the sea had left gaping holes big enough for entire schools of fish to swim through. One fish was so huge that Audun was sure that it, at least, couldn't fit through the openings. Nearly twenty feet long, the fish's gaping mouth took up most of its pointed face and was filled with dragon-sized teeth. It swam with the confidence of being the biggest predator around. Audun watched as it passed over the wreck and back again. Finally, it seemed to grow bored and swam away, but the young dragon waited until it was out of sight before heading down to the wreck.

He didn't want to startle the witch, so he swam around the wreck quietly, wondering how to find her. At the squared-off back of the ship he found the window that he'd seen in Wave Skimmer's bowl of water. He peered through the window, trying to see the dim interior, and suddenly there she was, staring back at him with eyes like dark, bottomless pits. The witch's pale, green skin looked taut and ageless, but it was her cloud of nearly colorless hair and her horrifying eyes that made her look so old.

"What do you want?" Nastia Nautica demanded.

A jellyfish undulated past Audun, trailing ribbonlike tendrils behind it. Squinting her eyes in annoyance, the sea witch pointed a finger at the creature. The tendrils flailed and began to tie themselves in knots while the jellyfish wobbled in agitation.

Unable to bear the creature's agony, Audun hoped that distracting the sea witch would make her leave the jellyfish alone. "I've come to trade something for a musical instrument that you have in your possession. I have something I believe you would like."

"What musical instrument?" asked Nastia Nautica, turning back to Audun and letting the jellyfish get away. "I have lots of them. I'm a very musical person."

"It's called the Sea Serpents' Flute."

"Really? Now why would a dragon want to torment a sea serpent until it flees? Is it anyone I know?"

"I doubt it," said Audun. "Are you interested in making a trade?"

"What do you have? That flute is one of my most prized possessions. I won't let it go for just . . ." When Audun held up the covered egg, Nastia Nautica leaned out the window saying, "What's that? Unwrap it and let me see."

Audun was reluctant to unwrap the egg. After seeing what the witch had done to the poor jellyfish, he knew that she liked hurting living creatures. But he had been sent to get the flute and he wasn't going to go back without it. Gritting his teeth, Audun slowly unwrapped the egg, revealing the distinctive mottled shell.

Nastia Nautica gasped. "Is that what I think it is?" she said, crawling halfway out the window. "Give it to me! I have to see if it's alive."

"The instrument . . . ," said Audun.

"I'll get it! Just let me see that egg!"

Audun would have held on to the egg, but he was taken by surprise—the sea witch snatched it from him, and shook it hard. Placing her ear against the egg as she retreated into her wreck, she listened for a moment, then chortled with glee. "I've finally got it! Now that little witch will learn a lesson she'll never forget."

"About the trade . . . ," said Audun.

The sea witch sneered at him. "You're a fool, dragon. You should never have given up the egg so easily. Here's your trade!" Holding the egg with one hand, she made circling motions with the other and a dark, solid-looking bubble formed on her palm. Audun was backing away when she hurled it at him. The bubble exploded, its force flipping the dragon head over tail all the way to the bed of seaweed.

As a black fog dragged at his mind, he thought about Millie. She'd never let magic stop her and neither would he. Shaking with the effort, Audun fought against the darkness, willing it away until he was able to raise his head from the silt of the ocean floor. Looking around, he spotted Nastia Nautica swimming in the opposite direction with the egg clutched in her hands. He would have to follow her, but first there was something else that he needed to do.

Audun was angry. The sea witch had taken something he wasn't even sure he wanted to give up. Knowing it was a living creature that she would probably mistreat made it that much worse. And for all he knew, she might have swum away thinking that she had killed him.

Audun didn't have time to find his way through the witch's ship to the room where she kept the flute, so he decided to use the window. It wasn't big enough for a dragon Audun's size, but he drew away from the wreck, tucked his wings tight against his body, and used powerful strokes of his legs and tail to propel him through the water and smash through the window frame, splintering the wall around it.

In an instant Audun flipped open the lid of the trunk he had seen in Wave Skimmer's image. What he hadn't seen in the image, however, was the nest of sea snakes writhing in the bottom of the trunk.

The snakes hissed and stared up at the dragon with their cold eyes.

"I don't have time for this," Audun growled, as he reached toward the trunk. The sea snakes might be venomous, but they would break their fangs before they'd ever pierce his scales.

"Ordinarily, we wouldn't say anything," said one of the snakes, raising its head above the rest, "but you're one of the great ones and worthy of our respect."

"The sea witch has cast a spell on us," added another. "We must stay in this chest and guard the flute. Please don't blame us if we can't let you have it."

"What if I set you free?" asked Audun, his talons poised over the chest.

The snakes shivered in ecstasy at the thought. "Can you really do that, Great One? Do you really have the power? We would be forever grateful if only you could help us!"

"Just watch me," Audun said, as he turned around. Dragging his tail in front of him, he swung it around with a *whump*, pulverizing the chest and sending the sea snakes flying around the room.

"We're free!" cried a snake. The other snakes cheered.

Audun plucked the flute from the shards of splintered wood while the sea snakes gathered around him. The flute was bigger than he had expected, but he was still able to fit it in the pouch under his wing. Squeezing back through the hole where the window had been, he turned to follow the sea witch's scent through the water.

"What about us?" asked the snakes. "What should we do now?"

"It seems to me that you have two choices," said Audun, glancing at the little faces clustered at the splintered window. "You can stay here and let the sea witch know how you feel about being locked in a chest, or you can go back to wherever it was you came from and get on with your lives." Audun could hear them hissing among themselves as he swam away.

Following a scent through water wasn't much harder than it was to follow one through air. It helped that the amulet made breathing underwater so easy. Sea creatures gawked at the blue and white dragon as Audun coursed back and forth, tracking the sea witch. Her smell was slightly sour and distinctive enough that he didn't confuse it with other odors.

Moving as silently as possible, Audun followed the sea witch into a cave. After only a few yards, the cave narrowed into a tunnel that headed downward before abruptly changing direction and angling up. He moved more cautiously as the tunnel became so narrow that he feared he might get stuck, but it soon widened into a high-roofed chamber. The tunnel had been dark, but the chamber was filled with a pale green light that seemed to come from green stones embedded in the walls. Strange plants and animals grew in the cave, but any creature that could move fled when it saw Audun.

The dragon had gone only a few feet into the cave when he saw the sea witch. She was crouched beside the egg, which had already begun to crack. *I'm too late,* he thought, certain that the baby bird would drown if it hatched here, at the bottom of the sea.

A hole appeared in the shell and the baby's yellow beak poked through. More cracks appeared and the baby emerged, its beak opening and closing as if it were gasping.

Audun rushed farther into the cave to try to save the baby bird but slowed as he realized that the hatchling was growing rounder and fatter. By the time Audun had taken three steps, the baby that had started out smaller than a human boy's fist was as big as Audun's head. Three more steps and the bird was twice that size. It was soaking up water just as its siblings had at the oasis, but with water all around, this baby was doing it much faster.

"You're going to kill it!" Audun shouted.

Nastia Nautica whipped her head around, making her

hair swirl behind her. "So you followed me. And I thought my sharks would be fighting over your carcass by now." The baby bird continued to grow as Nastia Nautica swam back and forth in front of Audun, blocking his way. "It might die, it might not. It will soak up some of the water; the rest it will turn into air. What difference does it make as long as it does its job before it dies?"

The little bird burped and a bubble floated out of its mouth. Suddenly, the sea witch darted forward and ripped the amulet from around the dragon's neck. With a flick of her fingers, she encased the amulet in a bubble and sent it shooting out the entrance of the cave. Sneering at the dragon, the sea witch said, "You'd better hope that the bird doesn't die until it empties this cave or you'll die with it. What a dilemma—save the bird and you die, or let it finish soaking up the water and filling the cave with air and you live, for a little while at least."

Audun knew just how long he could live on the air in his lungs. It was enough to let him get to the surface, if he left right away. "You can't do this," he said, and watched the precious air bubbles trickle past his lips.

Nastia Nautica laughed. "I can do whatever I want, and you won't be able to stop me. You're going to be too busy sucking up air," she said, pointing at the ceiling where the water level had already dropped.

Audun growled at the witch as she swam to the side and let him pass. He was picking up the baby bird when Nastia

Nautica backed into the cave entrance, saying, "You really aren't very bright, are you? I wanted this cave empty of water so I could use it as a cell for a little thief who thinks she can get away with stealing my pearl. Do you see those green stones in the walls? They give off light, but that isn't all they do. They wipe out any magic used around them, so neither my prisoner's spells nor your magic will work down here. I bet you didn't know that your amulet stopped working the moment you entered this cave. You've already used up most of your air! Once again, you've helped me out through your stupidity. You'll be my test case. If the cave will hold you, it should hold my little prisoner as well. Oh, and by the way, you won't be able to get out even if you can breathe underwater. Not after I do this!"

With a flick of her tail, the sea witch turned and darted down the tunnel. A moment later, Audun heard the rumble of stones falling as she blocked off the entrance to the cave.

They were trapped! Now Audun would never see Millie again and . . . He took a deep breath of the air at the top of the cave and tried to calm himself. The baby bird made a chirruping sound and waddled a few steps closer. The little creature didn't seem to mind being underwater. His body was so big now that his head looked like a tomato resting atop an enormous pumpkin and his legs were two little twigs that probably couldn't have held him up if he had been on dry ground.

Bending his neck until his eyes were level with the

bird's, the young dragon said, "How are you doing, little fella?"

"Mama!" said the bird, gazing at Audun with a look of adoration.

Audun jerked his head back. "I'm not your mother. My name is Audun and I'm going to rescue you."

The little bird bobbed its head up and down as if in agreement. "Mama!" it said again.

Audun was about to protest, but he felt a growing tightness in his chest. The air in his lungs was almost gone. If he didn't do something soon, he might actually die down here. Glancing up, he saw that the water level had dropped by a third. While the baby bird continued to swell, Audun swam above the water and took a deep breath. The air smelled like fish and seaweed, both of which Audun liked. At least he could breathe while he tried to think, but he still didn't have long. If they didn't go soon, the baby bird would be too big to fit through the tunnel even if it wasn't blocked. And the sea witch was bound to discover that he'd taken the instrument and freed the snakes. He was sure she'd come back then, but if Audun had his way, he and the bird would both be long gone.

Ten

$\mathcal{L}$eaving the baby desicca bird on the floor of the cave, Audun slipped down the tunnel to see if it was truly blocked. He was able to get past the point where the angle of the tunnel changed direction, but only a few feet farther he ran into a plug made of boulders. Knowing that the sea witch's word was worthless, he tried to use his magic to move the boulders aside. Try as he might, he couldn't budge even the smallest pebble. He was still trying to make the boulders move themselves when the sea snakes arrived.

"What are you doing?" asked the first snake to wriggle through a crack between the boulders.

"Trying to get out," said Audun.

Another snake appeared, and another and another until a mass of squirming bodies filled the water around Audun and he couldn't see his talons in front of his face. "Why don't you go between the rocks like we do?" asked one of the snakes.

There were too many snakes to tell them apart, and the way they kept sliding over and around one another would have made it impossible, so Audun didn't even try. "I'm too big. Now get out of my way so I can see what I'm doing."

"We want to help you," said a snake.

"How can you . . ." Audun stopped when he began to feel the tightness in his chest. Knowing that he didn't have any air to waste, he shuffled backward until he reached the cave behind him. By now the baby bird was nearly as big as he was and the water level was so low that the dragon had only to stretch his neck to breathe. When he dropped his head again, the water around him was once more filled with sea snakes.

"Why are you here?" he asked them.

"To help you," said one.

"We have to," said another. "We tried to go home, but the witch's magic won't let us."

"We have to protect the flute, no matter where it is."

"You have the flute, so we have to stay with you."

"What can we do to help?"

Audun sighed. He knew that a magic compulsion could be very strong. Even if his magic was working, he wasn't sure he'd be able to break it. If he didn't want the snakes getting in his way, he'd have to give them something to do, although he doubted they could really help him. "Why don't you go see how many boulders the sea witch put in front of the opening?"

"We can do that!" said a snake, and they all turned and swam into the tunnel in one apparently solid mass.

"Are you all right, little one?" Audun asked the baby bird. He couldn't see its legs at all now under its grossly engorged body.

"Mama!" cried the baby bird, rocking toward Audun.

The dragon looked up as the first sea snake returned. "How many boulders did you see?"

"A whole lot!" said the snake.

"Can you give me a number?" Audun asked. "You can count, can't you?"

"What does that mean?" asked another snake.

"Never mind," Audun said. "You just stay here and keep your eyes on the bird. Don't let anything happen to it."

"But we need to stay with you!"

"Not this time," said Audun. Rising up on his toes, Audun filled his lungs with air until he couldn't hold any more. After giving the baby bird a gentle pat, he backed down the tunnel so his tail would be toward the boulders. When he reached the plug, Audun moved his tail to the side, rested his weight on his front legs and kicked hard with the back ones. One kick shifted the boulders, making debris swirl around him. It took two more kicks before the boulders shot out of the tunnel, startling a school of orange and white striped fish.

Some of the sea snakes had followed him despite what

he'd said. They cheered, writhing in joy. "Now you can get out!" said a snake, twining around his ear.

"Not yet," Audun said, and he hurried down the tunnel. There was very little water left in the cave when he arrived and Audun wasn't sure he'd be able to get the bird out, but when he touched it, the water in its belly sloshed around, changing the bird's shape enough that he thought he might have a chance.

The bird was so big now that Audun could no longer get a grip on it. Instead, he rolled it toward the tunnel, letting the little bit of water left in the cave support some of its weight. When he reached the entrance to the tunnel, he had to push and squeeze, pinch and shove the bird through the narrow opening. He thought the bird was stuck at the point where the tunnel changed direction, but a little more pressure on one side and its round, spongy body squished through.

Audun was relieved when the baby bird popped out of the tunnel like a cork out of a bottle. Although he was no longer afraid that the bird might drown, he was worried about what would happen to it out in the ocean where the volume of water was so huge. He didn't have much air left himself, after working so hard to get the bird out of the cave.

There hadn't been enough space in the tunnel for the sea snakes to help him much, but once in the open ocean they gathered around, waiting to be told what to do. "You can help me push it to the surface," he said.

With the snakes pushing alongside him, Audun was

making good headway when the fish with the pointed face appeared from the direction of the sea witch's wreck. Audun wasn't afraid of the fish, but he could already feel the tightness in his chest from lack of air.

"Shark!" hissed the snakes, moving away from the bird to place themselves between the dragon and the fish.

"I know you want to protect me," said Audun, "but I need some of you to push the bird to the surface while the rest go find my amulet. It's a piece of gold on a chain that the sea witch took from me."

"We can find it," the snakes replied, and a moment later half of them were swimming back toward the bottom of the sea. Audun watched to make sure that the remaining snakes were indeed pushing the bird, albeit more slowly, before he turned to face the shark.

"Why are you here?" Audun asked, trying to ignore the tight feeling in his chest.

"I'm hungry," said the shark. "I want to taste that thing you were pushing. Get out of my way or I'll eat you instead."

"Just try it!" Audun snarled, baring his fangs.

Suddenly, Audun felt the overwhelming urge to inhale. His air was gone. He'd have to surface or drown. Either way, he wasn't going to be able to help the baby desicca bird any longer. If only . . .

And then the shark was there, jaws snapping and teeth grazing the scales on Audun's neck. The dragon fought back in a desperate frenzy. His fangs pierced the rough skin of the shark even while white lights exploded in the darkness.

The shark writhed, its tail whipping the water as Audun released his grip and bit again, deeper and harder, only to feel his jaws grow slack as he began to lose consciousness.

"We got it!" a snake's voice whispered in Audun's ear as the shark broke free and turned to rip at the dragon's side. Something cool settled around Audun's neck while the shark snapped at him, trying to penetrate the rock-hard scales. Within a few seconds, the dragon was able to breathe. He could feel the scrape of the shark's teeth even as he started to come around, and then the dark fog was gone and he was back. With one swipe of his tail, Audun knocked the shark spinning through the water.

The shark shook itself and turned to charge at the dragon again. When it was only a few yards away, Audun threw back his head and roared. Ripples of sound hit the shark like mallet blows to its snout, forcing it to turn aside. Audun was preparing to fend off another attack when the shark shook its head and sped away.

The sea snakes cheered, their tails slicing through the water, but Audun wasn't ready to celebrate yet. All the while he had been fighting the shark, the baby bird had been soaking up more water, becoming wider and harder to move. It took all of the young dragon's strength and that of the sea snakes as well to shove their charge to the surface of the water, and even then the bird grew heavier and heavier as they propelled it toward the nearest island. When they finally rolled the baby bird onto the sandy beach, Audun was so tired that he was close to collapsing.

"Get rid of that water!" he told the bird, and gave it one last shove. Then, while the sea snakes watched from just beyond the surf, Audun lay his head on the sand and let the darkness overwhelm him.

Eleven

*I*t was morning when Audun came fully awake, although he seemed to remember more than one sunset since he first lay down. The baby bird was nestled against his side, muttering about being hungry. It was back to its normal size. Audun raised his head and saw that he was only a few yards from a pool of water that hadn't been there before. A deep channel had been etched into the beach where the excess water had drained into the sea. Apparently the baby bird had rid itself of the water right where it landed.

Audun was stiff and sore when he stood, but he had one more trip to make before he could return to King's Isle to present the flute to the council. Picking up the baby bird, he carried it past the island's tree line to the underbrush, where insects would be easy to find. While the hatchling ate, Audun returned to the ocean for a quick breakfast of fish, then retrieved the bird and rose into the sky. The oasis where he'd found the egg was at least two days' flight away, but he had to return the little creature to its mother.

🐉

Audun had been gone for over a week by the time he returned to King's Isle with desert sand still grating between his scales. Finding the mother bird hadn't been easy, but it had been well worth the effort to see her joy when she finally saw her hatchling for the first time. Fortunately for Audun and the baby bird, the mother had accepted it back, although the baby still seemed to think that the dragon was its mother, too.

The first dragon Audun ran into when he set foot in the king's stronghold was Frostybreath. The big ice dragon seemed happy to see him, patting him on the back so hard that Audun nearly lost his footing. "Welcome back, young dragon. You were gone so long that we thought we'd never see you again. The king and his councillors are going to be happy to see you. And so is Loolee. Make sure you ride the chute with her. It's all she's been able to talk about since you left the last time."

"I will," said Audun. He didn't want to disappoint the little dragoness again.

"I'll go on ahead and let the king know that you're here, but you might as well go down to the antechamber. I'm sure he'll want to see you right away."

Audun was on his way down the ramp when he passed

115

a gaggle of dragonesses going the other way. They all seemed happy to see him, but it was Hildie who stopped to talk while her friends continued on. "What have you been doing?" she asked. "You look different."

"I've been in the desert," he replied, thinking that she must be referring to the sand he was still shedding as he walked.

"Hmmm," Hildie said, looking him up and down. "I didn't know a desert could do that to you."

Audun excused himself and continued down the ramp, but somehow he knew that she was still watching him.

Audun had never thought much about his appearance. He'd always been the average length for whatever his age happened to be and he'd always kept his scales fairly presentable, but he'd never preened the way some dragons did, or paid someone to burnish his scales to a semi-sheen. It came as a surprise, therefore, when he paused long enough to see his reflection in the ice and it wasn't at all what he'd expected. True, his scales were the same blue and white they'd always been, but now they gleamed in the torchlight like well-polished metal. He also looked older; he'd lost the rounded cheeks of a teenage dragon and acquired a more angular, adult look. Although he hadn't grown any longer, he seemed bigger, with well-defined muscles and broader shoulders. When he turned this way and that to see himself better, it was obvious that he had been working hard and eating little. Perhaps that was what Hildie had meant.

Frostybreath was waiting for him on the ramp. They nodded once at each other, then the older dragon ushered him into the audience chamber and left, shutting the door behind him.

Audun felt uncomfortable as he stood before the king and his councillors, waiting for his turn to speak. He wasn't happy with them for sending him on a mission that had endangered an innocent life. It was hard to think of a diplomatic way to tell them this, though, while they talked among themselves. Their voices were too quiet for him to hear except for a few phrases like ". . . not at all what I expected," ". . . couldn't have been nicer . . . ," ". . . someone will have to go . . . ," and ". . . know that you have fish eggs on your chin?"

Finally King Stormclaw turned to the young dragon and said, "I've been reminded that I haven't properly introduced my councillors to you. You've met Frostweaver and Wave Skimmer, and of course you know Song. This," he said, indicating the gray-and-white-scaled dragon seated beside Audun's grandmother, "is Vision Seeker, a truly gifted dragoness who is sometimes able to see into the future."

Audun dipped his head in respect, but the old dragoness just snorted and said, "Did you get the flute?"

"I have it here," he said, holding it up so everyone could see it.

"Did you have any problem with the sea witch?" asked Wave Skimmer.

"Nothing I couldn't handle," said Audun. "She wanted the egg so she could make it hatch and use the baby bird to suck the water out of a cave. Did you know why she wanted it before I went? Did you know that she wouldn't care if the hatchling lived or died?"

Wave Skimmer shook her head. "We didn't know what she wanted the egg for, although we had a good idea, considering the nature of the bird. What happened to the hatchling?"

King Stormclaw leaned over the edge of his slab to glare at Audun. "Did you leave it with the sea witch?"

"I couldn't," Audun said, straightening his back and returning the king's glare. "I took it back to its mother in the desert."

King Stormclaw looked satisfied. He glanced at Song and nodded. "You were right about him."

Audun glanced from the king to his grandmother, confused.

"I told King Stormclaw that you would not only get the flute from the witch, but also keep the baby bird safe," said Song of the Glacier.

"We needed the flute," said the king, "but we had no intention of hurting the baby."

"You could have told me," Audun muttered.

"Yes, and we should have," said his grandmother. "You must excuse us. We've had other things to worry about of late."

"Tell him!" said Wave Skimmer. "If you don't, I will!"

King Stormclaw nodded. "There's something else you should know. We've had a most unexpected visitor in your absence. Princess Emeralda, the Green Witch, came to see us. It seems that her daughter is pining away. She refuses to eat and doesn't sleep, so her mother came looking for you. I didn't know how powerful the witch's magic was until she said that she used it to trace you here."

"She says that her daughter swears she loves you so much that she will never love another," interrupted Wave Skimmer. "I must admit, the girl sounds like a true dragoness. When I was young, I had a number of friends who swore they would rather die than give up the one they loved. I think it's so romantic!"

King Stormclaw cleared his throat. "The Green Witch is a much better human than I expected. And a much better dragon," he added, at a small sound from Song. "Word of the war between East Aridia and Aridia has spread. The Green Witch has heard of our ties to Aridia and understands our concern. She explained that she doesn't care about jewels, and that Greater Greensward has had difficulties of its own with the East Aridians. She came to the stronghold to offer us a pact of alliance should we need it."

"I thought it was so nice that she asked," said Wave Skimmer.

"We told her that we would discuss it and send her word of our decision when it had been made," said the king.

"What about Millie?" Audun asked anxiously. "Is she all right?"

"I'm sure she is now," said his grandmother. "Her mother said that she's going to withdraw her objections to her marrying you."

"Imagine a human objecting to her daughter marrying an ice dragon!" snapped Vision Seeker. "She should be grateful an ice dragon wants to marry her!"

"Can I go see Millie?" Audun asked, suddenly so excited that he found it hard to stand still.

"Actually, we have another task for you," said the king. "The girl's mother understands that we're in the midst of a difficult time and will tell her daughter as much."

Audun held the flute out to the king. "What should I do with this?"

"Take it with you," said King Stormclaw. "We need you to deliver it to a family of giants traveling on the Eastern Sea. They have been friends to ice dragons for many years and we are happy to help them when they find themselves in need. Frostybreath will give you the directions."

❧

Frostybreath was waiting for Audun outside the chamber, but he wasn't alone. Loolee was there, wriggling with anticipation and talking nonstop about sliding down the chute. Hildie was there as well, along with another dragon that

Audun had never met before. Unlike Ice Rider, the dragon Hildie had introduced him to during his last visit, this one was much older and not nearly as athletic. He looked closer to Audun's father's age than to Audun's, and his ponderous belly was encrusted with jewels, a typical dragon way of showing off wealth and protecting his more tender regions.

"Audun," said Hildie, pushing herself in front of the others, "this is—"

Loolee grabbed hold of Audun's leg and clung to it. "I'm ready to go down the chute," she cried, her eyes wide with excitement as she gazed up at him. "Can we go now?"

"Loolee!" Audun had never had a younger sibling and neither had any of his friends, so a playful little dragoness was new to him.

"Audun, I wanted you to meet—," Hildie tried again.

Loolee began bouncing up and down, crying, "You promised, Audun, remember?"

Audun sighed. "I can go with you one time today."

Shrieking with delight, the little dragoness took off up the ramp. Audun was about to follow her when he remembered something. "You have some directions for me, Frostybreath?" he asked, turning to the big dragon.

"You go ride the chute," the big dragon replied. "I'll meet you at the door and tell you how to get to the islands."

"But, Audun," wailed Hildie. "I need to talk to you!"

121

"Sorry, but I'm already short on time. It will have to wait until I come back." Audun may not have had a lot of experience with young dragonesses, but he did know that he didn't want his name added to Hildie's list of suitors.

Twelve

$\mathcal{F}$rostybreath was good at giving clear directions. For the first half of the trip, Audun found himself flying over familiar territory. He saw the distant mountains where the witch's servants had imprisoned his family, and flew over the plains and forests that he had crossed while looking for Millie. Later that same day he looked down to see a marshy area where a dragonlike beast called a knucker was chasing an unfortunate deer. He circled for a minute, wondering if he should look for fish in the marsh, but continued on, his stomach growling from hunger. Just beyond the marsh lay a forest of scruffy pine which continued to the rocky shore of the sea. It wasn't as blue or as clear as the sea where he'd found Nastia Nautica and he couldn't see as far into its depths, but he did see schools of fish from time to time. He had a full belly by the time he reached the island where the giants' boat was beached.

The giants' ship was much bigger than the wreck that was the sea witch's home, with a mast at least fifty feet tall.

It rested on a beach of silvery sand with shallow ditches on either side. Two enormous boys were standing where the wavelets washed onto the beach, tossing rocks as large as Audun's head into the water. A woman was seated on the sand, with her head bent so that her long, brown hair hung over her face. She was sobbing and her shoulders shook with every breath she took. It was obvious that something was terribly wrong. Suddenly, Audun regretted taking the time to slide down the chute with Loolee.

The young dragon was trying to decide where to land when he noticed ripples of water arrowing toward the beach, aimed directly at the woman. "Watch out!" Audun shouted. Thinking that a sea monster was about to attack her, he tucked his wings to his sides and plummeted to the sand, pulling up short in front of the giant woman. Audun turned his back to her and faced the water, preparing to fight.

He had already tensed his muscles and spread his wings to make himself look bigger when the ripples faded away and another giant stood up, shedding a torrent of water. At least twenty-five feet tall, he was bigger than the woman and the boys. "Who's this?" boomed the giant, brushing his dripping hair out of his eyes and looking warily at Audun. Thick sheets of water sprayed across the beach, drenching Audun and making him stagger.

Audun bowed his head and said, "King Stormclaw and his council sent me. I brought you this." Reaching into his flap, he took out the flute and laid it on the ground at the giant's feet.

"Ah," said the giant, giving Audun a halfhearted smile. "I was afraid he hadn't gotten my message. I'm not sure it will do any good now. It's been so long . . . I didn't see anything," he told the woman seated behind Audun.

The woman's crying became so loud that each sob hurt Audun's ears. He moved away when the giant gestured for one of the boys to pick up the flute. Although the boys looked just like the giant, they weren't nearly as tall. Audun decided they must be his sons.

Audun had to brace himself as the earth shook from the giants' footsteps and it wasn't until they were all sitting down that he was able to say, "May I ask what happened?"

"Our daughter is gone," said the woman, dabbing at her tears. "The sea monster took her."

"Let me explain," said the man. "My name is Hugo and this is my wife, Mona, and our boys, Clifton and Tomas. We'd been visiting the islands, seeing if we'd like to settle here, when we stopped to take on more fresh water and supplies. Mona and I were collecting seaweed with the boys just over there," he said, pointing down the beach, "when our little girl, Penelope, disappeared."

"She's only three," wailed her mother.

"We think a sea monster took her. Shortly before she disappeared we saw a hideous beast with a long, whiplike tail jump out of the water as if it was trying to get a good

125

look at us. We've been searching for her for days, but all we've found are some prints in the sand."

"Don't forget the picture," said Clifton, the taller of the two boys.

Hugo sighed. "The boys found a picture made of seashells. They thought it looked like their sister."

"It did look just like her, Papa!" said Tomas. "It was so good an artist must have done it."

Hugo shrugged. "I didn't see it myself. The waves had washed most of it away by the time I got there. If it was as good as the boys say, whoever made it must have seen Penelope. We thought they might want a ransom, but they never sent us a message of any sort. However, it wasn't the picture that interested me as much as the marks in the sand. They were just above the waterline; the waves hadn't reached them yet. It almost looked as if someone had pressed a cup over and over into the ground. The only thing we could think of was that a sea monster must have left the marks."

"Which means that some horrible fiend had the sea monster carry her off," said Tomas. "Those monsters aren't smart enough to do a picture that good."

"We don't know anything for sure," said Hugo. "Just that we think a sea monster was involved somehow. That's why I asked an eagle to carry a message to King Stormclaw. I'd heard of the Sea Serpents' Flute and knew Stormclaw could get it if anyone could. I thought we could find out what happened to her if we could talk to the sea monster."

Clifton held up the flute, which looked like a child's tiny toy in his hands and would have been lost in his father's. "What happens if I blow into this?"

"The sea witch who I got it from said that it would torment sea monsters and make them leave," said Audun.

Hugo looked puzzled. "I'd heard that it will calm sea monsters so you can talk to them."

"That may be true," Audun replied. "I wouldn't trust anything that sea witch says; she's a notorious liar."

"Do you still think you should use it, Hugo?" his wife asked. "We wouldn't want to torment them and drive them off if they have Penelope with them. They might hurt her . . ."

"If they haven't already," murmured Clifton.

His mother's chin wobbled, but she managed to say, "Or abandon her, and then we'd never find her."

"That's a good point," said Hugo.

Audun cleared his throat. "Maybe I can help. I'm pretty good at tracking things, even underwater. If sea monsters took her, I should be able to find her. Can I see something of hers, as well as the place where you found the prints?"

"I'll get something that belongs to Penelope," said Mona, her eyes glistening with hope.

"And we'll show you where we found the picture and the prints!" exclaimed Tomas.

The ground shook so much as all the giants got to their feet that Audun couldn't stand. He was stumbling around when he finally spread his wings and rose into the air, although he didn't go very high.

It looked like it was going to take Mona a few minutes to get something of Penelope's, so Audun followed the boys. When they crouched beside something on the sand, Audun landed and bent down to look. Clifton said that he had placed spindly pieces of driftwood around the marks on the beach, but there were only a few indentations and the blowing sand had made them indistinct. Audun examined them for a moment, noting the acrid scent of whatever had made them, then the boys showed him where the picture had been. Most of the shells had washed away; Tomas had stacked the rest in a pile just beyond the water's reach. Audun picked up one of the shells and sniffed it. The shell carried the same scent as the marks in the sand. He set it down when Mona arrived with Penelope's shoes, which the girl had taken off while playing on the beach. They, too, had a very distinct smell.

"I think I'm ready now," said Audun. "But first, tell me, can your daughter swim?"

"Like a fish," said Hugo, who had come with his wife. "We made sure all three children could swim before we set sail."

"Where did you spot the sea monster?"

Hugo pointed out to sea. "Just past those rocks. There, where the waves are breaking."

"Then that's where I'll begin," said Audun. After

assuring himself that the amulet was still around his neck, he told the family of giants that he would do his best to find Penelope, and dove into the middle of a curling wave before it could crash over his head.

Although he had hoped to find Penelope's scent, it was the smell from the beach that Audun detected first. It was stronger than any other scent he found, as if whatever had made it had just passed by. Audun followed the trail like a hound would a rabbit, with his nose quivering and all his attention focused on that one telling odor.

The water was colder here than where Nastia Nautica lived, but Audun liked it better this way. The water farther south had been so warm that it had made him drowsy, but the cold water rushing against his scales as he sped beneath the waves now was invigorating. The fish weren't as brightly colored here, but there were more of them, and he would have been easily distracted if he hadn't been on such an important mission . . . or hadn't just eaten.

The scent grew stronger as Audun swam and he was convinced that he must be getting close. Suddenly, he glimpsed something nearly as big as himself swimming just above the edge of a rocky outcropping. Drawn by the scent, Audun followed the creature, noting the long whip-like tail that propelled it through the water. The beast was easy to see against the browns and grays of its surroundings because its long, thin body was colored a contrasting orange and yellow. As Audun drew closer, he saw that rows of thin legs ending in suckers were tucked under the monster's body, and its eyes, when it turned to look at him, were enormous.

The creature blinked, as if in surprise at seeing a dragon, and began to swim more rapidly. When it looked back a short time later and saw that Audun was still following, its tail became a blur and it sped away faster than Audun would have thought possible. Sure that he had found the sea monster that had taken Penelope, Audun raced after it.

The creature twisted and turned, swimming around obstacles as it tried to lose the young dragon. When it sped through a school of fish so quickly they didn't have time to get out of the way, so did Audun. When he raced through a gap in the side of a shipwreck, so did Audun. They passed islands and a peninsula that jutted out into the sea without Audun losing sight of the monster.

The water became deeper and colder. They circled the peak of a mostly submerged mountain, startling huge fish that flashed blue and silver as they changed direction. Every so often the sea monster would turn to see if Audun was still behind him, and each time the dragon was a little bit closer. Audun wasn't aware of how far they had traveled until they entered a trench that split the floor of the sea in two. He had heard about the Mary Alice Trench, named after two mermaids who had entered it on a bet and never returned, but he didn't know anyone who had actually gone there. Loathsome creatures supposedly inhabited its depths, which ran deeper than Audun had ever gone, but he followed the monster, not wanting to lose it.

The water around them grew even darker as they traveled downward, and Audun began to feel pains in his chest and limbs. When the sea monster's swimming became more labored, the dragon was sure that the creature was feeling similar discomfort, but they continued to go deeper until Audun could scarcely see. Strange creatures swam past, illuminating their way with lights they carried on their bodies. Some had little lanterns dangling from their heads while others had rows of glowing spots on their sides. A few darted away at Audun's approach, while one with ferocious teeth set in huge, gaping jaws swam a little bit closer, but none were brave enough to come after a dragon.

It was so dark now that Audun was following the sea monster by its scent alone; and then he encountered a strong mineral smell that nearly overwhelmed all the other odors. A few minutes later, he spotted the glow of a fire in the water ahead. Thinking he'd seen the sea monster pass in front of it, he swam toward the light, but it was so bright that it made him blind to everything beyond it.

Enormous plumes of fire and gas were erupting from a hole in the seafloor, heating the water. Clusters of tall tubes sprouted from the ground around the hole and Audun wondered what they might be. A slim, wormlike creature poked its head out of one of the tubes and eyed him. When he did nothing more threatening than look back at it, the worm said, "Hello!" in a cheery voice.

Instantly, a hundred other worms popped out of a hundred other tubes.

"Who are you talking to?" some said.

"Are you talking to me?" asked a dozen others.

"Look, we have company!" said the worms who had noticed Audun.

"Are you a fish?" asked three or four, while twenty wondered aloud what he could possibly be.

"I'm Audun," replied the young dragon, who had been taught to always be polite. "I'm a dragon."

"Ooh!" exclaimed nearly every worm. "A dragon!"

"What's a dragon?" only one was bold enough to ask.

"I'm sorry. I'd like to stay and chat, but I'm looking for someone. Have any of you seen a sea monster with a whiplike tail who passed by here just a moment ago? We were together, but I seem to have lost him."

"What's a sea monster?" asked some.

"What's a whip?" asked others.

"What's a tail?" asked the smallest worm in the shortest tube. When the rest turned to look at him, snickering, he disappeared into his tube and refused to come back out.

"We saw something big go that way," said the first worm. It jerked its head in a direction Audun never would have guessed. "It wasn't nice like you. It didn't stop to say hello."

"They rarely do," said another worm.

"How true," said at least a dozen, sounding mournful.

"Thank you very much," said Audun. "You've been very helpful."

"You're welcome," said all the worms at once.

"Good-bye," Audun called, as he turned to follow the sea monster.

"Good-bye!" they all called back.

"Such a nice dragon," said one of the worms, as Audun swam away.

"What's a dragon?" asked a chorus of wormy voices.

Audun swam into the darkness, hoping the worm had been right, but he didn't have to go far before he picked up the sea monster's scent again. Soon light began to relieve the gloom enough that he could see the walls of the trench on either side. A few minutes later he spotted the sea monster in the distance.

Audun had just left the trench when he saw bubbles from a channel of water rushing by faster than the sea around it. He watched as the sea monster hesitated, then plunged into the current and was swept away. Determined not to be left behind, Audun darted forward and dove in after the already disappearing beast.

Although the current carried him forward at an amazing pace, it was carrying the sea monster just as quickly. Audun was exhausted, but he'd have to swim even faster if he wanted to catch up to the monster. It wasn't long, however, before the monster glanced behind him and saw the advancing dragon. With a swish of its tail, the beast slipped from the current. If Audun hadn't been watching closely, he would have been carried far past the monster, but he reacted quickly enough that he dropped out of the current only yards behind the monster.

The sea monster looked tired now, too, and didn't go far before turning to face Audun. Gathering his strength, the young dragon closed on the beast who met him with a slash of his tail. Audun bit the tail and the monster turned to grapple with him, fastening its suckers onto the dragon's scales. The beast pulled and would have ripped some of the scales from Audun's body if the dragon hadn't bitten one of the monster's legs, hard.

"Wait!" shouted the sea monster. "I have to know— why are you chasing me? What have I ever done to you? I don't even know you."

"You took a little girl," growled Audun. He was surprised to hear the sea monster laugh.

"Is that what this is about?" the beast said, relieving the pressure on Audun's scales. "Why didn't you say so in the first place?"

Audun shook the monster until its teeth clacked. "This isn't a joke," he hissed.

"Of course it isn't," the monster hurried to say. "If you mean that giant hulking girl, we didn't take her. She followed my friend Blooger. We've been trying to send her home ever since."

"What do you mean by 'followed'?" asked Audun.

"We were over by the island where the tastiest seaweed grows, resting after we'd eaten," said the monster. "Blooger was asleep in the shallow water when something grabbed one of the growths on his back and tried to pull it off. He swam away, of course, and it wasn't until he was almost home that he realized something was following him. He heard splashing and an awful wailing, and when he looked back he saw an enormous child floundering in the water. Blooger couldn't just leave the child there to drown! Anyway, he called to me and together we took the girl to our home, which was much closer than hers. That child weighs too much for either one of us to carry by ourselves and it was a struggle for the two of us."

"And so you just kept her? You didn't even try to take her back? Do you know how worried her parents are about her?"

"We tried to tell them! I went back to the seaweed island and left a picture of her on the sand. I drew arrows, too, pointing the way to our home, but they never came. Blooger and I were beginning to think they didn't want her. I've been back there every day hoping to lead them to her, but those people are always throwing stones and I can't get close enough to talk to them. I was on my way home after stopping by there when you started chasing me."

"Take me to the child," said Audun, releasing his hold on the monster. "Perhaps I can carry her."

"You're welcome to try," said the sea monster. "My name is Squidge, by the way. And you are . . . ?"

"Audun," he replied. "I'm from the Icy North."

"Well, Audun from the Icy North, let's hope you're a lot stronger than Blooger and I. The sooner we get that girl back with her parents, the happier we'll be!"

Audun wasn't sure how far he could trust Squidge, so he stayed close to the sea monster all the way to the entrance of a tree-shaded lagoon. The young dragon saw the giants' child right away. She was seated in the shallow water, playing with something that she held in her hands. Not wanting to frighten the girl, he climbed out of the water and walked toward her along the beach so that she'd have plenty of time to see him coming.

"Penelope," he said, as he got closer, "my name is Audun. I've come to take you to your parents."

The girl glanced up at him and smiled. It was obvious from the clean tracks on her cheeks where tears had washed away the dirt that she'd been crying, but she didn't look upset now. "We go see Mama and Papa?" she asked.

"That's right," said Audun, relieved that she seemed to be unharmed. He walked closer, wondering where the other sea monster was, and aghast that they would leave a young child alone in the water. Then he saw that she wasn't alone at all. What he'd thought was the sandy bottom of the lagoon was really an enormous oval of sand-colored flesh that rippled at the edges. Penelope was sitting on it, playing with a flower, although when he got closer he realized that it wasn't a flower, but a fleshy growth sprouting from the monster's back. A veritable garden of the growths dotted the monster, but most of them were too short to reach above the water.

"This is my friend Blooger, who I was telling you about," Squidge said, swimming to the shore where the dragon stood. Sticking his head under the water, the sea monster spoke to his friend. Although Audun couldn't see its eyes, he was sure that the beast was looking at him.

When he'd told Squidge that he would take the girl back to her parents, he hadn't even thought about her size—she was almost as big as Audun.

"So you'll tell her parents that it was all a mistake?" asked Squidge. "We didn't take her, she just sort of came to us."

Audun nodded. "I'll tell them as soon as I get her there. But that might be a problem. I thought I could fly her back, but I'm not sure I'll be able to lift her. She looks awfully . . . solid."

Squidge sighed. "I was afraid of that. I suppose Blooger and I could help you. We might be able to get her all the way there if three of us carry her. Although I don't know how . . ."

"I have an idea," said Audun. "Are there any vines on this island?"

"I don't know," Squidge said. "I haven't gone past the beach and Blooger never leaves the water."

"I'll go look," Audun said, already on his way to the trees.

He was back a few minutes later, laden with long, thick vines. Squidge helped him make a sturdy net big enough to hold Penelope. They were able to convince her to sit in the net only after Squidge told her that she could keep one of Blooger's flowers, much to his friend's dismay.

When everyone was ready, Blooger swam out of the lagoon with Penelope on his back, while Audun supported much of her weight from above and Squidge pushed from behind. Progress was slow as they crossed the sea between the islands, and they had to wait once for a whale to pass, but they eventually had the island in sight and could even see the mast of the giants' ship.

Audun was already thinking about taking a quick leave of the giants when the first stone hit the water, narrowly missing Squidge. "Penelope!" screamed the girl's mother from the shore.

"I'm coming, Audun!" bellowed Hugo, as he waded into the water. "Leave them alone, you miserable beast!"

It occurred to Audun that their little procession might not look quite right from the island. He doubted that the giants could see Blooger, so it probably appeared as if Audun was carrying Penelope in a net while another sea monster chased them.

"It's all right!" he shouted, ducking as another stone flew over his head. "The sea monsters are helping me!"

The barrage of rocks stopped as suddenly as it had started. While the giant family stood on the shore anxiously awaiting Penelope's arrival, Audun and the monsters labored to push, drag, and carry the now-laughing child through the waves to the beach.

"Mama!" she shouted. Pausing long enough to rip a flower from the monster's back, she hopped to her feet and scrambled onto the shore, where her family waited with open arms.

The sea monsters had no intention of sticking around, but Audun convinced them to wait long enough to tell the giants what had happened. Hugo and Mona listened, skeptical at first, but with growing belief when they saw their little girl's fascination with the flowers.

"And remember how she wandered off when we were cutting logs to build the boat? We found her in that meadow filled with wildflowers," Mona reminded her husband.

Hugo nodded and bent down to speak to the sea monsters. Keeping his voice soft out of consideration for the smaller creatures, he said, "I don't know how to thank you. My family is everything to me."

"We're so sorry for ever thinking that you had carried her off," Mona told them. "Is there anything we can do to make it up to you?"

"Just don't throw stones the next time you see us," said Squidge.

Although the giants promised never to throw anything at the sea monsters again, Squidge kept eyeing them warily and he and Blooger left soon after. It wasn't until the monsters had gone that Hugo turned to Audun and said, "Thank you for everything. You came so far, and helped us so much. How can we ever thank you?"

"There's no need," said Audun. "I'm happy I could help. I came on behalf of King Stormclaw and his council, so you can thank them if you'd like."

"But all they wanted you to do was bring the flute and you've done so much more. Tell me, where are you going next? Can we at least give you a ride in our ship?"

"Thank you, but it will be quicker if I fly," said Audun. "I'm returning to King's Isle. I'm helping the king so he'll agree to teach me how to become a human."

"Really? How very odd. Why would you want to do something like that?"

"Well, there's this human girl . . . ," Audun began.

"You're doing it for love! That's wonderful! Perhaps we can help!" Mona exclaimed. "Wait right here!"

Audun had no idea what the giant woman had in mind, and he was even more confused when she returned with a barrel in her arms.

"Here," she said, setting it in front of Audun. "Take this with you. It's a lotion I make myself. Giants have a very strong odor, but we don't like it any more than anyone else does. Slather some of this lotion all over yourself and you'll no longer smell like a dragon. We've known a few dragons who can turn into humans. Even when they have a human body, they still smell like dragons unless they use this. You won't have to use it often; once every few years should suffice."

"Thank you!" said Audun. "I never would have thought of this. Are you sure you can spare the whole barrel?"

Hugo laughed, making the ground shake along with his stomach. "That's one thing we'll never have in short supply!"

"I can always make more if we run out, which shouldn't be for years," Mona said. "Thank you again, Audun. We'll be forever in your debt."

Placing the barrel in the net he'd used to carry Penelope, Audun said farewell and rose into the air. Although he'd been working hard to do whatever the king and his council had asked of him, this was the first thing anyone had done to help him be like a real human. He wanted to stop running errands for everyone else and start on his own task. As soon as he got back to the island, he'd tell the king and his council that it was time he learned how to be a human.

Thirteen

Audun wasn't surprised when Frostybreath met him at the entrance, but he didn't expect the dragon to lead him down an extra level to Song of the Glacier's rooms. His grandmother was waiting for him and she greeted him with delight. "I knew you could do it! We saw part of your actions in Wave Skimmer's bowl of water. I'm so proud of you, Audun. All you went through to help that little girl!"

"She wasn't so little," Audun murmured, stretching to relieve the stiffness in his back. "I've worked hard to do what the king asked of me. Would someone either teach me how to be a human or tell me that I'm free to go see Millie?"

"That's one of the things I wanted to talk to you about," said his grandmother. "It has come to my attention that a young dragoness is interested in having you as her mate. You need no longer worry about learning to be a human just to win a mate for yourself. There have never been as many female dragons born as there were males, which is why many male dragons live their entire lives as bachelors. That need not be the case for you, however. If you are willing to forgo this scheme of yours to woo a human, you could have a marvelous and long life with a true dragoness."

"It's Hildie, isn't it?" asked Audun. "But that's just it. I already know that Millie is the one I want as my mate. She is a true dragoness *and* a true human. She is the one I love. I don't love Hildie. She doesn't stir my heart the way Millie does. I don't lie awake at night thinking about Hildie; the last dragoness I think about before I fall asleep and the first one I think about when I wake is Millie. I thought you, of all dragonesses, would understand."

His grandmother sighed. "Ah, but I do. I just thought you should know that you have a choice. If the girl is your true love, you are already on a path that you cannot change. Now, do you really still want to learn how to become a human?"

"Yes, of course!" said Audun. "I mean, I'm glad I got Millie's mother's approval, but there's still the rest of her family. And there's so much more of Millie's life that I can share if I can be a human with her."

"I'm glad to hear that," said his grandmother. "There's something I want to tell you that we should have told you long before this. We had you find the baby desicca bird because we wanted to make sure that you would be the best kind of human before we showed you how to be one at all. Turning into a human is easy, once you know what to do. The ability is inside every dragon, but not every dragon is capable of being a good one. However, you excelled at the task, and you did something else that we hadn't expected. You learned things while you were in Aridia that our regular contacts should have relayed to us. It wasn't until you told us about the fighting in Desidaria that we knew our contacts were in trouble. We have strong ties to Aridia; it's where the gem mine I told you about is located. Any upheaval in the kingdom affects us as well.

"When you came back with the egg containing the baby desicca bird, King Stormclaw saw how useful you could be to us. After that, he stopped testing you and has been giving you jobs that we've needed someone to do, only we're so shorthanded that we don't have anyone we can send."

Audun was incredulous. "You mean the king tricked me?"

"I mean we've needed your help and, at this point, *we* need *you* to learn how to become a human. You are the only one capable of going on a very delicate and important mission. Are you ready to learn how to make the transformation?"

Audun's heart began to beat faster as he realized what she was asking. "I sure am!"

His grandmother cleared her throat. "I was fortunate enough to be selected to help you." Opening her talons,

144

she revealed a ring bearing a large, green stone surrounded by smaller, red ones. "This will help you become a human the first few times you change. After that, your body will remember the way and you will no longer need the ring. At that point, all you'll have to do is will it to happen. For now, however, put this on."

Audun trembled as he took the ring from Song and slid it over a talon. He was examining the ring when his grandmother stepped so close that their foreheads were touching. "Now, I want you to close your eyes and think about what it is that you want to become. Think about being a human—with only two legs, no wings, no scales, no ridge . . ."

Audun laughed self-consciously. "You make it sound as if I will be losing so much and gaining nothing."

"You understand at last," his grandmother said, but her voice was only a whisper because Audun was already beginning to change.

What began as a hum inside his head grew louder and louder until he could hear nothing else. His heart had already been beating rapidly, but now it beat so hard that he feared it was about to pound itself right out of his chest. After the air in his lungs left his body in a *whoosh*, he found that he was unable to take a truly deep breath. When his muscles began to change and the skin beneath his scales to burn, he staggered and would have fallen if his grandmother hadn't been there to hold him up.

"Open your eyes," she said finally, only this time her voice was loud and clear.

When he did, everything had changed. His grandmother, who had always seemed small and delicate, now appeared huge and powerful beside him. His own body was small and helpless now, with his head reaching only as high as her chest and the span of both his arms together shorter than the length of her neck. He stood upright on only two legs, with a spine that held his head high. Raising the hand that bore the ring, he found that he had hair on the top of his head and ears on the sides. He had a nose instead of a snout, which struck him as funny. When he tried to speak, his voice came out sounding rough and raw. Although his ears were different, he could still hear well, although not as well as when he had been a dragon. His eyesight was different, too; things weren't nearly as distinct and colors didn't look the same.

"Try walking," said Song, her voice sounding loud in his ears even though she had moved to the far side of the room.

He moved a foot forward, but his joints didn't behave the way he expected them to and he had to grab hold of a table to keep from falling. The smooth wood felt odd and he realized that skin without scales was much more sensitive to texture. He took another step and, with his grandmother's encouragement, began to walk around the room, to stop and touch things, to look at them from a whole new angle. The furniture seemed bigger now, the room itself enormous, but as he stepped from one place to another he began to feel more in control.

"What do I look like?" he asked, running his fingers through his hair.

"See for yourself," said his grandmother. "There is a mirror in the drawer of that table."

Audun struggled to pull the mirror out of the drawer. Although it would have been small for a dragon, it was big and awkward for a human. He needed to use both arms to carry it to a chair where he propped it up so he could get a good look at himself. Taking a step back, he studied his reflection. Audun's shoulder-length hair was silvery white. He had a strong chin and prominent cheekbones, just as he did as a dragon. His eyes were the same vivid blue they had been in his dragon form, although he laughed to see eyebrows on his face. "I know all humans have these," he said, tracing one eyebrow with a fingertip, "but what are they for?"

Song of the Glacier shrugged. "I don't know. Perhaps to keep the rain from running into their eyes? They don't have two sets of eyelids like we do."

"That makes sense." Audun glanced down at his naked body, marveling at how vulnerable humans were, with nothing covering them but soft flesh. He prodded his well-muscled arm and pinched the skin on his bicep. "It's a wonder humans can survive at all. They have nothing to protect them."

"Except their wits," said his grandmother. "And for most of them, that's more than enough. Do you think you can handle walking as a human?"

"I think so," Audun said, nodding.

"Then I want you to turn back into a dragon. You need to be able to turn both ways as quickly as possible."

"All right," said Audun, and he closed his eyes again.

The transformation into a dragon was easier, and when Song had him turn into a human again only a few minutes later, he found that easier still. They spent the next few hours in the room while he changed from dragon to human and back again, and the more time he spent as a human the better he became at moving as one. After a time he was able to change in either direction in the blink of an eye. When his grandmother saw that, she took the ring away.

"You need to be able to do it on your own," she said, as she slipped the ring into a drawer in one of the tables. "A ring like that would give you away to anyone who knows what it means. And wearing an expensive-looking ring might not always be a good idea around certain humans, who are always aware of such things. Don't forget that even though you might look like a human, you are still a dragon at heart. Humans find it easy to lie, while honor is so ingrained in dragons that only those who are sick in their heart or mind may lie easily. Be careful if you find yourself in the position where you cannot tell the truth. Only bad will come of it if you do."

"I'll remember," Audun replied.

"So, are you comfortable enough as a human to go out in public as one?"

"I think so," Audun said, wondering what Frostybreath and the others would say when they saw him.

"Then put these on."

Audun had seen Millie change from a dragon back into a human, and each time she'd had clothes on when she became a human. As a dragon he had never worn clothes, so he'd been without them as a human as well. He supposed that he couldn't go out in public that way. Audun's grandmother helped him open the barrel that Mona had given to him. Dipping his hands into the barrel, he covered his body with the thick lotion that immediately soaked into his skin. Although he fumbled with the clothes at first, Song made some suggestions and he guessed the rests; he soon stood before her, dressed and ready to go.

"I had bumps on my skin before I put on the clothes," he said, rubbing his arms through the sleeves. "I guess that happens when humans are cold."

Song of the Glacier smiled. "You still have a lot to discover. Just don't let it overwhelm you." Crossing to the table, she opened another drawer and took out a small pouch. "Put this in your pocket," she said. "You'll need coins in order to buy anything."

Reaching into the drawer once more, she took out a rolled-up tapestry and spread it open across the top of the

149

table. "This is a map to the Magic Marketplace. No one knows where the marketplace is located and one may go there only through a map such as this. You're to go to the market as a human and buy a gift for a self-indulgent person. It's for a human male, so don't get anything for a dragon."

"Who is this man?" asked Audun. "Buying something for him would be easier if I knew something about him."

"We've learned that our contacts were killed in the war. Because we have no other way of learning what's going on in Desidaria, we were forced to piece together bits of information we've received from them in times past to learn what needs to be done now. All I know about the man for whom you're buying the gift is that he's the castle steward and indulges himself whenever possible.

"We're sending you to the Magic Marketplace because you can get just about anything there and everyone likes magical gifts. In your case, you can look around while you practice walking and talking as a human. Now, remember, you'll have to be careful not to draw undue attention to yourself or let anyone know what you really are if you want to survive. There are humans out there who hate dragons and would love to kill you while you're weak and vulnerable.

"To get to the marketplace, all you have to do is touch the fountain pictured in the tapestry. To return, you must touch the actual fountain. There are witches at the Magic

150

Marketplace, as well as other creatures, some who are in disguise, some who are not. Nearly everyone there has magic of some sort. Talk only when necessary, make your purchase, and return as soon as possible."

"I'm not sure I'm ready for this," Audun said, glancing down at his legs, which no longer seemed to want to move. "What if I forget how to be a human while I'm there?"

"You won't," said Song of the Glacier. "You are a dragon, no matter what you look like on the outside, and dragons can handle anything."

Fourteen

The Magic Marketplace wasn't at all what Audun had expected. It looked a lot like it did in the tapestry, but even a magic picture couldn't convey the noise, the smells, or the hustle and bustle of the real thing.

There were more humans there than he had ever seen in one place, but humans weren't the only ones who frequented the market. He saw a banshee buying ointment for red eyes and a centaur examining hoof polish at the same stand. A leprechaun was haggling with a stall owner over the price of a gold pot while only a few stalls away a nymph bought fruit from a goblin. There seemed to be more witches and wizards than anything else, but as Song had warned, not everyone was what they appeared to be.

"Move it, buddy," a goblin said, having arrived at the market right behind him.

Audun stepped out of the way, saying, "Pardon me," and bumped into a dog.

"Careful!" growled the dog, before stepping off the

raised platform surrounding the fountain and scurrying away.

Audun climbed down the steps carefully; he hadn't practiced with stairs and wasn't quite sure how to do them. When he reached the cobblestones that paved the streets of the marketplace, he stopped to get his bearings. He'd seen a few stalls that interested him from the height of the fountain, but now he wasn't sure which way to go.

He was looking around when a sultry voice called to him. "Might I interest you in some spices?" It was a witch with eyelashes and hair of real gold and a face too perfect to be real. "I have spice to make the nostrils burn and to cool a steamy temper. This one smells of a summer's day; sniff it and you'll hear bees buzzing and feel the heat of the sun. In this basket I have moregano and lessregano. Use one to fill a glutton's appetite and the other to make anyone hungry. Of course, I have the ordinary spices like frankincense and myrrh," she said, pointing from one basket to the next. "Can I interest you in cinnathinamin? One teaspoon a day and you'll lose weight in a trice. But then, I guess you wouldn't need that, handsome." The witch smiled and looked at him through her eyelashes in a way that might have made a normal man weak, but dragons are immune to such ploys. He shook his head and moved on.

"Maybe later," she called after him.

"Fabric for your sweetheart?" asked the fairy at the next stall. "Think of what she'd look like in a gown made of this!" Bolts of corn silk and spiderweb lace were piled atop woven goose down and a swath of cloth made of highly colored fish scales. Cloth of gold vied for space on the table with cloths of copper and lead. The fairy shooed a mouse away from the cheesecloth, but it had already nibbled a hole in one corner.

A man who looked as if he might be part ogre called from the stand across the way, "Get your bottomless tankard here! Fill it full of ale once and it will never be empty again!" Seeing a young mother carrying an infant in one arm, while holding the hand of a small child, he crossed to the other side of his table and held up what looked like a wad of cloth. "I have bottomless diapers as well! These diapers never need changing. They'll soak up anything . . ."

"Except the smell!" said a gnome at the stall beside his. "What you should be selling are bottomless trash cans to hold all the garbage you're spewing."

"Why, you little runt," the big man growled, showing fangs half as long as his fingers. "I ought to . . . Wait a minute. A bottomless trash can . . . That's a good idea. I can see everyone wanting one of those!"

Audun moved on, attracted by a sweet voice singing just a few stalls away. A marmoset was seated on the table, singing a song about blue skies and green leaves while a cat played a fiddle beside it. An old woman sat unmoving on a stack of crates behind the table, her eyes glazed over as if her mind was somewhere else. Audun peeked into a box on the table and was surprised to see three fully grown dogs no larger than chipmunks trying to jump out. Not one of them was making a sound, although their mouths were working as if they were barking. "Get your exotic pets!" shouted the cat with the fiddle when he saw Audun.

"Not today," Audun said, wondering if the cat was for sale, too.

Although Audun had seen many interesting things, he had yet to find something he liked. True, the object was supposed to be for a man, not a dragon, but Audun was waiting to find something special. He was passing a stand where a wizened, little old woman was selling shoes when he overheard a loud man's voice saying, "I don't care if you have phoenix feathers and unicorn horns. I need dragon parts. You wouldn't have any dragon scales, would you? Or perhaps a talon or two?"

A rack displaying necklaces made from various kinds of fangs and teeth stood between him and the customer, so Audun couldn't see him at first. "And why would you want a dragon scale?" asked the woman. "Don't you know that dragons never shed their scales? The only way you can get one is if they give it to you or they die and you pry it off them. You want some idiot to risk life and limb so you can pretend you killed a dragon?"

"Humph!" the man declared. "I don't have to explain myself to you, you knucklehead! But I can't believe you don't have the scales, at least. Dragons have an impeccable sense of direction. You carry one of their scales and with the right spell you can find anything, including people. Anyone with half a brain in his head knows the real value of a dragon scale! A simple yes or no would have sufficed. Now you've wasted my time!"

Audun's stomach churned at the thought of the man's shopping list. He half-expected to see some sort of horrible monster when the man stepped away from the stand and Audun saw his face for the first time. His skin was weathered as if from long exposure to the sun. A drooping mustache blended into a short beard, nearly concealing his mouth. Both mustache and beard were white, as was the fringe of hair rimming his shiny, bald scalp. *It's the wizard who made the mosaic speak in East Aridia!* Audun thought, and gasped.

Turning away, the wizard glanced at Audun and saw his horrified expression. "What's wrong with you?" the old man asked. "You look as if I'd asked her to skin your mother."

"I don't . . . I can't . . . ," Audun began. Too appalled and upset to think of what to say, he fled, unaware that the old man was still watching him.

Suddenly, the market no longer seemed quite so much fun. Audun wanted to leave. He would buy something . . . anything . . . for the self-indulgent man, and go back to the dragon stronghold as soon as he could. To think that there

156

were monsters walking around loose who would kill a dragon for its scales . . .

Thinking back on everything he'd seen, Audun decided to return to the stall where the man was selling bottomless tankards. Any self-indulgent man would surely love a tankard that never went dry. He was on his way there and was passing a stand displaying magic swords when he saw the old man's reflection in one of the shiny blades; the wizard was following him.

A large group of people were coming down the aisle, laughing and talking as they headed for the food stalls. Audun waited until they had almost reached him before stepping into their group, leaving the wizard stuck behind them. When he thought the man couldn't see him anymore, Audun slipped between two stalls and into the next row, where he had to wait for a procession of goats pulling heavy carts.

A stand selling seeds displayed its wares only a few feet from Audun. GIANT SEEDS! read one sign. BUYER BEWARE! read another. Smaller signs on each box described the contents within. There were beans for giant beanstalks for visiting friendly giants, peas for giant pea pods that could be turned into boats, pumpkin seeds for those wanting a new coach or small cottage, as well as onion seeds for recluses who wanted to keep everyone away from their cottages.

Audun stared blankly at the seeds as he tried to decide what to do. He had to get the tankard—it was the reason he had come and he wasn't about to go back empty-handed—but he didn't like the way the bald-headed man was following him.

"So what will it be?" asked a voice. Audun turned around. The bald-headed man had come up behind him and was studying the young dragon-turned-man the way a physician might a patient. "They don't sell seeds for gunga beans or hot flami-peppers here," the man said, smirking.

"I've never heard of either of them," said Audun, edging away.

The wizard followed him, sniffing. Audun was glad he'd used the giant's lotion and didn't smell anything like a dragon. When the man frowned and looked down at Audun's hands, the young dragon was grateful that Song had made him take off the ring, for this man acted as if he might actually know what it meant.

"I say we shouldn't take them, Ratinki," a woman at a nearby stall declared. Audun turned at the sound of the familiar voice. The two women who had flown their brooms out to meet him at the castle in Upper Montevista were standing in front of the magic-arrow seller and they both looked angry. "The last arrows we bought from him kept coming back," continued Klorine. "Who's to say these will be any better?"

"But those arrows were supposed to come back!" said the stall owner, a tall, thin man with a long, crooked nose.

"That's what made them so special. They were reusable arrows that you didn't have to look for. They returned to their owners when a magic word was spoken."

"And spitted them like trout on a stick!" exclaimed Ratinki.

The man glanced around, his eyes becoming frantic when he saw how many people had stopped to listen. "That's why I included a free shield with each purchase of ten arrows or more! Your soldiers were supposed to use the shields to catch them!"

"Well, they didn't! They used their bodies instead. Come on, Klorine, let's go find some arrows that work," Ratinki said, and the two witches turned away. "We have a big order to place, but we're not getting them here."

"I told you I'd give you three bundles of my new arrows to replace the ones you didn't like," the stall owner called after them. "Three bundles! That's a good deal. These new arrows glow when the archer says a magic word. It makes them easy to find after a battle."

"Glow schmo," grumbled Ratinki, as the two women neared Audun. "We need arrows that hit their target, not look pretty lying on the ground."

It occurred to Audun that the two witches might help him get away. Although he found it difficult to lie, that didn't mean he couldn't find a way to use the truth to his advantage. He waited until Klorine and Ratinki were close before stepping in front of them, saying, "Ladies, I wonder if I might ask you a question? Do either of you know why dragon scales are considered to be so special?"

"Because they're tough!" snapped Ratinki.

"Because they're pretty?" asked Klorine.

Audun shook his head. "I can't believe he's right about you two ladies."

"What are you talking about?" demanded Ratinki.

Audun stepped aside so the women could see the balding man behind him. "This man says that anyone with half a brain knows the real value of a dragon scale lies in its ability to help you find things!" he said, quoting the old wizard.

"He does, does he?" Ratinki said. "Why, if it isn't Olebald Wizard. Half a brain, huh?" The old witch advanced on Olebald and began stabbing him in the chest with one of her knobby, crooked fingers. "I'll tell you who the idiot is, you old sack of hot air! Why, I remember the time when you . . ."

As Audun joined a family group walking past, he couldn't help but smile at the look of frustration on Olebald's face. The old man was trying to speak, but neither of the witches would let him.

With Olebald no longer dogging his heels, Audun hurried to the stand where the tankards were being sold. Hoping to be gone before the wizard found him again, he plunked down his money, snatched one of the tankards, and dashed to the fountain.

"Stop," shouted the owner of the stall. Then he glanced down at the money and didn't say another word.

"That was awful," Audun muttered, as he reached for the lip of the fountain. "I hope I never have to go shopping again!"

Fifteen

A heartbeat later, Audun opened his eyes and found himself standing beside the tapestry in his grandmother's rooms with his finger still touching the picture of the fountain. He jerked his hand away as if the tapestry could burn him, and bumped into a slender statue of a dragon. The statue clattered to the floor, but luckily didn't break. A moment later his grandmother poked her head through the doorway.

"You're back!" she said, her eyes alight. "How did it go? Did you get the gift?"

Audun held up the tankard, saying, "I got a bottomless tankard. I hope it's good enough."

"It should do very well," said Song. "How was your visit to the marketplace? Did you have any problems passing yourself off as a human?"

Audun paused long enough to turn back into the more comfortable form of a dragon, then nodded and said, "There was an old man. I knew he was a wizard because

I'd seen him doing magic. He acted suspicious, and I'm pretty sure he thought I wasn't a human. I caught him looking at my hands and sniffing me. He followed me around until I got two witches to distract him."

Song of the Glacier sighed. "I was afraid something like this might happen. Humans never can mind their own business, especially the ones with magic. I want you to tell me exactly what happened. This may be nothing, or it may mean we're in real trouble."

The young dragon told his grandmother how he'd overheard the wizard asking about dragon scales and how he'd followed Audun. She looked interested when he told her about the two witches, but it wasn't until he told her that they'd called the man Olebald Wizard that she really looked worried and began to pace the width of the room.

"What did he do when you left the stall?" she asked, turning around. "Did he follow you again?"

"Not that I saw," said Audun. "But then, I didn't stay around to make sure. I bought the tankard and came straight back here."

"I don't know many wizards," Song said, pacing again, "but even I've heard of Olebald. He's a tricky old man without many scruples who'd do just about anything to get what he wants. If he really suspects that you might be a dragon, he might try to follow you. Humans are always looking for dragon lairs. Sometimes it's to steal our treasures. Other times it's to steal pieces of our bodies in the hope of tapping into our magic. Even the skull of a dead dragon has a powerful magic that few wizards can match.

"I'm not sure Olebald has the necessary magic to follow you here, but it wouldn't hurt to take a few precautions. Roll up the tapestry and bring it with you. We need to put it somewhere safe."

"Like in a treasure chest?" asked Audun, as he rolled the tapestry into a long tube.

"That might work," said Song, "but I was thinking more of tossing it into a deep pit or setting it adrift on an ice floe. Hurry. We might not have much time."

Audun gathered up the tapestry and followed his grandmother out the door in time to hear her call to the guards. The two guards on duty came lumbering around the corner with Frostybreath close behind. "We may have a problem," Song told them. "A wizard may be coming here through my tapestry."

"Can we destroy the tapestry before he gets here?" asked one of the guards.

Song shook her head. "Magic tapestries are not easily destroyed."

"Audun!" called a feminine voice. He looked away from his grandmother, who was still explaining the problem to the guards, and saw Hildie hurrying down the corridor. "I heard you might be here," the young dragoness said, brushing past the big dragons. "We need to talk."

"This isn't a good time, Hildie," Audun replied, noting

that the guards' expressions were turning fierce as Song told them about the wizard.

"That's what you always say!" Hildie yelled. "The last time you were here you said we would talk the next time you came and you're here now! You're not getting out of talking to me this time!"

"Audun," said his grandmother, "we need to go now. The guards think the ice floe is our best option."

"I'll talk to you later, Hildie," Audun said, shouldering the tapestry as he tried to walk around her.

Hildie stepped in front of him, blocking his way. "You're not going anywhere until we talk about this! I have to know—are you going to declare yourself, or am I going to have to choose one of my other suitors?"

Audun was so surprised that he fumbled the tapestry and almost dropped it. "I'm sorry, but there must have been some sort of misunderstanding. I never was one of your suitors and I'm sorry if I gave you the impression that I might be. I think you're a wonderful dragoness, but I'm in love with someone else."

"I thought that might be it! Is it one of the dragonesses here? It isn't Patula, is it? Why, I'll . . ."

"No, Hildie, it's not. She's not anyone you know. It's—"

A heavy weight hit Audun's shoulder, almost knocking him down. "Audun, watch out!" his grandmother screamed.

The weight was still there, so the young dragon rose onto his back legs and heaved the thing off. Olebald went flying and hit the wall with a *thunk*. Audun was backing away when the old wizard staggered to his feet, shaking his head and swearing. The two dragon guards converged on the wizard, who raised a gnarled magic wand and waved it in their direction. A gray haze filled the air and the guards began floundering around as if they couldn't see.

Olebald had turned toward Audun when Frostybreath sprang in front of him and exhaled at the wizard. The air crackled around him as his beard turned stiff and cold and frost sparkled on his bald head. Olebald's movements were slowed, but he was still able to raise his wand. Frostybreath exhaled again. A thicker layer of ice formed on the old man, and he grew still, his eyes glazed over.

"I don't know how long this is going to last," said Frostybreath. "I thought one breath would be enough to hold him."

"Watch him," said Song. "If he so much as twitches, breathe on him again. We're going to have to find somewhere we can lock him away where he can't get out. As for you, Audun," she said, turning to her grandson, "give me the tapestry. You have to leave before the old fool can cause any more trouble."

Gesturing for the young dragon to follow her, she led the way back into her suite of rooms and closed the door. "Take this," she said, handing him the tankard and a sack

166

to put it in, "and go to the capital of Aridia. Look for the human girl who doesn't belong. She's an orphan and we believe she's living in the castle."

"Song of the Glacier!" shouted Frostybreath. "He's moving!"

"Then breathe on him until he's an ice cube!" she called back. Turning to Audun one last time, she pointed at a door he hadn't noticed before. "That will take you to another corridor. I don't have time to tell you anything else. Go now—and hurry!"

Sixteen

The royal castle of Aridia had been built with thick walls and blocky towers to withstand the desert storms. Tall dunes had settled against the walls of Desidaria, making it almost indistinguishable from the desert itself. As Audun circled the city from a distance, he wondered if the presence of the dunes had helped or hindered the invading army.

In early evening Audun landed behind a dune not far from the main road into Desidaria. Burying himself in the sand so that only his face was exposed, he waited until the gates were closed and the caravans that arrived too late to gain entrance had begun to set up camp for the night. He was about to crawl out of the dune when he realized that anyone riding a magic carpet would be able to see him from above, so he waited until dark, when the traffic in flying carpets had died down, before he shook off the sand and turned into a human.

Careful to avoid the more heavily guarded camps, Audun slipped among the tents looking for groups that seemed to feel safe enough to relax and enjoy themselves. While the men sat by the fire drinking and telling stories in increasingly loud voices, Audun rifled through their saddlebags until he found the clothes and coins he was seeking. He was sneaking out of the camp when he overheard a man telling the others about what life had been like under the old king.

"King Cadmus was fair, I'll give him that much," the man said in a gruff voice. "My brother worked in his kitchens for twenty years. He said Cadmus cared about his people and always made sure no one went hungry."

"He had to," said a man with a whiny voice. "He was stingy with his wages, despite his hoard of precious gems. Cadmus's, brother, Dolon, pays better. I'm glad he's king now. I've heard he's hiring, which is why I've come looking for work."

"Cadmus wasn't stingy. He was careful with the royal treasury. Mark my words—Dolon'll spend it inside a year."

"You can bet Dolon won't be spending his money on paying work crews to push the dunes back," said the man with the gruff voice. "He'll get King Beltran's wizard to do it. He's nearly as old as the last wizard we had and I've heard that he's almost as powerful."

"I have no stomach for wizards," whined the second man, "but wizard or no, I'm going to get a job in the castle. It's the best pay around and no one else is hiring. I heard Smugsby, the steward, is the man to see."

"That's right," said a different man. "Just make sure you take him something good. The better the gift, the better the job."

Some of the men left the campfire after that and Audun had to hurry to get out of their way. As he hid behind one of the tents with the clothes and coins he'd stolen, two men went past, talking in voices so low that no one, other than a dragon, could have heard them. "I don't know much about King Dolon," murmured one of the men, "but I doubt he'll run out of money soon. His men contacted me last week to say that my nephew had been orphaned and I needed to come get him. It took me a few days to gather the money. They called it a gift for King Dolon, but for all their demanding ways and the amount of money they want, it's ransom if you ask me."

"Hush!" said the man's companion. "You never know who's listening these days."

A few minutes later Audun was back behind the dune changing from the clothes he'd been wearing into ones that matched those of the other travelers. After tucking away the small sack of coins he'd stolen, he turned back into a dragon and buried himself in the dune once again. The temperature dropped and Audun drifted off to sleep, smiling as he dreamt of Millie.

Audun woke the next morning before the sun was up, but not before the caravans had already begun to break camp. He turned back into a human and slipped into line behind other travelers even as the gates were opening. The crowd surged forward, shoving Audun to the edge, near where a group of soldiers on horseback waited to enter. He was nervous at first, remembering how the horse had reacted when he arrived in the castle courtyard in Greater Greensward, but when nothing happened and the horses ignored him, he stopped worrying that the animals might give him away.

Intent on their own business, none of the people around him showed any interest in a boy dressed in a plain, brown tunic, dusty leggings, and the typical head covering of desert dwellers, which suited Audun just fine. He moved forward, shuffling one step at a time as the people in the front of the line were admitted. As he waited, he listened to the chatter going on around him. Most of it seemed unimportant, but he began to listen in earnest when he heard soldiers lolling by the side of the road mention missing children.

"You see these blisters?" one soldier asked of another. "The day after I got here they sent me with a patrol to look for Cadmus's brats. I nearly died out there, it was that hot. My brain was cookin', my skin was sizzlin', and I got blisters poppin' up like mushrooms on manure. The captain wouldn't let us turn around until we found those kids, but they'd disappeared like magic had carried 'em off. We were out there a whole week."

"Stop your bellyachin', Narwool," said the soldier

behind him. "We've all been out in the desert. We know what it's like. I was in the patrol that had charge of the wizard's enchanted vultures that he sent out to look for the children. He had little crystals tied around their necks. I heard the old man could see through those crystals as if he was there himself, no matter how far or high the birds flew. Of course, those birds splattered gook on the crystals every time they ate. It was our job to keep the crystals clean. Do you know how revolting it is to clean up after a vulture? It was the worst job I've ever had."

"They never did find those kids," said the soldier beside Narwool. "I was there when King Dolon heard they were missing. I've never seen him that angry before. He hates those kids with a vengeance. Do you think he would have killed them if they hadn't disappeared?"

"Those brats got out just in time, if you ask me."

Audun would have liked to have heard more, but the crowd had moved forward and it was finally his turn to pass through the gate. Three soldiers guarded the entranceway, yet only the oldest turned to look at Audun. The other two were more interested in talking to a pair of young women who didn't seem interested in leaving.

"So what do we have here?" demanded the soldier. Audun's breath hitched in his throat and he gazed at the man blankly, wondering how he could possibly have known that the young dragon masquerading as a human wasn't what he seemed. But then the soldier added, "Why are you here, boy—business or pleasure?" and Audun exhaled in relief.

"I'm looking for a job," he said, glad he had heard the men talking the night before. Obtaining a job in the castle would be the best way to get inside and would give him a legitimate reason for being there while he looked for the girl.

"Do you have a trade? What is it you do? Nobody is going to employ a boy your age who doesn't have any skills."

"I'm going to see the steward, Smugsby, at the castle. I understand they're hiring."

The soldier nodded, suddenly looking bored. He held out his hand and grunted, then seemed annoyed when Audun didn't respond.

The woman in line behind Audun bumped him with her basket and whispered, "Don't you know anything, boy? Give him a coin. There's some of us what's in a hurry."

Audun fumbled for the small purse in the folds of his tunic. He had no idea how much the coins were worth, so he hoped the one he took out would be enough. The old soldier grunted when he saw it, and glanced at his companions, who were still talking to the young women. When they didn't look his way, he tucked the coin into his own pocket. Giving Audun a slightly more respectful look, he nodded and let him pass as the woman behind him shuffled to the front of the line.

Although Audun could see the castle towering above the much shorter buildings of the city, the streets were laid out in such a confusing way that he kept finding himself in dead ends and roads that looped around to take him back to where he'd started. As a dragon he would have spread his wings and flown straight to the castle, but now he had to walk wherever he wanted to go and he wasn't used to it. Soon his feet hurt and his legs ached, neither of which had ever happened to him before.

The area around the gate had been crowded, but the farther he went into the city, the fewer people he saw. Many of the buildings had been damaged or destroyed by fire. Abandoned possessions, broken and trampled into the mud around some of the larger, more prosperous-looking homes, gave evidence of looting. The few people that he passed hurried away once they saw him returning their gaze.

After a time Audun heard voices; he followed them to a square, empty except for women who were hauling buckets of water from a well. The castle was so close now that it blocked half of the sky. He could make out the damaged battlements, but they weren't in as bad shape as he'd expected.

If the group of women hadn't been there, he might have gotten a drink from the well, but he was still too self-conscious about posing as a human to want to start a conversation. He was about to continue on to the castle when he thought he saw Owen, the boy he had rescued from the roc, crossing the far end of the courtyard.

"Owen!" he yelled, drawing all eyes in their direction.

The boy stopped and stared, appearing stricken at hearing his name. Audun started toward him, but the boy took off, running into one of the alleyways that led from the courtyard. Audun had become adept at walking with human legs and feet, but running was another matter. After taking only a few running steps, his feet went out from under him and he sprawled on the smooth cobblestones. The women laughed at his clumsiness, making him feel even more self-conscious.

"Walk much or just practice a lot?" shouted a girl nearly his own age.

Peals of laughter rang out and Audun's face reddened. He was never going to be able to pass as a human long enough to find the girl. Scrambling to his feet, he fled the courtyard, forgetting about following Owen as he made his way to the castle once more.

᠅

A crowd had already gathered by the time Audun reached the entrance to the castle, and once again he had to stand in line. Fortunately, only a short time later a guard led the job seekers into the castle, where he left them in a room too small for their numbers. While some of the men began to argue over the few available benches, Audun took a seat on the floor. Even in human form, he was taller than most, and stronger than all of them. He could have won any fight with ease, but dragons rarely fought unless it was over something of great importance.

Audun hadn't been there long before he recognized the voices of some of the men from the night before. They were talking about the jobs they hoped to secure even as they were led one by one to meet with the castle steward. Only a handful of hopeful faces remained in the room when it was Audun's turn.

A pinch-faced little man led him down the corridor to another room, where two men sat behind a wooden table looking tired and bored. His escort said, "Master Smugsby, sir, here is the next applicant," then waited while the larger of the two men set a scrap of meat on a platter, licked his greasy fingers, and nodded. The nervous-looking assistant seated beside him took a sheet of parchment from a pile and glanced up at Audun, his quill pen in his ink-stained hand.

Smugsby, the steward, looked as if he'd never denied himself anything. A golden chain gleamed from the folds of a tunic made of deep red fabric embroidered in threads of blue and yellow. Each finger of the hand resting on his bulging stomach bore a glittering ring and when he burped he patted his mouth with a delicate lace handkerchief. Behind him rested a treasure trove of bags and boxes, evidence of the applicants who had visited the room before Audun.

"What's your name, boy?" Smugsby asked Audun, as the other man dipped his pen into a pot of ink.

"It's Audun, sir," he replied, glancing at the man who had begun to scratch on the parchment with the pen. "I'm from the north."

Smugsby snorted and said, "I don't care where you're from, boy, just what you can do for me. What jobs have you had in the past?"

"None, really," said Audun. Performing tasks for the dragon king and his council didn't seem to count as a job.

"A son of the privileged class? There are a lot of you looking for work just now. We'll try not to hold it against you." Smugsby chuckled with his mouth open, showing Audun the gaps between his teeth. Turning to the other man he said, "Write that down—no prior work experience. What about skills?" he asked, turning back to Audun.

The dragon-turned-human thought hard. As a dragon he had plenty of valuable skills. He could fly, swim, hold his breath for a long time, find things by their scent, and slide down the ice on his belly. As a human he couldn't do any of those things, except maybe the belly sliding. He could grip small items easily now and his skin was more sensitive without his scales, but he didn't think the steward would find either of those things impressive.

"I assume from your silence that you don't have any skills," said Smugsby, as the other man's pen scribbled away. "So tell me, lad, why should I hire you?"

177

Audun's expression brightened. Here was a question he could answer. Swinging the sack onto the table, he took out the tankard and handed it to Smugsby. "Because I brought you this."

Smugsby glanced at the tankard and scowled. "I should give you a job because you brought me an ordinary tankard? The thing isn't even made of silver! Do you honestly think I'd demean myself by accepting anything less?" He glanced at the man beside him, who was writing down every word. "Scratch that out, Pringle. I told you there have been rumors that the king might start looking at the books."

The man beside him looked pained. "I'll have to redo the entire page. Scratch-outs aren't allowed in the official records."

"So do it," snapped Smugsby. "But first you can escort this young scallywag out of the castle."

Pringle sighed, crumpled the piece of parchment, and stood up. "Come with me, young man. You shouldn't have wasted Master Smugsby's time like—"

"But you haven't even tried the tankard!" Audun told the steward. "Fill it with your favorite ale. Or wine if you prefer," he said, talking faster as Pringle came around the table. "It's a magic tankard. Fill it once and it will never be empty again."

Smugsby quirked one eyebrow. "Magic you say? Now, where would a boy like you get a magic tankard?"

Audun was about to tell him that he'd bought it at the Magic Marketplace, but Smugsby waited only a heartbeat or two before saying, "I like a man who can be discreet. Pringle," said the steward, as the other man reached for Audun, "do as he says. Fill it with ale—no, make that an expensive wine just in case, then bring it to me. If this boy is telling the truth, he'll be rewarded with a job, but if he's lying to the king's steward, I'm sure they can find room for him in the dungeon."

While Pringle went to do the steward's bidding, Smugsby sat back in his chair and smiled at Audun. "You've provided me with entertainment, boy, something I rarely get these days. If you are telling the truth, I'll have a magic tankard and a boy working for me who has enough skill to beg, buy, or steal one, any of which would be useful to me. If you are lying, I'll see you thrashed and thrown into the dungeon for the rest of your days, which would be diverting in itself. Ah, there you are, Pringle. I hope you got me something tasty. I've worked up a thirst talking to the young scamp."

Smugsby took the filled tankard, being careful not to spill a drop. Tilting his head back, the portly man began to drink. Both Audun and Pringle watched his Adam's apple bob up and down as he took one gulp after another. Audun glanced at Pringle as the steward continued to drink. The man had looked skeptical at first, but his eyes grew wider and his jaw began to sag as Smugsby showed no sign of stopping. When the steward finally lowered his hand, smacked his lips, and sighed, Pringle ran around the table to look in the tankard. Even from where he stood, Audun could see that wine filled the tankard to the brim.

"Excellent!" Smugsby said, wiping his face, which had grown pinker with each gulp. "It looks like I've got a bottomless tankard, and you, my boy, have got yourself a job."

"What should I write down?" asked Pringle, picking up a new sheet of parchment.

"Write that the boy is intelligent and will do admirably as my new assistant," said Smugsby. "Then take him to get a new suit of clothes and his sleeping assignment." He smiled as he turned to Audun. "You'll start work in the morning. Come see me then."

"But what do I do about the other applicants?" asked Pringle. "Don't you want to see them?"

"Not today," said Smugsby, smiling into the depths of the tankard. "Tell them to come back tomorrow. I'm going to be busy for the rest of the afternoon."

Seventeen

Pringle took Audun down another corridor and into a small room where he dug through a trunk and found a plain blue tunic and brown leggings, much like the ones he was wearing himself. He handed over a pin identifying Audun as one of the steward's men and said, "You'll sleep in the room at the end of the corridor. Take one of those pallets," he added, indicating a pile by the door, "and find a space on the floor. You'll be eating with the rest of the servants. At first light, be in the room where you spoke with Master Smugsby to get your instructions for the day. Now, be off with you. I'm a busy man and you've already taken up too much of my time."

Audun nodded, too excited by his success at getting a position in the castle to think of all the questions he should be asking. While Pringle retreated down the corridor, Audun picked up the cleanest-looking pallet and hefted it onto his shoulder. A trio of maids so alike that they had to be sisters watched him walk to the end of the corridor with obvious interest, but Audun simply said hello and continued to the room, mindful that these girls looked as if they belonged together. Although he really didn't know what a girl who didn't belong would look like, he was certain that she wouldn't have family around.

The room was larger than the one he'd been given when he first arrived at the dragon stronghold, but the walls were lined with rolled-up pallets so Audun knew that come nightfall he'd be sharing the room with quite a few others. In the meantime, the remaining hours until supper were his own and he decided that it was the perfect opportunity to go exploring and begin his search for the girl. Hoping to blend in, he changed his clothes and tucked his old ones inside the bedding on the pallet before setting it against the wall. He would find the girl right away, if he was lucky, and never have to come back to this room again.

Audun headed toward the Great Hall first, having passed the entrance in the corridor when he was walking with Pringle. Song of the Glacier had told him to look for an orphan girl who didn't belong. Galen, one of the boys he'd found in the desert, had told him that all the children who'd been left without parents had been brought to the castle. Didn't that mean that none of them really belonged? He'd have to find the orphans and see if one of the girls stood out from all the rest.

Once he stepped inside the Great Hall, he realized that it was bigger than the dragon king's audience room. He stood gaping at the high ceiling and weapon-decorated walls until he heard a group of pages and younger squires making rude comments about the peasant from the country.

"Don't pay them any mind," a dirty-faced boy with scruffy brown hair said, stopping by Audun's elbow. There was a smudge of ash on his upturned nose and one of his front teeth was chipped. He looked as if he couldn't be more than nine or ten years old and the top of his head scarcely reached Audun's chest. Obviously a servant, he was carrying rags and a bucket and was dressed in a soiled tunic and patched leggings with shoes so ragged that most of his toes were showing. Although humans rarely washed and usually smelled of body odor or perfume, this boy smelled like he'd rolled in a pigpen *and* hugged an old billy goat. Audun didn't care. He thought most humans smelled bad, anyway. "They want everyone to think they're sophisticated," the boy continued, "but half of them are from the country themselves."

"I'm surprised there are so many people here," said Audun. "Did they all come with King Dolon?"

"Just the ones who are acting all puffed up like they're something special," said the boy, glancing at a young woman walking heedlessly through a cluster of people who stepped aside as she'd obviously expected them to do. "That's Dolon's daughter, Gabriella. She used to be called Gabby, back when her uncle was king. The nobles who are here were either Dolon's friends or the ones who changed allegiances as soon as they saw which way the wind was blowing."

"What about you?" asked Audun. "It sounds like you've been here awhile."

"I have, one way or another," said the boy. "My name is Jim."

"I'm Audun," he replied. "I'm pleased to meet you, Jim. But should you really be telling all these things to a stranger?"

Jim shrugged. "Why not? No one cares what someone like me thinks. To most of the people here, I'm practically invisible unless they need me for something. You will be, too, once you stop gawking and making yourself obvious. Just act like you've been here for years and know exactly what you're doing."

"Good point," said Audun. "I'll have to try harder."

"You do that," Jim said, backing away. "See you around," he added.

Audun watched as Jim slipped through the crowd without anyone looking his way. People in the Great Hall made him feel uncomfortable, so he followed Jim's suggestion and tried to act like he knew what he was doing as he started to leave the room. He had almost reached the door when it occurred to him that the Great Hall might be just the place to find the girl, since it seemed that nearly everyone passed through it. Instead of leaving, he walked to the wall as if to inspect a tapestry that he'd seen from a distance, intending to watch the comings and goings from the side of the room.

The sound of a scuffle in the middle of the Hall drew his attention. Jim was on his knees, cleaning up spilled ale. The same pages who had mocked Audun were now gathered around Jim, calling him names and trying to push him over with their feet.

"The filthy pig reeks! He'd do well to dump that water on himself, not the floor."

"Maybe we should help him. Hand me the bucket, Ronald, and we'll give him a bath!"

"I wouldn't do that if I were you," said Audun, putting his hand on the page's shoulder. "No one deserves to be treated like that."

"Who are you to talk to me that way?" asked the page. "You're new, but I can tell from your clothes that you're just a servant. You shouldn't even be talking to me. I'll report you and see that you get punished for this."

"Really?" said Audun. "And while you're reporting me, you should add that you were trying to keep another servant from doing his job, and because you both live off the king's treasury, you've been wasting the king's money. Just how kindly do you think he'd feel about that?"

"Why I . . . We were just . . ."

"I thought so," said Audun. "If you don't like the way someone smells, then stay away from him." Nodding to each of the boys, Audun walked away, leaving the pages staring.

"We'd better get out of here," Jim said, tagging along at Audun's side. "They could easily change their minds and report you."

Audun shrugged. "I'm not afraid of them."

"Maybe not," said Jim. "But I am. I appreciate what you did. No one has stood up for me for a long time, but I'm afraid this will only make things worse. Take my advice and steer clear of them. That's what I do." The boy gave Audun a pat on the arm, leaving a dirty handprint, then ran off through the door leading from the Great Hall.

Audun was disappointed in himself. He shouldn't have butted into a conversation that didn't involve him if he didn't want to be noticed. But then, he couldn't just let those older boys pick on Jim. It was getting harder and harder for him to blend in. Someone was sure to ask questions about him if he kept drawing attention this way. Taking Jim's advice, Audun left the Great Hall.

He drifted through the corridors, learning his way around the castle while keeping an eye out for the girl, but when the light outside the narrow windows began to fade, he followed the scent of cooking food to the kitchen. Audun was a door away when he once again heard familiar voices and peeked into a room just off the kitchen. Nearly a dozen people were seated at a long table and among them were some of the men who had sat with him in the waiting room that very morning. Seeing Audun in the doorway, one of them called out, "So you got a job, too! Congratulations! Come in and join us."

When the man slid over to make room for him, Audun took a seat, not knowing how to refuse.

"I'm John, and the ugly cuss on your other side is Gib," said the man who'd moved over. "What job did you get?"

"I'm working for the steward," said Audun, as he accepted a platter from a pretty girl with freckles and a friendly smile. Although supper wouldn't be served for over an hour in the Great Hall, the servants who would be doing the serving there were already sharing their meal with a few friends and acquaintances.

"Lucky you!" laughed John. "I'm a server, until I find something better. I didn't know it until I got here, but my brother Patrik got his old job back. He's head baker and the best one this castle has ever seen. Here, try some of his bread. Then tell him how good it is. That's him in the doorway."

Dragons don't eat much besides meat and fish, but Audun took a small hunk of bread and bit into it, just to be polite. The outside was crusty while the inside was soft and chewy, much like an oyster. He thought it was probably very good, if you liked bread, so he had no problem calling, "It's delicious!" to the man in the kitchen doorway.

Patrik grinned and nodded, making Audun feel as if he'd finally done something right. No one seemed to notice that he didn't finish the bread, although they made comments about how much sausage he was able to eat.

Seated with the new people were servants who had been there during King Cadmus's reign. Audun learned that although the king, his family, and many of his nobles had run away or been killed, many of the servants who had stayed behind had continued working in the same jobs they'd held before.

As Audun listened to the conversations around him, it was the older servants who proved to be the most informative. While some gossiped about the love lives of their fellow servants and others talked about members of the nobility who had recently moved in, it was the woman seated at the end of the table who really sparked his interest. "I don't care what you say about Princess Gabriella. She doesn't hold a candle to my little Shanna! I was nursemaid to all four of Queen Floradine's babies and was there when the good queen died at Shanna's birth. That little one stole my heart. It was nearly the death of me when I heard that the poor darlings were lost in the desert."

"She doesn't seem very upset now," Audun whispered to John.

Gib must have heard him, because he leaned closer and whispered, "There are rumors that the children still live. They say that those rumors are all that keep her going. Meg couldn't stop crying the day they disappeared. We all thought their uncle Dolon had had them executed, but no one does that and then spends so much time looking for them."

A man on the other side of Gib nudged the woman beside him and whispered something in her ear. She glanced toward the doorway and her mouthed crinkled in distaste. Audun let his gaze follow hers and was surprised to see Jim. When Audun smiled, the boy waved a greeting, but didn't cross the threshold until Meg called, "Come in, boy. Look at you! You're all skin and bones. I've seen boiled chicken bones with more meat on them than you have. Patrik, serve up a plate for our Jim, won't you, please, darlin'?"

"He'll do it, too, seeing that Meg asked," Gib whispered to Audun. "Patrik has been sweet on Meg for years. He told me all about her long before I ever came to the castle."

"Wouldn't he give the boy a plate, anyway?" asked Audun.

Gib shook his head. "No one goes near the boy if they can help it, except Meg, that is. The rest of us stay away from him and he stays away from us. Get a good whiff of him and you'll know why."

Audun watched as one of the scullery maids handed a plate to Jim. The boy ducked his head and whispered his thanks, but the maid had already hurried away, holding her nose. Jim sighed and took the plate to the corner, where he sat on the floor with his back to the wall and tore the meat with his teeth. Audun decided that the boy must be ravenous.

"What about Davie?" asked someone farther down the table. "Any word on how he's doing?"

"Dolon beat him the night before last when the poor man was slow to refill the tankards at the head table," Gib told Audun. "No one's seen him since."

Smithson shook his head. "It wasn't Davie's fault that he was late. It was his turn to take the food to the south tower. You know he has a soft spot for those orphans, locked away waiting for their families to come for them. He always dawdles when he goes there. We've been short-handed," he said, glancing at the new servants. "It'll be better now that you're here."

"What's this about orphans?" asked another man who had also been hired that day.

"After he took over the city," said Gib, "Dolon had his soldiers go through the streets, looking for orphans from wealthy families. The children were brought here to the castle. He said it was so he could take care of them, but he locked them in the south tower and sent word to their relatives that they should come fetch them. He told the head cook that we weren't to give them but the smallest portions of food. 'Let their relatives bear the brunt of their expenses,' he said. We do what he orders us to, officially, but we can't stand to see the wee mites go hungry, so we take a little extra when we can."

"He's stingy with the orphans because of all the prisoners he's got locked away in the dungeon," said another voice. "Not that he gives *them* much to eat."

"Anyone know how many are down there now?" asked Gib.

Someone Audun couldn't see said, "I used to know, but they haven't let me down the steps since Dolon took charge."

Audun noticed a look pass between Smithson and the head cook, who had come to the door. "That's it, everyone," the cook said abruptly. "Time to take the supper to the Great Hall. You've had your share of food and gossip. Now, let the mighty lords and ladies enjoy theirs!"

Eighteen

Audun woke early the next morning hoping that he could locate the girl and be headed back to the dragon stronghold before the end of the day. He had found his way to the south tower the night before, although it had been heavily guarded and he hadn't been able to get in.

He reached Smugsby's office before anyone else, then had to wait for nearly an hour before Pringle showed up to tell him that the steward was feeling ill and wouldn't be in until later. "He has a bad headache," he said, giving Audun an accusing look. "I daresay it's because of that tankard you gave him yesterday. He should be back by this afternoon. Come here after the midday meal so he can tell you what to do. In the meantime, familiarize yourself with the castle if you haven't already. Master Smugsby will expect you to know your way around, given you've had so much free time."

"Yes, sir," said Audun. Of course, he had something else in mind.

The kitchen was bustling with activity when Audun reached it just a short time later. It was still early, so he didn't think anyone had carried the orphans' meal to the tower yet. He found the baker, Patrik, in the heart of the large, chaotic kitchen. When Audun asked if he could help out in any way, perhaps by taking the orphans their food, the baker seemed happy to accept the offer.

After collecting the pot of porridge and some bowls, Patrik handed him several loaves of hot, crusty bread. "Take these for the guards. They'll be more likely to let you take the food to the children if they have their own breakfast to eat. You'll want to go up the tower to make sure the orphans are being treated well, and that the food is really going to them. Oh, yes, and these are for the cat." Audun couldn't understand why the man handed him three pieces of meat wrapped in an oiled cloth, but he wasn't about to object. Surely a cat wouldn't need all three pieces, in which case, he could have a taste himself.

It wasn't until after he had given the bread to the guards positioned outside the door and had started up the steps that he understood about the cat. He had climbed only half a dozen steps up the narrow spiral staircase when something landed in front of him, yowling like a banshee. It was an orange tomcat as big as a large dog and it had three very different heads. The one in the center was big and blocky with a ragged ear and a scar down one side of its face. It was spitting and snarling at Audun. The one on the right was more refined, although it was growling deep in its throat. The third head was rounder and had short, little ears. Its sweet face had a more pronounced nose that it kept in the air, sniffing the meat.

Audun reached into the pocket where he'd stuffed the cat's breakfast. He'd seen the length of its nearly dragon-like claws and the sharpness of its daggerlike teeth, and he felt sorry for any unprepared intruder coming up these stairs to take a child home without paying the ransom. Whoever the wizard was that was helping King Dolon, he seemed to know what he was doing.

At the top of the tower, Audun found the children playing with a few broken toys while an old woman with a sour face watched over them. Her eyes lit up when Audun gave her the last of the bread, and she retired to a chair in the corner to eat.

The children gathered around Audun as he served their porridge, smiling shyly whenever he looked their way. None of the five little boys or three little girls appeared to be more than seven years old. If they'd been wearing any-thing of value when they were found, it had been taken away; they were dressed in clothes much like those of the servants. Even so, everything they wore was clean and they looked healthy.

While the children ate, Audun squatted down beside them, and spoke to them in a kind and encouraging way. Although they had been shy at first, they soon told him their names and what toys were their favorites. Then a little boy named Ortzi told him that his uncle was coming for him that very day. When the other children told Audun in excited voices about the impending arrival of their relatives, he began to wonder how any of them could be the one he had been sent to find. The little girls were the most animated, and although they didn't belong in the castle, they did have someone with whom they belonged. Nothing seemed particularly out of place. Surely none of them needed to be rescued.

There was no sign of the cat when Audun returned down the stairs carrying the empty bowls, which was just as well because he was trying to remember exactly what his grandmother had said in those few hectic moments before he left the dragon stronghold. He was sure she had said that the girl was an orphan, but he couldn't recall her saying anything else about her. If only that wizard hadn't shown up and they'd had more time to talk.

Audun returned the bowls to the kitchen and swiped a chunk of raw meat for himself while the cook had his back turned. Next, Audun decided to look around outside. He took the closest door leading into the courtyard and found himself near the stables. As Audun passed an open door, he glanced inside and saw a boy entering an empty stall a little farther in. The boy was the same size as Owen and had the same color hair. Audun was wondering if he should say anything when the boy raised his head. It *was*

Owen and he didn't seem happy to see Audun. He took off, running into the dimly lit depths of the stable.

Audun was peering into the darkened stalls when Owen stepped out of a doorway and they both stumbled. While Audun was trying to get them both back on their feet, he felt Owen's arm wrap around his neck and the cold blade of a knife press against his throat.

"Why are you following me?" Owen demanded.

Audun inched his hand between them, ready to break the other boy's grip. "I want to help you," he said. "I don't mean you any harm."

Owen pressed the knife a little harder. "Who are you? I've never seen you before."

"Yes, you have," said Audun, as he shoved the hand that held the knife aside, and jumped out of Owen's reach, keeping his eyes on the boy. "It's just that I didn't look like this then. I helped you once before. I want to help you now. What are you doing here? You are the prince they're all talking about, aren't you? It's too dangerous for you to be anywhere near this castle."

"I'm not telling you anything!" Owen said, waving the knife in Audun's face.

Realizing that he wasn't going to get anywhere without revealing who he was, Audun said, "I helped you escape from the roc's nest. My name is Audun."

Owen looked confused. "How is that possible?"

At least, thought Audun, *there's no one around to hear this.*

Shrugging, he said, "Humans have their magic, we dragons have ours. So why are you here?"

Owen lowered the knife and used the back of his other hand to wipe sweat from his forehead. "I heard that my father isn't dead after all. He's still alive and locked in his own dungeon. I've come to free him. Did you mean it when you said you want to help me?"

"Any way I can," said Audun.

"Then come back here tonight at midnight. You can go with me to get him out of the dungeon. I could use the help of someone like you."

"I'll be here," Audun said, even as Owen slipped into the shadows and disappeared. He was scarcely out of sight before Audun realized he should have asked if Owen had noticed a girl who didn't belong. He hurried after him.

Audun walked behind the stable and had almost reached the top of the manure pit when he heard someone shout. A slight figure was standing on the edge of the pit waving its arms in the air. Audun realized it was the boy, Jim. "What are you doing?" he shouted, just as Jim jumped into the pit below. Audun ran as fast as he could to the edge. To his amazement, Jim was rolling around in the smelly mixture, coating his clothes and body and making small grunting noises.

Seeing Audun, Jim stopped rolling long enough to sit up and shout, "Hello!"

"Are you hurt?" Audun asked, although he could tell

that the boy was fine even before he began to pick his way down the slope.

Jim was laughing when Audun finally reached him, looking happier than Audun had ever seen him. His laughter transformed his face, making him look less like a lost waif than a mischievous prankster.

"I'm right as rain," Jim said, climbing out of the pile.

"Physically, maybe," muttered Audun, running his eyes over the boy's thin frame. "But you must be crazy to jump in that."

"No, I'm not. Meg made me take a bath today," he said, as if that explained everything. When Audun's expression remained blank, Jim added, "Most people don't bother me when I smell. I mean, honestly, would you?" Raising one of his arms to his face, Jim took a deep sniff. Rolling his eyes, he stuck his tongue out of the side of his mouth and pretended to faint.

"I thought you were on fire or someone was chasing you," said Audun. "If I'd known you were just being an idiot, I never would have gotten so worried."

Jim blinked and looked up at Audun. "You were worried about me?" he said, as if he were pleased. "No one ever worries about me."

"Meg does," said Audun, giving Jim a hand out of the manure.

"Meg worries about everyone," Jim said. "I think it's part of her job."

"And what's *your* job exactly?"

Jim shrugged. "I clean up messes that no one else wants to touch. I run errands that no one else wants to do."

"In other words," said Audun, "you make yourself invaluable."

Jim gave him a sideways glance as if surprised that someone had figured it out. "I guess you could say that."

"And what else do you do?" Audun asked. "You have complete run of the place. I bet you know everything that goes on here."

"I guess you could say that, too," Jim said with a smirk. "I know that Smugsby has a killer headache and that he blames a certain person who gave him a certain tankard. I'd tiptoe around him if I were that person."

"Thanks for telling me. Now, tell me one more thing: have you seen a girl who doesn't belong here? One who might be in danger?" Audun asked, trying to sound casual, as if the question weren't uppermost in his mind.

Jim glanced away, but not before Audun could see that his eyes looked troubled. "No. I don't know anyone like that."

Audun nodded. He didn't want to scare the boy off. "Well, then, what about places? I bet you know your way around this castle pretty well."

Jim snorted. "Better than anyone. I know more secrets about this place than the men who built it. There are secret passages everywhere. I know three ways to get into the king's own chamber, and only one of them is through the door."

"What about the dungeon? How many ways do you know to get in there?"

"You aren't asking about the front door, where you have to go past two sets of guards and a trapdoor that would send you straight to the netherworld if you took one wrong step, are you? You want to know about the back way, where no one can see you and you have to watch out for rats and things that give you nightmares even during the day."

"That's right," said Audun.

"Did you want to see these places yourself?"

Audun nodded. "Now, if you have the time."

Jim took his mission very seriously. He warned Audun to be quiet and, once they had passed the stables, looked high and low to see if anyone was watching them as they approached the far side of the castle. They had rounded the corner of the keep when Jim stopped suddenly and said, "That's odd. Those weren't there when I was here last." He pointed along the back of the keep to a group of figures that were standing in their way.

"What are they?" Audun asked, squinting into the sunlight. They looked like tall, thin people with upraised arms, but they were too tall and too thin to be real.

"They're some kind of plants," Jim said, approaching them cautiously. "Look, they're covered with prickers."

"How long ago were you here last?"

"Right after I came to live at the castle. Before the wizard came. Do you think he had something to do with this?"

"I wouldn't be surprised," said Audun.

As they got closer, Audun saw that they really were plants. Gray green in color, they each had two armlike branches that reached toward the sky and sharp, spike-like growths that covered them from top to bottom. Jim and Audun were almost among them when the plants began to move.

"Watch out!" Jim shouted, as the plant closest to Audun swung a branch at him.

Audun jumped back, and the branch barely missed him. Drops of liquid quivered on the tips of some of the spines. "We're not going any farther now," said Audun, taking another step back. "Where exactly is the opening to the dungeon?"

"There," Jim said, pointing at a patch of tall, normal-looking weeds by the base of the wall. "There's a hole with a grate in front of it. The hole is small, but it gets bigger inside. We'll never get there, though, not with these plants guarding the opening."

"I'm sure you're right," said Audun, but he was already thinking of ways he could do just that.

The sun was high overhead by the time they returned to the stables. "Thanks," said Audun. "You were a big help. Just don't tell anyone what you showed me."

"Who—me? You're the only person I've talked to since Dolon took over. No one else is worth the bother. Say, aren't you supposed to go see Smugsby soon? I've heard he has a whole lot of things for you to do." Grinning at Audun once more, Jim darted off around the manure pile and up the hill to the castle keep.

Jim was right; it was time to go see Smugsby. Only a few minutes later, Audun was passing the Great Hall. He heard the commotion of an excited crowd. Lords and ladies dressed in fine clothes pushed past him to stand shoulder to shoulder with scullery maids and undergrooms while the words "marvelous" and "wonderful" rang out around them. Audun worked his way into the crowd and finally, after crawling under a table and stepping on a few toes to get people to move, he was able to see Princess Gabriella and the man he assumed was her father, King Dolon, greeting someone he had yet to see. It wasn't until the crowd parted so that the new person could come forward that Audun saw his face. To the delight of everyone except Audun, Olebald Wizard was back.

As the old man's head turned his way, Audun ducked and melted into the crowd.

Nineteen

*J*im had been right about something else, too: Smugsby was in a very bad mood.

"Someone who hates me sent you with that blasted tankard, I know it!" he growled, when Audun walked in the door. "Either I didn't give him a job, or he didn't get what he thinks he deserved. You brought me that . . . that *thing* so I'd drink myself to death!"

Audun shook his head. "That isn't true. I brought it because I thought you'd like it."

"I do, and that's the problem," Smugsby said, rubbing his temples. "I wouldn't be too pleased with myself, though, if I were you. Every time my head pounds, I'm going to think of more work for you, and right now it feels like it's the midsummer celebration and everyone is dancing on my skull! Go see Pringle. He's got a list of things I want done today. And don't dawdle if you want to keep your job."

True to Smugsby's word, Pringle kept Audun running

all afternoon. He took a message to the captain of the guard, then brought back his reply. He rushed to the city with a note for a man who sold wine, and as soon as he returned he was sent back to the city with a note for a wool merchant.

Audun was relieved when Pringle finally told him that the rest of his errands would be inside the castle. He was walking through the Great Hall when the floor beneath him trembled and a loud rumble filled the air. A passing guard smiled in a knowing kind of way and said, "Must be that wizard. I expect we'll have a lot of that kind of thing going on with him in the castle."

Audun frowned. It had been easy enough to forget about Olebald Wizard while he was in the city, but he'd have to remember to stay on guard if he didn't want the wizard to see him.

Late that afternoon Audun was returning with a message from the king's chancellor when he saw an enormous man come out of Smugsby's office. His shoulders were broad and his arms and legs muscled as if he lifted heavy objects daily. Although Audun was sure he'd never seen the man before, there was something familiar about the way he held his head. He nodded at Audun and winked, as if about to say something, and might have if Pringle hadn't stuck his head out the door and told Audun to come in.

"Who was that?" Audun asked, shutting the door behind him.

"A new guard," said Pringle. "He's big enough to intimidate anyone, don't you think?"

"Indeed," said Audun.

He wouldn't have thought any more about the new guard if the man hadn't kept popping up. Audun saw him while passing through the Great Hall on two different trips, then once outside the kitchen, and again in the corridor by the room where he'd left his pallet. Although the man never spoke, Audun could sense his eyes following him every time they met. At first he thought the man might be working for Olebald Wizard, but he discarded that idea when the man didn't approach him and neither did anyone else. Surely if Olebald knew he was there, Audun would no longer be walking around freely. But, the man made him nervous.

The sun had already set when Audun finally finished his work for the day. After making sure that no one, including the new guard, was following him, he slipped through a door and hurried around the side of the castle. He was about to do something he had told himself he wouldn't do while on the castle grounds, but it was the only thing he could think of that would take care of the spiky plants. For just a few minutes, Audun was going to have to turn back into a dragon.

He waited until he was in the deepest shadows close to the wall of the keep before closing his eyes and thinking about being a dragon. When he next looked up, his eyesight was back to normal; washed in a pale light, the plants were no longer the dull grayish green they'd appeared through human eyes, but now showed patches of ultraviolet and a white so bright that Audun had to look away. The plants seemed to be watching him. He took a step closer and they swayed in his direction ever so slightly—as if a gentle breeze had blown them. When he was a few yards away, they began reaching for him.

If Audun had been a fire dragon, he would have blasted them with a heat so intense they would have blackened and withered like daisies in a forest fire. But because he was an ice dragon, he coughed. It wasn't a loud cough, just the kind that ice dragons do when they are mixing the noxious gas stored in a sac near their lungs with the air they are about to exhale. When he did exhale, the gas formed a small cloud that was colorless and nearly invisible. As the cloud drifted through the cluster of plants, they jerked back and then began to shrivel and die. Not a single desiccated plant stirred as Audun walked between them to the grate in the wall.

About two feet across and built into the wall for drainage, the grate covered a round opening at the bottom of one of the walls. Time and rust had loosened it so much that Audun was able to lift it free with no effort at all. The opening was too small for a dragon as big as Audun, and since he had to change back, anyway, he crouched down and, a moment later, tried to see if his human form could fit. Although it was tight, he was able to wriggle inside. He thought about going to look for the king himself, but he had no idea what the man looked like or what he would do with him once he got him out, so he wriggled back through the opening and set the grate where it belonged. Midnight was only a few hours away and Audun guessed Owen would be furious if he rescued the king without him.

The full moon was peeking over the castle wall when Audun returned to the stable yard. Owen had yet to arrive, so Audun sat on the ground to gaze up at the sky while he waited for the prince. It wasn't long before he heard someone approach, but the boy who sat down beside him was Jim.

"I wish I could fly away from here," Jim said, sounding wistful.

"Where would you go if you could?" asked Audun.

"Somewhere I wouldn't have to hide and could just be myself. The problem is, I wouldn't know how to get there."

Audun felt sorry for the boy. He pretended not to notice Jim scrub his eyes with the back of his hand as he climbed to his feet.

Jim straightened his back and glanced at Audun. "Where's your friend?"

"What friend?" asked Audun.

"The one who's meeting you at midnight. I told you I know everything that goes on around here."

"He should be here soon," said Audun.

"Who is that?" said a voice out of the near-darkness. "I told *you* to come. I never said you could bring someone else."

Audun waited while Owen came close enough that they could see each other clearly. "I didn't invite him, but it might not be a bad idea to have him along," said Audun. "Jim knows his way around the castle better than anyone."

"He doesn't know it better than I do," Owen snapped. "Look at him—he's a kid. He'll just get in the way."

"I can help!" Jim rushed to say. "And I bet I know ways into the dungeon that you've never seen."

Owen narrowed his eyes. "He told you we were going to the dungeon?"

"No, I just know a lot of things," Jim said. "And I'm small. I can fit places you can't."

"All right," Owen said. "Since you already know all about it, you can come, but stay out of my way. And it's up to you to keep an eye on him," he added, glancing at Audun.

"No problem," said Audun, giving Jim a pointed look.

Owen acted as if he knew where he was going, but when they reached the base of the first tower, he stopped and kicked at a pile of gravel. "I know it was here," he said. "I found the tunnel years ago when I was playing with my friends. It was behind a couple of big boulders."

"I think Dolon had it filled in after he took over the castle," said Jim. "If it were daylight out, you'd see the new stones and mortar."

"There was another, smaller entrance," said Owen, "but it had a grate over it. I don't recall exactly . . ."

"It's this way," said Jim. "Follow me!"

He took them around the castle wall to the side he had visited with Audun earlier that day. It was darker there because the tower itself was blocking the moonlight, but with his sharp dragon eyes, Audun could see the ground where the spiky plants had been standing. It looked ghostly in the gloom, as if a patrol of guards had been mown down and deflated at the same time.

"What happened to them?" Jim asked.

"Looks like something killed them," said Audun.

Jim glanced at him in exasperation. "I know that! I just wonder how."

Owen nudged the limp remains of a plant with the toe of his shoe. "Could have been a lot of things."

The prince seemed to be having difficulty determining where to step, so when he stumbled and nearly fell, Audun set his hand on his arm to guide him. Owen tried to shake him off, saying, "I don't need your help."

"What harm is there in accepting what little help I can give you? Or would you rather trip over a rock and break your neck so that your father rots in the dungeon for the rest of his life?"

"Well, if you put it that way . . . ," said Owen.

"It's over here," Jim called from the middle of the dead weeds.

Audun helped the prince down the slight incline, the weeds crunching beneath their feet. Releasing his grip on the prince's arm, he lifted the heavy grate as easily as if it were made of paper, then bent down to peer into the opening.

"It's a tunnel," said Jim, squatting beside him. "It opens into another tunnel that goes all the way under the dungeons. It smells in there and there're a lot of rats, but there's water running through the bottom."

"An underground river runs beneath the city," said Owen. "It's why Desidaria was built here and why we rarely run out of water. I've seen it on my father's old maps." Reaching into his tunic, he pulled out a candle and flint. "We can light this in the tunnel. Stay here. I'll go first."

"I think I should go first," said Audun. "You never know what you're going to find in a place like this."

"I'm not going to argue about it," Owen said. "Just stay here until—"

"Come on in," Jim called from inside the tunnel. "There's plenty of room in here."

"People are supposed to listen to princes," Owen grumbled, as he crawled through the opening. Audun followed, reaching back to grab the grate and pull it roughly into place. When he turned around again, Owen had lit the candle and was holding it up to examine their surroundings. The tunnel was wider than the opening to the outside, but still not big enough to allow them to stand. It went back only a dozen yards or so before ending in a mound of stone and gravel. The sound of rushing water was audible even near the opening and grew louder the farther in Audun went.

"The other tunnel is this way," Jim said, as he scurried off, still doubled over, into a side passage. "We'll have to go down because it's under this one and . . . Hey! It's filled with water! It wasn't the last time I came here, I swear it!"

"I believe you," Audun said, squeezing in beside Owen and Jim. The tunnel was short, ending in a hole in the ground as wide as the tunnel itself. Water rushed only a foot or so below them. "I bet the wizard brought the water level up just so people couldn't get into the dungeon through these tunnels."

Owen nodded, the flickering light of his candle making his shadow on the wall nod with him. "The whole castle shook this afternoon. I even felt it outside."

"What are we going to do?" asked Jim. "I know of two other ways in, but if this tunnel is flooded, they will be, too."

"I'll go," said Audun.

"Don't be ridiculous," Owen said, scowling. "You won't be able to breathe in there and there's no telling how far you'll have to go before you reach air again."

Jim shook his head. "You can't go in! I've been down there and I can tell you that it's a really long way. I suppose we can check the other openings. Maybe one of them . . ."

"You said yourself that if one is flooded, the others will be as well. I'm a strong swimmer and can hold my breath for a very long time, much longer than either of you. I'll have the best chance of getting in there and back out again." Although Owen knew that Audun was really a dragon, Jim had no idea. The last thing Audun wanted to do was let someone else in on a secret that no one was supposed to know.

Owen held up his hand in protest. "It's my father and—"

"Exactly," said Audun. "I don't want to be the one to tell your father that you died trying to rescue him. Don't worry, I know what I'm doing."

"You won't have any light," said Owen. "How will you see where you're going? I have another candle, but it won't do you a bit of good underwater."

"I can see in the dark better than you can," said Audun. "There is one thing, though. I've never met your father or seen what he looks like. How will I know who to bring back? From what I've heard, Dolon has been collecting prisoners in the dungeon since the day he took over the castle."

"Here," said Jim, reaching into the neck of his tunic. "I have this." A jeweled locket lay on his palm and when he pressed a tiny knob on the top it split in half, revealing a miniature picture on each side. "That's my father," Jim said, pointing to the picture on the right. The man was dressed in heavy robes with a jeweled chain around his neck. Jim tapped his finger against the other picture. "And that's King Cadmus. He and my father were friends." The king was a distinguished man with hair as blond as Owen's.

The prince glanced up and gave Jim a searching look. "Your father was the gem merchant, wasn't he? My father counted him as a good friend."

"This should help," said Audun, examining the miniature portrait of the king closely. "There is one other thing that might be useful. Would you happen to have something of your father's, Owen? Perhaps a piece of clothing that you took with you when you left?"

Owen looked thoughtful but shook his head. "The only thing I have of my father's is this ring," he said, holding up his hand. "He gave it to me for safekeeping just before Dolon's men took him away."

"That might work," said Audun. He pulled Owen's hand closer as if to get a better look, and quickly sniffed the ring. When he had a good sense of its owner, Audun turned and lowered his legs into the water before anyone could stop him. It was warm, with a strong current that Audun hadn't anticipated.

"Are you sure you want to do this?" asked Jim. "I

mean, you're the first friend I've made since I got here and I really don't want to lose you."

Audun grinned. "I don't want to lose me, either. Don't worry, I'll be back before you know it." The last thing he saw before the current carried him away were the worried faces of his two new friends.

As the water swept Audun under the castle, he considered changing into a dragon, but the space was narrow, and he didn't know how wide it would be up ahead. He'd never taken off the amulet that allowed him to breathe underwater, so he wasn't worried about air. However, his human body was far more fragile than his true dragon self, a fact he'd forgotten when he had said that he would go. The current was fast, and if it hadn't been for his dragon strength he would have been hurled into the wall. As it was, it took all of his efforts to stay in the center of the channel while avoiding the debris that churned in the water around him.

After what seemed like hours, Audun finally saw a glimmer of light ahead. He was swimming toward it, hoping that it was an opening into the dungeon, when he sensed a change in the current. Something big was coming.

Even with the eyesight of a dragon, Audun couldn't see more than a few feet away in the darkened water. He was turning in a circle, trying to see what was coming up behind him when a tentacle wrapped itself around his neck and jerked. Audun flailed his arms as the tentacle dragged him backward. There was a loud sucking sound and he slid down the gullet of a river monster.

The tentacle let go with a slurp and Audun slid on his back down a bumpy surface. He was stunned. He'd never been swallowed before and it wasn't at all what he would have expected: he hadn't been chewed into bits, nor was he dissolving in a vat of stomach acid. Instead, he floated in water that smelled faintly of rotting fish and was warmer than the water he'd just come from. The light he'd been trying to reach was still visible, although it was wavery, as if he were looking through a thick layer of ice. The roar of the underground river was muted.

Audun twisted his body around until he felt footing below him. Using his hands and feet, he tried to climb up the bumpy surface, but it gave too easily under pressure; he felt like he was climbing in old fish pudding. He could always turn into a dragon if he had to, but the thought of doing it inside another living creature made his stomach turn. There had to be another way out.

Water sloshed around him every time the creature moved. With his hand touching the inside of the beast, Audun could feel its body slosh, too, which made him realize just how much of the monster was made of water. It seemed more like a water-filled bladder armed with a tentacle than like the sea monsters Audun had met near the islands. And if it really was mostly water . . .

Audun reached into the satchel where he'd hidden the

215

objects he usually carried in the pouch under his wing. The piece of ice felt colder in his human hand than it had in his dragon talons and he dropped it sooner than he'd intended. It fell into the water which instantly turned slushy with the cold. The monster shivered and Audun's human body shivered with it.

A groaning sound filled Audun's ears and he looked up as a wave of warm water washed over him. It took only moments before this water had turned slushy as well. Hoping that the monster would groan again, Audun doubled his efforts as he fought his way to its mouth. He was ready when the creature's jaws gaped open. Grabbing hold of the creature's lip, he somersaulted out of the beast and into the underground river which was already turning colder. Although he kept his head down, he grazed his back on the ceiling of the tunnel, cutting through his clothes and scraping away skin.

With powerful thrusts of his legs and arms, Audun swam away from the monster toward the light in the ceiling. It was another wide hole covered with a metal grate. Audun struggled against the current, trying to stay under the opening long enough to grab hold of the grate. It took all his strength, but Audun was able to push it aside and pull himself out of the river with a *whoosh!*

He stood for a moment, trying to get his bearings as water sluiced off his clothes. Squelching with every step, he began to search for Owen's father.

The only light in the otherwise dark dungeon came from smoking torches that sputtered at the slightest puff of air. At first, Audun caught only a faint whiff of the king's presence, and thought it might have been left from visits in times past. That changed, however, when Audun reached the intersection of two corridors and the scent became much stronger.

Although he tried to be as quiet as possible, even the small sounds he made drew the prisoners to the doors of their cells. A few of them watched him walk by in silence while others cried out, asking for his help, yet each time he tried to talk to one of them, they were too frightened and distrustful to listen to what he had to say.

Finally, he noticed a man who pressed his face against the bars in the square window of his door and didn't hide when Audun approached. "Be quiet, you idiots!" the man shouted, making his long, scruffy beard bob up and down. "Can't you tell—that's a dead man walking there. You don't want the kind of help he can give you!"

"Pardon me," said Audun, "but I was wondering if you know where the king is being kept."

"Why?" asked the man. "Do you want to drag him off to drown him so you'll have company in your watery grave?"

"Not at all," Audun replied. "I'm not dead and I don't want to hurt anyone. I'm here to help the king escape."

"Really? In that case, I'm the king. Which one are you looking for?"

"King Cadmus," said Audun.

"Well, then, I'm King Cadmus! Let me out."

Audun sighed. "I can't take everyone in the dungeon, and if I let you out they'll all want to go. I'm here to rescue the king. Once I get him out, I'm sure he'll do his best to come back and free the rest of his subjects."

"Why would he want to do that? There are murderers and cutthroats down here. Most of these men deserve to be right where they are. I'm different, though, so let me out."

"Why are *you* in here?"

"Because I'm King Cadmus, remember? You have a very short memory, don't you, boy?"

Audun peered at the man. He was old and wrinkled and his beard must have taken years to grow. The man in front of him didn't look anything like the clean-shaven man in the picture and he smelled so awful that Audun's eyes teared. "Never mind," Audun said, as he turned away. "I'll just have to keep looking."

"Don't be a dunderhead!" yelled the man. "I'm Cadmus and you have to get me out."

"No!" shouted a prisoner on the other side of the corridor. "I'm Cadmus. Take me with you!" Audun glanced at him, but he was much too young to be the king.

While voices up and down the corridor clamored that they, too, were Cadmus, Audun went from window to window, trying to find the prisoner who looked like the man in the picture. None of them were right, however. Some were too young, some too old, some had eyes too far apart or noses too small, yet now that they knew that Audun was there to free the king, every one of them claimed to be King Cadmus. Unfortunately, they all smelled horrible.

Reaching the end of the row, Audun closed his eyes. Taking a deep breath, he tried to sort out the awful smells. There, that was it. It was true, Cadmus was here, but he was behind him. Audun retraced his steps all the way back to . . . Audun groaned. The crazy old man he'd been talking to was Cadmus after all.

"I told you so," said the king.

"Why don't you look anything like the picture you gave the gem merchant?" asked Audun.

"Is that the picture you saw? I must have given that to him six or seven years ago. I pass out so many of those things that it's hard to keep track. I've had a beard for the last five years at least. Now, how about letting me out?"

"I'm doing this on your son's behalf," Audun said, wrapping his fingers around the window bars. With one powerful jerk, he yanked the bars from the window, but left the door still in place.

"Is that the best you can do?" asked the king. "I can't fit through that little hole. I may have lost weight, but I'm not a skeleton like that guy." Audun peered behind the king at the skeleton sitting in the corner. Someone had rearranged his bones so that he was in a sitting position, with one knee resting on the other and his hands palm up beside him. An old metal cup had been placed on one of his hands so that he looked as if he'd been drinking.

"I'm not finished," said Audun. Bracing his feet against the wall on either side of the doorway, he gripped the door through the window hole and pulled. The top of the door broke free, leaving the bottom intact.

"You're not very good at this, are you?" said Cadmus. "Why, if it were up to me—"

"Pardon me, Your Majesty," Audun said, as he reached through the opening and picked up the king. "We don't have time for criticism."

Slinging the king over his shoulder, he turned and started down the corridor while prisoners shouted and pleaded for him to take them, too. He really would have taken them with him if he could have, but he knew that the return trip wasn't going to be easy. In view of what had happened on his way in, he was already considering how he was going to carry the king back with him. It had been difficult enough to fight the current when he was by himself, but carrying this old man would make it that much harder . . . unless, of course, Audun was a dragon.

Putting aside the concerns that had made him refrain from changing into a dragon earlier, Audun resolved that he would have to return to his normal shape if he were to have any chance of reaching the outside world. He had even thought of a way to keep the king from seeing his true form. He hoped the old man wouldn't be able to feel the difference between human and dragon once they were in the water.

After setting the king beside the opening to the tunnel, Audun took Frostweaver's fabric from his satchel and held it up so King Cadmus could see it. "We're about to go into some very cold water. This magic fabric will keep you warm, but you have to keep it over your head, so you won't be able to see anything. Don't struggle while I carry you, or I might lose my grip and drop you. Do you understand?"

"Of course I understand," grumped the king. "What kind of idiot do you think I am? You're going to carry me to who knows where and I won't be able to see where we're going until we get there. And if I try to get away, you're going to drop me." King Cadmus peered over the edge into the ink-black water where chunks of ice floated by. "I see what you mean by cold. I thought you were making up excuses for wrapping me in a blanket so I couldn't see where we were going. Who would have thought there'd be ice in the desert? So how am I going to breathe down there?"

Audun didn't think he had any choice; he had to tell the king about his amulet. "I'm wearing something that lets me breathe underwater. I believe you'll be able to breathe, too, as long as I'm carrying you. It's an—"

"You *believe*? You mean you don't know? Now, isn't that a fine kettle of fish! I'm supposed to trust you with my life and you don't even know what you're doing! And this is all on my son's behalf? Which son is it? I have three, you know. Do they know what you're up to? Maybe they're out to kill me, too. Never mind. They're all good boys. We'd better get out of here before those fool guards wander down this way in one of their drunken stupors and trip over us. Hand me that fabric. I'll do it myself. I don't trust you not to . . . There, that's it," King Cadmus said through the fabric. "I'm trussed up like a goose and ready to go. I don't care how you get me out of here. Just do it! Hey, are you going somewhere? You're not going to leave me here!"

Audun had slipped into the river feet first and was treading water. While the king flopped around like a blindfolded fish, Audun changed back into a dragon. It was a relief to be himself again, and the current that had felt so strong and cold before now seemed gentle and refreshing. Because the hole was too small for him to fit through as a dragon, he reached up with both forelegs and plucked the king off the floor. Careful not to poke the man through the fabric with his talons, Audun dove into the river and swam upstream, easily maneuvering around the debris.

The king had begun to struggle as soon as he entered the water. Audun worried at first, but the old man continued to shout and thrash around long after he would have drowned if the magic hadn't been working. Satisfied that the king was all right, the dragon sped through the water, reaching the hole in the ceiling near the outer wall in minutes.

With a powerful heave, Audun tossed the king through the opening onto the floor of the tunnel. He heard Jim and Owen shout, but by then he was so busy focusing on turning back into a human that he missed whatever they were saying. A moment later he pulled himself out of the water, landing on his stomach beside the partly unwrapped king with an *oof!*

"You got him!" Owen shouted, pounding Audun on the back.

"You shouldn't have doubted me," Audun said, although he'd had moments when he'd doubted he could do it himself.

"Your friend swims like a fish," said the king, as he kicked the cloth off his feet. "I wouldn't have thought he was human if I hadn't seen it with my own two eyes. Didn't feel like a human, though." He rubbed his chest where Audun's talons had pressed against him. "Strongest grip I ever felt."

Owen put his arm around his father's shoulders. "Thank goodness for that. But now we have to get you out of here, Father. I have a horse waiting in the city. You two should come with us," he added, glancing from Jim to Audun. "This is no life for you here, Jim. And I can use your help, Audun. My father and I are going to get his throne back."

"Jim should go," Audun said. "But I have to stay here. I came to Desidaria to find someone and I'm not leaving until I do."

Twenty

The sun was coming up as Audun helped Owen hide King Cadmus in a wagon that would take him off the castle grounds. After wishing his friends well, Audun sneaked through the back door of the kitchen behind a yawning scullery maid and trudged down the corridor to the Great Hall. His clothes still damp, he sat on a bench to wait until it was time to see Smugsby.

Exhausted from the sleepless night, Audun dreaded all the tasks the steward was bound to have waiting for him. He thought about abandoning the job altogether so he could focus on looking for the girl, but then he would probably be kicked out of the castle. Perhaps he could hunt for the girl while he was working, provided he wasn't too obvious about it. He'd already decided that he would talk to every girl in the castle if he had to, in order to find the one he was meant to rescue. After that, he would go straight to Greater Greensward and tell Millie how much she meant to him, and this time nothing was going to get in his way.

Audun was about to get off the bench and go see Smugsby when four guards approached him. The big man who'd been made a guard just the day before was among them. Audun thought they were headed for the next table, and was surprised when they stopped beside his.

"You're coming with us," said one of the men. Audun recognized him as a guard from the orphans' tower.

"What's this about?" Audun asked, getting to his feet.

"Treason," the guard answered. He refused to say anything more, even as they hustled Audun through the Great Hall, along the corridor, and down the steep stairs to the dungeon.

Audun wasn't worried when they marched him into an empty cell and manacled him to the wall. He knew he could get out at any time: he was sure that the chains couldn't withstand a dragon's strength, but he was curious enough to want to know why he was being named a traitor. They couldn't know of his actions during the night, unless . . .

Audun sniffed the air. Could they have captured Owen and Jim while they were helping King Cadmus off the castle grounds? If so, they would be in the dungeon as well, but he couldn't sense either of the boys, and with such a distinctive odor, Jim would have been easy to smell.

Audun watched the guards as they prepared to leave the cell, taking the torches they'd brought with them. Although three of the guards hurried out of the cell without a backward glance, the new guard paused at the door, letting the light of the torch he carried play over his features. And he winked.

Audun's jaw dropped. He wanted to ask the guard who he was and why he had winked, but the man was gone before he could get the words out. As the door slammed shut, Audun closed his eyes and shook his head. He'd really messed things up this time. Not only had he not found the girl, but he'd gotten himself locked away, and now he'd have to free himself without revealing his true nature. He was wondering how things could have gone so wrong when he heard footsteps. Light filled the small square window again.

His answer came when two visitors unlocked the door and one of them, a man dressed in a billowing robe decorated with spinning silver stars, jerked his cupped hands into the air, sending a ball of pale, blue light through the cell to bob just above Audun's head. Ever since he'd seen Olebald in the Great Hall, Audun had suspected that it wouldn't be long before the wizard knew of his presence in the castle. He had hoped, however, that it would take a little longer than this, and that he might actually be able to leave before the wizard could find him.

As the two men drew closer, he recognized the other man as the one who had greeted Olebald on his arrival, the one he'd assumed was King Dolon. Shorter than his brother, Cadmus, Dolon's hair had yet to turn from silvery gray to white and his beard was just a fringe on his chin.

"So this is the one who's come to kill me," said Dolon, peering nearsightedly at Audun. "He doesn't look like an assassin."

Audun's head shot up. "What? I never tried to kill anyone."

Olebald snorted and stomped across the filthy floor to glare down his nose at Audun, even though the boy was a good eight inches taller and the wizard had to tilt his head back to do it. "Don't lie to us, boy. Why else would you be here? You got a job under false pretenses—bribing a court official with a forbidden magical gift."

"Oh, dear," said King Dolon. "Is it really forbidden? I was so hoping to get one for myself. I've heard those bottomless tankards are wonderful, especially when you plan to entertain, and you know my wife intends to have all her relatives visit now that she's queen. Those people can drink more in one hour than a ship's crew the first day in port."

"Well, of course *you* can have one, Your Majesty," said Olebald. "I'll get you one myself if you'd like."

King Dolon looked pleased. "Very thoughtful of you, old fellow. I'd like mine filled with mead. I'm partial to it myself, and I don't see why the wife's brother can't drink mead instead of the imported wine he's always demanding."

Olebald sighed. "As you wish, Your Majesty. Now, about the boy . . ."

"What boy? Oh, yes. Him. He looks like a nice enough boy. Handsome, too. Just the sort my daughter would be interested in meeting. Do you suppose you can arrange that as well?"

Olebald ground his teeth and, in an obvious effort to remain patient, said, "He's here to kill you, Your Majesty. That's why he's in the dungeon."

"I told you, I'm not here to kill anyone!" said Audun.

"Then why are you here, if not to overthrow King Dolon and put his brother back on the throne?"

King Dolon nodded. "Someone set Cadmus free last night. Was it you? Because if it was, I'd like to know how you did it. Quite an amazing feat actually, what with the river and the monster and all. I was astounded when Olebald thought of so many marvelous traps. I never would have come up with any of them in a million years."

"That's why I'm here, Your Majesty," said Olebald. "To protect you from nefarious scoundrels like him."

"I'm not here to hurt King Dolon!" Audun said again.

"He certainly is vehement. Are you sure he isn't innocent?" asked the king.

"Don't listen to him, Your Majesty. He has to lie about it. It's part of the assassins' code. They never admit that they've come to kill someone, even under torture."

"Oh, dear, we're not going to torture him, are we? You know I don't like that kind of thing."

"We could torture him," said Olebald, "to try to learn

if he has any accomplices, but I don't believe it would work. No, we'll just execute him quietly, if that's all right with Your Majesty."

"Yes, indeed, that's much better," King Dolon said, looking relieved. "You'll handle all the details, won't you, Olebald?" The wizard nodded, and the king added, "That's a good fellow. I knew I could depend on you. Now, if we're finished here, I suppose I'll be off."

Olebald ran to the doorway and stood just inside, watching the old king go. "I thought he'd never leave," he said, once the king's footsteps stopped ringing in the hall. The old wizard waved his hand, creating a blue cloud that drifted to the door, closed it with a *whump!* and remained to swirl in front of the window, preventing anyone from seeing inside the cell. Turning back to Audun, Olebald rubbed his hands together, saying, "Tell me what it would take to get you to turn back into a dragon."

Audun shook his head, not sure he had heard him correctly. "Pardon me?"

"You can either show me your own true self right now, which would save us both so much trouble, or I could show you a way I've devised that will change you, whether you want it to or not."

"What are you talking about?"

Olebald smiled, but in a not-very-friendly way. "Some time ago I came across a spell that would give me exactly what I'd been dreaming about for years. A nasty little witch exiled me to a tropical island where the memories of a group of witches had been kept. Although most of them had been freed, I found one bottle still intact, buried in the sand. I freed the memories in exchange for the witch's strongest spell, one which will turn me into the most fearsome dragon alive. All I need are a few key ingredients and I'll never again have to follow the orders of a sniveling king who has no idea how to rule a kingdom. I'll be the one with all the power and everyone will have to listen to me!"

"Do you honestly think a simple spell is going to turn you into a dragon? There's a lot more to it than that."

"Really? Like what?" Olebald said, his eyes lighting up.

"I'm . . . not sure," said Audun.

"Why don't you turn into a dragon and show me? I'm sure you're a most handsome beast."

"Why do you want *me* to turn into a dragon so badly?"

"Would you believe—I'm curious?"

"Not in the least. And I doubt it's because you want to see what I look like while I change. Unless . . . What precisely did the spell say you needed to turn into a dragon?"

"Just a dragon scale, a dragon talon, a dragon eyeball, and a dragon jaw. Nothing you'll miss too much."

"Sorry, but even if I wanted to give you the scale and the talon, I believe I'd really miss the eye and the jaw."

"I wasn't asking for them," said Olebald. "I was just telling you what I'm going to take once you change back into a dragon."

"You're crazy. Why would I turn back knowing that you want to tear off bits of me? I'm not going to do anything to help you."

"I can see you aren't going to cooperate," Olebald said with a sigh. "Fortunately, my plans don't depend on your goodwill." Reaching into his robe, Olebald took out a silk pouch and opened it, revealing a green stone the size of a large man's fist. Bathed in a pale light, the stone illuminated the cell like an eerie, flameless fire. The moment the stone left the pouch, the ball of blue light that had been bobbing above Audun's head flickered and went out and the silver stars on Olebald's robe stopped spinning.

Audun recognized the stone, having seen many just like it studding the wall of Nastia Nautica's underwater cave. What he didn't understand was what the wizard thought he could do with a stone that wiped out magic.

"This stone has many properties," said Olebald. "Even the sea witch I acquired it from didn't know them all, but I've been experimenting with it. I believe that while no one can do magic in its presence, if you were to swallow it, it would force you to turn back into a dragon. In essence, it can change your form only from the inside—and then only by returning you to your real shape."

Audun was incredulous. "You want me to swallow that rock? That thing is huge! I couldn't get it down, and if I did it would kill me."

Olebald shrugged and took a step toward Audun.

"Great discoveries often involve great sacrifices. I don't need you to be alive to get the parts I require. It will make it easier for me if you aren't. Now, open wide and we'll see if this fits."

"Mmph!" said Audun, pressing his lips shut and turning his head to the side. He struggled as Olebald grabbed his head and tried to pry his jaws far enough apart to shove the stone between his lips. Unable to use his magic in the presence of the stone, the old man had to rely on his not-so-great strength and was losing the battle when the cell door burst open, admitting a slender, young, blue and white dragoness with lovely green stripes.

"He hasn't hurt you, has he, Audun?" asked the dragoness. Audun wondered how this stranger knew his name. Only four feet long, she was probably about the same age as Loolee. Audun was certain that he had never seen her before.

"Mmph!" said Audun, still trying to keep his mouth shut.

"Get away from him, you horrible monster!" the dragoness roared. With one beat of her wings, she landed on Olebald and knocked him to the floor. She was so small, however, that once he was down, he was able to fend her off with one arm while the other clutched the stone to his chest.

"If I can't get . . . what I want . . . from one dragon," Olebald said, grunting with exertion, "then I'll get . . . it

from . . . another!" The old wizard shoved the little dragoness to the ground, pinning her beneath his knees. She
flailed at him with her wings, batting the stone to the floor
where it rolled well out of reach. With both hands free, the
old wizard tried to rip one of her scales loose. The dragoness screamed and snapped at him with her sharp baby
teeth.

Audun groaned. If only the stone had rolled in his
direction, he might have been able to toss it out the door
and turn back into a dragon. Now that the little dragoness
was in danger, he *had* to become a dragon to save her.
Whoever she was, she couldn't possibly know the danger
she now faced.

Audun dragged at the chains that bound him to the
wall and for the first time noticed that they were new and
not like the chains he'd seen in the cells while looking for
King Cadmus. These were made of bright, shiny metal
with no sign of rust; it was all he could do to bend them,
let alone break them.

While Audun thrashed around, jerking at the chains, he
called out to the dragoness, "Hold on! I'm coming!" When
the dragoness let out a pitiful mew, he threw himself
against the chains. With no scales to protect him, the metal
cut into his skin, making the manacles slippery with blood.

Audun turned his head as the floor shuddered under
the pounding of heavy feet. Suddenly, an enormous
dragon head filled the doorway, its mouth open in a

roar that shook the walls of the cell and made dust sift through the stone ceiling. Olebald looked up from the dragoness, his eyes as big as platters and his face turning pale. Snarling, the dragon thrashed its head from side to side as it fought to work its way into the room. With a sickening grating sound, the mortar that held the stones of the doorway crumbled and the dragon staggered into the cell.

The dragon was more than twice Audun's normal size, with burly muscles and a ridge as sharp as blades. When he roared again stones fell from the ceiling and screams of terror echoed from the neighboring cells. Audun had never been so happy to see anyone as he was to see Frosty-breath at that moment.

Olebald cowered against the floor with his arms crossed in front of his face as if they could protect him. The little dragoness looked just as frightened as she crawled toward the wall, away from both the wizard and the dragon.

"So you thought you'd get away," Frostybreath growled, thrashing his tail behind him as he strode toward the wizard. His tail hit an ancient skeleton, knocking it across the cell where it shattered against the far wall. "Did you really think I wouldn't find you again?"

The old man stammered, powerless against the dragon without his magic. He scuttled backward until he reached the wall and couldn't go any farther.

Frostybreath turned to Audun and shook his head, saying, "You certainly know how to get yourself into a mess."

The little dragoness's ridge was raised in anger when she flew at him shouting, "Don't you hurt my friend!"

"Who is this?" Frostybreath asked, as he caught the little dragon with his talons. She fought, scratching and biting.

Audun shrugged. "I don't know, although she seems to know me. Would you mind," he asked, pulling his arms as far from the wall as he could get them.

Frostybreath grunted. Stretching out his neck, he breathed on the chains, making them so cold that they became brittle. He was reaching out to break them when Olebald got to his feet. While the big dragon turned back to the wizard, Audun lunged against the chains, snapping them. He didn't hesitate, but dashed to where the green stone still lay and snatched it up from the floor. Running to the door, he pitched it down the corridor where it skidded through the dust and debris and finally disappeared through a hole in a grate to the water below.

Still in the doorway, Audun closed his eyes and turned back into a dragon. Hearing a gasp behind him, he turned around and saw the little dragoness looking from him to the blue cloud that had formed between the wizard and Frostybreath. The big dragon looked stunned. Audun didn't know why until he saw tendrils reaching from the blue cloud to wrap themselves around the dragon's throat.

The wizard had his back to Audun, who knew that he had only seconds before Olebald used the blue cloud against him as well. Without making a sound, Audun launched himself at the old man, knocking him to the floor. The impact stunned Olebald for a moment, which was just long enough for the cloud to falter and fall back in on itself. Released from the cloud, Frostybreath snarled and stalked toward Olebald. The old man was shaking his head when the big ice dragon breathed on him. A look of horror stiffened on his face as Frostybreath froze him as solid as an ice cube. The blue cloud imploded with a small *pop!* leaving the room too dark for a human to see. Fortunately, it wasn't too dark for dragons.

"I should have done that the last time," the big dragon said, sitting back on his haunches.

"You're a dragon!" breathed the little dragoness, staring at Audun.

He noticed that one of her front fangs was chipped. She reminded him of someone, but he just couldn't remember who. "Yes, I am," he said, still studying her face. "Thank you for coming to my rescue, but do I know you?"

The dragoness nodded and a moment later Jim stood in front of him, looking up at him with the same worshipful look that the dragoness had been giving him. Audun gasped and said, "Jim?"

"It's Gem, actually," she said, after turning back into a dragoness. "My parents raised me among humans. They were going to take me to the dragon stronghold in a few months. My big sister is already there, waiting for me.

237

When I was just a hatchling they taught me how to pass myself off as a human. They said I'd be safer if people thought I was a boy, so I started dressing like one when they brought me to Aridia."

"Why did they bring you here?" asked Audun.

"My parents were King Stormclaw's representatives to the king of Aridia. Ice dragons have mined the gems under the desert for centuries. We give some to the Aridian king and take the rest to the dragon stronghold. It's a big secret among the humans. My parents said that the king tells his son on his deathbed, but no one else is supposed to know. We were good at keeping secrets. King Cadmus and my father were friends, but even the king didn't know that my father was a dragon."

Frostybreath ruffled the crest on Gem's head with his talons. "What happened to your parents, little one?"

"Everyone knew my father was a gem merchant. Soldiers broke into our house, looking for the gems, but my father had hidden them all. The soldiers killed my parents when they couldn't find what they wanted. I hid until they left, then King Dolon's men found me and brought me to the castle with all the other orphans. When the king asked us for the names of our relatives, I told him that I didn't have any in Aridia, which was true, so he made me work as a servant. I didn't mind too much. It was better than being locked in the tower like the other orphans."

Audun nodded. If any girl didn't belong at the castle,

it was Gem. "Let me guess—you rolled in muck to mask your dragon scent, didn't you?"

"It was the only thing I could think of," she said. "My parents used a lotion to cover their scent. I didn't need it when I was young and now that I do I don't know where to get it."

"You're a very clever dragoness," said Frostybreath. "Your parents would be proud of you."

"And what about you?" Audun asked the bigger dragon. "You were the new guard, weren't you?"

"Figured that out, did you? I followed Olebald here after he escaped from the stronghold. I'm supposed to take him back with me so King Stormclaw and his council can pass judgment on him. He did some nasty things to a few dragons before he left and he's going to have to answer for that."

"Did you know that he was coming to Aridia?" asked Audun.

"Not until I got here, and then I was afraid he was coming after you."

"I met Jim my first day here, but I didn't know she was a girl," Audun said, before turning back to Gem. "May I accompany you to the dragon stronghold? You said that your sister was there, waiting for you. I bet she'll be happy to see you. What is her name? If I don't know her, I'm sure Frostybreath will."

"Her name is Loolee. She was my best friend before she left."

"I know Loolee!" Audun said. "She taught me how to slide down the ice chute. You'll like the ice chute. Frosty-breath made it so little dragonesses like you could have fun."

"Would you show me how to slide down it, Audun?"

"Of course," he replied, smiling. "And then I have something very important that I have to do."

Twenty-one

A wide grin stretched Audun's scaly lips when he finally spotted the royal castle of Greater Greensward from high in the sky. Although the castle wasn't as big as some of those he'd visited, it was by far the most beautiful. Green pennants streamed from the tops of the slender towers, and the white stone of the walls reminded him of home. Flowers grew in profusion along both sides of the road leading up to the drawbridge where guards kept watch over the people coming and going.

It had been more than three months since Audun had seen Millie. Although he'd planned to return to Greater Greensward sooner, Prince Owen had begged him to stay to help him and his father, Cadmus, regain the Aridian throne. Because of Aridia's ties to the ice dragons, Audun had felt obliged to help them in whatever way he could. Unfortunately, the short campaign they'd planned had lasted far longer than anyone anticipated and it had been many weeks before Audun was able to leave.

Through it all, Audun had spent hours thinking about Millie. Curled up under the stars trying to rest after yet another battle, Audun often lay awake, remembering how Millie had looked when he saw her last. She'd been so happy to see him when he first arrived, and later had looked as if her heart was being ripped apart when her mother whisked her away. Sometimes Audun tried to picture what she would look like when he finally saw her again; he was sure she'd be just as excited to see him as he'd be to see her. Yet now that the time was approaching, Audun was no longer quite so certain. They'd been apart for too many months. Could time have dimmed her memory of him? Or even worse, could she have met someone else?

No, he thought, bringing his wings down with extra force so that he shot toward the castle. After all he'd gone through, he wasn't going to let doubt mar their reunion. Millie was his one true love, his soul mate and the one with whom he wanted to spend the rest of his life. He knew deep down inside that she had to feel the same way. Now that he was back, he was going to do whatever it took to make sure nothing got in their way.

Audun circled over the courtyard looking for Millie, but the only humans in sight were the guards on the towers and some servants hustling from one building to the next. Folding his wings to his sides, Audun dove toward the pavement, pulling up short beside one of the outbuildings.

He was more concerned with landing where he wouldn't frighten the horses than he was in the humans who might be there, so he didn't notice a young man dressed in a cloth-of-gold-lined cape run down the steps, grab a spear from a nearby guard, and prepare to throw it.

Audun had barely set his feet on the ground when a voice shouted, "Don't worry, Princess! I'll save you!"

Audun's head snapped around just as the young man hurled the spear. After having spent so many days in battle in Aridia, the dragon sidestepped it easily.

"Beware, foul lizard," shouted the man, as he pulled his sword from its scabbard. "I, Prince Rudolfo, am about to slay you and rip your evil heart from your chest and—"

"Oh, for the love of fish!" Audun cursed. Although instinct told him to stand and fight, the last thing he wanted to do was hurt someone who might be a friend of Millie's. He wanted to make the best impression he could when he met her family again, and was sure they wouldn't take kindly to the sight of human blood on his talons.

A shadow moved in the open doorway, but before Audun could see who was there, the prince's sword came whistling through the air, and the dragon had to jump out of the way. Wondering if things had changed so drastically that dragons were no longer welcome in Greater Greensward, Audun turned and hid behind the outbuilding.

"Rudolfo!" shouted a familiar voice, but Audun was already changing and wasn't sure he'd heard correctly.

"Did you see that, Princess?" called the prince. "I sent the beast scurrying away with its tail between its legs! Wait here while I go finish it off."

"You'll do no such thing!" Millie shouted, as Audun came around the corner, now in his human form and dressed in the blue and white tunic that he'd chosen specially for their reunion. He looked up as Millie dashed down the stairs, saying, "If you've hurt him . . ." with a worried look on her face.

"Millie!" Audun said, reaching out his hand, but she ran right past him, stopping suddenly when she saw that there was nothing behind him between the back of the outbuilding and the castle wall.

"What happened to the dragon?" demanded the prince, who had also come running. He shot a glance at Audun and frowned. "Who are you?"

Audun nodded in Millie's direction. "I'm a friend of the princess's."

Millie gave him an odd look. "The dragon is gone. He must have flown off when we couldn't see him. But that's beside the point," she said, turning to glare at Rudolfo. "How dare you attack a dragon at my very door!"

"I was protecting you!" said the prince, falling to one knee before her. "I was going to slay him and lay his head at your feet and serve you his heart on a—"

Millie looked a little queasy as she shook her head. "That's enough, Rudolfo. I don't want to hear any more.

I don't need your help. I can take care of myself. As I said before, I appreciate your request for my hand, but we really aren't suited to each other. Please go before you embarrass us both."

"Embarrass!" said the prince, his brow creasing and his mouth turning down into a frown. He stood and gave her a stiff bow. "I have done nothing to embarrass myself. However, I do think it is time that I take my leave. Good-bye for now, Princess."

Both Millie and Audun watched Prince Rudolfo stalk to the horse that a stable hand had just brought out. They waited until he was riding under the portcullis and onto the drawbridge before turning to each other again. "All right," said Millie, "tell me what happened."

"I don't know what you—" Audun began.

"Don't act all innocent with me! Rudolfo may not have seen you change, but I could see it all from the top of the stairs. How is it that you're a human? Why didn't you tell me you could do this before? I can't believe you deceived me!"

"I didn't deceive you. I spent months learning how to—"

"There you are, Millie," said the older woman with the fading blond hair who had been so rude to Audun the last time they'd met.

Audun bowed to her, having remembered that this was Queen Chartreuse, one of Millie's grandmothers.

"So Prince Rudolfo has gone," she said. "I was hoping you had changed your mind, Millie. But I see another suitor has arrived. How delightful!" Leaning closer to her granddaughter, she added in a loud whisper, "You've already rejected most of the eligible princes in the known kingdoms. Try hard not to chase this one away as well!" Smiling a little too brightly at Millie, the queen nodded to Audun. "Welcome to Greater Greensward. May your stay be a pleasant one."

Millie frowned at Audun as her grandmother climbed the stairs. "I suppose I'll have to let you in now, although don't think I'm happy to see you. I hate being lied to, especially by someone I trusted."

"But that's just it," said Audun. "I've never lied to you and I never would! If you'd only let me explain—"

"Explain what?" asked Emma, Millie's mother, coming down the stairs. "I just saw my mother and she said Millie had a new suitor. Who are you, anyway?" she asked, eyeing Audun with suspicion. "I feel as if we've met before."

"This is Audun," said Millie.

"But I thought Audun was a dragon."

"Exactly!" said Millie, her eyes flashing. "Apparently he had hidden talents that he didn't bother to tell me about. I can't believe I was so gullible!"

Confused, Audun watched as Millie turned on her heels and stalked up the stairs, leaving him alone with her mother.

"Would you mind telling me what is going on?" Emma asked.

"I'm not sure I know, but I'll tell you what I can, Your Highness," said Audun, bowing. "The last time we met, I was a dragon. After I left here, I went to see King Storm-claw, as you know. Thank you for going to see him, by the way. I think your visit helped him decide to let me court Millie. Anyway, I asked the king and his council to teach me how to turn myself into a human. They did, after I performed several difficult tasks for them. I came back to see Millie as soon as I could."

"You mean you couldn't change into a human before?" asked Emma.

Audun sighed. "Don't you think I would have if I could have?"

"Then why didn't you tell Millie?"

"I was trying to! I wanted to come back sooner, but I had to help the king, and then they needed me in Aridia."

"I see," said Emma. "Millie was upset when you didn't come sooner. She was afraid you'd forgotten all about her. Explain to her what you've been doing and I'm sure she'll understand . . . eventually. It may take a while for her to calm down, though. She can be awfully stubborn at times."

"I know," said Audun, "but then, so can I."

Twenty-two

Audun wasn't nearly as confident when he woke the next day. All the previous afternoon and evening he had tried to explain what had happened, but each time he broached the topic Millie had invited someone to join their conversation or remembered a suddenly important errand that she had to see to right then. They hadn't been alone for a minute, and after a big, formal supper, Millie had slipped off to bed without even saying good night. He'd found it frustrating, but he had no intention of telling her all he wanted to say where anyone else could hear him.

Audun had spent much of the night trying to think of something he could do to get Millie to talk to him in private. He had a few ideas, but nothing he really liked, so he was still pondering the problem when he stepped through the door of the chamber where he'd slept. A page carrying a knight's sword and helmet almost knocked him over.

"What's the hurry, child?" Audun asked, as he helped the boy collect the gauntlet that he'd dropped.

"Haven't you heard?" asked the boy. "An army is advancing on the castle. The knights are preparing to defend it. They'd already lowered the drawbridge this morning, so they had to raise it in a hurry when soldiers appeared out of nowhere."

A passing serving man carrying a knife and an old-fashioned helmet stopped long enough to say, "The call has gone out for all able-bodied men. We're to bring what-ever weapons and armor we have and meet in the court-yard. With the Green Witch protecting the kingdom they probably won't need us, but they're having us get ready just in case."

"Whose army is it?" asked Audun.

The boy shrugged, but the man smiled wryly and said, "Some fool who thinks he can best the Green Witch with an ordinary fighting force. You'd think everyone would know better, considering our Princess Emma's reputation."

Audun nodded as the boy and the man went on their way. Even in far-off Aridia, Audun had heard rumors about the might of Princess Emma and the fire-breathing dragons that defended Greater Greensward. He'd never once mentioned that he'd met her or that she was the mother of his one true love. From everything he'd heard, anyone who would attack Greater Greensward would have to either be crazy or think he had some very special advan-tage that would allow him to defeat dragons and the magic of the Green Witch. If the latter were true, it was possible that the Green Witch might just need Audun's help, even if he couldn't breathe fire. Besides, with the alliance agreement between the Green Witch and King Stormclaw signed and sealed, he felt duty-bound to help her just as he had helped Prince Owen in Aridia.

Audun learned from a passing servant girl that Princess Emma had a tower of her own. He ran up the stairs, hoping Emma hadn't already left the castle, and didn't stop until he reached the door at the top. Hearing voices inside, he knocked and was relieved when someone called out for him to come in.

Although the room was fairly large, the end near the door seemed crowded. Millie and Emma were seated on a bench by the window while two men stood only an arm's reach away. Audun had met the men at supper the night before. The younger one had curly brown hair and a pleasant face. He was Prince Eadric, Millie's father and the crown prince of Upper Montevista, the northern kingdom where Audun had encountered the witches Klorine and Ratinki. The older man was King Limelyn, Emma's father and the ruler of Greater Greensward. His hair was graying and his skin was lined from years of worry, but he still had the commanding presence of a king who had seen many battles. Audun had liked both Prince Eadric and King Limelyn right away and had had the feeling that they liked him as well. Right now, however, they scarcely glanced at

Audun before turning back to examine a ball made of crystal that Millie's mother held cupped in her hands.

Audun ducked as a brightly colored bird the size of a chicken with long, trailing feathers and a curved beak swooped past his head to land on the table on the other side of the room. "Lover boy is here!" screeched the bird in a grating voice. "It's Millie's next suitor, come to spy on her and learn all her secrets! He wants to know why none of her other suitors have—"

"Be quiet, You-too," snapped Millie. "I don't have any secrets from Audun."

"Really?" said the bird. "Does he know that you—"

"I don't know why you keep this bird around, Emma," King Limelyn said, making a grab for You-too, who lurched off the table and fluttered out of reach.

Emma shrugged. "He was a wedding gift to Eadric and me."

"I'd say he was more of a curse," said her father.

"Look, that must be the one in charge," Emma said, pointing at something in the ball that Audun couldn't see from where he was standing.

Millie bent closer to the crystal ball. "Can you see his face?" she asked, frowning in concentration.

"Give it a moment," said Emma.

"There, he's turning this way," Eadric said, "and it's . . ."

"Prince Rudolfo!" they all exclaimed in unison.

"He must have had his soldiers waiting for him on the other side of the border," King Limelyn said. "And went to fetch them when Millie turned him down."

"I told you I didn't like him," muttered You-too. "He had shifty eyes."

"You never said any such thing!" Millie said.

The bird shuffled sideways on the back of the chair where he had perched. "Yes, I did. You just didn't hear me!"

Emma shook her head. "I wish I had seen those men sooner. The first thing I do every morning is check our borders with this," she said, tapping the farseeing ball, "but I didn't see anything out of the ordinary today. I can't believe so many men made it all the way through the forest before anyone noticed them. If we hadn't heard their horses we wouldn't have known they were here until it was too late. Even then I had to cast a spell to make them visible. They must have a magic user of their own, but I can't seem to find him."

"My friend Frostybreath froze Olebald, but the wizard was able to use his magic to escape after he'd thawed just a little," said Audun. "He fled into the desert, where he gathered a group of soldiers and used a spell to hide them right beneath our noses by changing the color of their skin and clothes to match the colors of their surroundings."

Millie gave him a quizzical look. "How did you see the soldiers to fight them?"

252

"We didn't, at least not at first. But I sent a small puff of poison gas their way. Smaller doses of an ice dragon's poison gas makes humans ill without doing permanent harm. Soldiers who are violently sick to their stomachs aren't effective fighters."

"Poison gas?" screeched You-too. "I thought there was something odd about you. There," he said, turning to Millie. "Did I say it loudly enough for you this time?"

Eadric strode to the window and looked out. "Rudolfo's men are drawing closer to the moat. I don't think they've spotted your moat monster yet, Emma."

"Do you see anyone who might be a magic user?" asked Millie.

"Not from here," her father said, craning his neck.

"I'll try again," said Emma, turning back to the ball. Audun noticed for the first time that it was attached to a gold chain that she wore around her neck. He took a step closer, taking the place of Prince Eadric, who was still looking out the window. Audun could just make out a swirling light before the Green Witch touched the ball and the light disappeared. Even with his dragon hearing, he couldn't make out what she said as she whispered under her breath and tapped the ball again. A faint image appeared. It blurred and shifted and looked like it was about to become a face when it dissolved in a blue fog. Suddenly, the ball went blank.

Emma shook the farseeing ball, but nothing happened.

"There must be a magic user out there, but I can't tell you who it is. Whoever it is has done something to my farseeing ball. It's not working anymore."

"I need more information," said her father.

Emma nodded. "I could turn myself into a bird and go look for the magic user. It would be easy to gather information without anyone noticing."

"Just as easy as it would be for a magic user to find you, or for an archer to shoot you down," said her father. "No, there has to be another way."

"I'll go through the secret tunnel to look around," said Eadric. "I'm glad we put it in. I knew it would come in handy someday."

"What secret tunnel?" squawked You-too.

"You think we'd tell you?" Eadric asked. "You have the biggest beak in the kingdom."

"I'll go with you, Eadric," Emma said. "Just give me a moment while I change."

Audun glanced at the door. "Perhaps I should leave."

"Why?" said Millie. "She's not going to change her clothes."

"While you see what you can learn outside the wall, I'll go to the parapet," King Limelyn said. "Perhaps I'll be able to find out what Rudolfo wants."

A pale, green light had begun to shimmer around Emma, but it faded away when her father said he was leaving. "I need to renew your protection spell if you're going outside," she said, taking her father's hand in hers. "I know I put one on you just a few months ago, but they don't generally last very long. This should do the job."

> Keep him safe from point or blade,
> From all that's magic or man-made.
> Deflect their aim, repel their blows,
> Let him be well where'er he goes.

Bright green sparkles dusted the air around the king, melting on his head and shoulders as if they were tiny, colored snowflakes. King Limelyn smiled and patted her hand. "You're a good daughter, Emma."

Audun watched as she kissed the king on the cheek, something that made them both smile. The young dragon was surprised by the feelings the sight of such a simple sign of affection stirred inside him. Millie had kissed him twice before, once as she was about to enter the Blue Witch's castle, and again when she was leaving the mountain range. They were the only kisses he'd ever received and they'd given him a warm feeling inside, which was unusual for an ice dragon.

"Emma, perhaps you should change in the dungeon," Eadric suggested. "You always complain that the stairwell is too small when you're a dragon."

"Good thinking," Emma replied. Something heavy hit

an exterior wall, making the castle shake. "We'd better go. It sounds as if someone is trying to get our attention."

Emma and Eadric were already out the door when Millie started after them saying, "I'm going, too. I'm sure you'll need my help."

"Not so fast, Millie," said King Limelyn. "I want to ask your young man about the poison gas he mentioned."

"Yeah," said You-too. "Do you have it in a bottle, or do you make it yourself? And if you make it, does it come out your mouth or your—"

"That's enough from you!" declared the king. In two strides he crossed the room, snatched up the bird, tossed him into Emma's storage room, and slammed the door. Turning to Audun he gave him an apologetic smile and said, "I understand you have the same ability as my daughter and granddaughter."

"That's true, sir, although I breathe poison gas instead of fire."

"Ah," said the king. "And that's because you become an ice dragon."

"Actually, sir, I'm an ice dragon who can become a human. After I last saw Millie, I spent my time earning the right to learn how to make the change."

Millie inhaled sharply, but Audun kept his eyes on her grandfather.

King Limelyn rubbed his chin and looked at Audun

speculatively. "I didn't know that such a thing was possible. Either way, we can use a man like you in the family."

"Grandfather!" exclaimed Millie. "He hasn't even asked me yet!"

"You go with Millie and keep her safe," the king told Audun. "She's very dear to me."

"To me as well," Audun replied, turning his gaze to Millie.

Twenty-three

Millie and Audun accompanied King Limelyn down the tower stairs, separating when the king headed for the parapet while they descended the stairs to the dungeon. "Did you tell my grandfather the truth?" Millie asked. "Did you have to earn the right to learn how to become a human?"

"Of course it's true. Dragons don't lie!" Audun said.

"And you did it for me?" asked Millie.

Audun nodded. "Your grandmother made it clear that we couldn't be together as long as I was a dragon. Since you'd become the most important person in my life, I had to find a way to be with you."

"You really feel that way?" Millie breathed.

"Dragons don't—"

"Lie. I know. You already told me."

"When your mother told King Stormclaw that you were pining for me, I knew that you truly did feel the same way about me that I feel about you. I meant to come to you sooner, but I had to perform tasks for the ice dragon king, and then there was the war in Aridia . . ."

"So you came as soon as you could. I believe you, Audun." Giving him a smile that made his heart miss a beat, Millie took Audun's hand in hers and led him down the last of the stairs.

They had just reached the dungeon when Audun heard voices up ahead. Two of them sounded like Emma and Eadric, but the others were too faint to make out. As they walked deeper into the gloom broken only by the light of flickering torches, the voices grew louder. Millie smiled. "You're about to meet my great-grandparents. I can hear my parents talking to them."

"Why didn't I meet them last night when I met everyone else?" asked Audun.

"They rarely leave the dungeon. You see," she said, as they turned a corner and saw two hazy figures facing Emma and Eadric, "they're ghosts."

"I didn't know ghosts were real," breathed Audun. "I've never seen one before." He peered at the figures, trying to see them better in the dim light, but their wavery forms seemed to fade away at the edges as he and Millie approached. The ghosts were gone altogether by the time the two young people stood before Emma and Eadric.

Sometime after leaving the tower, Eadric had acquired a sword and tarnished armor, which Emma was now helping him put on. "Wasn't this Great-grandfather's?" Millie asked, running her finger over the scabbard leaning against the wall.

Emma nodded as she helped her husband pull up one of the jointed metal gloves. "Grandfather insisted that Eadric use it. My grandmother put so many protection spells on it over the years that some of them became permanent and now it's virtually impenetrable. There, that ought to do it," she said, setting the helmet on Eadric's head.

"You forgot one thing," said Eadric. Lifting the visor, he gently touched her chin with one hand and raised her face so that he could give her a tender kiss on the lips. Emma ignored the hard metal encasing his body and wrapped her arms around him, deepening the kiss. When she stepped back a moment later, Audun saw the way they looked at each other, as if nothing else in the world mattered at that moment. He wondered what it would be like to kiss someone on the lips—something most dragons would find distasteful.

"We need to go," Emma said softly, as the air began to shimmer around her. A heartbeat later a lovely green female dragon swung her tail out of the way and started down the corridor behind a knight in not-quite-shining armor.

"We should change now, too," Millie told Audun, as she stepped back to give him room.

It had never occurred to Audun that he would have to

change in front of Millie, at least not quite so soon. Not knowing how he looked when he did it, he was reluctant at first, but when she gave him a brilliant smile and started her own change into dragon form, he began his change as well. Although he had changed back and forth many times over the last few months, this time he was left feeling breathless and exhilarated. He was gazing at Millie when she glanced toward the ceiling and he became aware of the sounds coming from above. Fighting had started in earnest.

"The tunnel is this way," Millie said, hurrying in the direction her parents had gone. The corridor that had seemed wide just moments before now seemed cramped with two dragons in it. He could hear Millie's scales scraping the wall each time she bumped it and knew that it wasn't any more comfortable for her than it was for him.

When they reached what appeared to be the end of the corridor, Millie reached out and deftly pulled one of the blocks in the wall out part of the way. Audun heard a groaning sound before he saw that the wall had actually begun to move. Millie backed into him as the wall swung out, revealing a dank, lightless space. Although Audun couldn't see anything past the opening in the wall, he noticed that Millie ducked and lowered her tail before stepping into the tunnel.

"Hurry," Millie said, her voice loud in the confined space. "The door doesn't stay open for long."

Audun grunted and began to walk faster, but he was only partway through when he heard the door groaning shut. Not wanting to lose his tail, he pulled it as close to his body as he could and scurried forward until he finally bumped into Millie.

"We're almost there," Millie said. "See that light up ahead?"

Audun couldn't see anything with her body blocking the light, but he could smell fresh air and felt a hint of a breeze when he raised his head. With the next step he bumped his crest on a dangling root, and dirt showered around him. Audun jerked his head down, and was still walking hunched over when Millie pushed aside the canopy of leaves that hid the tunnel and they emerged into bright sunlight.

"Where are your parents?" Audun asked, blinking as his eyes adjusted to the light.

"Up there." Millie pointed to where a knight sat astride a flying green dragon as easily as he might a horse.

Stepping out from under the branches of the overhanging tree, Millie and Audun took to the sky. Once above the tops of the trees, Audun could see for miles and easily spotted the soldiers surrounding the castle. He saw King Limelyn as well, standing on the parapet above the drawbridge, looking down at the group of men clustered on the other side of the moat.

"Your demands are unreasonable!" shouted the king. "I'm not giving up my granddaughter or my castle."

"Be sensible! I'll let you and your queen depart unharmed if you lower your drawbridge now."

"Why should we go when we're perfectly happy where we are?" answered the king.

"Then you leave me no choice!" Prince Rudolfo shouted back.

At a gesture from the prince, the men who had been standing beside the moat opened sacks that they had hauled across the fields and began dumping rocks into the water. "What are they doing?" Audun asked Millie, who was flying only a wing tip away.

"They're trying to fill in the moat so they can use that," she said, gesturing to the tall wooden structure that another group of men were hauling out from under a copse of sheltering trees. "It's called a siege tower. They hope to push it up to the castle wall and climb onto the parapet."

"Shouldn't we stop them?" asked Audun. "You or your mother could burn that down with one puff of flame."

"The magic user has probably made it flameproof. But that won't make any difference," Millie replied. "Watch."

Audun glanced back just as two men shoved an extra-large rock into the moat and water shot up in a geyser. When the geyser failed to die down, the young dragon watched more closely. A tentacle rose from the center of the waterspout. It reached toward the edge of the moat, forcing the soldiers to back away. Two of the men weren't quick enough: the tentacle slapped the ground beside them and knocked them into the moat where they flailed about, struggling to reach the edge. The rock that they had just dumped in shot out of the water, hitting the siege tower with a thunderous *boom!* Soon the other rocks were hurtling out in a steady stream, demolishing the siege tower and chasing the soldiers across the fields and down the road.

The two soldiers still hadn't dragged themselves from the water when the last rock hit the ground and bounced across the field. Suddenly, the tentacle plucked the men from the moat and sent them screaming through the air only to land halfway across the field in a stack of freshly baled hay. Whimpering, they scrambled out of the hay and limped as fast as they could across the field.

At first, when Audun saw the prince riding away, he thought that Rudolfo had given up, but then more soldiers came out of the woods carrying bows and full quivers. The archers had assembled only a short distance from the castle when the prince gave a signal and they opened fire, raining arrows down on the parapet where King Limelyn was retreating into the shelter of one of the castle towers. Seeing the approaching cloud of arrows, the soldiers around the king held up their shields to protect him, but Emma's spell was already working. Although the arrows rushed at them with frightening speed like a cloud of deadly hornets, when they were a dozen yards from the king, they bounced suddenly as if hitting stone and fell to the ground, broken and useless.

"Now what?" Audun asked, as the archers reached for more arrows.

"Since they're being so persistent, Mother will probably want to chase them off. See, I was right. There she goes now."

Audun glanced up to see Emma come roaring out of the sky with Eadric bent low across her back, his sword in his hand. With an answering roar, Millie joined them as they plummeted toward the now-scattering soldiers, who were running before even a hint of flame left the dragons' mouths. Prince Rudolfo had already disappeared into the forest.

Audun was tempted to fly with Millie and her parents, but they didn't seem to need his help. He was circling overhead, watching the fleeing soldiers, when he noticed one figure heading in a different direction. Instead of running away from the castle, he was moving furtively around the side, stopping every now and then as if to see if he was being watched. The figure was already close to the entrance to the secret tunnel. Audun was about to follow him to see what he was up to when a dark shadow blotted out the sun. Even before he raised his head, Audun knew what was up there. Only one thing could cast a shadow big enough to darken an area that size. A roc had come to Greater Greensward.

Cupping the air with its wings, the great bird screamed as it approached the castle. The soldiers who hadn't already run away did so now, shedding heavy armor as they tried to outrun their friends. The roc wasn't after them, however. Bellowing so loudly that it hurt Audun's ears, the bird landed on the top of Emma's tower and began to rip at the roof with its massive beak. The tower sagged under the weight of the roc even as chunks of the roof fell into the courtyard below.

A green dragon swooped out of the sky, exhaling long tongues of flame at the roc. Eadric swung his sword and hacked at the bird as Emma flew past. They turned and were heading back for a second run when Millie joined them. As Emma and Eadric flew past the roc once again, Audun dipped his wing and headed back to the castle, arriving in time to breathe his poison gas into Millie's flame, making the air around the roc explode. Its feathers singed, the bird screamed and raised its head to lash at them with its beak. Millie and Audun dodged the blow and flew safely away.

On her next pass, Emma swung around to the other side of the bird. She had just started to exhale her flame when the bird turned and, with a powerful swipe of its head, knocked Emma and Eadric tumbling through the sky. Millie screamed and flew after them with Audun close behind. He was nearly even with Millie when Eadric fell from Emma's back. While Emma fought to right herself and Millie struggled to reach her father before he hit the ground, Audun pulled his wings to his sides and dove. Pulling up just below Eadric, he positioned himself so that he could lash out with his tail to catch the falling prince. With his tail securely wrapped around Eadric, he landed on the ground and gently laid the limp man on the grass.

Both Millie and Emma were there an instant later, their concern for Eadric plain on their faces. While Millie crouched by her father's side, Emma changed back into a human. Kneeling next to her husband, she placed her fingers on his throat. "He's alive," she breathed.

"Of course I'm alive," Eadric groaned, his eyes fluttering open. "I just had the wind knocked out of me, that's all."

Audun thought the prince might have protested when his wife fell on him and covered his face with kisses, but instead Eadric reached up with both hands and held her still so that he could kiss her.

"Your father is fine," Audun said, glancing at the young dragoness.

Millie smiled. "I can see that." Raising her eyes to the roc, she added, "But that overgrown crow isn't going to be if I can help it."

She was stretching her wings, preparing to leap into the sky when Audun barked, "No! You can't take on a roc all alone. You'll just get yourself killed if you try. If I thought I could get them here in time, I'd try to get ice dragons to help, but it would take a dozen dragons to challenge a roc and even then they probably wouldn't win. There must be a reason the roc is here and behaving that way," he said, gesturing to the bird that was clawing at the stones of the tower walls. Another huge piece broke away, making a tremendous racket as it crashed to the ground below.

"And how would we ever find out why that stupid bird does anything?" Millie asked. "You're not proposing that we go ask it, are you?"

"Not at all, but there might be someone we can ask. Let's see if we can find him." Spreading their wings, the dragon and the dragoness took to the air and circled once above the castle while Audun told Millie about the figure he'd seen sneaking toward the entrance to the tunnel. Together they landed beside the concealing tree and peered under the branches. There was no one in sight, so Audun pushed aside the leaves and entered the tunnel, not wanting Millie to be the first to confront whoever might be inside.

It took Audun a few minutes to find the block that opened the door. Even as the stone door groaned open, he could hear a man talking nearby. "Shh!" he whispered to Millie when she started to speak. "I recognize that voice."

Moving as silently as a dragon could in a stone-walled corridor, Audun and Millie crept toward the sound. Rounding the corner, they saw a man outlined in torchlight. He wasn't very tall in his long, flowing robes and his back was curved with age, but it was his distinctively shiny scalp that affirmed Audun's first guess. Olebald Wizard was standing with his back to them, trying to get past the ghosts who blocked his way down the corridor.

"I don't know why you keep trying, you old coot," said a wild-haired ghost dressed in rags. He brandished a long chain with manacles attached to the end. Judging by the grating sound they made on the floor, they were far more substantial than the ghost. "My friend and I aren't letting you by, no matter how much you wheedle and whine."

"Quite right, Hubert," a well-dressed ghost pointing a rapier declared. "Imagine, thinking he can sneak in here and infiltrate our castle right under our noses. As if we wouldn't notice a buffoon sneaking around with a sack of rocks. We're not letting you go anywhere until someone in authority . . . Ah, here are Millie and her friend now. We found this scalawag sneaking into the castle. What would you like us to do with him?"

Olebald turned with a start and noticed Audun for the first time. "It's you," he said. "Well, you're too late. This castle is going to be destroyed and you can't do a thing about it."

"Is that so?" said Audun. He leaned toward the old wizard and exhaled a small puff of poison gas directly at his face. Olebald coughed and swallowed hard. Even in the wavering light of the torches, Audun could see the old man's face turn pale. The dragon stepped back as Olebald lost his breakfast onto the floor. The wizard looked awful as he straightened up and gave Audun a baleful glare.

"The next time I breathe on you like that, you won't be able to stand up again," Audun warned him, his voice a deep growl. "Now, tell me, how did you lure that roc here?"

Olebald tried to laugh, but the effort made his face green. Even so, he gave Audun a defiant look and kept his lips pressed tightly closed.

Audun shrugged. "It's your decision," the dragon said, taking a deep breath.

"No, wait!" Olebald rushed to say. "I made the roc think its baby had been stolen and locked away in that tower. It won't stop until it's torn apart the entire castle looking for its chick."

"Very clever," Emma said, as she and Eadric squeezed past Millie. "So this is how you'll get your revenge for the day I sent you to that island."

Olebald smirked. "This isn't about you—at least, not entirely. I wouldn't even have thought of coming here if I hadn't heard that the ice dragon was in love with your daughter. Just because King Stormclaw kept me frozen in his stronghold after I followed you from the magic market-place didn't mean I couldn't hear everything said around me. Those dragon guards were terrible gossips, but they couldn't keep me locked away forever. After I escaped and learned that Audun had helped the old king run my protégé out of Aridia, I couldn't resist coming back here and killing two dragons with one sack of stones, so to speak.

"I'm sure you recognize these, Audun," the old wizard said, kicking the sack that rested beside him so that a pile of green stones tumbled out. "But you wouldn't, would you, Emma? I had Rudolfo scatter stones like these throughout your castle while he was here pretending to court your lovely Millie. When I saw all of you come out of that hidden entrance, I couldn't resist bringing in more stones." Turning to Emma and Eadric, Olebald grinned. "You never did figure out that Rudolfo is Prince Jorge's nephew. The entire royal family of East Aridia hates you for defeating us when we invaded Greater Greensward and for making Jorge marry the troll queen."

There was another loud crash and the castle shook so that dust filtered down around their heads.

Olebald Wizard chortled. "That roc will have your entire castle down around your ears, and the stones Rudolfo planted will keep you from doing anything about it!"

Emma gave Audun an inquiring look.

"I don't know what the stones are exactly," he told her. "I just know that they keep magic from working in their presence."

"He may have planted some," said Emma, "but he

couldn't have put them everywhere. No one can get in my tower rooms when I'm not there."

"And that protection spell you put on Grandfather worked just fine," said Millie.

"Rudolfo couldn't have put them down here, either," Emma added. "Or you wouldn't be trying to do it now, old man."

"He tried to shove a stone in a crack in the wall, but Hubert and I stopped him and made him put it back in his bag. We've been watching him every minute," said the well-dressed ghost.

"In that case, I can take care of them right now," said Audun. Snagging the sack with one talon, he shuffled backward down the narrow corridor, turning when he reached the corner. He was back a minute later without the sack.

Everyone looked up as another chunk of the tower came crashing down.

"That roc isn't going to give up until it finds its baby," said Audun. "And since there is no baby to find . . ."

"We have to do something!" said Millie. "Mother, do you have a spell that could turn it into something else? A butterfly, perhaps, or a hummingbird?"

Olebald's eyes were bright with glee when he said, "Regular magic won't do anything to a roc. Even if she could change the bird, it could just become something worse."

"I'm afraid he's right," said Emma. "I tried to change a troll once. All I did was make him odder looking and give him a love of cheese."

"Then I say we should give the roc exactly what it wants," said Audun. "I know where there's a roc nest and there were chicks in it the last time I looked. For all I know, this might even be the parent of those very same chicks. We could go get one of those babies and bring it back here. The problem is that the nest is days away."

"My magic can take care of that," said Emma. "I can get us there in an instant, as long as you can give me a good description of the nest and the area around it."

"That won't be a problem," Audun said, remembering the distinctive stone formations that surrounded the nest.

"I'll have to go with you to bring you back," Emma added.

"I'll go, too," said Millie. "You might need my help."

"And mine," said Eadric.

"No!" protested his wife. "You're staying here. You've already fallen off my back once today."

"I wouldn't bother going if I were you," Olebald said, looking smug. "Magic won't do you a bit of good once you get there."

"You know, old man," Emma said, turning on the wizard with her eyes flashing, "I'm sick and tired of you and your pronouncements. I think you need to leave, and this

273

time I want your banishment more permanent. Let me see . . . How did that spell start? Ah, yes . . ."

> Go to the isle of sun-warmed sand
> Where I sent you once before.
> Stay there 'til your life is spent
> On that far and distant shore.

"Not again!" wailed Olebald, as a tiny whirlwind rose beneath his feet. "I hate getting sand in my clothes! And I think I'm allergic to shellfish! Don't do this to me . . ." The old man's voice trailed off as the swirling wind engulfed him and carried him down the corridor and out of sight.

"And now," said Emma. "About that nest . . ."

❧

Not knowing what they would encounter at the roc's nest, Emma turned back into a dragon before saying the spell that would carry them to Aridia. Audun's description of the nest and the stone formations around it were very complete, so it didn't take her long to find it. Her magic took them to a spot just above the nest so that they were looking down on it from the sky. Even at a distance, the two chicks looked enormous. Seeing that neither of the adult rocs was present, Audun and Emma decided to take the chance and assume that the roc destroying the castle was one of the parents.

"So," said Emma, eyeing the two chicks, "which one should we take?"

"They're both so big," breathed Millie.

Audun shook his head. The last time he had seen these babies they had been the size of large horses; they were now the size of full-grown male dragons. Even Emma, the oldest dragon there, was smaller than either of the chicks. "We should take that one," he said, pointing to the smaller of the two.

"Audun and I can distract the other chick while you take that one back, Mother," said Millie.

"I shouldn't be long," said Emma. "I already know what I'm going to say."

While Emma descended to the edge of the nest closest to the smallest chick, Audun and Millie began harrying the larger of the two babies. Millie dove past and the baby snapped at her with its wicked-looking beak, but didn't come anywhere near her. It was ready, however, when Audun flew close, because it hopped into the air three times higher than he would have thought possible and almost caught him. After that, Millie and Audun were more cautious and tried to keep its attention from a distance.

"Is everything all right?" Audun called to Emma when more than enough time had passed for her to have taken the baby back.

"No, it's not," she replied, sounding exasperated. "My

magic isn't working. I've tried and tried, but I can't move this bird."

"I was afraid of that," said Audun. "You heard what Olebald said about magic not working here? He probably planted some of those stones in this nest."

"You mean like that one?" Millie asked, pointing at a stone buried so deep among the intertwined branches that it would have been impossible to remove.

"And those," Emma said, gesturing toward a scattering of smaller stones in the bottom of the nest.

Seeing how many stones there were, Audun wondered why he hadn't noticed them before, even if he had been kept occupied with the baby bird. "We won't be able to move the chick with magic, at least not from the nest. We'll have to get it far enough away from here that your magic will work again, Emma."

"It looks awfully heavy," said Millie.

"I'm sure it is, but we can lift it if we all work together. I've done something like this before," he said, failing to tell them that that time it had been in water.

Pulling out some of the enormous vines that held the nest together wasn't easy. It was even harder to tether the larger chick to the opposite side of the nest to keep it away while they wrapped more vines around the smaller of the birds, pinning its wings to its sides and securing its lethal beak and talons. Once the baby roc was trussed up like a chicken, Audun took a loop of vines in his own talons and beat his wings, struggling to lift the chick high enough that Millie and Emma could get underneath. With the two dragonesses pushing from below, they were able to raise the bird to one of the neighboring pinnacles, where it struggled to get free while they caught their breath.

"Where are you going...to put the baby?" Millie asked her mother.

"The base of...the tower," Emma replied. "If it's still there."

Audun held his breath as once again Emma tried to take the chick back with her magic, exhaling loudly when both dragon and chick disappeared. He'd scarcely had time to wonder if he and Millie would have to fly back when Emma reappeared and touched her wings to theirs and then all three of them were perched on the parapet where King Limelyn had been standing only hours—or was it minutes—before.

"Look!" Millie said, gazing down at the rubble where the tower had stood for hundreds of years. After screaming her rage for so long, the mother bird's cry was a hoarse bleat, but even those unused to the sound of a roc's voice could tell when it changed from anguish to delight. Peering down through a gap in the floor below her, the roc cooed to her chick, ripped up the floor with her beak, and plucked the hefty youngster into the air with her massive talons. Screaming in triumph, the enormous bird beat her wings and rose into the clouds, heading west toward Aridia.

Although most of the castle's inhabitants had fled into the surrounding fields and forest as the roc demolished the tower, they returned now, singly and in groups, laughing aloud in their relief that the attack was over. "Do you see your father or your grandparents?" Emma asked, looking worried.

The three dragons sat side by side, watching for members of the royal family. Audun was turned around when he heard a small sound behind him. Something moved beneath a patch of crushed stone, which shuddered and fell in a small avalanche down the side of the wreckage. A moment later, You-too emerged, fluffing his feathers and preening with his beak.

Noting the dragons perched on the parapet, You-too flew up to join them. "Look at you three, sitting up here like you own the place! Well, I guess you do, sort of. I could have used your help, though! I was locked in this little, bitty room while a horrible monster tore it down around me! I'm going to have nightmares for weeks!"

"It wasn't a monster," said Millie. "It was a roc."

"That thing was a bird?" You-too said, sounding incredulous. "I knew rocs were big, but, wow! Say, you know what this means, don't you? Your father was wrong when he said that I have the biggest beak in the castle. Speaking of your father, isn't that him now?"

Everyone turned as Eadric emerged through the castle door. With a whoop of glee, Emma spread her wings and swooped down to join him, turning into a human again even as her feet hit the ground. She stumbled and almost fell, but her husband caught her, wrapping her in an embrace that looked as if it would never end. When Emma raised her face and Eadric began to kiss her, You-too turned away in disgust. "Ick!" he said. "I can't watch this!"

Audun didn't notice the bird fly away; he was too busy looking at Millie. "Your parents do seem to kiss a lot."

Millie shrugged. "They've always been like that. I guess they do it because they love each other so much."

"Do all married humans kiss like that?"

"No," said Millie. "My grandmother and grandfather hardly ever kiss. But then, they don't talk to each other much, either."

"When we're married, we'll kiss all the time, too," Audun announced.

"Is that your way of asking me to marry you?"

"Only if you'll say yes."

"Well, then, here's my answer," Millie replied. Sidling closer so that her scales touched his, Millie, the fire-breathing dragon, kissed Audun, the ice dragon, full on the lips. And he liked it.

A Prince among Frogs

One

Millie leaned back against the dragon's side, enjoying the coolness of his bluish white scales on the hot summer day. The dragon, Audun, was curled around her with his head resting on the grass near her feet while Felix, her baby brother, lay on the blanket beside her, cooing at the tip of the dragon's tail that dangled over his head. Millie glanced down when the baby batted at the tail with his chubby hands.

"As far as I'm concerned, the smaller the wedding the better," she said to Audun as she reached out to stroke the baby's red gold curls. "I want it to be intimate, with just us and our immediate families."

"Don't you want our friends there, too?" Audun asked.

"Well, yes, of course, at least our closest friends, like Zoë and her parents and Ralf and his parents and your friends Frostybreath and—"

"Do you see what I mean? It's going to be nearly impossible to have a small wedding. I don't have a lot of relatives, but I do have lots of friends I want to invite."

"Speaking of relatives," said Millie, "I'm not sure what to do about my father's side of the family. My uncle, Bradston, is all right, but I've told you how much my grandparents hate dragons. They can't even accept the fact that *I* turn into a dragon. I can only imagine what they'll say when I tell them about you!"

"Millie!" called her mother, Emma, from where she was kneeling in the garden, supervising the weeds that were pulling themselves out of the ground. "Don't let the baby put that thing in his mouth! You have no idea where it's been. No offense, Audun."

"None taken," the dragon replied, moving his tail out of the baby's reach. Felix began to fuss, so Audun pulled a golden chain from around his neck and held the dangling amulet over the baby. "Here, you can play with this instead." The ice dragon council had given the amulet to Audun to allow him to breathe underwater, and the rolling waves that decorated it soon caught the baby's eye.

Millie's great-aunt, Grassina, sat back on her heels and wiped the perspiration from her forehead. "When we finish this, I'm going to add a new section to the garden. I want to have plenty of fresh flowers for the wedding," she said, smiling at Millie.

"We have to invite all the dragons who helped us, too, you know," Audun said, nudging Millie's foot with his chin.

Millie turned her head to watch Grassina gesture, making a strip of ground crumble until it was well worked and ready for seeds. The seeds flew from the witch's hand, burrowing into the soil. Another gesture, and a dozen willow wands pushed into the soil beside the seeds and wove themselves into a delicate fence.

"Like who?" Millie asked Audun.

"King Stormclaw, for one. If he hadn't given us permission to marry, we wouldn't be having this discussion."

"That's true . . . ," Millie said.

"And then there's his council . . . ," said Audun.

"His entire council?" Millie said, sitting up abruptly. A lock of her long blond hair had gotten caught around one of Audun's scales, and she winced when it yanked at her scalp.

Audun moved his back legs, and his tail twitched closer to the baby. "My grandmother is one of the members, and they all voted to let us get married."

Millie sighed as she reached back to free her hair. "I suppose we'll have to invite them, too, but we can't include everyone we know."

"I didn't say we had to. I just want—YOW! Watch it, kid. Those scales are attached, and I'd like them to stay that way!"

Millie giggled. Her baby brother was just an infant, but his tiny fingers were already strong. She adored the little boy and was still surprised and delighted that he had become part of her life. Although most royalty relegated the care of infants to nursemaids, Millie and her parents spent as much time with Felix as they could. When Emma and Eadric were busy with the demands of the kingdom,

Millie often visited the nursery on her own. Sometimes she felt almost as if she were the baby's third parent.

"Excuse me," Audun said, edging away from Millie as he got to his feet and put the golden chain back around his neck. "My back is getting stiff. I think it's about time for a change." Like the air above a sun-heated boulder on a hot afternoon, the air shimmered around Audun as he turned from a dragon into a young man with silvery white hair and vivid blue eyes. He was handsome whether he was a human or a dragon, with a strong chin and prominent cheekbones.

When Felix's smile melted away and he began to fuss, Emma looked up from the growing pile of weeds and muttered under her breath. Butterflies flitting around the garden rose above the blossoms and flew to where the baby lay. The multihued cloud descended over the baby, fluttering just out of reach of his flailing fists. Felix chortled and his smile returned even brighter than before.

Audun had just taken a seat on the blanket when the shadow of a large bird passed overhead. Millie glanced up. Her heart rate quickened when she saw that it wasn't a bird at all, but a witch with long white hair whipping behind her as she darted to a landing on her broom made of palm fronds tied to a stick.

Millie was used to visitors arriving at all hours of the day and night. Her mother was the Green Witch and in charge of dealing with the magical issues in Greater Greensward. Because Emma was married to Eadric, crown prince of

Upper Montevista, she had to watch over that kingdom as well. Witches, fairies, and normal humans were always stopping by to tell her about yet another problem. Millie wouldn't have minded if their arrival didn't usually mean that her mother was going to be called away once again, leaving Grassina and Millie to deal with whatever problems might crop up in the two kingdoms. So far Grassina had been able to deal with it all, but there was always the chance that Millie would be called upon to help, and that the small amount of magic she was able to use wouldn't be enough.

Millie tried to stay calm as the visiting witch, who appeared to be nearly ninety, hopped off her broom like a spry sixty-year-old and brushed her snarled hair back from her face. She was a pretty woman with tanned, not-too-wrinkled skin. When she spoke, her voice was unexpectedly husky. "Which one of you is Grassina?" she asked, peering at the women. "My eyesight isn't so good anymore."

Grassina stood, dusting off her hands. "I'm Grassina, and I know who you are, Cadmilla. How can I help you?"

"You can offer me a drink and a seat in the shade," said the witch. "I've been on that pitiful excuse for a broom since yesterday, and my joints ache worse than a whale with a sick belly." She sighed and shook her head. "Listen to me. I've spent so much time with those old crones on the island that I'm beginning to sound like them."

While Grassina hurried into the cottage, Emma helped Cadmilla to a bench under the spreading branches of the oak that grew at the river's edge. "I must be a sight," the old witch said, fussing with her sleeves as she made herself comfortable. "I got caught in the rain yesterday. It took forever for my clothes to dry out."

Grassina emerged from the cottage, carrying a large tankard. "Why were you looking for me?" she said, handing the woman the drink.

Cadmilla took a long sip. "I didn't want to come, and I wouldn't have if the old biddies back on the island hadn't left me the short straw. I think they cheated and used magic to make their straws longer. I would have, too, if I'd thought of it soon enough. I came because of that sea monster. Wrecked our cottages and drove us into the woods. The ugly beast won't leave us alone. It's been coming for a week and hasn't shown any sign of leaving."

"If you and your friends are witches, couldn't you have gotten rid of a sea monster on your own?" Audun asked.

Cadmilla curled her lip in exasperation. "Don't you think we tried? But either our magic is getting as feeble as we are, or the monster is stronger than all of us put together. All our spells and potions didn't affect Old Warty one bit. That's what we call it, because of its warts."

"And you came here because . . ."

"We heard that Grassina had taken it upon herself to get rid of all the monsters around that town Chancewood . . . Chanceworld . . . something like that."

"Chancewold," said Grassina. "Tell me about the monster. What does it look like?"

6

"It's gray and has a floppy body like a half-empty blad-der covered in warts. It stays in the water most of the time, but when it does come out, it crawls around on three big flippers. It has long tentacles with leaf-shaped tips, and it smells like a slop bucket that hasn't been emptied for a month."

"That's one of mine, all right," Grassina said, frown-ing. "I guess I won't be able to work on the garden after all. If you'll excuse me, I need to get ready to go."

"I remember that monster," said Emma, placing her hand on her aunt's arm. "I'm the one who sent it away. If anyone should deal with this, it's me."

"Don't be absurd. I created the monster, so I'll take care of it."

Emma shook her head. "You can't go alone. I'll go with you and—"

"You'll do no such thing. Haywood will go with me. You're the Green Witch and your responsibilities are here in Greater Greensward. Don't worry. I've dealt with many monsters over the last few years. Haywood and I will be back before you know it."

Although Emma didn't look happy, Millie relaxed and gave an unconscious sigh of relief. She didn't mind helping her mother if she needed it, but then her mother very rarely needed help. All Millie wanted to do was plan her wedding; with her mother there, she just might get the chance.

Two

*B*efore she met Audun, Millie had thought she knew everything there was to know about being a dragon. But after they fell in love and Audun had had to earn the right to learn how to be a human, she discovered there were a lot of things she didn't know. Most of them, like how ice dragons differed from fire-breathing dragons, were interesting, but only a few affected her directly. Her sweet tooth was one such discovery. She'd always thought it was part of her human side, so she'd been surprised when Audun, who had been a dragon at the time, nibbled a honey-laced confection and declared that it was the best thing he'd ever tasted. It had never occurred to Millie to try anything sweet as a dragon, but when she did, she discovered that dragon taste buds amplified the flavor so that her entire mouth tingled. After that, Millie got in the habit of fetching a huge bowl of porridge in the morning, dribbling a generous serving of honey over it, and taking it back to her chamber to eat. She was sure most of the other inhabitants of the castle would find it disconcerting to see a dragon eating breakfast in the Great Hall, and she didn't want to have to explain why she turned into a dragon just to eat breakfast.

She was in her chamber eating her porridge on the second day after Grassina's departure for the tropical island when she heard a knock on her door. Thinking that it was Audun, she left the bowl on the floor and shuffled across the room, keeping her wings tucked to her sides so she wouldn't knock anything over. Opening the door, she was surprised to find her grandmother Queen Chartreuse waiting on the other side.

After one glance at her granddaughter, the queen pursed her lips in disapproval. "Can't you refrain from turning into a dragon at least for one day? And if you can't restrain yourself, I wish you wouldn't do it inside. This castle was never built for creatures with your . . . bulk."

"Are you saying I'm fat?" Millie asked, backing into the room. Unlike her mother, Millie had never balked at speaking her mind to her grandmother.

"I'm saying that I'd prefer to talk to you while you're a human. There," said the queen as Millie obliged her by changing form. "That's better. Some people have come to see your mother. If you'd been eating in the Great Hall as you should be, you would know that she was called away to speak to a herd of centaurs who have been stealing horses from local farms. They call it liberating them, which is the silliest thing I've ever heard. Your mother had just left when these people came to see her. Ordinarily, I would send them to see Grassina, but she's away, as you know. Your grandfather and your father have gone hunting, leaving me to deal with everything, but I put my foot down when it comes to dealing with something like this. You're going to have to talk to them, so wipe the porridge off your chin and come with me."

"Who are these people?" Millie asked, following Queen Chartreuse down the corridor. Her stomach was beginning to clench—not a good thing when it was full of porridge. She doubted that she'd be much help in a magical way, and she dreaded telling people that she couldn't do anything for them.

"Fairies! Young people like you have no problem talking to them because you're used to it, but when I was a girl, they never came to visit the way they do now. And I'm not like your father's mother, Frazzela, who dotes on fairies. I have no idea what to say to them. Then there's the wing issue. If they have wings, I try not to stare at them, but I know I will anyway, which is rude. And if they don't have wings, I wonder why not—I always do—and then I lose track of whatever they're saying. They shed fairy dust, too, which is so untidy. Now you go on ahead," the queen said as they reached the bottom of the stairs. "You'll find them just outside the door leading from the Great Hall into the courtyard."

"No one invited them in?" asked Millie.

"Of course not," the queen said, wrinkling her nose with distaste. "You'll see why when you meet them. Oh, and by the way, you *have* gained a few pounds lately. You really must cut back on the sweets."

Three fairies were waiting by the stairs in the courtyard, looking as if they weren't sure they should be there. They turned to face Millie as she reached the bottom step. She'd met the fairy dressed in the soft green gown and matching floppy cap before. Moss had visited her mother and even come to some of the parties at the castle, but the other two fairies were unfamiliar.

"Good day, Millie," said Moss. "Is your mother, Princess Emma, here? We have a problem and we think she's the only one who can handle it."

Millie shook her head. "She left this morning and I have no idea when she'll be back. Maybe I can help," she added, more because she thought she should than because she wanted to.

"You can if you're as powerful a witch as your mother," said the fairy with the pale skin and gown made of shiny green leaves. The nostrils of her thin, arched nose flared when she looked at Millie, giving the fairy's narrow face a scornful expression.

"I'm sorry, I should have introduced my friends to you," said Moss. "This is Poison Ivy, and this is Trillium," she added, indicating the shorter fairy with dark red hair that hung down her back almost to the ground. Her flower-petal dress was only a shade or two lighter than her hair, and it glistened as if sprinkled with dew.

"It's nice meeting you," said Millie. "But I'm not a witch."

11

"I knew coming here was a waste of time," Poison Ivy said, tilting her head back so that she looked down at Millie.

Taking a deep breath, Millie tried to tamp down the irritation welling up inside her at Poison Ivy's rudeness.

Trillium sighed and said in a whispery soft voice, "Perhaps we should go."

Millie started to agree with her. If the fairies thought they needed powerful magic to deal with their problem, Millie probably couldn't help. Aside from her dragon magic, she had very little magic of her own. She could find lost items, but only if they were things she used all the time and had lost recently. She could turn the pages of a book with the wave of a hand, but only one at a time. She could even blow out a candle from across the room, but she couldn't light it again unless she turned into a dragon. Millie wanted to tell the fairies that they'd have to return when her mother was home, but then she glanced at Poison Ivy again and knew from the curl of her lip that the fairy expected her to back down. The irritation she'd felt before flared into a spark of anger.

For most of her life, before Millie had learned how to control her temper, she turned into a dragon each time she got angry. Even now, controlling her temper wasn't always easy. She knew that if she let little things bother her, even the smallest spark of anger could flare into full-blown rage. Millie glared at the narrow-faced fairy, then purposefully turned toward Moss. "If you tell me what the problem is, I might be able to help."

Moss shook her head, and her cap slipped down over her eyes. She pushed it back with a rueful smile and said, "That's very nice of you to offer, but I don't see how you can possibly help us. It's a plant problem, you see, and not a nice plant, either."

"Is it one of your plants?" Millie asked, glancing from one to the next but letting her gaze linger longest on Poison Ivy.

"Don't look at me!" Poison Ivy declared. "My ivy has nothing to do with this. I only came along to help."

"There's no need to act defensive," said Moss. "I'm sure Princess Millie didn't mean anything."

"Ha!" said Poison Ivy.

"It's not one of our plants at all," whispered Trillium. "It's a plant so nasty that it doesn't *have* a fairy to watch over it."

"That's right," said Moss. "No fairy wants anything to do with it. It's new to the enchanted forest. We think some horrid person brought it here to stir up trouble. Thank goodness there's only one."

"It comes from a rain forest far away," Poison Ivy added. "Too bad it didn't stay there."

"What's so awful about this plant?" asked Millie. She was intrigued now. A plant couldn't be that bad, could it?

"What plant?" asked Audun as he descended the steps behind her.

"Are you a wizard?" Poison Ivy said, looking Audun up and down. "Because we could really use a good one."

13

"This is my betrothed, Audun, and he's not a wizard."

"Even so, I'm sure we can deal with a plant," Audun told them.

Poison Ivy snorted. "Not this plant!"

Trillium tugged on Poison Ivy's sleeve. "We could show it to them," she said in a voice so soft that Millie had to strain to hear it.

"I'm not sure . . . ," Moss began.

"Why not?" said Poison Ivy and sneered at Millie. "I'd suggest that you follow us on your broom, but you're not a witch, so—"

"Would a magic carpet do?" Millie asked, anger building inside her again. "I'll be right back."

She left Audun talking to the fairies while she went to her chamber to fetch the carpet her mother had given her for her last birthday. It was also an excuse to leave the fairies for a few minutes. Generally, the only people who were rude to Millie were those who didn't know either that she was a princess or that she could become a dragon at will. Moss had mentioned in Poison Ivy's presence that Millie's mother was a princess, so it couldn't be that. However, there was a good chance that Poison Ivy might not know about Millie's dragon side; Emma had been using magic for years to keep it a secret. Millie was tempted to turn into a dragon to show the fairy just whom she was dealing with— which was exactly why she couldn't let herself do it. Once she was a dragon, the temptation to fry Poison Ivy would be hard to withstand.

The magic carpet was right where she'd expected to find it—buried under all the things she had tossed into the back of the storage room. She pitched the old shoes to the other side of the room and set the broom she'd never been able to fly next to the basket of toys she'd loved when she was younger. Maybe she'd give a few of the toys to Felix.

And then there were all the things she kept because she was sure she would need them someday: her great-grandmother's old chipped scrying bowl; the bouquet of crystalline flowers that her great-aunt, Grassina, had given her and that Millie had broken with one accidental swipe of her tail; the troll-hide trunk that her mother had wanted to throw out; her great-aunt's old magic mirror. Millie had propped the mirror against the wall to keep the magic carpet from unrolling, but the dark wood frame was so heavy and awkward to move that she considered getting someone to help her. Instead she turned into a dragon just long enough to lift the mirror aside as if it weighed nothing at all.

She would have remained a dragon long enough to carry the carpet out of the room, but she was too big to turn around in the small space, so she had to change back into a human. When she was finally able to drag the narrow carpet into the center of her chamber, she spread it out on the floor and sat down in the middle with a sigh. This was not at all how she had meant to spend her day! Now all she had to do was remember the magic words to control the carpet and she could take care of this silly errand. The fairies

15

were worried about a plant, for goodness' sake. Even she could handle a plant!

Because Millie didn't have the kind of magic to control a carpet herself, her mother had given it a simple set of commands. All the princess had to do was repeat a few words and the carpet would go wherever she wanted. It wasn't as much fun as flying in dragon form, but there were certain places where a royal princess would be welcome whereas a dragon would not. Her parents had made her promise never to leave Greater Greensward in dragon form unless another dragon accompanied her. Too many people feared and hated dragons, and she wasn't safe outside her own kingdom. Millie never even flew to Upper Montevista as a dragon. The royal archers still shot at dragons that dared to fly near the castle, which didn't bode well for relations between Millie's Upper Montevistan grandparents and her future in-laws.

"Rise and leave!" Millie said, bracing herself because she expected the magic carpet to levitate. When nothing happened, she tried again. "Climb and depart!" The carpet remained motionless on the floor. It had been many months since Millie had used the carpet. She knew the phrase her mother had chosen was short and to the point, but that didn't help if Millie couldn't remember the words. "Float and flee!" "Ascend and fly away!" she said to no avail.

"I can't believe this!" she declared out loud. "All I want to do is make this carpet get up and go!" The carpet lurched into the air, sending Millie toppling onto her back. Flinging her arms wide, she grabbed hold of the edges and held on while the carpet shot through the window, only to hover two stories above the ground. "Ah," she murmured. "I think I remember it now."

The magic carpet wobbled beneath her as Millie sat up and looked around. She hated that things like this happened whenever she tried to use ordinary magic.

Millie shifted her weight the way her mother had shown her, making the carpet change direction. She straightened her clothes as the carpet floated around her parents' tower and into the courtyard outside the castle keep. The fairies were still there talking to Audun. Though Moss and Trillium both looked worried when they saw her, Poison Ivy only managed to look smug. "So you did come back," the fairy said as if she'd tasted something nasty. "I thought you might have been frightened into running away."

"I'm sorry it took me so long," Millie replied, turning to face Moss and Trillium, "but it took me a while to get my carpet out of storage. Audun, if you're ready . . ."

Millie leaned forward and the carpet drifted to the ground, allowing Audun to climb on behind her. He gave her a searching look as he sat down and crossed his legs. After all they had been through together, he was attuned to her moods more than anyone and often seemed to know just what she was thinking.

"This should be fun," she said over her shoulder, giving him an encouraging smile.

Audun nodded, although his eyes showed that he didn't believe she meant it. She'd told him many times how worried she was about her lack of nondragon magic and how ineffective she felt in a family where most of the women were witches.

"Then let's go!" Poison Ivy announced. The next instant she was no bigger than Millie's little finger and sported iridescent green wings. She was the first to dart over the castle wall with Trillium only a heartbeat behind her.

"I'll show you the way," said Moss, and then she too was tiny.

Millie had never flown with fairies before. By the time the carpet rose above the walls, both Poison Ivy and Trillium were out of sight. Moss was careful to stay where Millie could see her, however, although she had to circle back if Millie and Audun didn't move fast enough. Soon they landed in a small clearing in the heart of the enchanted forest.

"Where is this plant?" Millie asked, looking around her as she climbed off the carpet.

"It's a tree, actually," said Moss, settling on the forest floor a few feet away. The air shimmered as she turned back into a full-sized fairy in time for her to raise her arm and point. "It's down that path. Just look for the tree with the red berries and the dead bird by its roots."

"Aren't you coming with us?" Millie asked, feeling a touch of unease.

"We wouldn't go near that thing for all the pollen in the kingdom!" said Poison Ivy, who was already back to full

18

size. "It's up to you now. We just wanted to make sure that someone came to take care of it. Come on, Trillium, I hear they have a new batch of dandelion wine at the old stump."

Moss shook her head as the other two fairies darted away, tiny once again. "I'm sorry, but she's right. We're not able to go near that tree safely. Thank you so much for coming. We weren't sure that even a strong witch like your mother could handle this. Let us know how it goes!"

The air had begun to shimmer around her when Audun called out, "Are the berries poisonous?"

"Maybe," called Moss, her voice becoming fainter as she shrank. "I don't know. But it's not poison you have to worry about." And then she was gone, leaving Millie and Audun alone in the enchanted forest.

"What do you suppose is wrong with this tree?" asked Millie. "What could be so awful about it that no fairy will claim it?" Now that Poison Ivy was gone, Millie's temper had cooled and she started to wonder what she'd gotten herself into.

"Is that what they said?" said Audun. "I thought every plant had a fairy to watch over it. It must be pretty serious if none of the fairies likes it."

"Maybe we should go back," said Millie. "The fairies said this would take really strong magic. My mother should be home soon and we can bring her here, now that we know where to come."

Audun frowned. "You shouldn't second-guess yourself, Millie. There's no need to worry. We're dragons. We can handle anything. Unless it's your human side speaking now, in which case—"

"Are you implying that my human side is any less than my dragon side?" Millie asked.

Looking surprised, Audun backed up a step. "You're the one who has doubts. Lack of confidence is rarely a dragon trait. As far as I know, humans are the only creatures who are ever uncertain about their own abilities."

"I'm not uncertain!" said Millie. "It's just that my magic isn't very strong and that's what we need to take care of this plant."

"I'll tell you what we'll do," Audun told her. "You stay here, and I'll go look." He started down the path, glancing from one side to the other.

"I will not!" Millie said as she hurried to catch up. "I came here on my mother's behalf, so *I* have to take care of this. You're the one who should stand back and wait for me to look into it!"

"Look," said Audun, gesturing at a tree a few yards away. "Is that the tree they were talking about? It has red berries."

It was a pretty little tree that couldn't have been more than seven feet tall. Its leaves were nearly heart shaped, and the branches bore clusters of red berries.

"They look like raspberries," said Millie, reaching out to pick one.

Audun knocked her hand aside. "Don't touch it!"

"Moss said it wasn't poisonous."

"She said she didn't know if it was poisonous, but she still thought it was dangerous. There's the dead bird she was talking about."

"And there are three more dead birds over here," Millie said.

"I saw some plants once that had branches like arms. The plants could move around. I wonder if this tree can, too."

Millie shook her head. "It doesn't look like it."

A breeze sprang up, shivering the leaves of the trees around them. Audun slapped at his cheek. "Something just stung me!"

Millie took a step toward him. "Let me see," she said. A flurry of loose leaves broke free from the tree and fluttered through the air. One brushed against her upraised hand. Millie cried out as blinding pain tore through her. She stared at her hand in horror, stumbling back until she bumped into the solid trunk of an old oak.

"What happened?" Audun asked, his hand pressed to his cheek.

"I don't know," Millie gasped. The pain radiating up her arm was so intense that she could think of nothing else.

"It must have something to do with that tree. We have to change, Millie. Do it now!"

"It hurts so much!"

"The change might help. Please, you have to try!"

Millie's entire body vibrated from the pain. It was hard to concentrate, but she forced herself. The transformation seemed to take forever, but then her skin turned from the soft flesh of a human to tough dragon hide and the pain ended with surprising abruptness. Millie turned to face Audun, who was now a dragon as well.

"Are you all right?" he asked, his voice heavy with concern.

"I am. Are you?"

Audun nodded. "Look," he said, striding closer to the tree. "The entire thing is covered with fuzz—the berries, the leaves, the bark—everything."

"Like a peach?" asked Millie, joining him beside the tree. She arched her neck for a better look. Dragon eyesight is far better than human, and she could now see things that she couldn't before.

"Not at all," said Audun. "Peach fuzz is soft. This stuff is more like tiny needles."

Millie glanced down at her front foot. She could see her dragon hide forcing the needles out even as she watched. When they were fully expelled, she exhaled a puff of flame, melting them like molten glass. "I can see why the fairies were afraid of the tree."

"They should have told us what to expect," said Audun.

"Fairies rarely do what they should," said Millie. "They don't think about things the way we do."

A breath of air rustled the leaves again. This time Millie could see the cloud of tiny needles that swept from the tree into the surrounding forest.

"What do you want to do about the tree?" Audun asked.

"Burn it to the ground," Millie said, backing away. "The fairies were right. This tree is too dangerous and shouldn't be here."

Audun stood to the side while Millie blasted the tree with fire, letting her flame wash over it so that she burned the tiny needles as well as the plant itself. When she was finished and there was nothing but ash, Audun stepped forward and began digging up the ground where the tree had stood. "Remember those plants . . . I . . . told you about?" he asked, puffing with exertion. "I thought I'd killed them . . . but just a few weeks later . . . they started to grow again. If we really want to . . . get rid of this tree . . . we have to destroy . . . the roots as well."

"Good idea," said Millie.

A dragon's talons are tougher than metal yet refined enough to pluck a gnat from the air without hurting it. Millie watched as Audun dug up the roots, knowing that he would find every one. She waited until he was out of the way, then burned every scrap of root to ashes, too.

"That was awful!" Millie said as they returned to the spot where she'd left her magic carpet.

They flew back to the castle side by side. Millie was delighted with what she'd been able to accomplish, but she couldn't help wondering what she would have done if the task had required the kind of magic she didn't have.

۶۶

Millie was relieved when she found her parents waiting for her in the Great Hall and couldn't wait to tell them what had happened. But before she could say a word, her mother kissed her on her human-again cheek and said, "Your father and I are leaving. Grassina and Haywood should have returned by now. I told your father I was worried, and he suggested that we go to the island to see if they need our help. I'm sure your father is right and nothing bad has happened, but I can't help thinking that we should have heard from them."

"And when we get there and your mother sees that everyone is fine, she and I might just take a few days to enjoy the beach," said Eadric, Millie's father. "We haven't been there in years."

"We shouldn't be gone long," said Emma. "Your grandparents will be in charge of any nonmagical issues, but I'm depending on you and your cousin, Francis, to help out if any magical problems come up. And keep an eye on Felix, too, if you would. His nursemaid has everything under control, but I'd feel better if I knew you were watching over him as well."

"Of course I'll keep an eye on Felix, but are you sure you have to go?" Millie asked, and immediately felt selfish and petty. This was her great-aunt and great-uncle her mother was talking about, people who were very dear to her. If they needed help, her parents had to go. But being left alone to deal with all of the magical problems . . . Francis would be there, but she couldn't imagine that he'd be much help. He was so preoccupied with becoming a knight that he never spent much time on his other magical studies, even though he was more gifted than Millie. If she had half the magic he had, she would have studied every book and parchment she could get her hands on . . .

"Don't you worry about a thing," Audun told her parents, pulling Millie to his side and giving her a reassuring hug. "I'll be here to help Millie and Francis if they need it. I'm sure there won't be any problems that the three of us can't handle."

Three

Two days later, Millie learned that something was harassing the residents of the tiny village of Dewly Glen. She hurried to her aunt's cottage to ask Francis to go with her, but he was sound asleep in bed.

"You'll have to go without me," he mumbled when she shook him awake. "I just got back from chasing will-of-the-wisps out of the swamp. It took me all night to get rid of them."

"But Francis," she said as he closed his eyes again, "you're the one with the magic!"

"You'll manage, I'm sure," he said, pulling the covers over his head.

Millie turned to Audun, who was waiting by the door. "I don't even know what I'm going to face. The man who left word was gone before I could talk to him."

"Don't look so worried," Audun said, taking her hand. "When I was little, my grandmother Song of the Glacier always told me, 'Dragons can do anything if it's worth doing.'"

"I didn't know it until recently, but apparently my grand-mother Frazzela used to say that the only good dragon is a dead dragon. That's one of the reasons we didn't see her very often."

"Huh," said Audun. "Song of the Glacier used to say the same thing about humans, which is probably why she hasn't warmed up to your family yet."

"You didn't tell me she hates humans! Maybe we shouldn't invite her to the wedding."

"I wouldn't go that far," said Audun. "I'm sure she won't do anything unpleasant, and there's no use worrying about something that probably won't happen. Like what-ever's bothering the people of Dewly Glen—you shouldn't worry about how you're going to handle it until you know what it is. It might not be much at all."

"I suppose," said Millie. "Or it could be something really nasty. Being dragons helped us last time, but that doesn't mean it always will. One of these days I'm going to run into a problem that fire and strength can't solve."

Audun shaded his eyes as they stepped outside into the bright sunlight. "Maybe, although it's hard to imagine what that might be. We should probably take your magic carpet again."

Millie nodded. "Especially since we'll have to talk to people this time."

Dewly Glen was on the far side of the enchanted for-est, nearly two hours by magic carpet from the castle. Millie and Audun spent the time holding hands and talking as the carpet skimmed just above the tops of the tallest trees.

"Do dragons have family names?" Millie asked.

"No, we don't. Our mothers give us our first names, then we choose our own adult names when we're old enough."

"How old is that?" asked Millie.

"That depends on the dragon," he replied. "It could be anywhere from twenty years to two hundred. My father didn't choose his until he was sixty-three. What's your family name?"

"Verderia. It's from my mother's side. In Greater Greensward, the crown goes to the eldest daughter, unless her parents declare her unfit or she marries and moves far away. That's happened only once, and they say that princess had never wanted the crown. Her younger sister became queen and was said to be a good one. All the women of Greater Greensward had only daughters for as long as anyone could remember, until Great-Aunt Grassina had Francis and Mother had Felix."

"Why would a girl be declared unfit for the crown?" Audun asked.

"Lots of reasons, but usually because she'd fallen victim to the curse that said that girls in our family would become nasty hags if they touched a flower after turning sixteen. Our family history would have been a lot different if that curse had never been cast. I'm so glad my mother was able to end it. If she hadn't, my parents would never have gotten married and I wouldn't exist."

"Then I'm glad she got rid of the curse, too. My life would be nothing without you in it." Audun leaned closer to kiss her and Millie turned halfway around to face him. When they looked up again, they were both smiling. "Go on," he said. "I think your family history is interesting."

Millie cleared her throat and said, "There isn't much else to tell. The daughters who inherit the crown take the name Verderia to show that the line is unbroken, unless they move to their husband's kingdom and take his name."

"What about your father's side?"

"The crown is always passed down through the sons in Upper Montevista. The old ruling line died out almost three hundred years ago, and my father's ancestor won the crown through combat. His family name is Highwall."

"Since I don't have a family name, I guess you would keep the name Verderia, or would you choose Highwall?" asked Audun.

"It would have to stay Verderia. I don't have the magic to be the Green Witch, but I'm still the oldest daughter so I'll probably be queen someday. Felix will be the next heir to the throne of Upper Montevista after Father."

"Verderia. I like the sound of that," Audun said, kissing her on the tip of her nose. "Now tell me, where exactly is Dewly Glen? We haven't passed it, have we?"

"Not yet," said Millie. "But we should be close."

Although Millie had flown over Greater Greensward as a dragon countless times and knew where every village was located, she had never actually visited Dewly Glen.

She preferred seeing villages for the first time with her mother, who, as the Green Witch, had made a point of visiting them all long before Millie was born. People knew her mother and were comfortable talking to her; no one in Dewly Glen knew Millie.

It was a small village on the edge of the forest only a few miles from Greater Greensward's eastern border and the kingdom of Soggy Molvinia. Tiny cottages with thatched roofs and walls of sticks and dried mud lined a narrow dirt road running through the center of the village and south past the ancient trees of the enchanted forest. Beyond the last of the cottages lay a scattering of small, cultivated fields where men and women tended the crops.

Millie landed her carpet in the middle of the main road amid a cloud of swirling dust. She and Audun stood up, coughing, and, when the dust cleared, were surprised to see an elderly couple watching them from under the eaves of a nearby cottage.

"Hello!" Millie wheezed as she tried to catch her breath.

"Huh," grunted the old man.

The old woman continued to bounce the infant she held in her arms without saying a word. A small child peeked through the doorway but didn't come out. Another young child began to wail inside the cottage. The old woman turned and went in. A moment later the wailing stopped, leaving only the strident chirring of insects.

"Where is everyone?" asked Audun.

The old man spat into the dust, then jerked his chin toward the small patches of farmland that lay beyond the village. "In the fields," he said.

Millie peered into the shadow under the eaves. The man's face was scratched, as were his neck and wrists. He had purple smudges under his eyes as if he hadn't gotten much sleep. "I'm Princess Millie and this is my betrothed, Audun," she said. "We're here on behalf of my mother, the Green Witch. I understand you've been plagued by some kind of beast. We've come to help you."

"We don't need your help," he said, wiping his chin and lower lip with the back of his hand.

Millie sighed. "Even so, I need to see what—"

A loud blast of discordant notes drowned out the sound of the insects. Both Millie and Audun looked around, startled, but the old man didn't seem surprised. Before they could ask him what had made the sound, the man hustled back into his cottage and closed the door.

"Now I'm really curious," said Millie. "Let's go find someone who's willing to talk to us."

They had taken only a few steps in the direction of the fields when a creature the size of a six-month-old kitten launched itself at Millie, digging its claws into her leg and trying to climb her like a tree. She thought it *was* a kitten until she saw its face. Although the creature was covered with a thin layer of gray fur, the face was shaped like a man's and had a man's nose, mouth, and eyes. Millie reached

31

down, trying to grab the little creature by the scruff of its neck, and it opened its mouth to bite her. She jerked her hand back when she saw that it had three rows of very sharp teeth.

"Get off me!" said Audun.

Millie looked up to see Audun shaking his leg, too, trying to dislodge a small, orange-striped beast. When the creature climbing her leg dug its claws in to go higher, she yelped, grabbed it, and pulled it away from her body. She examined the spitting, snarling creature and was surprised when it spoke to her in a man's voice. "Let me go, or I'll tear out your gizzard and eat it for my midday munchies!"

"You'll do no such thing," said Millie. "If I put you down, I expect you to behave yourself. And tell your friend to behave himself, too."

"What is this thing?" Audun asked. He raised his arm and held the orange creature upside down by the ball attached to the end of its tail, making the little creature yowl and thrash.

"Put me down!" it screamed, swiping at Audun with its claws extended. "How dare you treat me like this! Don't you know who I am?"

"You're a baby—"

"I'm no baby! My babies' babies are having babies! Put me down before I—"

"I think they might be manticores," said Millie. "Or at least they're descended from a manticore. Grassina told

32

me that when she was young, she conjured up a manticore from a tooth my great-grandmother had given her. When the beast wouldn't go away, Grassina cast a spell and made it kitten-sized. It must have mated with a cat and these are its progeny. Do you suppose that someone in the field could tell us . . . Oh, they've all run off!"

The people who had been working in the field just minutes before had disappeared while Millie and Audun were occupied with the odd creatures. They had been in such a hurry that they left their tools on the ground behind them.

"Then we'll go talk to the old man," Audun said, his face looking grim. "I don't care if he wants to talk to us or not."

Still carrying the little creatures at arm's length, Millie and Audun returned to the cottage and knocked on the door. They could hear muted voices inside, but no one answered.

"If no one comes to talk to us, I think we should open the door and toss these little monsters in," Audun said in a loud voice. "One . . . two . . ."

The old man opened the door muttering to himself. A little boy about eight years old pushed past him to stare wide-eyed at Millie and Audun. He looked much like the old man must have when he was a boy.

"Is this what you didn't want to talk about?" asked Audun, holding up the wriggling ball of teeth and fur.

The old man flinched and placed a hand on the boy's shoulder, pulling him back a step.

Millie gave the man her sternest look. "Why didn't you send word to the castle that these creatures were harassing you? Don't deny they are, because I can see the scratches."

The old man coughed into his hand and seemed unable to meet their eyes. "It's kind of embarrassing-like. What were we supposed to say—we've got a plague of kittens drivin' us crazy? Every time we come outside, they pound on us with those balls on the end of their tails, an' rip into us with their claws. You can't walk under a tree without the little monsters landing on your head and bitin' at your ears. No one can get a wink of sleep, either, what with the racket they make soon as the sun goes down."

"What racket?" asked the creature dangling from Audun's hand.

The one that Millie still held twisted around in her grasp to face the old man. "Those are love songs!" it said, sounding indignant.

The old man eyed the little beasts warily. "They don't sound like love songs to me. They sound like a whole bunch of people blastin' away on broken trumpets."

"Tell 'em about the dogs, Grandpa," said the little boy.

The old man nodded. "We tried handlin' it ourselves—borrowed some top-notch huntin' dogs—but the darn cats drove 'em off and now we have to pay the hounds' owner. Good hounds don't come cheap, let me tell you! Those blasted kittens—"

"They're manticores, not kittens!" said Millie.

"Whatever you want to call 'em, the hounds ran off with their tails between their legs the first time the little monsters yowled. Then we tried trapping the . . . manticores . . . , but they were too smart for us. They sprang the traps, stole the bait, and left the traps in the road. We heard 'em laughin' at us when we came out in the morning."

"It was funny!" said the orange-striped manticore.

"How many are there?" asked Audun.

"I don't rightly know," the man replied. He rubbed his chin and added after a moment, "Couple dozen, I expect. They come out a few at a time during the day, but they all come out at night, leastwise it sounds that way."

"Then that's when we'll come back," said Millie. "One more question before we go. What do they eat?"

"Just about anything, I think. They ate all our chickens, and we haven't seen nary a mouse nor a rat since they got here."

"They ate all the frogs in the pond, too, Grandpa," said the little boy. "And I saw one eat a snake yesterday."

"They may be small, but they've got powerful appetites."

"It sounds like it," said Audun. "Do you have somewhere we can keep these two for now where they can't get away?"

"I have an empty barrel you can use if you'll put 'em in and take 'em out. But if you come back tonight, watch your step. Those little monsters like to trip you in the dark."

❧

They were seated on the magic carpet flying over the enchanted forest once again when Millie asked, "You have a plan, don't you?"

Audun nodded. "We'll trap them, but our trap won't look like one. I caught a desicca bird by hiding in the sand once. With the right kind of bait, I should be able to catch some miniature manticores the same way. We just need to get a few things at that fishing village I saw on the river last week and we'll be all set."

It was dusk when they returned to the village of Dewly Glen. This time they arrived as dragons, flying so high over the forest that anyone looking up would see little dots and think they were birds. Even from high up, their dragon vision could make out the tiny figures in the village going about their business. Millie and Audun waited, gliding on updrafts until the last door was closed and the last window shuttered. Moving as silently as wind and wing allowed, they spiraled down, landing in a grove of trees.

They waited until they heard the voices of manticores coming from the village before creeping to a mound of dirt just beyond the last cottage. Keeping an eye out for the little beasts, Audun curled up in a circle and lay still while Millie covered his body with dirt. When only his face was exposed, Millie stepped to the center of the circle and set down a large wooden box made to trap fish. She opened the lid and a torrent of mice poured from the box. Before

36

they could scurry off, Millie untied a cloth bag and took out a wheel of cheese, which she dropped on the ground beside the box. Their noses quivering, the mice turned to the wheel of cheese. With a beat of her wings, Millie rose into the air and returned to the trees, where she hunched down, waiting for Audun's signal.

Both dragons lay still, their ears pricked as they listened to the cacophony of the manticores' voices. Nearly half an hour passed before a manticore came close enough to smell the scent of the mice. Blaring the news of his discovery, the beast summoned his friends to the feast. Millie's limbs twitched as she readied herself to fly to Audun, but she didn't open her wings until he raised his head and coughed, a loud sharp sound that made mice and manticores freeze where they stood. Only a few heartbeats later she was landing beside Audun, who had shaken himself free of the dirt and was catching manticores and stuffing them into the wooden box through a small door on the side. The beasts became frantic when they discovered that the door didn't open outward and that they were trapped. The little creatures in the box filled the air with the ear-shattering din of their distress, while the ones outside fought with tooth and claw, neither of which could penetrate the dragons' hide. It took both dragons' efforts to collect the beasts and shove them into the box as they tried to escape.

When the last one was in the box and the door was securely fastened, Millie sat back with a sigh. "Remind me never to do that again. My great-grandmother shut wasps and bees in a crate once. I think this might have been worse."

"Wait, here's another one," Audun said, dragging a particularly stubborn manticore away from his tail, where it had been gnawing with much effort and no effect.

Millie opened the door so he could shove the little beast inside. The noise in the box was so loud it made even the dragons wince. "Do you think that was all of them?" she said, looking around.

Audun refastened the latch on the box. "I hope so, but there's no way of telling, at least not tonight."

"We'll have to come back in a few days and ask the villagers," said Millie.

"Let us outta here!" shouted a voice from inside the box.

"We will!" Millie shouted back. "As soon as we get where we're going."

"And that can't be any too soon," said Audun. He sniffed the air, his nostrils flaring. "We need to finish this and get back to the castle before dawn. I think a nasty storm is headed this way, and I don't want to get caught in it if we can help it."

When they took off, Millie carried her magic carpet in her claws while Audun lugged the box. The flight north was a familiar one, although neither of them had passed that way in more than a year. The two dragons flew side by side, soaring over grasslands, forests, and a few scattered villages where only the sleepless would have seen the dragon silhouettes against the bright disk of the moon. They reached the mountains in the early hours of the morning, when the air was still and every sound seemed loud. Tall mountain peaks surrounded the valley where they landed and set down the crate. Although it was midsummer and there was grass under their feet, the air was chilly enough to turn to fog with each puff of Millie's breath. A stream ran through the center of the valley, its water nearly as cold as the ice from which it came, but the dragons bent down to taste it and found it pure and sweet.

Audun opened the crate, releasing the kitten-sized beasts. Once out of the crate, the manticores made such a clamor that the echo seemed to shake the mountains themselves, yet the beasts had no interest in either attacking or fleeing from the dragons. Instead they stood in a group, peering into the dark while the balls on the tips of their tails twitched in agitation.

"What is this place?" asked one as Millie and Audun prepared to leave.

"Somewhere that you can do anything you want without hurting anyone," said Millie.

"You should be fine here," Audun added. "There are caves where you can live when the snows get deep, and you'll find plenty of fish in the stream."

"And mice!" said a manticore just before it pounced on something small and furry rustling the grass.

"Good luck!" said Millie as she and Audun took to the air.

"They're going to need it if they try crossing those mountains," Audun told her. "Those peaks are higher than they look."

❧

They were on their way back to Greater Greensward when Millie said, "I've been thinking. Why do you suppose no one saw the manticores until now? I mean, if they were descended from that one Grassina changed, why didn't they make their presence known before this? It's been years since Grassina was a girl and used her magic on that manticore."

"That's a good question," said Audun. "It does seem odd that they'd appear so suddenly."

Millie nodded. "Like that awful tree with the spines. All this *would* have to happen while my mother and Grassina were away!"

"Yes," Audun said, looking thoughtful. "It's almost as if someone had planned it that way."

❧

The storm that Audun had predicted caught up with them as they were flying south over the Bullrush River. A gentle rain pattered on their backs for a few minutes before turning into a torrent. Water pelted their faces and sluiced down their scales, running into their eyes so that they had to close their second set of eyelids to see. Although the lids were transparent, they made everything look a little less distinct. The wind grew fierce, pummeling them. Lightning flashed as the dragons flew over the enchanted forest, and they landed at the castle in a deluge that had already made the moat overflow its bank and created small rivers within the castle grounds. The sky was so heavy with thick, gray clouds that even if the sun were high, its light couldn't have gotten through.

Millie was convinced that it had to be past dawn when she and Audun landed in the courtyard and ran up the castle steps. They both changed back to their human forms as soon as they were inside, shuddering in the pounding rain that soaked them to the skin even as they worked together to close the door against the force of the wind.

Sighing with relief, Millie led the way to the Great Hall, a shortcut to the stairs that led to their rooms and dry clothes. Although Millie wasn't surprised to see the torches lit as if it were still night, she didn't expect to see a murmuring crowd gathered around her grandmother in the Hall. Queen Chartreuse was wringing her hands as tears streamed down her pale cheeks. Guards strode purposefully through the Hall, their expressions somber.

"Grandmother, what's wrong?" Millie asked, running to the side of the queen.

"Felix is gone!" sobbed Queen Chartreuse. "Someone came in the night and stole him away!"

Four

"What do you mean, someone stole Felix?" asked Millie. "Are you sure, because one day last month I went to see him and he'd been fussy and his nursemaid had taken him for a walk. I was sure he'd been kidnapped until I found them in the garden."

A middle-aged woman standing behind the queen wailed and buried her face in her hands. Sobbing loudly, the woman ran from the Hall.

"What's wrong with her?" said Audun.

Millie frowned, staring at the door through which the figure had just disappeared. "That was his nursemaid. I guess that means she's not with him. Can someone please tell me what happened?"

A tall, distinguished-looking man with white hair and a trim white beard had just come into the Hall through a different door. "I can tell you," King Limelyn, her grandfather, said. "His nursemaid said she'd heard a strange sound in the corridor outside your brother's chamber. She went into the hallway to investigate and found nothing unusual. When she tried to go back into Felix's room, the door was locked. She ran down the corridor to call for the guards; the door was standing open when they arrived. They hurried in to investigate and found the baby's crib empty. I've had my men search every floor, but so far we haven't found even the smallest clue as to what might have happened."

"I knew your mother shouldn't go away!" the queen wailed. "Those old witches had no right to ask Grassina for help and she had no right to go. And then your mother went traipsing off after her! Both of my daughters are more interested in helping others than they are in seeing to their responsibilities here at home. If they had been here, none of this would have happened."

"That's not fair, Grandmother," said Millie. "My mother does what she feels she has to and so does Great-Aunt Grassina. They work hard for Greater Greensward and you know it."

"Your grandmother is just upset, Millie," said the king. "We're all very worried. If my men don't find your brother, we may need to ask for magical help."

"Audun and I can look, too," said Millie. "There has to be something that can tell us what happened to Felix."

Millie and Audun ran up the steps to the baby prince's room. Guards were inspecting the doorway and the corridor, but the room inside was empty. The prince's crib stood against the far wall, holding nothing more than a light silk blanket and a golden rattle shaped like a frog. "Poor Felix,"

Millie said with a catch in her voice as she touched the blanket with tentative fingers. "Whoever took him had better not hurt him. If they do, I'll hunt them down myself. This is my fault, you know. My mother asked me to look after Felix, and I let someone kidnap him!"

"You didn't *let* anyone do anything," said Audun, wrapping his arms around Millie and pulling her close. "Your mother also asked you to take care of the kingdom, which is what you were doing. And now we'll deal with this. We'll find your little brother before anything can happen to him."

"But what if something already has?" said Millie.

Audun's expression became cold and hard. "Then the monster who hurt that baby will have two dragons who won't stop until every last scrap of him is torn to shreds. But before we plan his demise, let's see what we can find. Our eyesight is better as dragons. Maybe we'll see something everyone else has missed."

Millie nodded. "Unless it was a ghost, he must have left some sign that he was here, and a ghost can't carry off a baby."

It took them only a moment to turn into dragons. The room had looked well scrubbed and spotless while they were human, but now Millie could see every speck of dust on the chair backs and the lid of the trunk, every smudge on the floor, and every piece of lint on the baby's bedding. Her hearing was better, too, and she could make out the distinct sound of each raindrop hitting the wall outside the window.

While Audun inspected the area around the door, Millie moved toward the window, casting back and forth, with her nose inches from the stone surface. "Look here," she finally said, pointing to a spot just under the window ledge. "There's dirt on the floor here that I haven't seen anywhere else in the room."

"Let me see," Audun said, lumbering toward her.

"What do you think?" Millie asked as Audun sniffed the dirt.

Using his talon, he poked the little clump until it fell apart. "Looks like dirt to me."

Millie sighed and sat back on her haunches. "I don't know what to do, Audun. If my mother were here, she could say a spell and have the walls tell us what happened."

Audun laughed. "From what I know about the Green Witch, she could have the dirt talk to us and tell us where it came from. You should hear what the dragons back on King's Isle say about her!"

"I wish she were here," said Millie. "Grandmother was right, in a way. This probably wouldn't have happened if Mother had been home."

The rain that had been pouring so fiercely just minutes before had begun to slack off. Millie was looking out the window at the now-brightening sky when she heard the faintest of sounds. *Scritch! Scritch!* She turned around, bumping into Audun as he too turned to see what was making the sound. *Scritch! Scritch!* The sound came again.

45

"It's coming from the trunk," said Millie. "Maybe it's a mouse."

Something thumped in the trunk. "It would have to be an awfully big mouse," said Audun. He lifted the lid and jerked his head back in surprise. "Millie, I think this might be a friend of yours."

Millie peered into the trunk and gasped. Two small bats lay on top of the folded baby clothes. "Zoë!" Millie exclaimed. "Li'l! Who did this to you? Are you all right?" Her two friends were struggling to sit up when Millie reached into the trunk and lifted them out.

"I could hardly breathe in there!" said Zoë.

"Did you find your brother yet?" Li'l asked, her eyes frantic.

The air shimmered around Zoë as she changed back into her human form. Her mother, Li'l, had married Garrid, a vampire, which was why her children could become human.

"What do you know about Felix?" said Millie. "Did you see whoever took him?"

Zoë shook her head. She picked up her mother and carried her to the nearest bench. When Li'l fluttered to her daughter's shoulder, Zoë sat down with a sigh and said, "We didn't see much of anything."

Li'l stretched her cramped wings, groaning softly. "That's true. We were out catching bugs when we saw a strange light coming from that window," she said, pointing with a wingtip at the only window in the room. "We flew in to investigate and a blast of air hit us."

46

"It felt like a giant had slapped us to the ground," said Zoë.

"When we came to, we were in the trunk—"

"Like old clothes," Zoë added.

"And we couldn't get out."

"We could hear everything, though," said Zoë. "We heard the guards talking about how Felix was missing. We both shouted, but I guess the rain was so loud that no one could hear us."

"Whoever took your brother must have already been gone by the time we woke up," said Li'l.

"So we're no closer to knowing who took him," Millie said.

"Yes, we are," replied Audun. "Whoever took him must have used magic to do it, which was more than we knew a minute ago. We should go tell your grandfather so he doesn't waste his time searching the castle."

"And *we* should go home," Li'l told her daughter. "Your father probably won't be able to get a wink of sleep until he knows that we're all right, and he should have gone to bed hours ago."

Zoë stood and turned to Millie. "Let us know if there's anything we can do."

"We will," Millie promised.

A moment later Zoë was a bat again and she and her mother were flying out the window.

❦

Millie and Audun went to the Great Hall, but it was nearly deserted. They learned from a passing guard that the queen had retired to her chamber and the king had gone into the dungeon.

"Do you suppose he went to consult with the ghosts?" Audun asked Millie as they descended the dungeon steps.

Millie shook her head. "Neither of my grandparents likes talking to the ghosts. My grandmother still tries to pretend they don't exist. Grandfather isn't quite so bad, but he avoids them whenever possible. I don't think it would occur to him to ask a ghost for help or advice. No, I'm sure he's down here for another reason."

The dungeon felt especially damp after the downpour. Millie knew the dungeon as well as she did the upper floors of the castle and could find anything, even when errant magic had relocated the doors or opened holes in the floors. There wasn't as much wild magic running loose in the dungeon as there had been when her mother was young, but it still showed up now and then. Because of the bottomless pits that appeared occasionally, it was never wise to run through the dungeon, no matter what was chasing you; when the air suddenly turned cold and an aged ghost came toward them, Millie told Audun not to move.

The ghost ran down the corridor, shrieking with rage at Millie and Audun. His long hair streamed behind him, and his ragged tunic flapped around the vague shape of his emaciated body. "Come to steal my medallion, have you?"

he screamed, brandishing a ghostly pike. "I'll show you what happens to thieves!"

Audun gasped as the ghost ran him through with the pike. The dragon looked down in horror, then glanced up in confusion when he realized that he hadn't felt a thing.

"He can't hurt you," Millie told him. "Most ghosts can't do more than frighten you into doing something foolish, in which case you might hurt yourself. Hubert," she said, turning to the ghost, "why do you think we want to steal your medallion?"

"Because there's a thief in the castle and it might be you!"

A tall, elegant-looking ghost dressed in a peaked cap and overtunic glided down the corridor to float between Hubert and the princess. "Hubert thinks that because someone took your little brother, they want to steal the valuables, too. If anyone is going to steal your medallion, Hubert," he said, turning to the first ghost, "it would be the hamsters. If you're so worried about your medallion, go watch over it and stop bothering the princess," he said, making shooing motions with his hands.

Grumbling to himself, Hubert disappeared through a wall.

"Thank you, Sir Jarvis," said Millie. "I didn't know that Hubert was so worried about his medallion."

The noble ghost sighed. "It was his most prized possession. The first princess Millie, the one you were named after, gave it to him for bravery. Just a few years before you were born, your family had the bones in the oubliette buried, but Hubert insisted the medallion stay here in the castle. Your mother hid the medallion in a special place. Though Hubert forgets everything else, he never forgets where that special place is located."

"So you've heard about Felix," said Millie. "Does anyone down here know who might have taken him?"

Sir Jarvis shook his head. "No one has been aboveground in days. Your great-grandparents are away at a meeting of the council of ghosts. We know only what we've heard people talking about when they visit the dungeon. Your grandfather passed through just a short time ago on his way to the secret passage. He was talking to his guards about your brother. They said—"

A roar so high pitched that it reached the very limit of what a human can hear echoed throughout the dungeon. Audun whipped his head around, and even Millie, who had heard it before, felt her heart leap in her chest. "That's the shadow beast," she said, taking a step toward Audun.

The air that had been cold before turned frigid as unseen figures rustled by them. Audun pulled Millie to his side when it sounded as if a crowd were passing them in the corridor.

"Everyone is headed toward the shadow beast. I'd better go help them," said Sir Jarvis. "We've been trying to capture the beast for the last few days. All of us other ghosts stand watch over the secret passage and warn the guards when the wall between the dungeon and the moat

50

springs a leak. We think it's about time the shadow beast contributed, too, instead of just scaring our visitors."

As Sir Jarvis floated away, Millie and Audun began walking toward the end of the dungeon where the secret passage was located. "You haven't seen the shadow beast yet," said Millie. "No one knows what it was originally, because all you can see of the beast are its eyes and a shadow. It's a ghost, too, but the odd thing about it is that you can touch it, although only Grassina and my mother actually have. And if we can touch the beast, it can touch us, so everyone is afraid of it. The beast has never bothered me, but I've heard that it almost got my grandmother when she was young."

The roar rang out again, louder this time, as if the beast were coming closer. Millie glanced down the corridor and saw a shadow pass beneath the flickering light of the torches on the walls. "It's here!" she whispered, reaching for Audun's hand.

Audun took a single step forward. "Where?" he murmured. And then reddened eyes appeared in the shadow as the beast loped down the corridor.

"Watch out!" shouted Millie, but the beast was already on them.

It knocked Audun to the side with one powerful blow. He staggered and fell against the wall. It wasn't until the beast's eyes turned to Millie, however, that Audun's expression hardened and he began to change into a dragon. The change wasn't complete when the beast launched itself at

Millie, but Audun didn't wait—he threw himself between them even as his skin hardened into scales and his nails into talons.

Aside from its eyes, the beast looked like little more than a deepening of the shadows. It was hard to fight something he couldn't really see, but Audun managed somehow. Whipping his tail, he hit something with a good, hard *thwack*. A powerful swipe of his talons elicited another high-pitched roar. The beast leaped onto Audun's back, forcing him to the ground, but Audun shook off the weight and turned to face the shadow again. Another swing of his tail and the beast hit the wall hard enough to crack stone. The red eyes blinked, then moved from side to side as if a great beast were shaking its head.

"There it is!" shouted Sir Jarvis, appearing in the darkened corridor as a pale blue glow.

The beast backed away, its eyes watching the advancing ghosts as one blue glow after another joined Sir Jarvis. The ghosts began to take shape, becoming a little less transparent, although Millie could still see the walls of the dungeon through them. More appeared, coming through closed doors and solid stone walls. One materialized right in front of Millie. "Pardon me, Your Highness," he said, tipping his dented metal helmet.

Soon more than a dozen ghosts were crowding the shadow beast, and it began to pace as if looking for a way out. When the ghosts moved closer, the beast leaped, soaring over Audun and Millie and disappearing in the shadows behind them.

A shout went up from the ghosts and they gave chase, turning back by twos and threes into pale blue wisps that poured down the corridor after the shadow beast.

"You were amazing," Millie said, standing on tiptoe to kiss the dragon on the cheek.

"I wish I could exhale ice like Frostybreath can. That might have slowed the beast down," Audun said, turning back into his human form.

"Or done nothing at all," said Millie. "The shadow beast is a ghost, after all."

They found the king on the other side of the secret passage door talking to Millie's cousin, Francis. The king looked up as the door creaked open. "Any news?" he asked, sounding hopeful.

"No news of Felix, but we did learn something about the person who took him," said Millie. "He—or she—is a magic user." She continued by telling him what had happened to Li'l and Zoë.

King Limelyn didn't look happy. "I was afraid of that. If someone used magic to whisk Felix away, he or she could be anywhere by now. Francis and I have been inspecting the secret passage to make sure the kidnapper didn't go this way."

"We haven't found anything here, but then we wouldn't have if the kidnapper used magic or went out the window," said Francis. "I'm sorry I'm not more help. I've been focusing my study of magic on ways to make myself a better knight. I should have listened to my parents and broadened my studies to include a wider range of magic. I can't do much unless I can see my enemy."

"If we need magic to help us find magic," Millie said, "we'll have to go ask someone who can do the right kind of spells. I'm going to the enchanted forest to see if any of the three witches are home."

Five

The cottage lay in the heart of the enchanted forest, far from any other human or witch dwelling. It had once belonged to a would-be witch who had captured Millie's mother after Emma had been turned into a frog, but now it was the home of three real witches, two of whom were sisters. Although all three witches were friends of her family, Millie was especially fond of Azuria, the Blue Witch, and it was Azuria whom Millie and Audun first saw when they landed in the field beside the cottage.

"Hello, Millie! Hello, Audun!" the witch shouted as she ran past, waving a butterfly net. A sapphire blue butterfly zigzagged just out of reach as the elderly woman lunged after it, her net snapping in the air.

The air around them shimmered as the two dragons turned into their human form and stood waiting for Azuria to come back. When the old witch continued to dart around the field, Millie looked at Audun and shrugged. "Maybe we should talk to someone else."

They could hear voices arguing inside the cottage as they drew closer, so they knew that the two sisters were home. Millie's mouth watered at the scent of fresh-baked cherry pie, and she smiled when Audun raised his nose to sniff. She knocked on the door, and a moment later it opened with a bang. A woman with gray hair and bright blue eyes greeted them, reaching out a flour-covered hand to gesture them inside. Her name was Oculura and she carried a large wooden batter-filled bowl. She was stirring her wooden spoon with so much energy that the batter sloshed over the sides, splattering her clothes, the walls, and the floor. "Come in, come in and make yourselves comfortable," said Oculura. "Dyspepsia, clear off that bench so our guests can sit down."

"Don't you tell me what to do!" said an even older white-haired woman as she swept a pile of clean clothes off the bench and into her arms. Scowling at her sister, she stomped across the room and kicked the wall. The fireplace slid back, making a grinding sound and revealing another room beyond it.

"But that's an outside wall," Audun murmured into Millie's ear. "That's not possible."

The room they were standing in seemed bigger than she remembered it, and she thought the way the fireplace moved was definitely new. "They're witches," whispered Millie. "Anything is possible for them, which is why we came." In a louder voice, she said to Dyspepsia, "We need to talk to you."

"I'm busy," said the old woman. "Talk to Miss Bossy over there." Grumbling to herself, Dyspepsia flung the clothes through the doorway and kicked the wall again. "I'll deal with them later," she said as the fireplace swung back. Millie had to jump out of the way when the witch grabbed a broom and began to beat the floor with it, sending up thick clouds of dust.

"We need your help," Millie said, crossing the room to where Oculura was dumping batter into a pan.

"Dyspepsia, mind that dust!" shouted Oculura. "If you keep that up, there will be more dust than flour in this cake!"

"That would be an improvement," Dyspepsia replied.

"I can't talk to you now," Oculura told Millie. She scuttled across the room, moving a pan of cooling tarts from a table to the windowsill. "We couldn't sleep last night, what with that storm booming and banging, so I tried something new and made us all cups of sleep-tight tea. It worked very well because we slept like logs—"

"We slept like the dead," said Dyspepsia. "The house could have collapsed around our ears and we wouldn't have noticed. I told her this morning that that wasn't a good thing, but does she ever listen to me?"

"There's only one problem with sleep-tight tea," Oculura continued. "When you finally do wake up—"

"We slept hours past our usual get-up time," declared Dyspepsia, emphasizing each word with a *thwack* of the broom at whatever object was closest. Audun hopped out of the way when she turned in his direction.

57

"When you finally do wake up," Oculura repeated, "you have so much energy that you can't sit still. Azuria went outside to catch blue butterflies for a potion she invented, and I decided to cook. Dyspepsia said she's going to clean, but all she's done is make a bigger mess than before."

"That's not true!" snapped her sister. "This place hasn't looked this good in years!"

"The extra energy isn't supposed to last long," said Oculura. "No more than an hour or two."

"Don't listen to her. It's been two hours and forty-seven minutes since I woke up." Dyspepsia jabbed the broom at an hourglass filled with sand, knocking it onto the floor so that it shattered, spilling sand across Millie's shoes.

Oculura began to crack eggs into a bowl. "Normally, I'd use magic for this, but I have to use all this energy somehow. You'll have to stay for supper. I've already made too much food for just the three of us."

"Actually," said Millie as she tried to get out of Dyspepsia's way when the old woman began to attack the spilled sand with a broom. "We're in a hurry, so—"

The door behind her creaked open and Azuria shuffled in carrying a woven basket with a wooden lid. She dragged her feet as she crossed the room and collapsed onto the bench, dropping the basket on the floor beside her. "Every muscle in my body hurts," she said, slumping against the wall. "My bones, too. I'm too old for this."

"See," said Oculura, "she's used up her extra energy."

Azuria shook her head. "That wasn't *extra* energy. I've used up every bit of energy I would have had this week and next. I don't think I'll be able to move again until spring."

"I'm still going strong," Dyspepsia announced. "When I finish sweeping, I'm going to . . ." She took a step and staggered. Reaching out her hand, she grabbed hold of the edge of the table for support. "I guess that's it for me. The end sure does come fast."

"I don't understand," said Oculura. "You both drank more tea than I did, but I still have loads of energy. Who would like a nice plate of . . . Oh, I see what you mean. It sort of hits you all of a sudden." Putting her hand to her head, she swayed on her feet until Millie helped her to a seat beside Azuria.

"Don't ever make that tea again," said Dyspepsia. "I haven't been this tired since those villagers chased me out of town back when I was young and spry."

Oculura nodded. "Sounds good to me. But at least we got a lot accomplished."

"And I got a good night's sleep," Dyspepsia admitted. "That's pretty rare these days."

So," Oculura said, glancing at Millie, "what was it you wanted to see us about?"

"Felix is gone," Millie said. "Someone kidnapped him during the storm."

The three witches looked shocked. "Oh no!" Azuria gasped. "That sweet little baby!"

"Who would do such a thing?" demanded Oculura.

"A no-good scoundrel who should be tied in a sack and tossed in a river," Dyspepsia said. "That's what I wanted to do to the last man who jilted me. I might still have the sack, if you want me to look for it."

"First things first, Dyspepsia," said Azuria. "We have to find dear little Felix and catch the horrid scoundrel before we can use your sack. Now, what can you tell us about the kidnapping?" she asked, turning to Millie.

"Audun and I were gone when it happened. We were taking care of a problem with manticores, and when we got home we learned that someone had distracted Felix's nursemaid and taken him from his crib. Zoë and Li'l said they saw a strange light in the baby's room and that a blast of air knocked them unconscious when they stopped to look. Mother and Great-Aunt Grassina are away, and so is my great-grandmother. Francis doesn't have the right kind of magic, so we are hoping you can help us find Felix."

"Of course we'll help!" said Oculura. "You're practically family! Would you mind getting my jar of eyeballs off that shelf? I'm too tired to move right now."

Millie ran to get the jar and set it on the table in front of Oculura. After taking a pair of milky white eyes from the jar, the old woman bent over the table and popped out her bright blue ones. With the new eyes in her sockets, she stared off into space, seemingly looking at nothing.

"Those are her seer's eyes," Dyspepsia whispered to Audun. "She can use them to see into the future or the past. They aren't pretty, but they get the job done."

Oculura sighed and reached for the jar. "Except for now. They aren't working. All I can see are clouds and rain. That storm seems to have blocked everything."

"Fetch me my scrying bowl, Millie," said Dyspepsia. "It's the shiny silver bowl on the top shelf. That's it. Now bring it here. Oh, and get me a dipper of water; I don't need much. Now step back and let me look." The elderly witch passed her wrinkled hand over the bowl, then leaned forward until it looked as though she was about to dip her face in it. Millie couldn't see what she was looking at, but it wasn't long before Dyspepsia sat back with a grunt. "It's as Oculura said—all I can see are rain and clouds."

Azuria fumbled at the neck of her tunic. "We're not finished yet. I've had this farseeing ball for fifty-two years and it's never failed me." Pulling out a golden chain, she showed Millie a small crystalline ball held in place with a clasp shaped like a pair of tiny blue hands. Holding the ball up so everyone could see it, she murmured something and breathed onto the clear surface. Nothing happened for a moment, and Millie was sure it wasn't going to work, but then an image began to form. She leaned forward for a better look. The image was blurry, and Millie was willing it to become clearer when the farseeing ball suddenly filled with clouds. Azuria frowned and shook the ball. Rain slashed through it, seeming to splash and run down the ball's inner surface.

"Drat," said Azuria. "That's never happened before." She sighed and replaced the ball under the fabric of her tunic. "You know what it means if none of us can see what happened, don't you, ladies?"

Oculura nodded. "That storm wasn't natural. Whoever took the baby created that storm to block anyone from seeing what he was doing."

"Or she," said Dyspepsia. "I know a few witches who could have done this."

"We need to call for help." Azuria grunted as she reached down to her wicker basket and took out one of the blue butterflies. Holding it carefully between her cupped hands, she whispered to the insect, then opened her hands and set it free. The butterfly fluttered around her head before flying to the window and out into the sunlight. "I laid a compulsion on that butterfly," said the old woman. "She has to go find the fairy Moth and ask her to come here. Moth goes out at night. She might have seen that strange light you mentioned. If she did, it would have drawn her like, well, like a moth to flames." Azuria chuckled to herself as she sat back on the bench.

"Do you mean she might be able to tell us who took Felix?" asked Audun.

Azuria nodded. "I hope so."

"While we're waiting," said Oculura, "would anyone like a fruit tart or a slice of pie?"

"No thanks," Dyspepsia replied, making a face. "Watching you cook has put me off food."

Oculura had put vivid green eyes in her sockets. They seemed to get darker when she glared at her sister and said, "I thought you liked my cooking!"

While the two sisters argued, Millie joined Audun by the window. The sky had cleared and the rain had washed away the dust, leaving everything looking fresh and clean. Droplets sparkled in the sunlight, but Millie soon noticed that one sparkle seemed bigger than the rest and was moving toward them. It drew closer until she could make out the tiny figure of a fairy.

Millie and Audun stepped back when the fairy flew through the window and landed on the floor. In an instant, she turned from a fairy no bigger than half of Millie's little finger to one who was human sized. Her soft white wings and pale blue hair were very pretty, but Millie thought it was her large, dark eyes that made her look unusual. She seemed shy at first and uncomfortable at the scrutiny of so many people.

"Moth, I'd like you to meet our good friends Millie and Audun. Millie's mother is Princess Emeralda, the Green Witch."

Moth smiled and visibly relaxed. "I know your mother, Millie. She's a good friend to fairykind. From what I've heard, you are as well. Thank you for helping my friends Trillium, Moss, and Poison Ivy. If there's ever anything I can do for you . . ."

"Actually, we need your help right now," said Millie. "My mother is away and someone stole my baby brother

63

during the night. We're trying to find out who took him."

"Did they leave another baby in his place?" the fairy asked.

Millie shook her head. "His crib was empty."

"Then it wasn't a fairy who took him. We always leave changelings to take the place of human babies."

Both Audun and Millie looked surprised, but the witches just nodded as if they'd heard it before. "You really do that?" said Millie. "I thought it was just a rumor."

"I never have, but I know other fairies who've done it. Human babies can be so cute!" said Moth.

Azuria cleared her throat. "What we really wanted to ask you was if you happened to notice a strange light coming from the castle last night. If you did, did you go to see what it was?"

Moth shook her head. "The storm was so awful that I spent the night in a hollow tree. I couldn't have flown in that wind if I'd wanted to, not without being blown halfway to the next kingdom. If I were you, I'd ask Raindrop. She learns a lot from listening to the falling rain."

"Of course!" said Azuria. "Why didn't I think of that? Thank you so much, Moth."

"I'm glad I could help," Moth said, shrinking once again. "We fairies do what we can!"

Six

The three witches were still debating how to contact Raindrop when Moth reappeared with Raindrop beside her. "I told Raindrop what you needed to know, so she insisted we go to the castle before coming here," Moth told them.

Raindrop nodded, her pale blue hair swirling around her delicate, pointy-chinned face. "Some people think I hear what the rain says only when it's falling, but I can hear it anytime, even after it's collected in a puddle!" She crinkled her nose and squinted when she glanced at Moth, as if to say that her friend was just such a person. "I wanted to listen to the raindrops where they collected in the puddles at the castle," she said, turning back to Millie. "I didn't know which window you meant, but I listened to each puddle till one mentioned a bright light. It told me that a person wearing a cloak came out through the high turret's window when the storm was at its worst. The figure was carrying a bundle, which could have been a baby, and flew off on a broom. I suppose the person was a witch. She went northeast, if you're interested."

"We're very interested," said Audun. "We have to find Felix and bring him back."

"I can go with you, if you want me to," Raindrop added. "The puddles will tell me where he went, but only for a little while. Once the rain dries up or gets soaked into the ground, it can no longer talk to me."

Millie felt as if a great weight had been lifted from her. She'd been so frightened that they'd never find her brother, but if the fairy could help find him . . .

"We're going, too," said Dyspepsia. "I wouldn't miss this for anything. We haven't had this much excitement around here since a boy griffin thought Oculura was a girl griffin and tried to carry her off."

"I was in the garden," said Oculura. "I don't know what he saw, but he sure liked it."

Dyspepsia chortled. "Maybe it was your feathered underwear."

"I didn't have any choice," said Oculura. "It was laundry day."

"We'll fly on our brooms, of course. I suppose you and Audun will travel by your usual method?" Dyspepsia asked.

Millie shrugged. "We have to. We didn't bring my magic carpet."

"What method is that?" asked Raindrop, quirking a pale blue eyebrow.

Audun and Millie smiled at each other as they stepped across the threshold and into the sunshine. "As dragons," Millie said as the air around them began to shimmer. She blinked as her eyes turned into those of a dragon. Colors looked different, and she could see the fairies even more clearly than before. Raindrop's blue hair had streaks of ultra-violet, a color Millie hadn't been able to see as a human.

Once everyone was outside, Moth decided that she wanted to go with them. "It looks like a party," she said, turning into her smaller self. "I can't resist a good party."

"It may take a while before I find more rain that can tell us anything," said Raindrop.

Moth zigzagged around her. "Then you'd best get started."

Millie, Audun, and the witches flew above the forest, circling while Raindrop looked for puddles. It took some time before she found one that could tell her about the cloaked figure. The tiny puddle was located in the crook of a tree and was nearly invisible to anyone in the air except a dragon or a fairy. The witches joined the two dragons to watch Raindrop scoop out a handful of water and bend down to listen as it dribbled back into the puddle. She looked satisfied when she glanced up to say, "The figure flew over this tree still headed northeast."

They moved more quickly after that, finding puddles in depressions in boulders, on top of witches' cottages, and in muddy dips in dirt roads. Moth finally grew tired of waiting for her friend and flew off, claiming that she was bored. The others followed Raindrop, anxiously awaiting her announcements each time she found the next puddle.

"Rain talks to all of us," she told them. "You just have to know how to listen."

They had left the forest behind when Azuria angled her broom so that she was flying next to Millie. "That's Soggy Molvinia," she said, pointing at the ground. "Most of the kingdom looks just like that."

Millie maintained the steady beat of her wings as she glanced down. Marshland stretched out in front of them for as far as she could see, making a crazy quilt of water and soggy patches of land. The bright colors of marsh flowers accented the mix of blues, browns, and greens like dabs of paint on an artist's palette.

Once again Raindrop flew down to listen to a shrinking puddle. She stayed on the ground for only a minute before darting back up to talk to Millie. "This is as far as I can go," she said. "The witch landed her broom on that hummock just as the rain stopped. She may have stayed here, or she may have gone on. Either way, I can't tell you what happened next. Falling rain notices everything, but puddles aren't very observant."

"Thank you so much," said Millie. "You've been such a big help."

"Just remember that," said Raindrop, "in case I need a favor someday." Bringing her hand to her lips, the fairy blew a kiss at Millie before darting back the way they had come.

"Now what?" asked Audun as the three witches gathered around them. "We can fly down there and look around, but that's an awful lot of ground to cover."

"I don't think we have much choice," Millie replied.

"I'm going to start by that hummock," said Azuria.

"We should all start there and work our way out," Audun said. "Millie and I will look from the air while you three ladies search the ground. If there's anything to find, we should be able to spot it with five of us looking."

"Oh dear," said Oculura. "I should have worn my blue eyes. These are fairly nearsighted, I'm afraid. I don't know how much help I'm going to be."

"And my back is hurting me," Dyspepsia whined. "I just can't ride a broom for long distances like I used to."

Azuria sighed. "Do what you can, girls. A child's life is at stake here."

"Yes, of course . . . ," said Oculura.

"I didn't mean . . . ," Dyspepsia protested even as Millie began to spiral closer to the ground.

While the three witches descended to the hummock, Millie and Audun began to search from the air. They didn't see much at first, but after a time Millie noticed a brown hummock much like the one where they'd left the witches. There was something odd about it, however, so she called to Audun and pointed at the little hill. "What does that look like to you?" she asked when Audun flew close enough to hear her.

"I don't know," Audun replied, squinting. "It almost looks like fabric, doesn't it? Let's get a better look."

The lower they went, the more puzzled Millie grew. It wasn't until the two dragons were about to touch the ground that she saw the brown mound for what it really was—a hunched figure wearing a cloak with the hood pulled up.

"It's the witch!" she breathed, but Audun had seen it as well, and he looked as if he was about to attack it. "No," said Millie. "You might hurt Felix."

Audun paused, his tail raised for a blow. He set it down reluctantly and, prepared to pounce, approached the seated figure.

"What took you so long?" asked the figure as he pushed back his hood. "I've been expecting you for hours."

Millie hissed as her breath escaped in a rush. It wasn't a witch at all. It was Olebald, the nasty old wizard. "Where's my brother? Do you have him with you?"

The old wizard shook his head and sneered. "I've put him where you'll never find him."

With a roar, Audun launched himself at Olebald and knocked him flat on his back. "What have you done with the baby?" the dragon growled.

When Olebald laughed, Audun pressed his talons against the old man's chest. Sweat broke out on the wizard's forehead and he gasped. "If you hurt me, that boy will spend the rest of his life in this marsh!"

"Where is he?" demanded Millie.

"Make Scaly Face get off me and I'll tell you."

The witches had noticed the commotion and flown closer to watch. Millie glanced up at them and saw Dyspepsia's mouth open in surprise. "Olebald, what are you doing here?" cried the old witch. "We were engaged to be married once," she told Millie.

"For about fifteen minutes!" said Olebald.

"Then he ditched me for a tree nymph!"

"And she tried to stuff me in a sack and throw me in the river!"

"It's too bad I didn't. Letting you talk me out of it was one of the dumbest mistakes I've ever made."

"That's saying a lot, considering how many dumb mistakes she's made," said her sister, Oculura.

Olebald's face was turning red when he shouted at Audun, "Let me go or I won't tell you a thing!"

Millie turned to Audun and nodded. Growling softly, the ice dragon sat back, freeing Olebald. The old man scrambled to his feet and straightened his cloak, revealing the broom he'd hidden under it. Snatching the knobbed wooden stick off the ground, he snickered and said, "You'll never find that baby. I turned him into a frog, and even I couldn't find him now. Do you know how many frogs there are in this marsh? Poor little princess," Olebald added, pretending to look sad. "Your brother is gone and so are your parents. You'll never see any of them again!"

Millie flinched as if she'd been struck. This time she didn't want to hold Audun back when he lunged for the wizard, but the old man was faster than anyone could have expected. Laughing triumphantly, Olebald smacked his broom against the ground . . . and vanished.

Dyspepsia squawked and nearly fell off her broom.

"Did you see that?" cried Oculura.

Azuria landed beside the two dragons, who were still staring at where Olebald had stood just a moment before. "He had it all planned, didn't he?" she said, using her toe to poke at a bristle that had fallen out of Olebald's broom. "He must have, to disappear like that. Olebald isn't a strong enough wizard to just vanish. He must have had a spell in place before we ever got here. All he had to do was tap the ground to put it into effect." She bent down to pick up a clump of dirt and crumbled it between her fingers. "If I'd had any inkling he was going to do it, I could have grabbed hold and followed him to wherever he went, but it's too late now. It was a one-shot spell. Ah well, live and learn. So, what did he tell you exactly?"

"He turned Felix into a frog," Audun said. "He set him loose in the marsh with all the other frogs."

"Oh dear," said Oculura.

"That's horrible," Dyspepsia declared.

"He said I'll never see Felix or my parents again," Millie said, sounding nearly as numb as she felt.

"You'll be able to find him, won't you?" Audun asked Azuria.

The Blue Witch shook her head. "It would take me weeks to find him among all the frogs here, and that's if he

72

doesn't swim farther away or get eaten. There are a lot of creatures in a marsh who consider frogs a delicacy."

Millie's face drained of color and she made a strangled sound. Her eyes looked stricken when she turned to Audun and said, "We have to find him soon!"

"Then we'll need your mother," said Azuria. "She's the most powerful witch I know."

"But I don't know how to get in touch with her," said Millie.

"You'll have to go get her. Do you know where she is?"

"She's on that tropical island where all the old witches were taken, but I don't know where the island is located."

"That's easy," said Azuria. "I've never been there myself, but I've heard that it's just past a string of islands that shoot melted rock into the sky."

Dyspepsia shook her head. "No it's not. It's all by itself halfway around the world, thousands of miles from anything."

"I was told that it was just off the coast of Grance," said Oculura. "They say the island is shaped like a rabbit with three ears and—"

"Never mind," said Millie. "I'm sure I'll find the way."

"You should go now, dear," said Oculura. "We'll stay here and look for Felix. Perhaps we'll be lucky and he'll come if we call him."

"Dragons know their names when they're babies, but do humans?" Audun asked.

Dyspepsia snorted. "I doubt it. But don't worry, we'll make sure nothing eats any of these frogs. Hey you, what do you think you're looking at? Shoo!" she shouted at a passing crow.

Millie thanked the witches, and a moment later she and Audun were airborne.

"It's good of them to help," said Audun. "Don't worry," he added when he saw Millie's expression. "Your mother will find him as soon as she gets back."

"That's another problem," said Millie, the creases in her brow deepening. "I still have no idea how to find the island."

Seven

$\mathcal{I}$t was late afternoon when Millie and Audun returned to Greater Greensward. They flew to the cottage where Francis lived with his parents, but he wasn't there so they continued on to the castle. Even from a distance Millie could see her cousin pacing the length of the curtain wall. He was wearing his armor as if expecting someone to attack the castle at any moment, and the polished metal reflected sunlight so that it hurt her eyes and she had to close her second set of lids.

"Any luck?" he called as she and Audun landed on the parapets.

Millie shook her head. "We know where Felix is, but we can't find him."

Francis looked puzzled. "That doesn't make any sense."

Agitated, Audun opened and closed his wings, making a sharp snapping sound each time. "It was Olebald Wizard who took him. I should have done something more permanent to him when we captured him in Aridia after the war over the throne. King Cadmus was sure he could keep him locked up, but Olebald is slippery and can escape from just about anything. He's been imprisoned in the dragon stronghold three times now. The last time he escaped, he sent two dragon guards to another time and place. No one has seen them since, and the king declared them both dead. After that the ice dragons were really out to get him. They'd be interested to learn what he's been up to lately."

Millie was changing back into a human even as she said, "Olebald turned Felix into a frog, Francis! He left him in a huge marsh in Soggy Molvinia. My brother is just a baby! He won't know how to find food or stay safe or anything! We have to find him right away, except we don't know how."

Francis reached up to scratch his head, and his fingers hit his helmet with a clang. He winced and shook his hand. "I want to help, but I don't know any frog-finding spells."

"Azuria, Oculura, and Dyspepsia are already looking for Felix. We think the best thing we can do is get my mother, only I don't know how to find the old witches' island. I was hoping you could tell me where it is."

"I don't know, either. My parents have gone there a few times, but they've never taken me with them. Is there any-one else you can think of who might know?"

"Great-Grandmother, but she's away with Great-Grandfather. There are probably some older witches in the retirement community who know, but I hate to waste time going door-to-door asking for directions."

"We might have to do that," said Francis, "unless... Does your mother still have the old carpet that used to belong to my mother? You know the one I mean—they used it the first time they flew to that island looking for Great-Grandmother."

Millie nodded. "It's in the back of her closet. At least it was when I went in looking for the basket with my old baby things. Mother saved all my clothes for when I have a baby, but she's using them for Felix now."

"You can use the carpet to find the island," said Francis. "Just tell it to take you to where it took your parents."

"That was a long time ago, Francis. My parents weren't even married then."

"Magic carpets never forget," said Francis. "I think it has to do with the way they're woven."

"It's worth a try," said Audun.

"I'll help you get the carpet started, then I'll see if I can locate a spell that would help me find a particular frog in a marsh full of frogs. But I think you're right; our best chance to find Felix is if your mother comes back."

༺6༻

Emma's storage room was nothing like Millie's. True, they were both small and dark, but Millie usually tossed things into her room, then had to hunt around for them later. Her mother was much more organized and kept her storage room so neat that it was easy to find things. Millie located the rolled-up carpet leaning against the wall in the back of the room, a thick coating of dust dulling the vibrant colors on the outside. She could have sworn it shivered when her fingers brushed against it, almost as if it couldn't wait to go flying.

The carpet was heavier than the one her mother had given her, and it proved to be much bigger once Audun and Francis wrestled it through the door and unrolled it. The scarlet, gold, navy blue, dark green, and cream were brighter than Millie remembered. She had ridden on the carpet with her mother when she was younger, but Emma had used it only rarely.

The old carpet would seat four people easily. Two heavy cords were attached to the carpet next to where the people riding in the front would sit. Grassina had put them there the first time Emma and Eadric had ridden on the carpet without her, but Millie had no idea how to use them.

"It's awfully big," said Audun, scratching his chin as he studied the magic carpet. "Will it fit through the window?"

Millie nodded. "When I rode on it with my mother, the window widened to let us through. Have a seat," she said as she stepped onto the carpet and sat down cross-legged.

"You don't happen to remember what your mother used to say to get this carpet to move, do you?" asked Francis as Audun joined Millie.

"Not really," said Millie. "She hasn't used it in a long time."

Francis shrugged. "It probably doesn't matter much. The older magic carpets are kind of funny that way. It's more the magic and the intent behind it than what you actually say. I know something I can use that should work. Are you all set?" When Millie and Audun both agreed, he raised his hand in a dramatic gesture and said,

> Take them to the island
> That her parents went to see
> When looking for the witches
> Who had gone through trickery.

The magic carpet shivered just as it had in the storage room, only this time Millie could feel it through her whole body. When it rose from the floor, the movement was so smooth that she might not have noticed if her eyes hadn't been open. Audun took her hand as the carpet rose higher, and she turned and smiled at him. He'd been so helpful ever since he arrived. She didn't know what she would have done if he hadn't been around when Felix disappeared. Just having him there was—

The carpet suddenly darted forward, only to slam into the sides of the window frame. Millie cried out as she nearly fell through the window, but Audun had a good grip on her arm. He pulled her back as the magic carpet backed up and prepared to try again.

"No! Stop!" shouted Francis.

"Hold on!" Audun cried, grabbing the edge of the carpet with one hand and wrapping the other arm around Millie's waist.

Taking hold of one of the heavy cords attached to the carpet, she gripped it so hard that her knuckles turned white. The carpet quivered and took off, ramming the window frame with even greater force than before. Millie and Audun bobbed back and forth like a pair of children's toys, but they didn't fall.

"Jump off!" Francis ordered.

Frantic, Millie looked around. The carpet was already backing up to the rear wall. Then suddenly it shot forward and was nearly halfway to the window when it tilted onto its side. Millie and Audun grabbed the upper edge and held on, their feet scrabbling to get a purchase on the now-vertical carpet. This time it slipped through the window with room to spare, although both Millie and Audun scraped their legs against the windowsill. Once outside the castle, the carpet righted itself and took off into the cloudless azure sky.

"Be careful!" Francis called after them.

Millie glanced back, but the carpet was moving so fast that the castle was already dwindling in the distance. They were passing over the closest village when she let go of the cord and reached for Audun's hand.

"Tell me about the island," he said. "What was that about witches going there through trickery?"

"It happened before I was born," said Millie. "Olefat Wizard, Olebald's brother, tricked some witches into going to a tropical island. Some of the witches liked it there and decided to stay. Cadmilla, the witch who came to get Grassina, is one of the few who still lives on the island."

"I visited a tropical island once," said Audun. "It was too hot for my taste."

Millie laughed. "Most tropical islands probably are."

Although Millie had flown great distances as a dragon, she'd never grown tired of seeing the countryside change beneath her. She leaned forward now, watching the land below them. They flew past the Purple Mountains, where she'd often attended the Dragon Olympics with her friend Ralf and his parents. When she saw pink clouds rising from the volcanic bowl where dragons practiced flame-breathing events, she smiled and pointed it out to Audun. "I'll take you there to look around sometime," she said. "We can go to the Olympics, too, if you can stand the heat."

Millie's muscles became stiff long before they reached the desert, and she leaned back to watch the clouds. After a while her eyes closed and she dozed, waking with her head nestled against Audun's shoulder in time to see the sky turn red and orange as the sun set. Night came and they watched the twinkling stars. They talked about their plans for the future, and the constellations above, but mostly about Felix and what they hoped Emma would do when she returned to Greater Greensward.

They drifted off to sleep, and when they woke they were flying over the ocean. Ralf's parents had brought her to swim in the great rolling waves and she'd always loved the way it smelled. She sat up now, breathing deeply, and felt Audun's gaze on her. He was still lying down and she turned her head to look at him. The warmth of his gaze made her blush, but she smiled at him, happy to have him along.

They both turned their heads at the sound of wings. A gull landed on the edge of the carpet. It tilted its head to eye them, then took off, leaving a single feather behind. "There must be land around somewhere," Millie said, although she looked in every direction and couldn't see anything but water.

"There are lots of islands," said Audun, covering his mouth as he yawned. "The trick is finding the right one."

They saw the occasional islands after that, but the magic carpet passed each one, heading farther and farther south. There were no clouds in the sky, and the sun seemed to burn brighter with each passing minute. Millie began to look at the water with longing, imagining what the cool depths would feel like on her hot skin.

She was considering tearing off a strip of fabric to protect her face from the sun when suddenly the magic carpet shuddered to a halt, flipped over, and dumped them off. "Help!" Millie screamed, tumbling head over heels. The skirt of her gown flapped in her face each time she turned right side up so that she had to fight to see where she was headed.

She turned over so that she was upside down for a moment. Her skirt gathered around her legs, allowing her to see Audun falling only a few yards away. "Change!" he shouted as the air began to shimmer around him.

When Millie flipped again, the fabric slapped her in the face; she shoved it out of the way and glanced down. The sight of the water rushing up at her with incredible speed was nearly paralyzing. The crack of Audun's wing beat made her whip her head around so that she was looking away from the water . . . and then she changed, too.

Millie's feet were aimed toward the water when her first wing beat cupped the air, pushing her higher. The next few beats carried her past Audun, who was flying so close that the scales on his wings brushed hers. "I was going to catch you if you didn't change in time," he said, his brow wrinkled with worry.

"Do you know what happened? Why did we fall?"

"I have no idea," said Audun. "One minute we were flying along just fine, and the next the magic carpet was flipping upside down. I see an island ahead. Do you suppose it's the one we wanted?"

"Do you think the carpet flipped on purpose? My mother told me that she and Father turned into frogs and fell off the carpet. I guess it brought us to the same spot where my parents got off. I just wish we'd had some warning. You don't see the carpet anywhere, do you? I'd hate to lose it."

"I think I saw it headed back the way we came," said Audun.

"Maybe it's going home. Mother might have put a homing spell on it in case it got lost or stolen."

"About that island . . ."

"That might be it," Millie said, squinting into the bright sunlight. "It certainly won't hurt to go look."

They flew to the island, startling a flock of seagulls headed in the same direction. Millie peered down at the ground, looking for the witches, but there wasn't anyone on the beach or among the trees or anywhere on the island as far as she could tell. She circled around again and saw some debris just inside the tree line, but no sign of any people. Green crabs scuttled out of her way as she glided to a landing on the white sands of a pristine beach and raised her head to look around. Audun landed beside her, raising a cloud of sand with the last beat of his wings.

Millie closed her second eyelids until the sand settled. "I didn't see any people from the air, did you?" she asked.

"Not one," Audun replied. "And there's no sign of humans near the water. Maybe this isn't the right island after all."

"But this was the closest island to where we fell off the carpet. This should be it."

"Are you saying that because you have a feeling or because you want it to be true?"

"Both, I think," said Millie. "Because if this isn't the right island, I don't know what we're going to do!"

"I think we should look around some more," said Audun.

"Fine, but we don't have much time. If this isn't the right island, we have a whole lot of ocean to search."

Eight

*I*t's not a very big island," said Millie as she followed Audun up the beach. "I would have thought we'd see someone right away. If there are any people here, they should have noticed us by now."

"I'm sure your parents would have come running if they'd seen us."

"Grassina and Haywood would have, too. I don't understand. Where is everybody?"

"It *must* be the wrong island," said Audun.

Millie watched a crab scurry under a fallen log. "Then how are we going to find the right one?"

"I can fly very high and look for islands from up there," said Audun. "If there are any more nearby, I should be able to see them."

"If there aren't any clouds," Millie said. "You know, we could go talk to those seagulls we just saw. They live around here and would know where to find the islands." She noticed a little crab sitting on top of another fallen log, waving its eyestalks as it watched the two dragons. Millie took a step toward the log. "Do you think these crabs might know something?"

"Maybe," said Audun. "Catch one and we'll see."

The crab began to scuttle off the log as Millie reached for it, but she was quicker than the crab and caught it between her talons. She was careful not to hurt the little creature, but the crab squirmed and tried to pinch her scaly arm as she carried it back to Audun. Millie looked up at a sudden rustling sound. A small sea of green was washing across the sand, from under logs and rocks and out of trees. Crabs seemed to be coming from everywhere, clacking their claws threateningly. A bird with a black-tipped orange beak that was nearly as big as its all-black body flew out of the trees with a raucous squawk.

As the crabs reached Millie and Audun, they swarmed up the dragons' legs and onto their bodies, jabbing with their claws and trying to pinch the scale-covered skin. The bird flew straight at Millie and landed on her head, where it pecked her with so much force it gave her a headache.

Millie cried out and shook her head, trying to dislodge the bird. It squawked and flapped its wings, but she couldn't get rid of it. She was trying to whack her body with her tail when she glimpsed Audun, who was also under attack. A crab that appeared to be bigger than the rest was tossing coconuts at him; he would have been able to dodge them better if he hadn't been covered with green crabs. Another crab picked up a coconut and hurled it at

Millie, hitting her on the tip of her nose. She blinked and took a step back toward a patch of fallen palm fronds. Another coconut hit her right between the eyes. Jerking her head away, she took another step onto the palm fronds and felt her feet slip out from under her.

Audun roared as Millie slid down a steep incline and fell over onto her back in a space barely wider than her body. Water partially filled the hole, and she had to hold her head as high as she could to keep her nose in the air. The crabs scrambled off her, scuttling up the incline to peer down at her from the edge of the hole. Water seeped from the walls and she began to worry that it might soon cover her. She was struggling to turn over in the narrow space when a flurry of sand showered down on her; the crabs were trying to bury her in the hole. Millie dug her talons into the wall, stopping when she saw that her efforts were bringing down more sand and water.

She pressed her lips together until they were thin lines. No crabs were going to get the best of them! Taking a deep breath, she blew a stream of flame at the wall, melting it so that it turned into a layer of glass, made rough from the still-falling sand. The glass steamed as she tried to right herself, making the rising water slosh. The sloshing water touched the glass, cooling it so that it hardened.

Pushing against the glass, Millie turned over and clambered out of the hole. She no longer cared if she hurt the crabs or not, so she swatted them aside when they tried to swarm over her again as she reached level ground.

"Audun!" she called and heard an angry snarl in reply. She turned in the direction of the noise and saw him curled up on the ground, nose to tail, with ropes made of vines wrapped around him.

"Are you all right?" she asked as she hurried to his side, but the vines were wrapped around his muzzle, too, so he couldn't answer.

She noticed movement out of the corner of her eye and turned to see more crabs scuttling her way. Once again she took a deep breath and exhaled a tongue of flame, this time drawing a line of fire right in front of the advancing crabs. The little creatures immediately turned and ran toward the waves creeping up the shoreline.

"Hold still," she said, turning back to Audun. Grasping the vines with her talons, Millie pulled them as far from his body as she could and exhaled a trickle of flame. One tug and they broke in two. She had to do it to three more vines before Audun was able to shrug all of them off and get to his feet.

Millie glanced up. The crabs had gathered around a pile of fallen logs while the birds watched from the trees. "Have you ever heard of crabs acting this way before?"

"I don't think so," Audun replied. "But then, I don't know much about crabs."

"My mother used to have a crab friend named Shelton, and I always thought he was nice. He even looked like these crabs, but they don't act anything like him. Look at the way they're watching us."

"That's odd," said Audun. "Do you see those logs? They look like they've all been cut to the same length."

"Maybe they didn't fall down," she replied and started toward the pile of logs. When the crabs clacked their claws at her, one small puff of flame made them retreat to the edge of the water. Audun reached the logs before she did and began to rummage through them. Each log bore a smooth cut at either end. Some were notched and a few had vines tied around them. They found logs that had been bound together with vines as well as sheets of tied-together palm fronds.

"These were huts," said Millie, holding up a piece of a crudely made door.

Audun nodded. "Someone definitely lived here," he said and placed a cracked cooking pot by her feet.

"Then it may well have been where the witches lived. What do you suppose happened to them?"

"I don't know," said Audun. "Someone either chased them off or ate them."

Millie shivered. "I doubt they were eaten! They're witches, after all. I'm sure they could find some way to protect themselves."

"What do you want to do now?"

"I don't know. Except—we've looked at this from a dragon's perspective, but maybe we should look at it through human eyes."

"Why? Do you think it will look different?" asked Audun.

"Not really, or at least not much. But I know when I'm human, I think of things differently. You don't have to change if you don't want to."

Audun shook his head. "We might as well both do it. But what about the crabs?"

"We can always turn back if we need to," said Millie. "On the count of three. One, two, three . . ."

The first thing Millie noticed after changing back into her human form was the heat. High temperatures never bothered her when she was a dragon, but now she felt as if she'd been stuck in an oven as the hot sun reflected off the heated sand. The only thing keeping it from being unbearable was the breeze blowing off the ocean, but even that was warmer than she was used to in Greater Greensward. Perspiration beaded her forehead as she turned to face Audun, and she noticed that he seemed to be suffering even more.

"So far, I'm not enjoying this perspective very much," he told her. "I was hot as a dragon, but at least my entire body didn't sweat."

Millie wiped her forehead with the back of her hand. "I wish we had something cold to drink. There must be drinkable water on the island somewhere if the witches were able to live here, but I don't know how we'd find it."

"There's a small stream that leads into a pond behind those trees," said a woman's voice. Millie's eyes grew wide as she turned to where the crabs had retreated to the edge of the water. Seven witches stood there now, their hair scraggly and unkempt, their tattered clothes hanging on their thin frames. They all looked tired, as if they had gotten little sleep, although their sun-bronzed skin kept them from looking unhealthy.

"Cadmilla?" said Millie, recognizing the witch who had come to Greater Greensward to ask for Grassina's help.

The old witch gave her a sad half smile. "We didn't recognize you when you were dragons. We'd heard rumors that there was a princess who could change like that, but we didn't know it was you. We wouldn't have trapped you if we'd known."

"You were the crabs?" asked Audun.

"And the toucan," said a witch with a long face and a very thin nose. "I think I made a good toucan, don't you, Septicimia?"

A witch with wild-looking eyes nodded and clasped her hands. "You were the best, Rugene!" she said in a breathless voice.

"But why?" asked Millie. "And where are my parents and great-aunt and great-uncle? Did they already head back to Greater Greensward?"

"Sit down, dear," said a kindly looking witch. "I'm afraid we have some bad news for you."

"I'd rather stand," said Millie.

"Suit yourself," Cadmilla told her. "Remember that monster I told you about?"

"It came at night when we were asleep and destroyed our cottages," said Rugene. "We were lucky to get out with our lives."

Septicimia wrung her hands in front of her chest. "It has these long tentacles, and it uses them like whips. It flung my poor Henrik all the way across the beach and into the ocean. He didn't stand a chance."

"He was a fish in a bowl. He just went back where he came from. I doubt he minded all that much," Cadmilla said.

"I took good care of him," wailed Septicimia. "I loved him and he loved me!"

"I'm sure he did," said Rugene.

Cadmilla sighed. "The sea monster comes every night when the moon is highest in the sky. After it destroyed our cottages, it still came back looking for us. We hid at first, but it crossed the island and we had to climb the trees."

"It was Septicimia's idea that we turn ourselves into crabs."

"The monster didn't bother us when we weren't human anymore," Cadmilla told them. "But we didn't want to spend our entire lives as crabs or birds, and we didn't want to leave the island. We were very happy here until the sea monster came, so we built our traps and waited for it to come back. We haven't seen it in a few days, though."

"When you showed up, we thought that the sea witch had sent you after us, too," said Rugene. "Our traps worked very well, don't you think?"

Both Millie and Audun looked puzzled. "What sea witch?" they asked at the same time.

"The one that rode the sea monster," said Cadmilla. "Did we forget to mention that?"

"We're not telling this very well," said the kindly faced witch. "You see, my dears, a sea witch came with the sea monster. She was a mermaid and her scales were the most ghastly shade of green."

"We told your aunt about the sea witch and her monster. She said that she knew what to do and left," Cadmilla told them. "Then your mother came and we told her exactly what we'd told your aunt. She took off right away, too."

"But what happened to my mother and Grassina? Where are they now?"

"That's the bad part, dear," said the kindly faced witch. "Your aunt never came back, and neither did your mother."

Millie swallowed hard and her voice shook when she spoke. "And my father and great-uncle? What happened to them?"

"Your uncle went with your aunt and your father went with your mother, of course," said Cadmilla. "They're all missing. I wouldn't be surprised if the sea monster ate them."

Nine

Millie didn't believe that the sea monster had eaten her family, despite what the witches said. Although she was sure they were in trouble, she was just as sure that they were still alive. "Call it dragoness intuition if you like, but I know we can save them if we hurry," Millie told Audun.

"What do you want to do? We can start looking for the sea monster. Perhaps some sea creature can tell us where it went when it left here."

"I guess that's what we'll have to do," said Millie. "Your amulet will work for me, too, won't it? I'll be able to breathe underwater like you can?"

"As long as we're touching," said Audun. "But we should go as dragons. We'll be much faster, and there's no saying what we'll run into down there."

"I hope we run into the sea monster," Millie said. "And I'd much rather be a dragon when we meet."

"Imagine that," said Rugene, who was still standing right there. "Being able to turn into dragons. It's amazing what young people can do these days."

"When I was a girl," Septicimia said, "I had a friend who tried to turn herself into a dragon. She changed partway, but it hurt so much that she got frightened and quit trying."

"Does it hurt when *you* change?" asked Rugene.

Millie laughed. "Not at all, although my mother said it hurt the first few times she did it."

"Do you mind if we watch?" asked Rugene. "I know we saw you turn back into humans, but it took us by surprise. Seeing you turn into dragons, well, I won't pretend I'm not curious."

"We don't mind," said Millie. "Just stand back. We wouldn't want you to get squashed by accident."

Septicimia gasped and the witches scurried back to the edge of the trees, then turned around to watch.

"They didn't need to go that far," Audun whispered to Millie. "What do they think we're going to do, turn into whales?"

"They'd probably enjoy that, too," said Millie. "We need to hurry and start looking, so let's do this together. One, two, three . . ."

They had gotten good at timing their turns at the same moment. The air began to shimmer around them, then their bodies began to elongate, their heads stretched, their limbs grew. Scaly skin replaced human flesh, and their teeth grew long and sharp. Their blinking eyes became larger, their pupils narrower. It all happened quicker than three heartbeats, and then they stood on the beach, water swirling around their scaled legs as their tails lashed the sand.

The dragons took to the air with the sound of the witches' applause. Millie could still hear them as she and Audun flew out over the curling waves to the deeper water that moved in small, barely discernible swells.

"Hold on tight," Audun said, taking her front talons in his.

They dove into the water and began to make a circle around the island. Millie held her breath until she remembered that it wasn't necessary. She felt a flutter of panic as she took her first breath, and relaxed when it felt natural.

Millie had gone swimming in the ocean as a dragon before, but she never grew tired of seeing what lay below the surface. Brightly colored fish darted around fantastic formations of coral, scattering as the dragons approached. Snaggle-toothed eels peered out from their hiding places, backing away when the dragons came too close. Large fish watched warily, keeping their distance. A curious shark came close enough to study the swimming dragons, then swam lazily away as if it had nothing to fear.

After swimming around the island once and seeing no hint of a sea monster, Millie and Audun expanded their search, swimming in ever-widening circles. As they moved away from the island, they no longer saw coral or the brightly colored fish, yet there was still life in the ocean around them. A strange flat fish nearly buried in the silt of the ocean floor watched them with one eye as they passed overhead. Fish as long as Millie's leg swam past in a school, their silver sides flashing as they changed direction. A huge crab scuttled across the ocean floor, leaving a trail of disturbed silt in its wake. And still they saw no sign of a sea monster.

They widened their circle, spiraling out from the island, which had now disappeared from sight. With nothing to use as a visual reference, Millie was glad that dragons had such a good sense of direction. No matter which way she turned, she knew where the island lay and even which way she'd have to fly to go home. Once she'd visited a place as a dragon, she could always find it again.

Lost in their own thoughts, Millie and Audun swam side by side in silence. That was one of the things that Millie liked most about Audun: he was great company even when neither of them had anything to say. She glanced at him and thought again how handsome he was and how good to help her with her family's problems. Most of the human princes she'd met would have helped her only if they themselves would have benefited in some way. Audun had told her that he did it simply because he loved her. She couldn't think of a better reason.

The ocean floor had begun to look monotonous, so Millie couldn't help but notice the seaweed. It started out as a few stray clumps but soon became a vast bed of long green plants swaying with the movement of the water, like saplings in a strong wind. Knowing that anything could lurk in the seaweed made her more cautious, but Audun plowed ahead, pulling her with him as they entered the forest that reached from the ocean floor to the water's surface.

The seaweed surrounded them immediately, muffling sound and blocking much of the light that filtered down through the water. Millie didn't like the way the seaweed hissed like a nest of baby snakes as it brushed against her scales, plucking at her limbs like long, green fingers. Even worse was the knowledge that some terrible beast could be only yards away and she wouldn't know it. She pulled her legs tighter to her body and discovered that she could swim faster with her legs tucked close and her tail moving from side to side to propel her. Powerful beats of her tail shoved the seaweed aside, tearing out the more persistent strands.

When they entered a thicker patch of seaweed, Millie felt increasingly anxious. She hurried Audun along, although they couldn't see where they were going. The only thing that kept her from panicking was having Audun close and hoping that nothing would want to take on two dragons at once.

They were racing through the seaweed when it ended suddenly and they emerged from the forest in a flurry of torn plants, nearly swimming into a mermaid. She looked terrified when she saw two dragons; turning tail in a swirl of long silver and dark blue hair, she sped away with only one quick backward glance.

"I know that mermaid," said Millie. "That's Coral. She's a friend of my mother's and Grassina's. I didn't realize we were so close to where she lives. Do you suppose my mother went to her for help?"

"It makes sense if your mother knew that her friend was close by. Maybe we should—"

"Let's go talk to her," Millie said, tugging at Audun.

"Did you see which way she went?"

"This way!" she said and let go of his talons to race after the mermaid.

"Millie!" cried Audun just as she realized what she'd done.

She turned and looked at him, suddenly all too aware of the weight of the water bearing down on her and that she had no air to breathe. Millie wanted to call out, but she stopped herself from trying, knowing that she'd lose her air that much faster. Although she could have held her breath for a few minutes and reached the surface with ease, it didn't occur to her to try. The only thing she wanted was Audun with his amulet. She couldn't believe how fast she'd become dependent on a small metal disk. Throwing herself toward him, she met him halfway.

"Don't let go!" he told her, pulling her into his arms.

Millie took a deep breath and smiled. "I won't!" she promised and kissed him, then turned and looked for

Coral. She saw the mermaid disappearing over a rise in the ocean floor. "Look," she said. "There she is."

This time Millie kept hold of Audun as they followed Coral. They were skimming over the rise when the mermaid stopped to look back. She shrieked and raced off to a castle visible in the distance.

"Wait!" Millie shouted, but the mermaid swam faster.

The two dragons followed her to the castle, reaching it while she was pounding on the door. Turning around, she brandished a long, pointed object that Millie thought looked like a unicorn's horn. "Stay back!" cried Coral, jabbing the horn in their direction. A stream of sparkling bubbles shot out of the horn, nearly hitting Millie and Audun as they lurched out of the way. The bubbles struck the rise with a loud boom, sending up a cloud of silt and debris.

"We just want to talk to you!" Millie screamed, but her voice sounded faint even to her own ears.

Coral aimed the horn at them again; they were already backing away. When the door opened behind her, the mermaid darted through the opening and slammed the door.

"That went well," said Audun. "Now what do you suggest?"

"I have to talk to her," Millie said. "But she's afraid of us when we're dragons. We have to let her see us as something a little less threatening."

It was the first time Millie had changed while touching anyone, and she wasn't sure she liked the feeling of someone else's hand altering its skin and shape while hers was doing the same. The contact also seemed to amplify the normal feelings and left her whole body tingling, like a foot or hand does when cut-off circulation is restored. Fortunately, the change seemed to go faster than usual, and she and Audun soon stood in front of the door as humans.

Millie was still feeling peculiar when Audun raised his fist. "Please let us in!" he shouted, pounding on the flat white surface. "Hurry, it's urgent!"

The door was a fragment of a giant seashell and had a single small bubble marring its perfect surface. Millie didn't remember the bubble being there, although it had been years since she and her mother had last visited the mermaid, so she leaned in for a better look. An eye suddenly appeared in the bubble, startling her so that she jerked her head back. The eye examined her for a moment before shifting to the side to study Audun. A moment after the eye disappeared, the door opened and Octavius, Coral's octopus butler, beckoned them in.

"What are you two doing out there?" he asked, sliding aside as they stepped across the threshold. "This is a terrible time to come visiting. There are monsters around and who knows what else."

"It's me, Octavius," said Millie. "I'm Millie, Emma's daughter."

The octopus looked at her as if he was affronted. "I know who you are, Princess. Didn't I dandle you in the highest tower of this castle when you were just a hatch-ling? Wasn't I the one who spent hours chasing you around the castle while your mother talked about magical things with Mistress Coral? And how many times did I have to undo the knots in your hair because that low-life crus-tacean Shelton hid there when we were playing hide-and-seek? I'd better warn you, Princess, he's getting ready to molt and is in a nasty temper."

"Shelton's here?" said Millie.

"And where else would he be?" Octavius asked, glid-ing down the floor in front of them. He was moving at an angle, as if the floor wasn't level, something Millie attributed to his age. "He's been here ever since your mother gave him to Mistress Coral, a dark day for us all."

"Shelton is the crab I mentioned before. My mother introduced him to Coral," Millie whispered to Audun. "They hit it off right away and Coral invited him to live with her. He came from the island where the witches live. He must be awfully old by now."

"You thought I was dead!" squeaked a voice by her elbow. "What a horrible thing to say about somebody! Although living here with that bloated bag who calls him-self a butler would be enough to shorten anyone's life. Did you know that he kidnapped me the other day and tried to stuff me down a hole in the ground bubbling with super-hot steam? I was lucky to get away with only a few toasted toes!"

"I wouldn't have done it if you hadn't glued my suckers to an electric eel, you vermin on a half shell. I'll probably list to the side for the rest of my life, shortened as it will be from living with you."

"Now, boys," said a melodious voice from another room. "How many times have I told you that I want you to get along? Who was at the door, Octavius?"

"Princess Millie and her friend," Octavius replied. "I think he's a very close friend, too. They've been holding hands ever since they arrived."

"Really?" said Coral, swimming into the hallway. She looked surprised and nearly dropped the seashell she was using to comb her long hair. Millie saw that the mermaid had already changed the seashells she wore on the top part of her body. "Ordinarily I'd be delighted to see you, but this isn't the best time for a visit. You didn't happen to see two horrible dragons when you came in, did you? I just had a very narrow escape! They were outside the castle a few minutes ago. I shot at them with my narwhal tusk. I put a repelling spell on it to keep the sea monster away, and I'm so glad I did. We've had such a terrible time of late. First the sea monster and now the dragons; who knows what's going to show up next?"

"Uh, should we tell her?" Audun asked Millie.

"I think we'd better," she told him.

Coral looked puzzled. "Tell me what?"

"That *we're* the two horrible dragons," said Millie. "I can turn into a dragon at will now, and Audun, well, he's a

104

dragon who learned how to turn into a human. We didn't mean to frighten you. We just wanted to ask you some questions."

Coral clapped her hand over her mouth. "I'm so embarrassed!" said the mermaid. "I know that your mother can turn into one and I'd heard that you could, too, but it never occurred to me that you might be one of the dragons outside my door! And you're Audun? Grassina mentioned you. You're a very brave young man—er, dragon—from what I've heard. Octavius, what are you doing?"

One of the octopus's long tentacles was edging across the floor, reaching for Shelton, who was too busy listening to Coral to notice. Octavius stopped now and flushed a deep red. "I was about to take out the trash?"

"You two will never stop, will you? Why don't you get us something to eat, Octavius? You must be starving," she said, turning to Millie and Audun. "I'm sure becoming a dragon takes a lot out of you."

"Actually, this isn't a social visit. We need to ask you about my mother and Grassina. They came to help the witches who live on an island near here. Did either of them come to see you by any chance?"

Coral sighed and nodded. "I was afraid that was why you were here. Come sit down and I'll tell you what I know, which isn't much, unfortunately."

Millie looked worried when she glanced at Audun and was grateful when he slipped his arm around her. They followed the mermaid into another room and sat down on a bench made of polished stone. Coral sat down opposite them and lowered her hand to pick up Shelton, who was tugging at her tail.

"Grassina and Haywood stopped by first," said Coral. "They said that a sea witch was using a sea monster to terrorize some other witches on an island. I told her that the only sea witch in the area, other than myself, of course, was Nastia Nautica. I haven't seen her in ages, and since her daughter, Pearl, moved away, I haven't heard a word about her. I assume Nastia still lives where she always has. Her shipwreck isn't far from here—just on the other side of the seaweed. Grassina left after I told her that, and I haven't seen her since, but a few days later your mother and father showed up asking the same questions. I told them what I'd told Grassina, and they took off in a tremendous hurry. I was hoping they had taken care of their business and gone home, but to tell the truth, I was getting worried. If everything was all right, wouldn't they have stopped to say good-bye?"

"I'm sure they would have," said Millie. "But everything is not all right. They never came home and the witches never saw them again. We need to find my mother. Olebald Wizard kidnapped my baby brother, Felix, and turned him into a frog. He set him loose in Soggy Molvinia and we don't know how to get him back. Mother needs to come soon, before an animal eats Felix or steps on him or something equally horrible! And now my parents and great-aunt and great-uncle have all disappeared and are probably in terrible trouble, too. Whatever happened, I need to go help them and take them to Soggy Molvinia as soon as I possibly can!"

Ten

e should start by talking to Nastia Nautica," said Millie. "Two dragons should be able to handle one nasty sea witch."

"I'll go with you," Coral said. "If you'll give me a few minutes to get ready, I'll show you the way."

Audun shook his head. "That won't be necessary. I've already visited her sunken ship. I should be able to find it without any trouble."

"But you'll still have to deal with Nastia Nautica herself," said Coral. "She's usually horrible to everyone, but if she's the one behind the sea monster attacks, then she's gotten worse. You need me to go with you."

"If you really think you should . . . ," Millie said. "It's awfully kind of you to offer."

"Kindness has nothing to do with it. I've been a friend of your great-aunt and your mother long enough to know just how upset they'd be if anything bad happened to you. Oh, and take Shelton with you, in case we get separated. You can always send him back to me if you need my help."

"A fat lot of good he'd do," muttered Octavius.

"That will be all, Octavius!" Coral snapped at her butler. "You may go."

The octopus looked deflated as he slunk out the door, his eyes turning to watch them as he left.

"I don't know if Shelton will want to go with us," Millie said. "We'll be going as dragons."

Shelton waved his claws in the air. "I'm not afraid of dragons! See here, I'm wearing my own suit of armor! Nothing can hurt me." He thumped his shell with his claws and tried to look fierce.

"I didn't think you'd be afraid," Millie hurried to say. "It's just that we'll be traveling very fast, and you might be in danger when we meet Nastia Nautica."

The little crab scuttled down Coral's fishy tail, across the white sand-strewn floor, and up the skirt of Millie's gown. "When do we start?" he asked.

"Octavius!" Coral called. The octopus appeared in the doorway as if he'd been listening in all along. "Our guests and I will be leaving now. Please see that there's nothing lurking outside the door that shouldn't be there."

"Right away!" said the octopus, and he disappeared from view.

"Thank you for your help," said Millie. "We'll come back to visit you properly when we have more time."

"Just take care of that baby brother of yours," Coral told her. "Olebald Wizard is a horrible old man to have kidnapped a baby like that. And to turn him into a frog . . .

The least I can do is help you find Grassina and your mother. Now, if you'll give me just a minute, I'll go get ready."

Octavius made them wait while he peered through the bubble, then went outside to look around. When he came back and reported that the area was clear, he blocked their way with spread tentacles and said, "Good luck finding your parents, Princess. I like your mother. She was always nice to me, even if she did bring that pest Shelton here."

"Who are you calling a pest?" Shelton asked, peering out from Millie's cupped hands.

"Thank you, Octavius," Millie said before the crab and the octopus could start arguing again. "I'm sure we'll find them." She tried to swim over Octavius's raised tentacle, but the octopus refused to budge.

"And as for you," Octavius told Audun, "I've known this girl most of her life. I'm holding you responsible for her safety. You take good care of her, or you'll have to answer to me."

"She'll be fine," said Audun, and he tried to brush past the octopus, but the creature was strong and Audun couldn't move him.

"Promise me you'll take care of her," said Octavius.

"On my honor as a dragon," Audun told him, looking into the octopus's two wandering eyes.

Apparently satisfied, Octavius slid out of the way, letting Millie and Audun pass. They waited until the octopus had shut the door before they turned back into dragons. Shelton was excited to watch the transformation and even more excited to ride on a dragon's back. Millie let him sit between two of her ridge bumps, warning him to hold on tight, but he squirmed so much that she began to wonder if it was a good idea.

The door opened and Coral swam out wielding her narwhal tusk. She looked startled to see the two dragons, but quickly composed herself enough to say, "It is you, isn't it?"

Millie smiled in what she hoped was a reassuring way. "It's us, Coral. We're ready if you are."

The mermaid eyed their linked talons and frowned. "Are you going to hold hands while you swim? I should think that would make it more difficult."

"The only reason we can breathe underwater is because Audun is wearing an amulet that the ice dragon council gave him," said Millie.

"I see. You have only one amulet, so you have to share," Coral said with a knowing smile. "Very good. Now follow me." She led the way toward the seaweed, stopping to part the long strands with the tusk. "There's a trick to this. You don't want to just barrel ahead, because you never know whom or what you'll run into. Swim slowly and as quietly as you can; that way you won't attract attention to yourself and you'll hear if anything else is swimming through the seaweed." The mermaid slipped between the swaying plants, gesturing for the two dragons to follow. "I'd avoid this area altogether if I could," she continued, "but Nastia Nautica lives just on the other side and it would take too long to swim

111

all the way around. This patch goes on forever. Well, not really, but if you get lost in it, it will certainly seem that way."

The mermaid stopped to poke something with her narwhal tusk, continuing on a moment later. "I was swimming through here once when I ran into an electric eel. It was quite a shock, believe me!" She turned around to see their expressions and seemed disappointed when they weren't laughing. "That was a joke," she said, facing forward once again. "I've never actually run into an electric eel, although I do have a friend who did. Her hair was straight before the incident and curly afterward. Her tail has a bad twitch now, too. Tsk! Such a shame."

Millie gritted her teeth, biting back a comment about people who talk after telling everyone else to be quiet. How were they supposed to hear something creeping up on them or even swimming in their direction if Coral wouldn't stop talking?

Suddenly the sound of hissing seaweed grew louder, and the mermaid stopped. Millie caught a glimpse of a narrow fishy face and a mouth filled with sharp teeth. A moment later the creature was racing away, leaving Coral screaming, "Stop! No! Come back here!" She swam off a little way, then rushed back to say, "A barracuda stole my narwhal tusk! I'll be back as soon as I can!" And then she was gone in a flurry of thrashing tail and tattered seaweed.

"I feel like we should go help her, but—," said Millie.

"She'll be fine," Audun told her. "We have something more important to do now. I've visited Nastia Nautica's shipwreck before, so I know the way."

"So do I," said Shelton. "It's over there."

Millie had forgotten that he was riding on her back ridge, and she curled her neck around to look at him. He was pointing straight ahead with one of his claws while holding on to her ridge with the other.

Audun looked annoyed. "I know. I told you I've been there before."

"Dragons have a fantastic sense of direction," Millie said, glancing back at Shelton. "For instance, Greater Greensward is that way." She pointed over her shoulder, then turned and pointed off to the right. "And the island where you grew up is that way."

The little crab climbed to the top of her ridge for a better look. "How do you know?" he asked. "Can you see that far?"

Millie shook her head. "We just know. Isn't there anything you know without seeing it?"

"Lots of things," said the little crab. "Like I know when Octavius is pretending he's mad and when he really is mad. And I know when I'm about to start molting. I should start in a few days. That's when I'll have to hide from that lousy butler."

The dragons swam with confidence, even when they had to change direction to get around a large rocky outcropping. When they finally emerged from the seaweed, they could see the shipwreck only a dozen yards away.

They approached the shipwreck slowly and without speaking. Eels slipped through gaping holes in the wooden walls. A large, flat, diamond-shaped creature swam past, dragging a whiplike tail behind it. Two small sharks circled overhead, leaving when they spotted the dragons.

"The last time I was here, Nastia Nautica was in a room at the back of the ship," said Audun.

Millie swam with him to the flattened stern and peered in the hole that had once been a window. Old sea chests sat against the walls alongside a wooden desk covered in barnacles. Tiny fish swam around and around in a tall, narrow glass jar that rested on the desk. A crooked bed occupied the corner, the bedding long gone. In the center of the room a high-backed chair faced the window, the perfect spot for someone to sit and watch the creatures of the sea swim by.

"She isn't here," said Millie.

"Maybe she's in another part of the ship," Audun said. "There was a big hole in the side. We can look in there."

They swam around the ship and peeked into the biggest hole, but there was nothing there except barnacles and a few fish that darted away. Peering into the other holes proved no more productive, and they wound up going to the far side of the hulk, where it rested at an angle on the ocean floor. When they peered through a small hole, they saw a big space with rotting barrels and crates jumbled on one side of the slanted floor.

"This wood is really decayed," said Audun when the piece next to the opening crumbled at his touch. "We could bash our way through if we really wanted to get inside."

"And let everyone for miles around know we're here?" Millie said. "What we need is someone small who can be discreet when he sneaks in and looks around."

When the two dragons turned to look at Shelton, the little crab jerked his eyestalks back and said, "You don't mean me, do you?"

"We wouldn't dream of asking . . . ," said Millie.

"He would," Shelton said, waving his claw at Audun.

"You *did* come along to help," Audun said.

Shelton grumbled as he released his hold on Millie's ridge. He swam toward the hole, gripping the edge with his claw, then turned to look back at the dragons. "I'm going, but if anything happens to me, it's your fault. Tell me, what exactly am I supposed to look for? You don't really expect me to find Nastia Nautica lurking in the hold of the ship, do you?"

Millie shook her head. "No, but since she doesn't seem to be here, now is a good time to look around. See if you can find something that will tell us what happened to my parents and my great-aunt and great-uncle."

"They might even be in there," Audun said, poking his head in partway. "If they are, I'll bash in the side and we'll get them out before the old sea witch gets back."

"You don't think she's kept them prisoner in there, do you?" Millie asked. "Hurry, Shelton! Go see if you can find them!"

Shelton disappeared from sight, reappearing now and then as he investigated the nooks and crannies in the hold. He swam back a few minutes later and said, "There's nothing here, but I saw another section up front. I'll go see what's up there."

"Hurry!" Millie urged the little crab as he swam off. "Nastia Nautica could be back any minute."

The ship creaked, making Millie back away in surprise. "Is it about to fall apart?" she asked Audun.

"Don't worry," he said. "Wrecks always make noises like that."

"But this one looks like it's in awfully bad shape."

Audun stepped back to take a long look at the hull. "It's been here for years and will probably be here for many more to come. Unless there's an earthquake or something, I don't think—"

"Come quick," Shelton said, so excited that his voice was little more than a squeak. "I found the sea monster in the front part of the hold. We'll find a way for you to get in and . . . Oh yeah. That'll work, too," Shelton added as Audun turned and pulled his tail to the side.

There was a loud boom as the dragon hit the hull with his tail, rocking the ship and creating a hole big enough for an enormous shark or a medium-sized dragon to pass through. Some of the debris rained down around Millie and some flew back into the hold, covering the tops of the barrels and crates. There wasn't room for them to swim side by side, so Millie held on to Audun's tail ridge as he

116

swam the length of the hold. He knocked aside everything that got in his way, shattering crates and barrels that had stayed intact over all the years that the ship had sat at the bottom of the ocean. Millie swam through clouds of sour-tasting pickle juice and long-fermented wine, around broken pottery and maggoty bread. When they reached the far end, Audun turned to face her in the cramped space and swung his tail as best he could, bashing another hole in the wall.

At first Audun's body blocked her view, but when he moved farther into the next room she could see the sea monster as well. It was just as Cadmilla had described it, with its warty body, three flippers, and tentacles with leaf-shaped tips. What the witch hadn't mentioned was that it was bigger than four dragons Audun's size put together and that it had two soulful-looking eyes like a puppy. Despite its size, the monster didn't look the least bit threatening as it lay cowering under Audun's fearsome glare.

"What did you do with the Green Witch and her family?" Audun roared.

The sea monster shrank back as if it had been struck. Its sacklike body quivered, sending ripples from one end to the other. "Urp!" belched the monster.

"Don't play innocent with me!" said Audun. "I know you've been terrorizing an island of witches. What did you do with the Green Witch?"

When Audun took a step closer, the sea monster fled to the wall, its flippers carrying it in an uneven rush to a hole no bigger than an ordinary loaf of bread. Squeezing one flipper through the hole, it oozed out, dragging its weight until it plopped through on the other side. Audun rushed to the wall with Millie close behind, but the monster was already swimming like a sea slug as it undulated out of sight.

"Should I go after it?" Audun asked.

"I don't think there's much point," said Millie. "I don't think it's fearsome enough to have attacked the witches on its own. Nastia Nautica must have been controlling it. She's the one we have to find."

Shelton had climbed back onto Millie's ridge. "Maybe Coral knows where else you could look," he said.

"We can go ask," Audun said with a sigh.

They were leaving the gloom of the wreck when Millie had the strongest feeling that something was watching them. She glanced back at the ship but didn't see anything peering out. The seaweed could have held an army of sea creatures, but nothing was making itself obvious. "I think something is here with us, but I don't see anything," she told Audun in a whisper.

"I do," he said, looking at the ground beside the ship.

Millie's eyes opened wide. Black lines that she had thought were cracks in the ground seemed to be wiggling. She rubbed her eyes with her front foot and looked again. The lines were coming closer, and as they drew nearer, they seemed to widen and take on features that . . . Millie realized with a start that they were sea snakes—

hundreds and hundreds of sea snakes. She watched as they rose up from the ground and swam toward them.

Millie backed away, ready to flee, but when Audun didn't move, she turned to him and stopped, her mouth hanging open. The snakes were swarming around him, making happy little sounds.

Audun looked just as happy to see them. "Hello, my friends! It's good to see you again, but why are there so many of you?"

"We stayed here waiting for your return," said one of the sea snakes. "Our friends and relatives came to join us once they learned that you had set us free. We are here to serve you, Great One."

"I don't have the flute anymore. I thought you helped me before only because I had the flute."

"When the flute left the ocean, we could no longer protect it and the spell was broken forever," said another sea snake. "We do not wish to serve you because we have to, Great One, but because we want to. Tell us, what can we do to help you?"

"I'm looking for some humans—two men and two women," he told the sea snakes.

"We don't know if they are men or women, but we do know where there are some humans," said a snake swimming past Millie's ear.

She shrank back, but it was paying no attention to her. When she glanced at Shelton, she noticed that he was holding on to her ridge with one claw while the rest of him was hiding in his shell.

"There are humans on the island and humans in your old cave," a sea snake told Audun.

"But you shouldn't go near any of them," said another.

"The humans on the island scream and run away when we swim past."

"And no one can get near the ones in the cave. The entrance is too dangerous."

"Our cousin tried to go in and was squashed when the roof to the tunnel collapsed."

"Two other cousins went in as well. We warned them to be careful, and they were. They didn't touch the tunnel walls, but more of the roof collapsed anyway."

"They were squashed, too."

"And what about the humans inside the cave?" asked Audun.

"They yelled when the roof collapsed, which only made it fall down more."

"Thank you, my friends," Audun said. "You've been very helpful."

"We have?" said one of the sea snakes.

"Indeed," Audun told them. "You have repaid whatever debt you believe you owe me."

"But we want to serve you, Great One!"

Audun thought a minute, then said, "Then wait here for my return, but live as you would anywhere else."

"Ooh," said one of the snakes. "We can do that!"

When Millie and Audun left, the snakes were writhing with happiness. Millie couldn't get away fast enough.

Audun obviously knew where he was going when he headed for the seaweed again. "We won't have to be in here long this time," he told Millie. "The seaweed doesn't grow very far in this direction."

"I assume my parents and Grassina and Haywood are the humans in the cave," said Millie, "but that doesn't make sense. My mother, my great-aunt, and my great-uncle all have magic. Why can't they get out? Unless . . . Oh, Audun, you don't suppose they're dead, do you?"

"I don't think that at all," said Audun. "You heard what the sea snakes said about the humans shouting when the tunnel roof collapsed. The tunnel is fairly long and the cave itself had plenty of room. They should be fine. As to why they can't get out . . . Do you remember the stones Olebald brought with him and tried to hide in the dungeon under your parents' castle?"

Millie nodded. "They were the same as the stones in the roc's nest. They prevented magic from working near them."

"The stones came from this cave. I saw them on the walls when Nastia Nautica tried to trap me in there. She must have given some stones to Olebald Wizard."

"So my family can't get out because their magic doesn't work. And the sea snakes say that no one can get in without making the roof collapse," said Millie. "We're going to need something to hold up the roof. Perhaps we could get some wood from Nastia Nautica's ship."

"That wood is too rotten," Audun said. "It wouldn't be strong enough to hold up the roof and support the walls for long. No, what we need is something strong that can hold up the roof from more than one angle."

"What can we use, then?" asked Millie.

"Not what, whom. And I know just whom to ask."

Eleven

$\mathcal{I}$t didn't take long for Shelton to return to the tunnel with Octavius. "I don't know why I have to do this," the octopus grumbled. "We could still go back to the castle and wait for Coral to return. I'm sure she'll be back soon, and with her magic you could—"

"Magic doesn't work in the cave," said Audun. "Or past the entrance of the tunnel. I know. I've been in it. We need you because you have all those strong legs. How many do you have, anyway?"

"Eight, but they're tentacles, not legs," Octavius said in a quarrelsome voice.

"Start at the front of the tunnel and work your way back to where the roof is weak," said Millie.

"Just leave room for us to get past," said Audun. "We'll have to haul out all the rocks that fell from the roof."

"Is there anything else?" asked Octavius. "I mean, if you want to stand here all day telling me what to do, I'll make myself comfortable and—"

"No, no!" Audun said. "That's all. You can go now."

"And be snappy about it!" Shelton said, snapping his claws like castanets.

Octavius turned one of his eyes toward the little crab. "Watch it or I might toss you into the tunnel to see if it's safe!"

Shelton scuttled behind Millie's tallest ridge and pulled his eyestalks into his shell. "Never mind!" he said and pulled the rest of himself inside, too.

Millie could hear Octavius grumbling all the way down the tunnel. When he stopped, he called back to them, "I found the first weak spot. Here goes . . . If I put one tentacle here and another over here . . . There's one there. I'll have to twist my body like this, but I might be able to reach it if I . . ."

"What are we going to do if he can't reach them all?" Millie whispered to Audun.

"I'm not going to worry about that unless I have to," Audun told her. "Let's just hope he doesn't run out of tentacles."

"All right!" Octavius called after a few minutes. "I think I have them all. You can come in now, but don't touch the walls and don't bump me, or the whole thing might come crashing down."

Audun entered the tunnel with Millie close behind, holding on to his tail. It was nearly pitch black inside the tunnel, but Millie could see with very little light. She followed Audun's example and hunched down so that she was

124

practically crawling on her knees. And then the tunnel got narrower and she *was* crawling. "Does it get any narrower than this?" she asked Audun.

"A little," he said. "But unless it's collapsed so much that we can't get through, we should be able to fit."

"That's encouraging," Millie muttered. "Ask Octavius if he can see anyone in the cave."

"I can hear you," said the octopus. "You can talk right to me, you know. I can't see anything from here, but if I twist this way a little . . . Nope. All I can see are rocks. I can try calling if you want me to. Emma! Eadric! Grassina! Grassina's husband whose name I can't remember!"

"He's my great-uncle and his name is Haywood," said Millie.

"Yeah? Well, it doesn't really matter. No one is answering me, anyway."

"Is there an opening big enough for Shelton to fit through? Maybe he can see inside the cave."

"Unh-unh," Shelton said. "You're not getting me to go up there until the opening is big enough for you. I'm not getting trapped in a cave when the tunnel collapses!"

Millie sighed. She was growing more anxious by the minute.

The sound of rock scraping on rock reached her ears. A moment later Audun pushed a pile of stones to her. Without letting go of his tail, she shoved the stones back with her feet, wishing she had longer legs to shove the rubble out of the tunnel. She glanced back to see how far from the entrance she had to carry them and saw something moving in the near dark.

"We have come to help, oh friend of the Great One," said a sea snake.

"In what way may we assist you?" asked another.

"Can you drag these stones out of the tunnel?" Millie asked, tapping the rubble with her hind foot.

"Yesss," a group of them said at once.

"Who are you talking to?" asked Octavius.

"Sea snakes," Millie replied.

Stones clattered up ahead as if Octavius had shifted. "I hate sea snakes," he said just loud enough for Millie to hear.

Millie would have loved to watch to see how the sea snakes moved the rubble, but Audun was already passing more rocks to her. She passed them on, then the bigger rocks that he shoved back one at a time. When Audun crept forward, she did, too, and the whole process started over. No matter how far they moved into the tunnel, the snakes were right there behind her, clearing away the rocks.

After what seemed like hours, Audun reached Octavius and began to inch past him. Millie heard only bits and pieces of their muttered comments to one another. "If you don't move that tentacle, you're going to have only seven." "Watch where you put that thing!" "You want me to go where?" "Ow! Your scales are sharp!" "You're not nearly as slimy as I thought you were."

Millie was tired, her back ached from crouching down for so long, and she'd already broken two talons on rocks. She had tried to be patient, but worry was making her temper shorter. She wanted to snap at Audun and Octavius and tell them to hurry up, but that would just start an argument and not help anything. Finally, trying not to let her impatience show, she asked, "How far are we now? Can you see anything yet?"

"Didn't you just ask that?" said Octavius. "No, I still can't see a thing."

"But I've almost reached it," Audun told her. "I'm out of the water now. Just a few more feet . . . There," he said, half dragging Millie past the octopus and into the cave as he lurched clear of the tunnel. He reached down and drew her up to join him and they stood side by side, looking around the enormous cave. It was dark, with a dim, pale green light coming from the green stones embedded in the walls. Water lapped around their ankles as they stepped farther into the cave. The remains of plants that normally grew in seawater hung dead and limp on the walls, as if the cave had once been filled with water. A few fish swam in the water on the floor, but they darted away at the dragons' approach.

The walls of the cave were uneven and bore ledges of varying sizes. There were shapes perched on some of the ledges; some looked just like rocks, the rest . . . ?

127

"Mother?" Millie called, the word catching in her throat.

One of the shapes groaned. Another raised a hand a few inches before letting it fall back to the ledge.

"It's them!" Millie let go of Audun and sped across the cave to crouch beside one of the figures. "My father is breathing," she said and inhaled, but the air smelled stale and she found herself gasping after the first few breaths.

Shelton climbed down off her back and looked around, waving his eyestalks.

"They've used up most of the good air," Audun said, placing his hand on her shoulder. "Let's not use up the rest. We need to get them out of here before it's all gone. Grassina is breathing, too."

"And here's your mother," said Shelton, swimming through the water covering the floor of the cave.

"Are they all . . . breathing?" Millie asked, almost too afraid to say it.

"Barely," said Audun as he straightened up from beside Haywood. He pulled off the chain holding the amulet and handed it to Millie. "Here, put this on. You can take your mother and Grassina out first. I'll stay here with your father and your great-uncle."

"But you won't be able to breathe!" said Millie.

"There's a little good air left. Just don't take too long!"

"I'll be as quick as I can," said Millie. "Help me get them to the door."

With Audun's help, Millie was able to carry her nearly lifeless mother and great-aunt out of the cave and into the tunnel. It was difficult getting the two women past Octavius, but he proved to be exceedingly pliable, and after some maneuvering Millie was able to squeeze them through the narrow space.

Millie was anxious to return to the cave to get Audun and the men, but first she had to see the women to safety. Because she was wearing the amulet, both Emma and Grassina were able to breathe again and both began to get color back in their cheeks. Neither woman was conscious, however, which meant that Millie would have to lug two dead weights to the surface and drag them through the waves to dry land. Swimming with her front legs wrapped around bodies was a difficult process and took far longer than she would have liked.

She was nearing the surface when she felt the presence of something behind her. After checking to make sure that the women were still all right, she bent her neck to look down. A large figure was coming out of the darker reaches of the water; at first Millie couldn't tell what it was. It wasn't until she saw an old mermaid with dark eyes like bottomless pits and wild, nearly translucent hair that she realized it was Nastia Nautica, and the blob that kept changing shape beneath her was the sea monster.

Millie curled her lip in a dragonish snarl. Nastia Nautica had already tried to kill members of Millie's family; she wasn't about to give the sea witch a second chance. Thrashing her tail as hard as she could, she swept her hind legs back in a powerful swoop and shot through the water, carrying Emma and Grassina into the open air. She tried to open her wings with their usual snap, but the water slowed her so that she fell back with a splash.

Something latched on to Millie's ankle and she shook her leg; whatever was holding on to her was strong, and it began to drag her toward the ocean floor. She glanced down and saw one of the sea monster's tentacles wrapped around her ankle.

Emma stirred in her daughter's grasp as the sea witch laughed with glee. "This is even better than I planned!" Nastia Nautica chortled. "Give the witch hope of escape, then take it away again. I'd heard the Green Witch's daughter could turn into a dragon, but I never thought I'd catch her, too! Swim, you misbegotten son of a monster's worst dream!" she screamed, prodding the sea monster with a curved whalebone. "We'll stuff them back in the cave and shut the entrance for good!"

Millie looked down again as she jerked her leg back and forth, trying to get rid of the tentacle. The sea monster held on, but it seemed reluctant to yank at Millie. Each time it hesitated, however, Nastia Nautica used the whalebone prod, poking the monster between its sad-looking eyes. Wincing from the blow, the sea monster tugged on Millie again.

"Millie?" Emma said, her voice so faint that her daughter almost missed it. "Is that you?"

"Don't worry, Mother," Millie told her. "Everything will be all right."

Even as the sea monster dragged Millie down into the ocean's depths, she was thinking about something else entirely. She thought about the Dragon Olympics and how she had come in second after Flame Snorter, Ralf's mother, the previous month. She thought about how it felt when fire burned hot in her belly and flame scorched her throat. She thought about what it was like to aim the flame at one point, narrowing it so that it shot in a straight line that nothing could extinguish. And then Millie arched her neck to look down at the still-laughing sea witch, and she flamed.

A tongue of fire shot from between the dragon's puckered lips, aiming straight for the sea witch. The flame lit up the depths as water boiled around it. Nastia Nautica screamed and turned the sea monster so the fire hit it instead. The monster shrieked—an unearthly sound that seemed to echo in Millie's ears long after it ended. Blisters appeared on its shapeless body and it writhed, letting go of Millie's leg and sending Nastia Nautica tumbling. The sea witch screamed and once again Emma stirred in Millie's arms.

Pulling herself upright, Emma cleared her throat. She pointed at the flailing sea witch and said, "Now it's my turn."

Spin around and spin around
Then rise into the air
Form a twirling tower
That will whisk away the pair
Carry them across the sea
To a place no human dwells
Where crashing waves will keep them
    trapped
Beneath the rising swells

Water began to swirl around the sea witch and the monster, catching them up and twirling them in an ever-rising circle, which lengthened, becoming a water spout. Millie backed away to watch the spout grow as it pulled more water into its spiral. Within seconds it had reached the surface and rose into the air, carrying Nastia Nautica and her monster with it. The monster cried out, a plaintive sound that tore at Millie. She turned her head aside, not wanting to see the look in the monster's eyes as the water spout rose higher until it disappeared from sight.

"Are they gone?" asked Shelton, peeking out from behind Millie's tallest ridge.

Millie smiled. She hadn't realized that Shelton was there, but she was delighted to see him. "Yes, they're gone, thanks to my mother. But I have a job for you now. Take this amulet to Audun," she said, pulling the chain off over her head.

"Tell him that we're fine and we're waiting for him here. Hurry! They didn't have much air left."

Shelton sighed and snagged the chain with his claw. "Why do I get all the dangerous jobs?" he said and turned to swim away.

Twelve

When Audun broke the surface of the water hauling Eadric and Haywood, who were pale but very much alive, Millie was sure they'd all be able to start back to Greater Greensward soon. The humans were still dazed and disoriented, so she and Audun shouldered their burdens and turned to the distant palm trees barely visible on the horizon. While the two dragons carried the humans toward the island, their lashing tails propelling them through the waves, Millie thought about what to do next. They'd go to the island, and she'd give her parents a few minutes to rest before telling them about Felix. Then they'd all go home, find Felix, and everything would be back to normal.

As they dragged themselves out of the water and onto the beach, she told Audun that they'd be leaving soon and that he needn't bother changing into his human form. Unfortunately, the four former captives were exhausted, ill, hungry, and desperately thirsty, so Millie waited as the old witches swarmed around them, offering them food and drink. When Millie tried to talk to her mother, Rugene shooed her away, saying that her parents needed to rest. Half an hour later, the women were still fussing over them, making sure that they had enough to drink and eat and were comfortable sitting on the witches' own feather mattresses dredged up from the nearly repaired ruins of their cottages.

Millie could scarcely sit still. She could feel the all-too-precious time trickling away like the sand she scooped from the beach where she sat beside Audun.

"Octavius feels terrible about what he did," said Audun, interrupting Millie's thoughts. "He told me so while we were waiting for you to come back."

"Why would he feel terrible? Without him we never could have gone through the tunnel to get them out," Millie said.

"He tried to talk us into waiting for Coral. If we had listened to him, all four of them might have died."

Millie shrugged. Any other time she might have worried about Octavius's feelings, but right now something else caused her far more concern. "But we didn't wait, so it worked out all right," she said. "He doesn't need to feel bad. I, however, feel lousy, and I don't see you worrying about me. I know that what you said was true—my mother asked me to watch over Greater Greensward *and* Felix, and I couldn't possibly be in both places at once, but I can't help feeling that I was still responsible. I was supposed to keep an eye on him and—"

135

"Do all humans fret this much?" asked Audun. "Dragons are much more sensible creatures. We don't dwell on what we did or didn't do, or at least not in our saner moments."

Millie's breath escaped with a gasp. "My brother was kidnapped by a lunatic and here you are calling me crazy! I can't believe that you would say such a—"

Audun shook his head even as he interrupted her. "I never called you crazy, nor did I mean to imply that you—"

"I'm not so sure about that," said Millie. "This is the second time you've told me how much better dragons are than humans. If that's really the way you feel, maybe we don't belong together. Maybe it's a good thing we haven't finished planning our wedding. Maybe we shouldn't have a wedding at all!"

Audun reached for her, his eyes stricken. "Millie, you can't mean that."

"I'm not sure if I do or not," she said, pulling away. "If you'll excuse me, I'm going to go try to talk to my parents again."

Millie walked away with her back stiff and her head held high. She was still upset as she worked her way through the group of witches to Emma, who must have seen the expression on her face because she stepped forward when Cadmilla tried to intercept the young dragoness. "Thank you for your hospitality," said Emma, "but I need to talk to my daughter."

Millie had thought long and hard about how she would tell her parents that their baby had been kidnapped. She'd wanted to break the news to them gently, but now, when she actually had to tell them, all she could do was blurt out, "I know you're tired and have gone through a terrible ordeal, but we have to go. I came looking for you because Olebald Wizard kidnapped Felix and took him to Soggy Molvinia."

Emma gasped and her hand flew to her mouth. She swayed until Eadric came up behind her and put his arm around her waist. "What's this about Felix?" he asked.

"Olebald Wizard kidnapped him," Millie said again. "He took him to Soggy Molvinia and turned him into a frog. The fairy Raindrop helped us follow him there, but he'd already released Felix into the marsh, where he's with a billion other frogs. Francis, Oculura, Dyspepsia, and Azuria are all looking for Felix, but Audun and I came to get you because I was sure that you would know what to do."

Eadric nodded and pulled Emma closer. "You did the right thing. We'll go there straightaway. Your mother can find anything, can't you, Emma?"

"Yes, but my baby! How could anyone do such a horrible thing? And of all the times for this to happen, why did Olebald have to do it now?"

"I think he was in league with Nastia Nautica," said Audun, who had come up behind Millie. He set his talons on Millie's shoulder and gave it a gentle squeeze. "They must have planned it together. She lured you away and trapped you in her cave while he kidnapped Felix. Who knows what else he has in mind?"

"That's right," Millie told them as she twitched her shoulder out from under Audun's touch and took a step away from him. "When Olebald brought the roc to Greater Greensward and tried to tear down the castle last year, he had green stones with him like the ones in Nastia Nautica's cave. If he got the stones from her, he must have known her for some time."

"We have to get to Soggy Molvinia as soon as possible," said Eadric.

"I have a spell that could carry us there in an instant, but it won't work on all six of us," Emma said.

"You two go, and take Grassina and Haywood," said Millie. "Audun and I will fly back. It won't take us long as dragons."

"We'll do that," said Emma, "but hurry. Olebald has obviously been planning this for a while. It sounds as if he's already wielded more powerful magic than I've ever seen him use before. I don't know if I'll be able to undo his spell. If that's the case, we're all going to be searching the marsh for Felix."

❧

Millie and Audun left the island just as her mother raised her hand and waved it in the air. In the next instant, the magic carpets and their riders vanished. The dragons turned and headed toward Soggy Molvinia, flying without talking for the first few miles. "I didn't mean that you were crazy," said Audun, finally breaking the silence. "I just wish you'd stop worrying so much. Worrying never helped anyone."

"But my baby brother has been turned into a frog!"

"I know, and we're going to take care of it. You've already done so much. You discovered that Olebald took Felix and that he put him in the marsh. You've also found your parents, and now they're on their way back to the marsh. No one blames you for any of this."

"My mother might, when she really thinks about it," said Millie.

Audun quirked one eye ridge at her. "Do you really think so? From what I know of your mother, she's a very practical person. I think she'd be the last one to blame you for what happened to Felix. Now, I've never met her, but I'd bet that your grandmother Frazzela would be happy to blame you, especially when you're a dragon."

Millie laughed. "Yes, and your grandmother Song of the Glacier would probably blame me when I'm a human. I don't know what we're going to do if they both show up for the wedding."

"You mean there is going to be a wedding even after I stuck my talons in my mouth?" Audun said.

"Yes, there will be a wedding," Millie said, smiling. "Everybody says things they don't mean when they're upset."

Audun looked relieved. "I know, and you were upset even before—"

"I wasn't talking about me!" said Millie. "You're the one who said what he shouldn't have. Just don't do it again," she added with a warning look.

When Audun closed his mouth with a snap, Millie couldn't help but smile.

They made good time flying over the ocean, but as they approached the shore, they saw dark, ominous-looking clouds looming over the land. "We could go around," Audun said as lightning split the sky only a few miles in front of them.

Millie shook her head. The clouds stretched as far as she could see in both directions. "It looks like an awfully big storm. Going around would take too long."

"We can try to go above the storm, although those clouds look enormous."

"Then we'll just have to go higher," said Millie.

Flying wingtip to wingtip, she and Audun spiraled upward, trying to gain altitude without entering the clouds. As the storm drew nearer, the air became rougher, buffeting them back and forth until Millie felt sick to her stomach.

"Just a little higher," said Audun, yet the clouds appeared to go on forever.

Millie looked around as lightning crashed so close that the air seemed to sizzle. The clouds surrounded them on all sides; when she looked up again, what had been clear sky above them was dark and ominous.

"I don't like this," Millie said, watching the clouds above them grow thicker.

"I don't, either," said Audun. "Let's get out of here. How fast can you fly?"

"At least as fast as you!" Millie told him.

They raced—first the lightning, then the torrential rain, and then, after they passed through the storm and out the other side, they raced each other. Neither one was faster, and they didn't stop until they had passed the border into Soggy Molvinia and the marsh lay just ahead.

"We're almost there," Millie said, glancing down at the first of the ponds that riddled the marshy land. Puddles, ponds, lakes of all sizes, and the thin ribbon of land that wound between them made patterns of light and dark in the pale haze of morning. If it hadn't been for their dragon senses, they might have become lost in minutes, but they flew on, landing on the same hillock where they'd spoken with Olebald Wizard.

When they'd left, three witches had been searching for Felix. Oculura, Dyspepsia, and Azuria were still there, along with Emma, Eadric, Grassina, Haywood, and another witch named Mudine. Oculura and Dyspepsia were stomping around the edge of puddles and ponds, poking through the mud as they looked for frogs, while everyone else was gathered around Emma and Eadric. The two dragons changed back into their human form before approaching the group, and Millie was about to call to her mother when the air sparkled in front of them and the Swamp Fairy appeared.

"I found some more," she said, jerking her thumb at two bewildered men who had appeared behind her. They were well dressed, although their clothes were out of date and didn't seem to fit very well. One crouched down into a squatting position and the other shivered and looked around, apparently too stunned to move.

"Let me question them before they join the others," said Eadric, breaking free from the group surrounding Emma. He noticed Millie and Audun then, and his lips shaped themselves into a weary smile. "There you are. We were beginning to worry about you. Before you ask—no, no luck so far. Talk to your mother, Millie, so she can fill you in."

Millie nodded. "I will, but first tell me, where's Francis? He said he was going to come here to help search for Felix."

"He was here," said Azuria, "but a fairy came to get him. She said he was needed at home. They went back to Greater Greensward together, and we haven't seen him since."

"That's odd," Millie muttered as she went to join her mother.

Emma looked even more tired than Eadric, with dark circles under her eyes and her brow etched with worry lines. She glanced up as the witches made room for Millie and Audun to pass. "I'm glad you're here," she said, running her fingers through her hair, making it messier than before. "I've tried everything I can think of, including the spell that I used to find Haywood when he was an otter, but none of my locator spells have done what they should and my summoning spells have been worthless. There were some other princes here, as you can see." She waved her hand at a group of men huddled together on another hillock. They looked as bewildered and just as out of place as the two the Swamp Fairy had found. "Unfortunately, Felix wasn't among them. Your father has been questioning the princes, but none of them know anything about my baby boy. There's only one thing left to try," said Emma. "I'll have to go look for him as a frog."

"Not without me, you're not," said Eadric from behind the witches. He worked his way through the group and took Emma's hand. "I've spent more time as a frog than you have. I know how to get other frogs to talk to me."

"And I'm going, too," Millie told them both. "He's my baby brother and I was in charge while you were gone."

"Actually," said Eadric, "you and Francis were in charge of magical problems. It was your grandparents who—"

"Yes, you can go," Emma said. "But stay near us. I don't want to lose both my children in this marsh."

"I can go, too," said Haywood. "Just turn me back into an otter and I can find any frog!"

"If you were an otter, you'd scare away every frog for miles around and we'd never find my baby," said Emma.

"Thank you for the offer, but I'd rather you stayed here and helped Grassina coordinate the witches' search. You could keep all the predators out of the marsh, too. The last thing we need is for a real otter to eat one of us while we're looking for Felix."

"Are you sure?" asked Haywood. "I could keep the other predators away better if I were an otter. Turn me back and I'll stay away from the frogs. I'd turn myself back, but I never did perfect the spell."

"I can't believe I'm saying this, but I'll turn you into an otter, Haywood," said Grassina. "Just be careful and stay out of the way."

Millie had never been a frog before. She was a human most of the time and she loved being a dragon, but it had never occurred to her to try anything else. Turning into a dragon had never made her nervous or anxious. Now, however, the thought of turning into a frog made her stomach churn, and she began to wonder if she was doing the right thing.

"Where should we look first?" Eadric asked Emma.

"I'm not sure," she replied. "That big pond over there looks promising, or we could try this one."

"We should try the one on the other side of that little hill where Audun and I met Olebald," said Millie. "I have a feeling about that pond."

Audun glanced at her, then turned to her parents and said, "You should trust her feelings. She's developing good dragoness intuition that has proven to be right more often than not."

"But she's not a dragoness now," said Eadric.

"Millie is a mixture of dragon and human," Audun said. "It seems the line between what she can do when she's one or the other is getting a little blurred."

"That pond is as good as the next," said Emma. "I think we should go with Millie's choice. Audun, I'd appreciate it if you could help Haywood keep the predators away."

Audun smiled, but he didn't look happy. "As the biggest predator around here, I'd say I'm very qualified for the job, but I can probably do it better from the air."

After trudging across the narrow strip of land connecting one hillock to another, Millie and her parents took up positions facing one another. "We should hold hands so the spell includes the three of us," said Emma. "Now, be friendly when you meet other frogs, so they'll talk to you. We're more likely to find Felix quickly if the frogs who live here are helping us."

Millie was already reaching for her parents' hands when the air shimmered around Audun and he changed into a dragon. She turned back to face her parents when her mother began the spell.

Green of skin,
And long of tongue,

With strong bespeckled feet.
Turn us into
Three fine frogs
That others want to meet.

Perhaps turning back and forth between human and dragon so often had made it easy for Millie, but for whatever reason, there was no pain or discomfort, and it happened so fast that she didn't think it had happened at all until she glanced down and saw that she was green and smooth and much smaller than either of her other usual forms. She blinked in surprise as her mother patted her hand with long green fingers.

"Follow us while you practice swimming," Emma told Millie. "I don't want to have to look for you, too." Then taking one hop backward and twisting her body halfway around, Emma jumped into the water with a tiny splash.

Millie shook her head in disbelief. Her mother knew that she could swim perfectly well as a human and even better as a dragon. Millie had been doing it for years and— She fell flat on her face, her long, thin feet tangled together. "Ow!" she exclaimed, rubbing the spot where she normally had a nose. Millie tried again, tugging until she'd freed her feet, then moved them carefully, one slow step at a time.

"It's not as easy as it looks, is it?" said her father. "Don't worry, you'll get it soon enough. Your mother didn't catch on right away, and neither did I, for that matter." He turned to look out over the water and frowned. "Where did she go? I'd better go find her. We'll meet you in the middle of the pond." Her father's splash was even smaller than her mother's.

Millie thought about hopping the way her parents had, but she couldn't manage more than a stumbling lurch. She ended up walking flat-footed to the water, then inching her way in until she was waist deep. Stretching her arms in front of her, she belly flopped into the water and kicked her feet. Her long legs felt awkward and uncomfortable, and she didn't go far.

Someone nearby began to laugh, a deep-throated sound that managed to seem good natured, even though Millie was sure the person was laughing at her. "I've never seen anyone do it that way," said a big bullfrog popping up beside her. "It helps if you bend your legs. No," he said when Millie tried, "not like that. Like this!"

Millie watched as the frog bent his legs to the side and straightened them with a thrusting motion. He sped past, waving at her with one hand. "I can do that!" Millie murmured, bringing her feet closer to her body. She kicked the way she'd seen the bullfrog do and was delighted when she actually moved forward.

"You're funny!" said a little frog as it swam circles around her.

"She's new," another, slightly larger frog said.

"What pond did you come from?" asked the little frog. "Are you going to live here now?"

"Actually, I'm just visiting," Millie began. "I'm looking for my brother. Have any of you met a frog named Felix? He's been here just a few days."

A crowd of frogs had gathered around her, bobbing in the water so that all she could see were their heads, which looked very odd when they all shook them saying "No."

"Two other frogs just got here, but nobody came before them," said the bullfrog. "Maybe your brother is in another pond."

"Maybe," said Millie. "But I have a feeling he's here somewhere."

One of the frogs giggled and splashed Millie. "Did you hear that? She has a feeling!"

"I have a lot of feelings," said another. "But that doesn't mean anything is going to happen."

"I just meant that something is telling me he's here. I'd appreciate it if you could all keep your eyes open for a little frog named Felix."

"She wants us to keep our eyes open. As if we don't already! Who says things like that?"

"She's with those humans clomping around in the shallows," said a female frog as she joined the group. "They took my boyfriend! We were sitting down to a nice mosquito snack when *zap*—he turned into a great galumphing human! He always said he was a prince, but I thought he was crazy like Peto. That fool claims he's really a snapping turtle, although I can almost believe *him*."

148

A froggy face rose above the back of the crowd and grinned evilly at Millie. He opened his mouth and snapped it shut with a loud *clack*. Even Millie could see how much he resembled a snapping turtle.

"I'm sorry they took your friend, but if he was a prince, he didn't really belong here," Millie told the female frog. "We'll all leave as soon as we find my brother. He's just a baby, you see, and can't take care of himself yet."

"A baby, you say? You should have mentioned that right away," said the bullfrog. "Baby frogs aren't frogs. Well, they are, but that's not what we call them. We call them little squirts, although I've heard them called polliwogs and tadpoles."

"I like 'polliwogs' the best," said the little frog. "It feels funny in my mouth when I say it."

Millie was so stunned that she let her legs drop straight down and she began to sink. She came back up spluttering and wiping the water from her eyes. "I never thought of that!" she said. "But it makes a lot of sense! I have to tell my parents. Thank you so much!" She started to swim away, then stopped abruptly and came back. "Where exactly would I find these polliwogs?"

"They swim in big groups in the shallows," said the little frog.

"Thanks again!" Millie shouted as she started toward the middle of the pond.

"I said they're in the shallows," the little frog shouted after her. "You're going the wrong way!"

149

"I have to tell my parents first," Millie called over her shoulder.

"Suit yourself. Just watch out for Old Gray. He hangs out in the middle of the pond until the sun gets high."

Swimming as a frog still wasn't easy for Millie, but she tried the bend-and-kick style and found she actually made some progress with it. Every now and then she raised her head to look around and make sure that she was still headed where she wanted to go. Finally, she chanced to look down as well and saw a shadow following her.

Unfortunately, it wasn't her own shadow.

"What is that?" she wondered out loud and stuck her face in the water for a better look. The shadow moved closer until she was able to see that it was a fish, not a shadow at all. It was hard to judge how far away the fish was or how big it might be, but Millie remembered the little frog's warning about Old Gray and decided that she really didn't want to learn any more about him.

She tried to swim faster, pulling her legs closer and kicking harder, and began to move at a better pace. Even so, when she glanced back down, she saw that the fish was drawing nearer and looked more threatening than before. Millie tried to swim faster still, but she had already been doing the best she could and he continued to come closer. Her heart pounded and her limbs felt like they were on fire when she realized that the fish was rising to the surface and was only inches behind her.

"Help!" she screamed. There was a *whoosh* and something enormous tore out of the sky. Millie shrieked and shot ahead as Audun plucked the fish from the water. "Thank you!" she shouted once she realized that it was him and that he held the flopping fish in his talons.

"No problem," said Audun. "I was hungry, anyway."

"Millie, are you all right?" her mother shouted, and she saw both of her parents swimming toward her, their eyes big with concern.

"I'm better than all right," she told them, "because I know where we might be able to find Felix." Her eyes shone as she told them about her conversation with the frogs, and by the time she had finished they were already swimming to the shallows.

They swam through the cattails edging the shallower water calling "Felix!" but for the longest time they didn't see anything that even resembled a tadpole. "Maybe I was wrong and he is in a different pond," Millie finally said.

"We're not giving up yet," her father told her with an encouraging smile.

Millie ducked when a blackbird darted overhead, and she bumped into something small and soft. A tadpole looked up at her with curious eyes before scooting off through a stand of water iris. Millie followed, pushing aside the iris as she forced her way through, and swam into the midst of the largest group of tadpoles she'd ever seen.

Startled, the tadpoles darted away, moving together like one much larger entity.

"I found them!" Millie shouted, and her parents hurried over to meet her.

"Felix!" called Emma as she drew alongside the tadpoles.

"Are you there, Felix?" his father called.

Millie glanced from one tadpole to another and shook her head. "It's impossible to tell them apart."

"It is, isn't it? And none of them answers to 'Felix,'" said Emma.

"Maybe we should try something else," Millie said. "He's ticklish when he's human. Do you think he might be ticklish as a tadpole, too?"

Emma smiled. "What a good idea! When I was a frog, Grassina tickled me and knew who I was by my laugh. I doubt any real tadpole would laugh like Felix. You start at that end of the group and I'll start at this end. Eadric, can you work your way out from the cattails?"

"How will we know which ones we've checked already?" asked Millie. "I know some have little legs and some are bigger than others, but I don't think I can keep them all straight."

"Dab some mud on each one after you tickle it," said Eadric. "Unless you can think of a better way to mark them."

"Mud sounds good to me," said Millie, bending down to get a big glob.

Although Millie thought that tickling tadpoles might be fun, she changed her mind after the first few. Some tadpoles squirmed to get away, but most of them just gave the frogs bored looks and swam off. An hour had gone by and her froggy fingers were sore when a dark shape shot out of the deeper water, scattering the tadpoles in every direction.

"Hello!" said Haywood, his otter mouth grinning. "I came to see how you were doing."

Millie didn't know a frog could look as angry as her mother looked just then. "We were doing fine until you came and chased all the polliwogs away!" Emma said, her froggy eyes bulging even more than usual.

Haywood looked confused. "What do polliwogs have to do with . . . Oh, I get it. You think Felix is a polliwog now! That makes sense because—"

"We can talk about it later," snapped Emma. "Right now I want you to get those polliwogs back. Go on, round them up and send them back here."

Haywood ducked his head like a little boy who'd just been scolded. "Sorry," he muttered. "I didn't know. I'll see what I can do." He swam off and in less than two minutes a flood of tadpoles surrounded the three frogs.

"How did he do it that fast?" asked Millie as she reached for a tadpole.

"He probably used magic," her mother said, trying to tickle two tadpoles at once. "Small magic has always been his specialty."

Millie gazed out over the sea of tadpoles that didn't show any sign of leaving. "He must have sent us every tadpole in the pond."

"Good," said Eadric. "Then Felix should be here somewhere."

Millie was getting sick of the sight, smell, and feel of tadpoles when her father finally tickled one that chortled with glee. Eadric called Emma and Millie over to see the tadpole. They recognized Felix's laugh even before they saw him and were both grinning when they gave the little creature a froggy hug.

"Now we have to get him to shore without losing him again," said Emma as they all tried to hold on to the squirmy tadpole. "The problem is, we have to keep him in water until I can change us back. I'm afraid I'll drop him if I try to hold him while I change."

Eadric looked around until he noticed a depression in the mud at the edge of the pond. "We can trap him in a puddle," he said. "Millie, come help me. We'll build up the sides so he can't get out."

"Hurry!" said Emma with her arms wrapped around the tadpole. "I won't be able to hold him for long. He's too slippery!"

Working as fast as they could, Millie and her father splashed water into the depression, then slapped mud around the edges, building them high enough to keep in even the most determined tadpole. When it was ready, they helped Emma lug the wiggly little creature over the mud wall and dump him into his own private puddle. Millie glanced at her parents and laughed. They were covered in mud, and so was she.

"Step back, everyone!" said Emma. "I'm going to turn us back first, and we don't want to step on Felix."

Millie scrambled out of the water, adding another layer of mud to her arms and legs. The three of them moved away from the pond and took hold of one another's hands again. The spell that Emma used was one Millie had heard before, only this time it applied to her, too.

> Turn us into that which we
> Long ago were meant to be.
> Make us human once again
> From head to toe and bone to skin.

Once they were human again, they stood beaming at one another for a moment before turning to look at the tadpole they were sure was Felix.

Emma knelt down beside the puddle to recite another spell.

> An evil man has turned my babe
> Into a polliwog.
> Change him back to the boy I love,
> A human, not a frog.

Millie waited, expecting the air to shimmer or lights to sparkle or something that would show the spell was working. Nothing happened, however, and the tadpole continued to swim in his little puddle.

"What's going on?" asked Oculura as the witches gathered around.

"Felix was turned into a tadpole, not a fully developed frog," said Emma. "I tried to turn him back, but my spell didn't work."

"Maybe you didn't say it right," said Dyspepsia.

"Mother always says it right and her spells always work," Millie told her. "Something else is wrong."

"Let me try," said Azuria.

Millie stepped aside as one witch after another tried to change the tadpole back. Standing by the pond, she let her mind wander. The pond had felt right, and now the tadpole felt right. That was Felix, she was sure of it. Whatever wasn't right wasn't anything they had done, it was Olebald. It had to be.

"Mother," said Millie. "Didn't you tell me that normally only the witch who cast a spell can undo it?"

Emma glanced at her and sighed. "Usually, yes, although I've been able to undo most witches' spells ever since I became a dragon friend. I was hoping that I could do it now as well, but it isn't working. The only one who can undo this spell is Olebald Wizard. We're going to have to find him."

Thirteen

They were flying over the enchanted forest when Millie slowed the beat of her wings so she could talk to her mother. Emma was riding on her magic carpet with Eadric, cradling the glass bowl that Grassina had created out of an old spell, a leaf, and a blob of mud. Pond water sloshed in the bowl, and the little tadpole swimming in the water sloshed with it.

Her mother was murmuring something to Felix when Millie appeared beside her. Emma glanced at Millie, then at Eadric, who was snoring softly, his head lolling at an angle. "My poor darling," said Emma. "He's exhausted. But then we all are today."

"Mother, I have to ask you, isn't your spell supposed to take us to Olebald?"

Emma was only half paying attention to Millie when she answered, "What's that, dear? Oh yes, that's right."

"But it looks as if we're going home," Millie told her. "I can already see the castle beyond the trees."

157

Emma frowned and looked up. "That's not possible," she said, her cheeks paling when she saw the castle. "This isn't good. It can mean one of two things; either my spell didn't work, or Olebald is here in Greater Greensward. I don't know which would be worse."

"If he's here, at least we won't have to go looking for him," said Millie.

᳀

They made a strange procession as they approached the castle: two dragons, two magic carpets each bearing a man and a woman, and four witches on broomsticks. Gliding over the battlements, they were aiming for the courtyard, but they seemed to hit an invisible barrier in turn and bounced a little before sliding off the side like a speck of dust on a soap bubble. They all ended up outside the castle wall, looking confused.

"What's going on?" Millie asked Audun as they met in the air above the moat.

"I don't know," said Audun. "But there's your cousin, Francis. He's waving to us."

Millie spotted Francis standing by the moat dressed in his best suit of armor. It gleamed gold in the sunlight, making him hard to look at. "Good," Millie said. "He should know what's happening." She turned on a wingtip and headed toward her cousin.

"Did you find Felix?" Francis called before they were even close.

"We found him, but we still have a problem," said Millie. "He's a tadpole and we can't change him back. We need Olebald Wizard for that."

"I've been told that he's in the castle, but I haven't seen him yet," said Francis. "Grandmother and Grandfather saw him for a few minutes before I returned."

When Millie tilted her head to the side in a quizzical way, Francis sighed and said, "Perhaps I should start from the beginning. I was helping the witches look for Felix when a fairy came to tell me that my grandparents needed me here. I hurried back and found everyone outside on the road leading to the drawbridge. Olebald Wizard had used an illusion spell in the middle of the night to make it look as if the castle were on fire. Everyone, including the guards, fled the castle. Once everyone was outside, Olebald closed the drawbridge and ended his illusion. Now no one can get inside. Stand back and I'll show you something."

Millie and Audun stood well back as Francis nocked an arrow in his bow, took aim over the castle wall, and let fly. The two dragons watched as the arrow arched over the wall with a whistling sound, hit something with a *twang!* and came flying back. Francis ran to the side, but the arrow headed straight for him. He dodged to the other side and the arrow changed direction. When it looked as if he wasn't going to be able to avoid it, he turned around and braced himself. The arrow hit him in the center of his back with enough force to knock him off his feet. Millie wasn't too worried however, because she knew he'd made his armor puncture proof.

"I thought you'd given up shooting arrows over the wall, Francis," King Limelyn said as he, Queen Chartreuse, and Emma crossed the well-trodden path around the moat to join them. The king acknowledged Audun with a single nod and patted Millie on her scaly cheek. "I'm glad you're back. Your mother told me about Felix. Did Francis tell you what Olebald Wizard has done here?'

"He did," said Millie. "Francis also said that you saw Olebald, but no one has seen him since."

"After he closed the drawbridge, he came out on the wall walk to gloat," said the king. "When he saw us watching him, he did a little dance and laughed so hard he had to lean against a parapet so he didn't fall over. Then he shouted down at us, 'I've finally done it. You think you're so smart, but I'm smarter than all of you. This castle is mine now and there's nothing you can do about it.' I can't believe that the old cuss tricked us into abandoning our home without lifting a finger to stop him. That fire illusion had me convinced. It crackled and flared and looked so real!"

"You could smell it, too," said Queen Chartreuse. "That wizard is evil, but he's very good at what he does. I was terrified! Olebald is a horrible old scoundrel to have frightened us all so. Now that you're back, you must kick him out of our castle. It's disgraceful. No queen should ever be seen in public in her nightgown, but the fire started so suddenly that I didn't have time to change."

"It wasn't a real fire, my dear," said King Limelyn.

"I know," said the queen, "but I thought it was, and that's what mattered."

"Have you tried to get in through the secret passage-way yet?" asked Audun.

"It was blocked," the king told him. "My men have done everything from trying to batter the door down to hacking at it with axes. Olebald Wizard must have used magic to protect it, too. As for the walls . . . I've given up counting how many places where we've tried to scale the walls and been repelled each time, even though no one is there."

"I'll see what I can do," said Emma. "Millie, you and Audun can take a look at the secret passage while I see about the walls. There must be some way we can get inside the castle."

Millie and Audun weren't far from the secret passage, so it took them only minutes to get there. Brushing aside the concealing vegetation, they entered the tunnel and followed it back to the door. A broken ax sat propped against the wall, and the dirt floor was churned up from the passage of many feet, but the door itself was intact and looked the same as always. Banded in iron and at least a foot thick, the wooden door was meant to withstand just about anything.

Millie waited while Audun tried the latch. When he looked back at her, she raised an eye ridge and said, "I'm sure someone already did that."

Audun shrugged. "You never know," he replied. "Stand back. I'm going to try to knock it down."

"But the soldiers—"

"Aren't as strong as I am. I bet they never tried this."

Millie backed down the tunnel, leaving Audun enough room to turn around. Pulling his tail back, he let go and hit the door with a *whump*. The door shook and dust billowed through the tunnel. When Audun cried out, there was so much dust that Millie couldn't see what had happened.

"Are you all right?" she asked.

"Fine," Audun said in a grumpy voice. "My tail came back and hit me, that's all." He took a step backward and groaned. "I think I sprained it."

The dust cleared, leaving the door looking just as it had before.

"I don't understand," said Audun.

"Move aside, please," said Millie. "It's my turn now."

The two dragons squeezed past each other to change places in the narrow tunnel. Millie eyed the door, then glanced back at Audun. "On second thought, you should probably go outside. It might get awfully hot in here—not at all the place for an ice dragon."

Audun nodded. "I'll go, but I don't like leaving you alone."

"I know, and I appreciate your thoughtfulness," said Millie, and she blew him a kiss. She waited until the sound of his footsteps had died away before taking a deep breath. Millie preferred fueling her flames with gunga beans and hot flammi peppers, but she hadn't eaten any in days and her only supply was in the castle. Now when she needed her biggest flame the most, her ordinary flame would have to do. She thought about her flame even as she filled her lungs with air. It needed to be hot and last long enough to test any magic the old wizard could have used. Anything less would be a waste of her breath.

Millie held the air inside her until she could feel the flame build, then closed her second set of eyelids, stepped back, and aimed for the center of the door. Dragon fire washed over the wood long enough to turn it to ash. Flame caressed the iron bindings and thick hinges until they should have melted into pools of liquid metal. And still she flamed, willing the fire to last. And then the last bit of air left her lungs and she gasped.

Millie blinked her second lids open and examined the door. It looked just as it had before she started. The stone walls around the door glowed red, however, and when she touched one, her talon sizzled.

The fire she had blasted at the door had washed back over her. Fire didn't bother fire-breathing dragons, but she was glad Audun had left when he did. Ice dragons could get burned just like humans, although they were totally comfortable with ice.

"Princess Emma? Is that you?" called a faint voice from the other side of the door.

"No, it's her daughter, Millie!" shouted the young dragoness. "Who are you?"

"It's Sir Jarvis! Someone has done something awful to the dungeon. The ghosts can't pass through walls or doors anymore. We're trapped wherever we were at midnight last night. Poor Hubert is stuck between one cell and the next. I was fortunate enough to be in the corridor at the time. Can you come in here and do something about this?"

"I wish I could," said Millie, "but Olebald Wizard has tricked everyone into leaving the castle and we can't get back in."

"Then he's the one! That dastardly rogue! This must be his revenge for when we foiled his break-in last year."

"Or he wants to make sure you can't help us now," she replied.

"Millie!" Audun called and she could hear him approach from down the tunnel. "Is everything all right?"

"It didn't work," said Millie.

"And we ghosts are trapped!" came Sir Jarvis's muffled voice.

"Then I guess we won't be asking them for help," said Audun. "Millie, I think you should come now. I heard a lot of shouting at the front of the castle."

"I'm coming," Millie told him. She turned and yelled at the door, "Tell the other ghosts that we're trying to get in. We'll help you as soon as we can."

"Please hurry," said Sir Jarvis. "Hubert hasn't stopped moaning since he was trapped. We'd end his suffering if he weren't already dead, so now we're trying to think of a way to drown out the sound of his moans."

"I'll do what I can," Millie called over her shoulder as she started back down the tunnel.

She heard the shouting as soon as she stuck her head outside the tunnel entrance. Although she couldn't make out what they were saying, it sounded as if a large group of men were arguing. She and Audun ran down the moat path and arrived by the drawbridge just as a makeshift siege ladder, propped against the wall, began to fall backward. Soldiers clung to the ladder as their legs dangled over empty air. Millie flew up to grab hold of the ladder, but Emma was there first, and she held it still while Millie and Audun helped the men down.

"We have an idea!" Oculura shouted to the dragons. "Come talk to us."

Emma sighed. "You go, Millie. I have to see what your grandfather wants to do next. I've been trying to talk him out of digging a tunnel that would come up in the dungeon. You should thank me. He already asked me to dig it with magic, and if that doesn't work he wants you and me to use our talons, with Audun's help, of course," she said, giving the ice dragon a halfhearted smile.

"You can tell Grandfather that it wouldn't do any good," said Millie. "The ghosts are trapped in the dungeon and

I'm betting any human who ends up down there would be trapped as well."

Emma's smile widened. "I'll be sure to tell him. Maybe that will get him to stop asking. Oh dear, he's talking to Azuria now. He's probably trying to get her to do it. I'd better go. Be careful, darling. People are coming up with all sorts of ways to get into the castle, and some of them are very dangerous."

Oculura, Dyspepsia, and Mudine rushed over to Millie when she landed. All three witches were quivering with excitement. "We've had the best idea!" cried Mudine.

"It was my idea, actually," Dyspepsia hurried to say.

"No, I think it was Mudine's," said Oculura. "I think she should be the one to explain it to Millie."

Dyspepsia scowled. "Does it really matter?"

"What is this idea?" Millie asked.

"It's quite simple," said Mudine. "We think Olebald must be directing invisible servants to repel attacks from the air. They are probably looking for the more traditional siege weapons, like ladders and catapults. However, we think we could sneak in when Olebald is distracted by the catapult."

"What catapult?" Millie asked, looking around.

"The one your grandfather is building with Azuria," said Dyspepsia. "Haven't you been paying attention?"

"I've been busy," said Millie. "So how do you plan to sneak over the castle wall?"

"Millie, can you come here for a moment?" her father called.

"I'll be right there," she replied, then turned back to the three witches. "Don't go anywhere until I get back. I want to talk to you."

"Millie, it's important!" her father called again.

She hurried to where King Limelyn was standing with her parents and the witch Azuria. No one acknowledged her, however, because her mother and grandfather were in the midst of an argument and everyone standing nearby was listening. "I told you that the tunnel isn't a good idea," said Emma. "I can't believe you had Azuria dig it. The way was blocked just like every other way has been, and now we're going to have to fill it in."

"It would have worked if Olebald hadn't put a spell on the dungeon," said Azuria.

Emma frowned. "I told you about the spell."

"After we dug the tunnel!" said the king.

"I didn't know you had even started!" Emma sighed and looked toward the field where a catapult was being loaded. "And when did you find the time to build a catapult?" she asked Azuria.

"I did that before I dug the tunnel," said the old witch. "I do so want to be helpful."

"And have you thought about what is going to happen when you use that thing?" asked Eadric. "Think about the arrows the men shot over the wall."

"The range is much greater," said Azuria. "The men will be fine."

The king scratched his head and looked doubtful. "I hadn't thought of that. To tell the truth, my head is getting a bit muzzy. Lack of sleep, I suppose."

"Well, I don't think it's a good idea," said Emma. "We should— Oh no, don't tell me they've started already!"

Everyone watched as a boulder hurtled from the cup of the catapult and flew over the wall. There was a smack like a paddle hitting a leather-covered ball and the boulder flew back over the wall, heading for the catapult.

"Run!" Emma shrieked and began a hurried spell to get the men operating the catapult out of the way.

"I did tell them to begin as soon as they were ready," the king said.

The men scattered, moving twice as fast as was normally possible for an ordinary human, and were well away from the catapult when the boulder hit, smashing it to bits. Emma lowered her arms and sighed. "Is there anything else I don't know about?" she asked her father.

"No, just that—"

"What on earth are they doing?" asked Azuria, pointing at the wall.

Oculura, Dyspepsia, and Mudine had flown their brooms across the moat and landed on the thin strip of ground circling the castle. Millie watched openmouthed as Mudine finished whatever spell she was saying and all three witches flopped down on their backs. Raising their feet, they pressed them against the vertical castle wall and began to walk up as easily as if on level ground, although their bodies were sticking straight out to the side like quills on a porcupine.

"They're crazy!" said Eadric, and everyone else nodded.

Even though they took slow, methodical steps, it wasn't long before the witches reached the top. They were raising their feet to step between the parapets when a strong wind sprang up, hitting them full force in the face and blowing them over backward. With only one leg firmly attached to the castle wall, the witches flapped like flags in a storm and couldn't move until the wind died down. A moment later they were running backward down the wall, flailing their arms and shrieking.

"I told them to wait," muttered Millie. "Some people just won't listen."

Fourteen

Emma glanced down into the glass bowl and frowned. "I'm worried about Felix," she said, holding up the bowl. "He's no longer swimming the way he should. Look."

Millie peered into the bowl and her breath caught in her throat. Although the little tadpole had been darting from one side of the bowl to the other the last time she'd seen him, he was now moving lethargically through the water as if it had turned into thick syrup.

"This can't be good," she said, feeling the first flutter of panic. Her baby brother *couldn't* die, but he would if they didn't do something soon. "We have to think of a way to get to Olebald!"

"Excuse me, but I think they're having a problem undoing the spell," Azuria said, pointing at the castle wall. "Perhaps I should go help them."

The witches were lying on their backs at the base of the wall, struggling to remove the bottoms of their feet from the stone surface. "Let them work it out," Emma said to Azuria. "It will keep them out of trouble." She peered down into the bowl again and shook it just a little. "Maybe it will help if I change his water."

Emma was hurrying to the side of the moat when Millie turned to Audun. "I have an idea. Remember how the door in the secret passage shook when you hit it with your tail? What if I hit it harder—I mean really, really hard?"

"We might be able to get through then, but there isn't room in the tunnel for you to swing your tail any better than I did before."

"I don't plan to use my tail. What if I dive from high up and hit the air above the castle full force? I've found that when I fly high and let myself drop from the sky, I end up moving at tremendous speed, like a hawk. With tremendous speed comes tremendous force. If I were to hit whatever is keeping everyone from flying over the wall, I might actually be able to make it through. I bet it's the same magic surrounding the entire castle."

Audun shook his head. "That's too dangerous. It's practically suicidal."

"But it could work?"

"I guess so," he said, sounding reluctant.

"Then it's worth a try," Millie said and took to the air.

"Millie, you can't do this!" said Audun, following her with a mighty sweep of his wings. "I can't let you risk your life this way!"

"Aren't you the one who's been telling me that I can do anything?" Millie asked him. "I thought you wanted me to believe in myself. Well, I believe in myself now and I wish that you would, too. You have to give me the chance to prove what I can do, and I know that I can do this. Look, it's not like I'd be hitting a really hard surface. We sort of bounced when we tried to land in the courtyard."

"Even so, I don't think—"

"Audun, we have to do something, and no one has come up with anything better!"

The ice dragon sighed and glanced down at the castle, then up at the sky above. "My father's special talent is that he can fly very high. I'm nearly as good as he is, if I do say so myself."

Millie reached out and touched Audun's cheek with her talons. "You'd risk your life for my family?"

"I'd do anything for you, Millie," he told her.

"And I for you," Millie said. "But you don't have to do this. It was my idea and I'll take the risk."

Audun shook his head. "We're doing it together. Two dragons are better than one, after all. If you can damage Olebald's magic, imagine what we can do together."

"In that case, the last one there is a rotten roc egg!" Millie shouted and turned her face toward the clouds high above. She began to spiral upward with Audun at her side. Flying wingtip to wingtip, they rose high into the sky, until the castle was no more than the tiniest speck when they looked down.

"Is this high enough?" Millie asked.

"Not yet," said Audun.

They flew higher until they were above the clouds, and when they looked down all they could see was a vast sea of puffy white. It occurred to Millie that they were higher than they'd been when trying to escape the thunderstorm on the way back from the island; going even that high had made her uneasy.

"Is this high enough?" Millie asked.

"Not yet," said Audun.

They flew until the clouds lay so far below them that they were white shapes over a background where the largest rivers were thin blue ribbons and forests were masses of green. And still they climbed until they could see the ocean sparkling far in the distance and Millie finally said, "One way or another, this is it for me. You may take after your father and be able to go to great heights, but I take after my mother and prefer seeing nice solid ground close enough to land on in less than a minute. So, if you don't mind, I'm heading back down now." Even as she talked, she was leveling out so that she could rest in a lazy glide.

"I was just about to say that we were high enough," Audun said, joining her. "We're directly above the castle now. If we tuck our wings to our sides and dive, we should be fine if we go straight. We're trying to smash this thing, not kill ourselves, so tuck your head in at the last moment. I don't want you to end up a smear on a tower roof."

"I know." Millie nodded. "And since I don't want you to be a smear anywhere, I want you to be careful, too."

Even from such a great height, Millie could sense exactly where the castle lay, so she knew that Audun was right; the castle did lie directly below them, but then so did her family, and if she missed the castle she could flatten them as well as herself, or at least leave them with a very bad memory.

"Are you ready? We won't be able to talk once we start."

"Ready," said Millie.

"Go!" shouted Audun, and they were off, their wings pressed against their sides and their legs to their bellies so they looked like arrowheads piercing the sky. They plummeted with their noses pointed directly at the castle while the wind whistled past them. And then the air grew thicker and the wind roared like a wild beast chasing them through a sky that was getting darker as the sun moved toward the horizon. A moment later they were passing through the layer of clouds and they could see the castle. It grew bigger and bigger until suddenly it was there in front of them and Audun was screaming, "Tuck your head in, Millie!"

Millie tucked her head close to her body just before she hit something that felt slightly squishy and made a loud booming sound in her ears as her momentum forced her ever lower. The next instant she was bouncing back into the sky, but when she looked down she could see a small fracture in the apparent nothingness that seemed to envelop the castle.

"Wow!" Audun shouted as he wrapped his front legs around her and they spun in circles in the air. "That was incredible! I half expected to die back there, but I never expected *that*! And did you see the rift we made in that thing?"

"But is a little crack enough?" asked Millie as they broke apart and spread their wings. "We're going to have to do it again, aren't we?"

"And I'm going with you," said a green dragon only a few shades darker than Millie.

"Mother!" said Millie. "Are you sure?"

"What you two just did is the only thing that's had any effect on Olebald's 'invisible nothing' that's keeping us out. I was appalled when I saw you diving, but I'm so proud of you for trying. If this is what it takes to get into our castle and make Olebald turn Felix back, there is nothing that could keep me from joining you. How high do we have to climb, anyway?"

"Higher than I'd ever gone before," said Millie.

Emma peered up at the darkening sky. "Then we'd best get started. The sooner I get my baby back, the happier I'll be."

This time there were three dragons climbing into the sky. Although they didn't go as high as before, it was higher than Emma liked, and she was gasping for air long before

Millie. They turned back when she could go no higher and together the dragons plummeted back to the castle. This time when they hit, the boom was louder and the crack wider, but it still was far from big enough to let them in.

"We need a lot more dragons," Audun said as they surveyed the crack that seemed to float in empty air.

"Remember how I said that I wanted a small wedding?" said Millie. "Well, I've changed my mind. I want an enormous wedding. I want you to invite all your dragon friends, and I want the wedding to be held tomorrow."

"Really?" said Audun. "If you're serious, we can send out word right away. The ice dragons would fly all night to make our wedding, but they'd fly even faster if we tell them that Olebald Wizard is here."

"Then by all means, tell them," said Emma. "I was going to ask if you were ready to make another run, but I must say that I like your idea better. I'll send word to the ice dragons and take care of the invitations to the others. I know a few fairies who love weddings, and we can round up enough bird messengers to carry the rest. Your grandmother Frazzela won't be happy to receive such short notice, and she'll be even more upset when she hears that dragons have been invited, but she loves Felix and will understand why we need to rush this. You really don't mind hurrying your wedding this way, Millie?"

"I don't mind at all," Millie said as she gazed into Audun's eyes.

"Then I have a lot to do," said Emma. "I'm glad Grassina is here. She's so good at this kind of thing. Thank you, my dears, for all your help. And congratulations! My daughter is getting married and we're going to teach Olebald Wizard a lesson all in one day. This is so exciting!"

Fifteen

Ralf and his parents were the first to arrive. When Millie spotted them, they were talking to King Limelyn, and she noticed that they'd brought Ralf's grandfather Gargle Snort, the king of the fire-breathing dragons. Millie was about to go greet them when Zoë and her family landed at the edge of the moat where everyone had gathered. No one seemed surprised to see a family of bats, however, because they were such frequent visitors to the court and everyone knew and liked them.

Zoë changed to her human form as soon as her feet touched the ground. "I'm so glad you found Felix!" she said, giving Millie a hug. "Is he all right?"

"Aside from being a tadpole, he's doing very well. Mother changed his water and he seems fine in the bowl now. Great-Aunt Grassina is holding on to the bowl until Olebald turns Felix back. We were afraid that if we set him down, someone might knock him over or drink him by mistake," she said.

"Where's your mother?" asked Li'l.

"Mother's a human again," said Millie, who hadn't bothered to change out of her dragon form. "She's with Grandfather, so just look for the biggest crowd and you'll find her."

"Thank you, sweetie. I'm so sorry we weren't here to help you with Olebald sooner," the little bat said.

"You're here now and I'm sure Mother will be happy to see you. Who is that?" she asked as a ghostly white shape emerged from the dark sky.

It was an ice dragon and Audun recognized him right away. "Frostybreath!" Audun shouted and ran to greet his friend. The two dragons met in the traditional dragon way of equals by bowing low and extending their necks along the ground. Audun had told Millie that this was a sign of respect. She'd told him that she thought it was so they could check out the opponent's vulnerable underbelly.

Millie was waiting for Audun to introduce her when a cloud of tiny fairies settled on the ground around her. Then the air sparkled and the fairies grew from thumb-sized to the size of full-grown humans. Moss, Raindrop, and Trillium were there, as well as a lot of fairies she'd known for years.

"Welcome!" Millie told them, but she knew better than to touch a fairy. Most fairies tried to avoid physical contact with dragons, even if they were the closest of acquaintances.

"We've come for the wedding," said the Swamp Fairy. "You know we never let ourselves get involved in the altercations of others."

"So I've heard," said Millie. "But you don't need to worry. There isn't going to be an altercation. All we have to do is get back in the castle and Olebald will have to give up. There are too many of us now for him to do anything else."

"Why is the Swamp Fairy talking to a dragon?" a voice asked in a fierce whisper, and Millie saw that Poison Ivy had also come.

"That's Princess Millie," said Raindrop. "I thought you met her already."

"Hello, Poison Ivy," said Millie. "I'm glad you were able to come." Unlike natural-born dragons, Millie didn't mind lying when the situation required it.

Poison Ivy's mouth opened in surprise. "You're Millie? I'd heard about the dragon princess, but I didn't know Millie, I mean you, were the one. Uh, it's nice to see you again."

Millie smiled her most insincere smile, certain that fairies couldn't tell the difference between one dragon smile and another. "It's nice to see you, too."

The first witch arrived a few minutes later, and soon there was a steady stream of witches and fairies setting down beside the moat. Millie wondered if Olebald was aware of their arrival or if he was sleeping through the whole thing.

It wasn't long before the largest group of dragons arrived, making enough racket that Millie was sure no one could possibly still be sleeping. King Stormclaw had come, along with four elderly dragonesses, two dozen dragon guards, and Audun's family. Millie had already met his parents and grandparents and was delighted that she was about to have the chance to meet his friends. She noticed that Song of the Glacier stayed away from the humans and gave disapproving glances when any passed by.

"There's the happy couple!" said the ice dragon king when he saw them. "I believe congratulations are in order." Millie smiled and opened her mouth to speak, but the king wasn't finished yet. "The Green Witch was just telling me about her plan."

"It was Millie's plan, actually," said Emma. "She's the one who came up with the idea to use dragon force against the 'invisible nothing' in the first place. With so many dragons here, we shouldn't have any problem breaking through the barrier. If we divide into three groups, we can take turns."

"Then we should organize now," King Stormclaw announced.

Emma was a dragon again when she organized breaking the dragons into groups. Millie and Audun were telling the last group what it needed to do when the witches Ratinki and Klorine swooped in on their magic carpets carrying the king and queen of Upper Montevista and their younger son, Bradston. Eadric hurried to speak to his parents, both of whom were scowling at the gathered dragons. Emma and Millie were in their dragon forms, so neither of them joined him.

"You did tell them that there would be dragons here, didn't you?" Millie asked her mother.

"Of course," said Emma. "I'm surprised Frazzela actually came. We'll just have to try to keep them away from the dragons, which includes us right now."

"I bet they leave early," Millie told her.

Emma smiled. "I wouldn't be surprised."

As the rays of the rising sun fanned out over the countryside, ten dragons rose into the air, including Audun, Frostybreath, and Audun's father, Speedwell. Millie watched as they beat their powerful wings and climbed until they were out of sight behind a scattering of clouds. Minutes passed and the next group readied themselves. Emma was the leader, and at her signal they followed the first group into the air.

"Look! There they are!" shouted one of the fairies, and everyone hurried to look where she was pointing.

Ten dragons plummeted toward earth like spears shot from the heavens, their wings tucked so tightly to their sides that their bodies looked wingless. They hit the "invisible nothing" with a boom that made the earth shake and the crack widen. Then Millie, Ralf, and his father, Grumble

Belly, took off with seven other dragons, racing into the sky as the second group began their descent. The two sets of dragons passed each other, but the second group was going so fast that all Millie could see were blurry shapes.

Millie's dragons had flown too high to hear the second group hit, so they climbed until she thought they had gone far enough and shouted to her companions, "Now!" As synchronized as if they had practiced for years, the dragons turned and began their descent. Once again ten dragons plunged toward earth, the cold air frosting their scales, then heating them as their speed increased. Knowing what would happen at the other end, Millie let herself fall to earth like a shooting star.

They hit with such force that the world seemed to shatter around them, but it was just the "invisible nothing" breaking under the impact of the final dragon onslaught. "Pull up!" Millie screamed when she realized that it wasn't like the last time, that there wasn't anything to cushion their fall or make them rebound.

Wings snapped open around her as she fought to spread her own, but the speed of her fall was so great that the rushing air kept pressing them closed. Arching her neck, she turned her dive into a climb; at the moment she changed direction, her wings opened so fast that it was painful. Millie angled her wings and swooped over the castle, trying to slow her momentum. She flew as far as the enchanted forest before turning back. Even then her heart was still racing and she was gasping for breath, but she wanted to make sure that all of the dragons who had flown with her were all right. Looking ahead, she saw them descend by twos and threes over the castle wall and the worry creating the knot in her stomach dissolved.

When she returned to the castle, the other dragons had already opened the drawbridge for King Limelyn's soldiers. She could hear the men's feet pounding across the wooden planks and watched them enter the courtyard with weapons drawn. They met with no resistance, however, and soon disappeared into the castle keep.

Millie searched for the only other green dragon, and when she saw her, she landed beside her mother. Emma's eyes were shining as she turned to her daughter, and a moment later they both began to change back into their human forms.

"I saw your dive," said Emma. "That was amazing! You had me worried, though. I didn't think you were going to make it for a moment."

"Neither did I," Millie admitted, running her fingers through her hair. "Have you seen Audun?"

Emma nodded. "He went into the castle with your father. There are so many people and dragons looking for Olebald that I didn't think they needed me in there as well. Apparently the ice dragons are furious with the old wizard, which is why so many of them came. They wanted to help us, especially if it meant they could get their talons on Olebald. He hurt some dragons when he escaped from their stronghold and they want him back in a bad way. I think he's in for it now. A vengeful dragon is a really nasty dragon. I doubt very much that he'll be able to get away this time."

"I hope not," said Millie. "I wouldn't want to have to deal with him ever again."

Sixteen

*I*t quickly became apparent that Olebald wasn't going to be easy to find. Every floor in the castle had been searched, including the towers, and yet not one dragon, human, or fairy had seen Olebald. No one wanted to search the dungeon, however, because the ghosts were making a racket horrible enough to chill the blood of even the hardiest soul.

"I think I might know what's wrong," Millie told her mother, who was about to investigate.

"Thank you, sweetheart. I want to see how Felix is doing. Grassina asked your grandmother to hold his bowl. I just hope she hasn't put it down somewhere and forgotten where she put it. She's been doing more of that kind of thing lately."

The sound from the dungeon grew louder as Millie opened the door and stepped onto the landing at the top of the stairs. Chains rattled, doors slammed, agonized voices howled and screamed and wailed. Millie would have been frightened if she hadn't heard some of those sounds every time she'd come to visit. "What's wrong?" she called, holding up her skirt with one hand while she hurried down the stairs. "Is Hubert still stuck between the cells? Are you still trying to drown out his moaning?"

Sir Jarvis appeared at the bottom of the stairs. When he held up his hand, the clamor died away to a few dragged chains, then stopped completely. "Hubert is fine. Everything went back to normal after the castle shook for the third time this morning. It was very noisy down here, I must say. Nothing like what we made ourselves, however. No, we just wanted to get your attention. It seems we have something that doesn't belong to us, and we want to give it to you."

Millie was puzzled. "Did I leave something down here? Surely this can wait until later."

"I think not," said Sir Jarvis as he drifted to a neighboring cell. "Please take a look in here and you'll see what I mean."

Millie hurried to the door and peeked inside. As her eyes adjusted to the deeper gloom, she saw a figure huddled in the corner with its face hidden in the depths of a hood. She thought at first that it was a dead body, and she started in surprise when it moved.

"Have you come to rescue me?" asked the wavering voice of an old man.

"Rescue you from what?" Millie replied. "And who are you?"

"The ghosts! Can't you see them? They chased me in here and nearly scared me to death with that horrible creature."

Millie turned to Sir Jarvis. "What is he talking about?"

"We finally got the shadow beast under control and set him to patrolling the dungeon. He makes a marvelous watchdog. In fact, he was the one who alerted us to the old gent's presence in the dungeon. We sent the beast away when we heard the door opening just now. We thought it was some guards coming down. No need to frighten them."

"I'm glad you finally have him under control," said Millie. "This . . . What *is* your name, anyway?" she asked the old man.

"Dogsbreath," he said. "I came to ask for a charitable contribution and was trapped down here when the fire broke out."

There was something about the old man that wasn't quite right, something that made her instincts tell her not to trust him. And when he tilted his head in a way she'd seen before, Millie knew her instincts had been right. She clenched her hands, fighting the urge to turn into a dragon, wishing she hadn't come into the dungeon so unprepared.

"You must be terribly hungry," said Millie. "Come with me and I'll get you something to eat."

"That would be wonderful, miss. You're too kind." The old man struggled to his feet, pressing his hand against the damp, grimy wall to get his balance. He wore the robes of a beggar, although his speech wasn't like that of any beggar Millie had ever met. "My legs have grown numb. Please excuse my clumsiness."

He took a step toward her and lurched almost to Millie's feet. She backed away as if to let him pass, then stayed where she was as he staggered to the door.

"He's lying, Princess," Sir Jarvis whispered in her ear as the old man tottered toward the stairs.

"I thought so," said Millie. "You would have told me sooner if a stranger had been in the dungeon all this time."

"Miss!" called the old man. "Could you help me up the stairs?"

"Careful, Princess," whispered Sir Jarvis. "He's got something in his hand."

"I'm afraid I can't help you," Millie called back. "My skirts are too long and I'll need both of my hands to hold them up."

"Ah, well," said Dogsbreath. "I'm sure I can manage. It just might take me longer."

Millie peeked out the door and saw the old man take his first unsteady step up the stairs. "Take as long as you need," she told him. "I'll be right behind you." Turning her head, she whispered to Sir Jarvis, "Make sure he didn't do anything to the dungeon or leave anything behind."

The ghost gave her an exaggerated wink and nodded. "I know what you mean. We'll see to it," he said and gestured at the ghosts floating in the corridor and emerging through walls.

Millie followed the old man up the stairs, holding her skirts with both hands in case he looked back. He paused frequently, and each time he did Millie paused as well, not wanting to get any closer to him. When he finally reached the landing, he waited as if expecting Millie to open the door.

"The landing is too narrow," she told him. "You'll have to open it yourself."

Dogsbreath groaned as if the effort was too great for him, but he pushed the door open and stepped out into a sea of soldiers.

"Grab him, but be careful!" shouted Millie. "He has some kind of weapon. We'll take him to my mother and sort this all out."

"No! What are you doing? I'm not— Get your hands off me, you rogues!" cried the old man as soldiers pinned his arms to his sides and hustled him down the corridor into the Great Hall. "Why did you do this?" he yelled at Millie. "I thought you were such a nice young woman!"

"Who is this?" Emma asked as the guards deposited the old man before her.

"The ghosts found him in the dungeon," said Millie. "I think it's Olebald."

"I told you my name is Dogsbreath!"

Emma nodded at one of the soldiers, who yanked the hood off Dogsbreath's head. The frail-looking old man with tufted eyebrows and a full head of white hair gazed back at them in confusion. A murmur ran through the crowd that had gathered around to watch.

Millie ignored the comments and sized up the old man. "I'm sorry for asking the men to bring you here like this if you are indeed who you say you are," she told him, "but I still think you're Olebald Wizard."

"Who?" Dogsbreath asked. The guards had loosened their grip on him and he took a step closer to Emma.

"Watch out," said Millie. "I told you he has something in his hand. I think it's a weapon."

"What? Do you mean this?" Dogsbreath held up his hand, revealing a simple gray feather. "It's my good luck charm. I was afraid of the ghosts so I held it in my hand, hoping it would keep me safe."

"A weapon!" one of the guards said, and a number of them snickered, earning them a glare from Millie.

"I know one way to set this straight," said Emma. Pointing her finger at the old man she said,

> If liars never prosper
> You have to show what's true.
> We want to see your real face–
> The old one, not the new.

Dogsbreath inhaled sharply, looking horrified. Then his face seemed to grow fuzzy and vague, his features shifted, most of his hair disappeared, and Olebald stood before them. There was a rustling of fabric, and angry voices spoke out in the crowd. The human guards reached for him again.

191

"No!" shouted Olebald, wrenching his arms out of their grasp. The old man held up his hand. What had looked like a feather was now a knife, its tip black with what must have been poison. Waving the knife in front of him, he forced the guards to step back. And then he saw his chance and ran straight for the door.

The dragons who had been watching from the back moved in, growling deep in their throats. It was a primal sound that had terrified humans since the beginning of time. Every human in the room edged away, looking for a place to run. Even though Millie was part dragon herself, she felt her heart skip a beat.

Olebald, of course, ran faster and had almost reached the door when the dragons were on him, knocking him down, wresting the knife from his hand, and pinning him to the floor with their sharp talons. "You're not getting away from us again," said one of the dragon guards.

"Wait!" Emma shouted. "You may take him back with you, but he has to do something for me first."

The dragons hauled Olebald to his feet and dragged him in front of Emma. The old man glanced from her to the dragons, fear plain on his face. After whispering something to one of the guards, she turned to Olebald and said, "I'm surprised you went into the dungeon, considering your run-in with the ghosts the last time you were here."

"I would have left the castle, but I had unfinished business," said Olebald. "Besides, your ghosts are so stupid that they didn't even suspect it was me."

"That isn't true," said Millie. "Why do you think they kept you in that cell and sent for me? They wouldn't have done that if they'd thought you were an ordinary stranger. And what did you mean by 'unfinished business'?"

"Nothing," said the wizard, unable to meet her eyes.

"You meant to cut someone with that poisoned knife, didn't you?" Millie asked. "You would have cut me with it if I'd come close enough to you in the dungeon."

Emma gasped and turned to glare at Olebald. "You really are a despicable old man!"

Olebald's face grew red and he pursed his lips as if trying not to speak. "Your family deserves to be taken down a peg or two!" he finally blurted. "You destroyed my life, and I want to do the same to you!"

"All we did was stop you when you tried to invade Greater Greensward and take our castle from us," said Emma.

"Twice!" said Millie.

"You sent me to that horrible island with those crazy old women!" he told Emma.

"How did you escape from there, anyway?" Emma asked. "You were supposed to spend the remainder of your life on that island."

Olebald smirked. "You think you're so smart, but I have friends, you know."

"It was Nastia Nautica, wasn't it?" said Millie. "She lives close to that island."

"You took a pearl from her and she wanted you to suffer for it," he told her mother.

Emma looked shocked. "I didn't take that pearl! I gave it to her daughter, Pearl, who was supposed to give it to her."

"Well, she didn't," spat Olebald, "and Nastia Nautica has hated you ever since."

"That explains a lot," Emma murmured to herself.

"We had an agreement," said Olebald. "She'd help me leave the island and use her skills to lure the Green Witch there, and I'd get to destroy the royal family of Greater Greensward. The thought of destroying this family was the only thing that's kept me going all these years."

"It was you who planted that nasty tree in the enchanted forest," said Millie.

"That tree was supposed to drive you insane with agony," Olebald said.

Millie shuddered. "It would have if I hadn't turned into a dragon."

"And the little manticores?" asked Audun, who had finally joined them.

"They did their job. They were a distraction to get her out of the castle while I took the baby," Olebald said, scowling at Millie.

"Ah, here he is," Emma said as Grassina strode through the crowd carrying the glass bowl. Taking the bowl from her aunt, Emma cradled it in her hands and turned to Olebald. "Before you go stay with the dragons for a very long time, you have to turn Felix back into a human."

A sly smile widened the old man's lips. "I'll help you on one condition. I'll turn him back if you promise to set me free. Otherwise he'll stay a frog for the rest of his life and you'll never—"

"The only bargain you'll get is one with us," said Frostybreath, who had come in from outside and pushed his way to the front of the crowd. "You turn the baby back into a human, and we won't rip you limb from limb this very minute! We don't have any patience for you, old man, so you have five seconds to decide. One!" All the dragons in the crowd smiled, showing their fangs. "Two!" The dragons tapped their talons on the floor. "Three!" The dragons began to growl softly. "Four!" The sound of growling swelled. "Fi—"

"All right, I'll do it!" Olebald screamed.

His hands were shaking when he reached into his robes and pulled out an intricately carved gold ring. When he slipped the ring on his finger, Frostybreath leaned close and whispered, "You try any tricks and I'll rip your head off where you stand."

When the dragon placed his talons on the old man's throat, Olebald gasped and said, "I won't! I promise!"

Frostybreath snorted. "As if your promises are worth anything! Go ahead—say your spell, but be careful!"

Emma dipped her hand into the bowl. She took out the squirming tadpole and some of the water, being careful to keep her hand cupped so that the water didn't leak through her fingers. Millie noticed that the tadpole had grown little buds that would turn into legs if he remained a frog.

Olebald opened his mouth to speak. He paused and a frown wrinkled his brow. "You've got me so rattled I can't remember what I said before!" he blurted.

"Try hard," Emma said, her voice cold.

"I'm not very good at making up spells," whined Olebald.

"Just do it!" Frostybreath growled.

"I'll . . . I'll try!" Olebald whimpered. "Let me see now. Oh yes, this should work."

> Turn this frog back into
> The baby that he used to be.

"That's it?" Millie said when nothing happened. "I could do better than that, and I don't even have that kind of magic."

"Try again, wizard," said Emma. "And he's a tadpole, not a frog."

"All right! I will!" Olebald squeaked as Frostybreath gave him a light cuff.

> This baby is a tadpole
> But he was born a human.
> Change him into what he was,
> A human, not a tadpole.

"That was worse than the first one!" said Millie.

"But it worked," said Emma as the air around the tadpole started to sparkle. When the little creature began to stretch and grow, there was a loud gasp as everyone held their breath. The little face widened, the eyes grew bigger, his mottled skin turned pink, the leg buds grew into human baby legs and feet, and his arms and hands sprouted. Suddenly he was Felix again, pink cheeked with red gold curls and blue eyes filled with wonder.

"Oh, my little darling!" said Emma, holding him so tightly in her arms that he began to squirm and whimper.

"Now you're coming with us," said Frostybreath as his talons closed around Olebald's shoulders.

"I'd take that ring from him first if I were you," Emma told the dragon. "I'm sure that's what gave him the power to change Felix and take over the castle."

Frostybreath grunted. "I was just thinking that. Give me the ring, old man."

"But I . . . ," Olebald began. Then the dragon squeezed just a little harder, and the wizard hurriedly removed the ring and held it up for Frostybreath to take.

"You keep it," the dragon told Emma. "If we have it at the stronghold, he'll try to get out of his cell and find it. Get some rope, boys!" he shouted at the other dragons. "We're tying him up and going home. I'm sorry I can't stay for the wedding," he said, turning back to Millie, "but the king put me in charge of Olebald. You and Audun should come visit me when you can."

197

"We will," Millie said and gave him a kiss on the cheek.

The big dragon looked flustered from the kiss as he turned away, and his voice sounded gruffer than usual when he directed his men in tying up Olebald. The dragons marched the old wizard out of the Great Hall just as Audun and Eadric came in.

"I heard you found Olebald," said Eadric as he watched him disappear down the corridor. "What about— Ah, there's my boy!"

The baby cooed when his father took him in his arms, then grabbed a hunk of Eadric's hair in his fist and yanked.

"Ow!" Eadric exclaimed. "It looks as if he's none the worse for his experience."

"He's fine," said Emma. "I'm going to take him up to the nursery now. Grassina is handling the preparations for the wedding. Do you see her anywhere? Ah, there she is! Millie, go talk to your great-aunt. I'll be back down as soon as I can."

"Can you smell that?" Eadric asked, inhaling deeply as he accompanied Emma and Felix from the Hall. "They've started baking for the wedding. I wonder if they have anything ready yet. Perhaps we should go see."

Seventeen

illie was crossing the Hall on her way to her great-aunt when Audun matched his steps to hers.

"Believe it or not," Millie told Audun, "our wedding almost seems like a minor event after all that's happened today. I'm almost too tired to get excited about it."

They stepped aside as a group of servants carrying benches from the Great Hall walked in front of them. Other servants staggered under the weight of tables until some soldiers went to help them.

"Wait until you see what they've done to the court-yard," said Audun. "I think it looks great."

"Why are they decorating the courtyard?" asked Millie as Grassina left a group of courtiers and linked arms with her.

"Because the weather is perfect and there isn't room for everyone in the Great Hall," Grassina said. "Come out-side, you two, and I'll tell you what I've planned."

Millie didn't realize how late it had gotten and was sur-prised to see that it was already growing dark out. The courtyard bustled with activity as fairies strung flower garlands and twinkling firefly lights between the buildings. Servants were filling bowls with even more flowers. Ralf's parents were lighting torches and King Gargle Snort of the fire dragons was already sampling fairy-made dandelion and herb wines with King Stormclaw of the ice dragons. Li'l and her children were helping the ladies of the court hang decorations from the parapets, while Garrid, Li'l's mate, helped Ralf drape banners down the sides of the towers.

"This is wonderful," said Millie, "but where are my grandparents?"

Grassina sighed. "Queen Frazzela is waiting in your grandmother Chartreuse's chamber until the ceremony begins. Eadric's mother refuses to go anywhere near a dragon, which is making things a bit difficult, I'm afraid. Your two grandfathers are directing the search for any magical traps or devices that Olebald might have set in the castle, which means that Francis and Haywood, who went with them, are really doing all the work while the two kings debate the best way to trap werewolves."

"And what is Bradston doing?" asked Millie. She had spotted her young uncle near the fairies, but he didn't seem to be doing anything.

"Ogling fairies," said Grassina. "Although he told me that he didn't trust them and would keep an eye on them for us."

Millie laughed. "That's Bradston, all right."

"It sounds as if you have everything well in hand," said Audun.

Grassina smiled and looked around with a sigh. "I believe I do, except for one thing: you. Clean clothes are waiting for you on your beds, so it's time for you to go change. Hurry now. I hear the musicians tuning up."

Millie felt more lighthearted than she had in weeks as she and Audun ran up the stairs to change. They parted at the top and Millie hurried to her chamber to see what Grassina had selected for her to wear. She had planned to get a new gown made for her wedding, but as she'd thought she'd have plenty of time, the gown had never been started. Throwing open her door, Millie ran to her bed and stopped. It was her grandmother Chartreuse's gown. Millie had seen it once when she was young, but her grandmother had told her that she wasn't allowed to touch it. Although her grandmother rarely showed affection, Millie knew that letting her wear the gown was a gesture of true love.

Millie reached out to stroke the gown with tentative fingers when one of her grandmother's ladies-in-waiting came to help her dress. The woman did her hair as well, and when Millie descended the stairs in the creamy white dress edged in pearls and decorated with pearl-outlined blossoms across the bodice, she looked and felt every inch a princess.

She had reached the corridor on the first floor when fairies arrived, bringing carefully selected flowers. It took only moments for them to weave the flowers into Millie's hair, then each one gave her a kiss on the cheek for good luck. The fairies left, and Garrid was there with his daughter, Zoë. They had brought her a necklace made of stones the exact shade of green as Millie's dragon scales. Millie bent down as her friend fastened the necklace around her throat. When she straightened up, both Zoë and Garrid gave her kisses on her cheek.

"For good luck?" Millie asked, her eyes shining.

"No, because we love you," said Zoë. "See you after the ceremony. I want to hear all about everything!"

Audun met Millie at the door leading into the courtyard. He looked so handsome in his clothes of silver and blue that her breath caught in her throat and she found she couldn't speak.

"You look beautiful," he said, raising her hand to his lips.

Millie smiled and suddenly her voice was back. "For someone who didn't know anything about kissing when we met, you've gotten very good at it."

"There's a reason for that," he said and kissed her full on the lips.

"Ahem," said her father. "I hate to interrupt, but isn't the kiss supposed to come after the ceremony? We have a courtyard full of people waiting for you two, so why don't we get started?" Taking her arm in his, he nodded to Audun and escorted Millie down the stairs.

Millie had expected to see the local pastor there to officiate, but she hadn't expected to see King Stormclaw waiting for her as well. It made sense, though, when she thought about it; Audun had told her that the king presided over all ice dragon weddings. She noticed that the pastor looked pale and cringed every time King Stormclaw glanced his way, but the king seemed to be enjoying himself.

Eadric walked Millie to a spot halfway between the pastor and King Stormclaw, and a moment later Audun was by her side. Although it wasn't part of the ceremony, he took her hand in his and squeezed. A warm feeling flooded through Millie; it occurred to her that she was very fortunate indeed to have met someone who could share both worlds with her and could understand her better than anyone else.

Lost in thoughts of Audun, Millie paid little attention to the ceremony itself. She spoke when prompted and assumed that everyone else said the right thing. But when the pastor and the king pronounced them husband and wife, and it was time to kiss Audun, Millie smiled.

After a kiss that lasted so long the guests began to fidget, Millie and Audun turned around, pausing to wave to everyone. The humans cheered and stomped their feet while the dragons roared so loudly that their breath knocked fairies from their perches on the flower garlands. The sound would have been deafening if the ceremony had been held indoors.

Millie and Audun looked out over the crowd seeing the smiling faces of their friends and family. It took a minute for

Millie to realize that one face was missing; Queen Frazzela, her grandmother, wasn't there.

"I don't think my grandmother came to the ceremony," she told Audun. "I don't see her anywhere."

"That's odd. I don't see mine, either. I wonder where they are."

Millie frowned. "I thought my grandmother might leave early, but I never thought she'd skip the ceremony altogether! I can't believe she did that!"

"I don't think she left. See, there are the witches who brought her." Audun nodded his head toward a group that included Klorine and Ratinki.

"And your grandfather is still here, so your grandmother must be, too," Millie said as she peered into the crowd. "I know they're biased against each other's kind, but I can't believe our grandmothers would fly all the way here and then not watch us get married."

"You don't suppose they ran into each other, do you?" asked Audun. "I'd hate to see what would happen if the two of them were left alone together."

"I'm sure they're fine," Millie said, although even she didn't think she sounded convincing.

The crowd thinned out as servants set food on the tables. When the guests started to sit down, Millie was pleased to see that the groups were mixed with humans sitting with fairies and dragons. She knew she should go from table to table, talking to her guests, but it didn't feel right that the grandmothers weren't there.

"I think we should go look for Frazzela and Song of the Glacier," she said, turning to Audun. "Frazzela may hate dragons, but she loves fairies and there are more than I can count here tonight. And I have this feeling . . ."

"I think you're right. Song of the Glacier wouldn't miss this unless something really important came up, but the king is here and so are the rest of his councilors."

Thinking that they could see better from the top of the stairs, Millie and Audun crossed the courtyard and started up the steps. "Millie, where are you going?" called Emma as she and Eadric hurried to meet them. "You should be out here talking to people."

"We haven't been able to find Grandmother Frazzela or Audun's grandmother Song of the Glacier. Have you seen either of them?"

Eadric had his mouth open to reply when they heard a muffled roar from inside the castle. "That sounded like my grandmother," said Audun, and they all turned to run up the stairs.

A human voice shouted, frantic and scared. As soon as they entered the corridor, a wind began dragging them toward Emma and Eadric's tower, growing louder with each step they took. They found the door to the tower standing open, and when they looked inside they saw the top half of Frazzela on the circular stairs with Song of the Glacier bending over her.

"Grandmother!" Audun shouted over the roar of the wind. "What are you doing? Leave that woman alone!"

"Don't be an idiot, boy!" Frazzela screamed. "Your grandmother is holding me up. If she lets me go I'll be sucked into this blasted hole. Help me, you fools! This poor dragoness can't hold me forever!"

Millie grabbed the door frame to keep from being dragged into the hole and tried to get a better look. Her grandmother was hanging on to the edge of a hole with her legs dangling below her. The wind was blowing around Frazzela, pulling loose items past her into the gap and creating an unearthly wail. Song of the Glacier stood with her back braced against the stairwell, straining to hold on to the old woman.

"What on earth— Mother, what happened to you?" Eadric shouted.

"I stepped on your stairs, that's what happened to me," the queen shouted back, sounding cross. "The step collapsed under me and I can't get out. Don't just stand there, help me!"

"And be quick about it!" shouted Song of the Glacier. "I can't hold her much longer."

The wind was growing stronger. Herbs that had been strewn on the floor in the Great Hall whipped past, stinging Millie's cheek when she turned her head to look.

"Olebald must have set a trap here!" Eadric shouted as he and Emma came to stand beside the hole with their arms wrapped around each other. "Audun, you lift Frazzela from that side and I'll lift from this one!" yelled Eadric. "You'll have to hold on to us, ladies, or we'll fall in, too. On the count of three. One . . . Two . . . Three!"

The veins stood out in Eadric's forehead as he strained to lift his mother, while Audun's face turned crimson. But no matter how hard they tried, they weren't able to get Frazzela out of the hole. Millie was afraid they were going to hurt themselves, and was relieved when they let go and stepped back.

"It's no use. We'll have to try something else!" Eadric shouted.

"Hurry up!" cried Frazzela. "I'm losing the feeling in my legs."

"Humans aren't strong enough to lift them out, but dragons might be!" yelled Millie.

Emma nodded. "Three should be enough."

It was the first time Emma had changed into a dragon in front of her mother-in-law, and the first time Millie had done it voluntarily, but Frazzela seemed more afraid of the hole than she was of any dragon. "Hurry!" was all she said as Millie reached under her arms.

The wind still felt strong, but not nearly as strong as it had when they were humans. Three dragons were able to lift the old woman out of the hole easily. When Frazzela was free, Song of the Glacier staggered back from the edge and sat down. "I must be getting old," said the dragoness. "When I was younger I could have lifted her out by myself."

"Not with that wind, Grandmother," said Audun. "You saw that it took the three of us just now."

"Thank you so much, Song," said Frazzela. "I would have died if it hadn't been for you."

"You're welcome, Frazzie. I'm glad I could help."

Millie's mouth dropped open and she glanced at Audun, who looked equally stunned.

"Take them out of here while I close this hole," Emma told Millie and Audun.

"But the wind . . . ," Millie began.

"The wind won't bother me as long as I'm a dragon. If I have to change back, your father will keep me from falling in. Now go! We're wasting time."

"You heard the dragon," said Millie as she and Audun ushered Frazzela and Song of the Glacier into the corridor. Audun ducked as a candlestick flew past, and a woman's veil came flapping down the corridor and got caught on Song of the Glacier's ridge. Millie and Audun had to work together to close the door. The moment it was shut, everything that had been flying in their direction fell to the floor, making it look as if a troop of vandals had visited the castle. The noise of the wind died down as well, although it left a ringing in Millie's ears.

"What happened in there, Grandmother?" she asked Frazzela.

The old woman looked away as if unable to meet Millie's eyes.

"We were taking a little look around," Song of the Glacier hurried to say. "Frazzie went first and the floor exploded out from under her."

"I could hardly hold on," said the old woman. "Fortunately, Song reached me before the wind got too strong or I would have been dragged into that horrid hole. Did you see how dark it was in there?"

"You have nicknames for each other?" asked Millie.

"Why not?" said Frazzela. "Song of the Glacier is the loveliest and most gracious dragon that ever lived. I'm honored to call her my friend. You know," she said, turning to the elderly dragoness, "I let only my best friends call me Frazzie."

"My grandfather can't even call her that!" Millie whispered to Audun.

"No one has ever called me 'Song' before, but I like it," said Song of the Glacier.

"May I call you Song now?" asked Audun.

"No," his grandmother said, giving him a frosty glance. "You may not."

"You know," Frazzela said, turning to the elderly dragoness, "you'll have to come visit me at Upper Montevista. We have such lovely mountains. I'm sure you'd enjoy seeing them."

"What a nice invitation! I may just take you up on that. And if I do, perhaps I'll take you for a sightseeing flight."

"Oh, I couldn't impose!" exclaimed Frazzela, although Millie thought her grandmother looked thrilled.

The two grandmothers walked away shoulder to shoulder while their grandchildren stared after them in amazement.

"You know your grandmother was covering for my grandmother," said Millie. "Frazzela was probably snooping around when she started up those stairs, and your grandmother heard her holler."

"That's probably true," Audun replied. "But Song of the Glacier would never admit it now."

"I did it," Emma said as she and Eadric came into the corridor. "I couldn't close it at first, but as soon as I put Olebald's ring on my finger, the spell worked and the hole closed right up. It was just in time, too. That wind was getting stronger by the minute. If I hadn't closed it I think it would have taken the entire castle apart stone by stone."

"I'm sure that was what Olebald wanted to happen if we were to get back into the castle," said Eadric. "I know Francis and Haywood checked our tower, but the trap was probably laid so that only a woman could set it off. We'll go over the entire castle again to make sure there aren't any more traps. However, I think we should get something to eat first. That food smells delicious. Let's go get some before it's all gone."

Emma laughed her distinctive laugh, which sounded almost like the bray of a donkey. It had been so long since Millie had heard it that she couldn't help but smile.

"You ate before the wedding," Emma protested as she and Eadric started toward the door to the courtyard. "How can you be hungry again?"

Audun waited until his in-laws walked out the door before he pulled Millie into his arms and said, "Alone at last!"

"This has been a most interesting day," Millie said, leaning against his chest. "We caught Olebald, made him change Felix back, and got married. And to top it off, my grandmother finally likes dragons!"

"And my grandmother likes your grandmother enough to offer her a ride on her back. That's the most improbable thing of all."

"This is our wedding day, so I really don't mean to argue, but I'd have to say that you're wrong about that. The most improbable thing is that you and I found each other. I thought I'd never meet the man who was right for me. Who would have thought that a human and a dragon could make such a perfect match?"

Acknowledgments

I would like to thank Victoria Wells Arms for her wisdom and patience, Caroline Abbey for all her help, and Kalissa Haff and Kitty Hamilton for their marvelous name suggestions.

Thanks also to *Wicked Plants: The Weed That Killed Lincoln's Mother & Other Botanical Atrocities* by Amy Stewart, which provided inspiration for the stinging tree. It is a very real tree that grows in Australia and a few nearby islands, with tiny "hairs" that contain a neurotoxin. Brushing against these hairs can cause unbearable pain that sometimes lasts as long as a year!

About the Author

E.D. Baker wanted to be an author from a very early age and wrote many stories before she made her international debut with *The Frog Princess*, the inspiration for the hit Disney movie *The Princess and the Frog*. As well as the *Tales of the Frog Princess* series, E.D. Baker has written *The Wide-Awake Princess* and *Fairy Lies*, the sequel to *Fairy Wings*. When she needs a mini-break from writing, E.D. Baker likes to play games on her computer or take care of her dogs, cats, goats and her ducks, Quackers and Fromage. She lives on a small farm in Maryland, USA, where she and her family breed horses.

To find out more, visit www.talesofedbaker.com

For more magical stories don't miss . . .

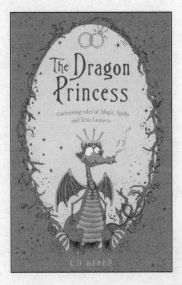

Tales of the Frog Princess   The Dragon Princess

www.bloomsbury.com

And also . . .

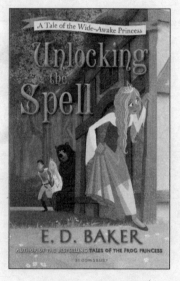

The Wide-Awake Princess   Unlocking the Spell

www.bloomsbury.com